Treasure in a Tin Box

A Novel

"…where your treasure is there will your heart be also" (Matthew 6:21).

Dorey Whittaker

This is the Back Story for Dorey's popular novel, *Wall of Silence*

Copyright© 2015, by Dorey Whittaker
Treasure in a Tin Box
Dorey Whittaker
Dorey@DoreyWhittaker.com
www.doreywhittakerbooks.com

Published 2015, by

Paperback ISBN:
Ebook ISNB:

ALL RIGHTS RESERVED

ISBN: 1517622166
ISBN 13: 9781517622169
Library of Congress Control Number: 2015917834
CreateSpace Independent Publishing Platform
North Charleston, South Carolina

NOTE: All names, companies, cities and events in this novel are fiction when combined with the characters within this novel. Any similarity to anyone living or dead, except for Public Figures, is purely coincidental.

This novel is dedicated to Sandra Upton, whose belief in my talent has been unwavering, and to Linda Stubblefield, my superb editor.
This novel is also dedicated to all fifteen of my faithful "Treasure Readers." You kept me going during twenty-six months of grueling research and development. Thank you for your encouragement and patience; and for loving the Bascom family almost as much as I do.

Table of Contents

SECTION ONE

The Invitation
1954

CHAPTER 1

❧

The Invitation

TOBIAS SMILED AS he parked his brand-new '54 Chevrolet Bel Air in front of his house. He locked his car and made a run for his front door. Three straight days of downpours in Atlanta could not erase the smile from his face. Fifty-seven years old and today he had taken possession of his first brand-new car. He had owned many other cars since his first purchase in 1926, but they had all been well-used before he got his hands on them. Unlike most men his age, cars had never been very important to him. They were simply a means to get from here to there, so he was quite surprised at the euphoric feeling which overtook him as he drove this car home. He quickly unlocked the front door, reached over and pulled the stack of dampened mail from the letterbox, and closed the door behind him. He dropped the mail on a chair and hung up his drenched overcoat before removing his shoes. He knew better than to walk around Ruth's house in wet, soggy shoes.

Turning on the living room light, he couldn't resist peeking out the front window to admire his shiny Biscayne-blue car sitting out front. The wide whitewall tires glistened in the rain, and the memory of the ivory interior's new-car smell still filled his nostrils. His intention had been to trade-in his '37 Chevy for another used car, but a few years newer one. He had learned that with labor and hours under the hood, he could usually get a solid seven or eight years out of used cars, but the war had forced him to keep this one far longer than the rest. He never minded driving someone else's leftovers, but he had to admit this purchase felt special.

While staring at his beautiful car parked in front of the house, suddenly trepidation replaced the feeling of euphoria. He knew he had not been impulsive; he could afford this shiny, new car. Tobias could not help but admire it, but he also knew it would draw too much attention. Being a black man who lived on Chesterfield Street in the Darktown section of Atlanta, he knew it was never wise to flaunt your success—not to your neighbors and especially not in front of the struggling whites of Atlanta. For three long years his deacon board had pressed him to get a new car. As pastor, he was always being called upon to drive out in the middle of the night to take someone to the hospital, visit a grieving family, or pick up someone at the train station. "You need a dependable car," they had stressed.

He knew Ruth would have loved for the car to be Chevy's new Romany red with an India-ivory top, but Tobias knew that the dark Biscayne blue would draw less attention; brand-new is still brand-new. As he walked away from the window, he chided himself, "Tobias, you are over-thinking this."

All of his life he had been taught to work hard, do right, help others, and keep a low profile and that advice had served him well. "It is only a car, Tobias, don't make this bigger than it is," he chuckled as he checked his watch, "I have thirty minutes before I leave to pick up Ruth."

He grabbed the mail, headed to the kitchen, placed the mail on the table, and poured himself a glass of water. As he flipped through the clutter of junk mail, he spotted a strange return address on an expensive-looking envelope. He pulled the envelope out of the pile and studied it. The return address read "The Shepherd's House, Washington, D.C." He inwardly groaned to himself, "Who in Washington, D.C., would be sending me a letter? I've heard of The Shepherd's House. That's a large black church up in D.C. Why would they be writing to me?"

Tobias tore open the envelope and quickly unfolded the letter to check the signature on the bottom. As he did, something slipped from the letter and fell to the floor. He bent down and picked up what looked like two very fancy tickets. He tucked them back into the envelope and focused on the letter, which had been sent from a Michael Stoddard, the events co-ordinator for The Shepherd's House. "I remember Michael," he thought.

"He was one of Aunt Pearl's boys. I'm glad to see him doing so well. We lost track of him after Aunt Pearl passed away."

Tobias thought about how this church was known for being very political—an avenue he had always tried to avoid. He wondered why he was being invited to their biggest event of the year—the celebration of the passage of <u>Brown v. The Board of Education</u>. Curiously, he read the letter.

Dear Pastor Bascom,

You probably do not remember me, but I had the distinct honor of being one of Ms. Pearl's first brigade boys back in 1928, and her influence changed the direction of my life. I was ten years old and heading for trouble when she challenged me to join her new brigade. Eleven boys showed up that first day, and I was one of them. At first, all of us boys mocked and jeered at this elderly woman, but not for long. I remember her saying, "Reading can take you places this world will not let you go and will open doors for you that no one can close." Ms. Pearl repeated this phrase at the start of every brigade meeting until every young boy understood what it meant. My adopting that mantra has certainly been proven true in my life.

As a young black boy growing up in Darktown, neither my mother nor I saw any value in school. I loved my mother, but she, like so many others, believed that learning was only for whites. Ms. Pearl proved we were both wrong, and she did it brilliantly. I understand that for many years now—at least in the Darktown, Ms. Pearl has been lovingly referred to as "The Reader." Those of us who joined her first brigade are now grown men. We had the privilege of sitting at her feet and listening as she made books come to life. As she shared the gift of reading with us, indeed doors were opened that no one can ever close again. I am not telling you anything you do not already know.

I am sure you are aware of all the hard work Thurgood Marshall has done to bring down the "separate but equal" laws throughout this country. He has spent his legal career fighting this injustice. In December of 1952, he argued his case before the Supreme Court. He reargued the case <u>Brown v. The Board of Education</u> before the court on December 9, 1953. Victory finally came to us this past May 17, 1954. The law has finally been struck down, but we are far from feeling its reality. We will continue to fight for the implementation of justice; however, we are also aware of another fight we must address- and win—if this new law is to become successful—hence, the reason for this invitation.

During a strategy meeting, I shared your great-aunt's story with the committee, and we feel it is something we need to promote. We can fight for new laws, but if our own people do not believe that education is our pathway to freedom and equality, the laws will lie dormant. Ms. Pearl understood this and awakened the love of learning in the hearts of young boys who had been told learning was a waste of time. She did not lecture us; she simply read exciting stories that fueled our imagination and drove each of us to want to read.

We would like to start many "Pearl's Book Brigades" all around the country, and we would be honored to have her last surviving family member in attendance when we announce this plan. Would you and your wife honor us with your presence? Would you consider addressing the audience? We would love to hear her story as told by someone who truly knew her. We have set aside between seven and ten minutes in the schedule for you. Would you be willing to do this? If so, we would be honored to put you up at the home of one of our members and provide a driver to take you around Washington.

Pastor Bascom, Thurgood Marshall himself has stated he would be honored to meet the grand-nephew of Ms. Pearl Bascom-Lagolaei.

Yours Respectfully,
Michael Stoddard
Events Coordinator for "The Shepherd's House"

Tobias sat stunned for a moment. Names like Thurgood Marshall were not casually tossed around in his world. Never one to seek attention, Tobias knew this invitation was not about him; rather, it was all about the remarkable work done by his Great-Aunt Pearl. Noticing the time, he put on his overcoat and shoes, grabbed the letter and headed out to pick up his wife.

Tobias pulled up to the back entrance of the Atlanta General Hospital as Ruth walked out of the back door. Tobias chuckled to himself, "Funny how quickly things can change. Forty-five minutes ago, all I could think about was showing Ruth our brand-new car, and then I read this letter. Now the car is of little importance because I cannot wait to share this letter with her. Having known both Aunt Pearl and Aunt Ruby for most of her life, Ruth loved them dearly and will appreciate this letter as much as I do."

Ruth made a dash toward Tobias' usual parking place. She has been the head bread-and-pastry chef at the hospital for sixteen years, and every day at the end of her shift, Tobias has been waiting for her. She smiled at the look of excitement on his face, assuming it was because of the beautiful new car in which he was sitting. Ruth was instantly thankful that because of the rain, she had made sure she dusted off all the cake flour from her shoes and uniform before stepping outside. Nothing was like a Georgia rainstorm to turn cake flour into sticky glue. She made a dash for the car and climbed in. "Wow! Tobias, this is beautiful!"

Barely acknowledging her comment, Tobias shoved the letter into Ruth's hand and said, "Read this, Ruth."

Not grasping the importance of the letter in her hand, Ruth smiled as she looked at the fancy dashboard and questioned him. "I thought you were going to buy another used car, Tobias. Didn't you tell the deacon board we didn't need a new car?" Rubbing her hand across the spotless ivory interior, Ruth added, "I'm not complaining, mind you. I've said you deserved one for several years now."

Seeing the look of consternation on Tobias' face, Ruth asked, "What is it, Tobias? Did the salesman pressure you into buying this car?"

"Of course not, Ruth, you know me better than that. It was a good price and is a well-built automobile." Pointing back to the letter, he again pleaded, "Just read that letter, Ruth."

After reading it Ruth laid back her head and uttered, "Oh, my goodness, Tobias! What a wonderful honor!" Then overcome with giggles, she added, "And oh, how Aunt Pearl would have hated it."

Joining Ruth in laughter, Tobias agreed. "Yes, she would have. Even though the Brigades were Aunt Ruby's idea, Aunt Pearl's tenacity made the idea happen. All my life, Aunt Pearl said I should write down the Bascom family story. She wanted the world to know what my Great-Grandma Hannah went through as a slave. She also wanted the world to know how wonderful her big brother, my Grandpa Samuel, was. She did not want any attention; she wanted the focus on people like her twin sister Ruby, Ms. Estée, Joseph, Arthur, and Mr. Washington."

Ruth turned and looked directly at her husband. "You *are* going to accept this invitation, aren't you, Tobias?"

"Yes, of course, I must. I just don't know how I can do it in the allotted seven to ten minutes they have offered me."

"Tobias, you can't tell her whole story, so simply focus on how rare it was for a slave child to become a reader and how she used reading to help so many others." Checking the letter again, Ruth gasped, "This event is set for six weeks from now. Are you thinking of driving this new car up to Washington?"

"No, Ruth, it wouldn't be wise. I think it would be best if we were to take the train. There are so few places we can safely stop along the way to eat and even fewer places will rent us a room. A black couple driving a shiny new car through the Carolinas is just asking for trouble. Michael Stoddard has arranged a driver for us up in Washington, so we won't need a car there."

"Are you nervous about talking in front of so many important people, Tobias?"

"No, I'm not nervous; I'm completely undone. Those people will surely intimidate me, but my greatest problem is my speech. Not so much deciding what to say, but rather, what to leave out."

⚜

CHAPTER 2

The 6:05 to Washington

AT FOUR IN the morning, every light was on at the Bascom house on Chesterfield Street. For the past six weeks this trip was the main topic of discussion on Chesterfield Street. All of Darktown knew that today was the day Tobias and Ruth were heading for Washington. Ms. Pearl had been well-loved and admired in this community since 1869, when the Bascom kids moved in, all the way until her death in 1932. This neighborhood remembered its own. Darktown was a place where not only did a neighbor know his neighbor; he more than likely knew his neighbor's momma, his auntie, and his grandma as well. This "Southern way," as it was termed, was certainly true on the colored side of town—and especially on Chesterfield Street. The houses on this street have been proudly owned and occupied for generations. Their deeds read like a genealogy of their families. Sitting on one of these porches on a Sunday afternoon is like signing up for a history lesson, served up with pride and sweetened iced tea.

At 5:00 a.m. Tobias walked into the kitchen. "Ruth, you have been baking all night. Are you just about done?"

"Yes, just have to box things up. I have a box of goodies for our host, and one for our Washington driver. Also, should I have an opportunity; I have made one for Thurgood Marshall." With a giggle, she added, "Did you ever imagine we might meet that man, let alone be able to talk with him?"

"Ruth, I would remind you that he puts his trousers on one leg at a time like every other man, but I know how you feel. I feel a little starry-eyed as well to think he knows who Aunt Pearl is or was."

"Honey, I have also made goodies for the train ride. I will be ready on time, I promise."

Tobias chuckled as he left the kitchen. "Ruth, you could feed the whole train with what you baked last night."

Confident that everything was packed and ready to go, Tobias made one last check of his list: Train tickets, his speech, a change of clothes, sleepwear, toothbrushes, travel funds, and a street map of Washington, D.C. He then closed the case and mused to himself, "That is everything except the most important things." He smiled as he heard his wife in the kitchen, packing the bag to take on the fifteen-hour train ride from Atlanta to Washington. He had one last item to pack before heading out. Ever since the decision was made to accept this invitation to go to Washington, he had been gathering every important item he intended to take with him. A casual glance of his desk would create more questions than answers. Why would he take these things to honor his Great-Aunt Pearl?

First, Tobias opened the tin box that had always held a place of honor in his life. It was the oldest and dearest possession ever owned by any member of the Bascom family; and its condition belied its age. As with all those that had gone before him, Tobias took great care of this beautiful tin box. He gently wiped it out with a clean, dry cloth. The tin itself dated back to about 1802, and a damp cloth on such an old tin would prove disastrous. Satisfied the tin was clean; he began filling it with his precious possessions. First, he picked up three buttons on his desk and placed them carefully in an envelope before putting them in the box. Next, he picked up the old whistle with a very old shoelace still attached to it and placed it in the box. He then picked up an old tattered page of the *New York Times*, dated June 1905. The article and photo were about an Italian woman shopping at the old neighborhood Italianna store on Lexington Ave. This item had obviously seen many years of handling, yet Tobias carefully wrapped it in tissue and placed it inside the tin box. With great tenderness, he picked up a mother-of-pearl lapel pin and slipped it in its own envelope and gently placed it next to the whistle. With a warm smile, Tobias picked up a stack of well-read letters wrapped with a faded red ribbon and six family photos wrapped in tissue paper and placed them on top of the newspaper article. Finally, he picked up the three books he had planned to take along. The first was Ms. Pearl's 1859 copy of *The Count of Monte Cristo*, and he slipped his speech inside its pages. Not being a first edition and showing serious signs of use, the book held little monetary value; however, the care with which Tobias handled it spoke volumes. The second book was a well-worn 1910 copy of *Treasure Island*. The third book, which had only recently been published, had been written by an unknown author and was still wrapped in the printer's tissue. He carefully placed these books in the tin box and secured the latch with a wedge of wood.

With these precious items safely packed, Tobias decided to start loading the car. Checking his watch, he realized he had taken much too long packing the tin box. He and Ruth needed to get a move on.

Ruth locked the door behind her and joined her husband at the car, "Tobias, did you remember to pack your speech and the invitation?"

"Yes, Ruth. I put them with our train tickets after I sent the thank-you note accepting Rev. Wilcox's generous invitation to let us stay at his home. His son, William, is meeting us at the station tonight and was kind enough to offer to show us around Washington tomorrow."

Tapping his suit-coat pocket, Tobias reassured her, "I have our tickets right here, but my speech is inside the book, and that is in my tin box. Ruth, I can't believe it was fifty years ago when I passed through the Capitol, but I wasn't able to stop and see anything back then. The truth is, at seven, I would not have been able to appreciate anything I would have seen."

Noticing the size of the goodie bag Ruth placed on the back seat, Tobias teased, "Sweetie, are you planning on feeding everyone at the nation's Capital tomorrow?"

With an uncharacteristic edge in her tone, Ruth responded, "Tobias, six months ago we celebrated the ninety-first anniversary of the signing of the Emancipation Proclamation; this weekend we are celebrating the take down of 'Separate but Equal.' Yet here we are in 1954, and Negroes still cannot use the dining car on that train."

He knew the pressure of meeting and mixing with so many important people this weekend was beginning to show itself in Ruth's response. In order to keep the situation light, he chose to ignore the irony of this sad truth. Instead of being drawn into the seeming injustice of the situation, he teased, "But Ruth, we couldn't possibly eat all of that food. Ah, let me guess, you're planning to feed every hungry Negro on that train, right?"

"If I have the good fortune to do so, yes, Tobias," Ruth teased right back. "You, and my daddy before you, preach sermons to reach people's hearts for God. I, on the other hand, feed their hungry stomachs to reach their hearts. Jesus said, 'Feed My sheep.' We just do it differently, that's all." Ruth smiled and then quoted dear, sweet Great-Aunt Ruby, Pearl's twin sister. *"Toby Boy, not everything is right in this world; that doesn't mean you don't do what's right anyway."*

"So Tobias, I can either fuss about not being able to use the dining car or I can use the situation as an opportunity to love on some hungry people today."

Having been reared by Ms. Ruby, he had heard this saying many times throughout his life. Every time he tried to use some unfair injustice in the world as his excuse not to do right, he heard that quote. As a boy, he had resented its truth, but he never resented Great-Aunt Ruby.

Tobias started the car, adjusted the rearview mirror, and then noticed something odd happening. All along the street, people were pouring out of their homes and lining the block. Most in this community would have loved to be in attendance when one of their own was being honored, but that simply was not possible. Therefore, they had all decided to show their respect for Ms. Pearl by standing at the curb and waiving as Tobias and Ruth drove off to catch the 6:05 to Washington. Men, women, and children stood tall and proud as Tobias slowly pulled away from the curb. As his car passed by, everyone held up books and waved them above their heads. Tobias and Ruth smiled all the way to the train station.

They arrived at Peachtree Station a good twenty minutes before the train was to arrive. Tobias made sure everything from the car was safely inside the station before moving the car to the parking lot. Since they only had one suitcase, he decided to keep it with them rather than check it into the baggage car.

The train was due into the station in about ten minutes, so he gathered up their belongings and they headed out to the platform where the other passengers were already standing in line. Neither spoke as they quietly walked over and stood in the line marked "Colored."

The conductor's shrill whistle signaled that all passengers could now board the train. As Ruth reached the steps that would guide them into the "Colored Car," Tobias took her goodie bag from her hand and warned, "Use both hands, Ruth. I will hand you the goodie bag as soon as you get up the steps. Be sure to turn to the right. I'll be right behind you."

He quickly double-checked his suit-coat pocket for their tickets. As soon as Ruth cleared the gangway, he hoisted their suitcase up onto the landing, pushing it back far enough to have a place for his feet, and started to climb up the four steep steps. He quickly realized that even for him, he would need both hands. Reluctantly, he placed his beloved tin box beside the suitcase and hoisted himself up. That box had been with him his whole life. As a little boy living in Harlem, the box sat beside his bed and held all his trinkets.

The conductor's whistle reminded him of the day he was given that tin box. He was only three years old when his Grandpa Samuel brought home the shiny new whistle that still called his tin box home. Grandpa had tied an old shoe-string to the whistle and placed it around his neck. "Now, Toby Boy," he warned, "don't you ever blow this whistle in the apartment or Grandma will toss it out. But if you ever feel in danger, I want you to blow this whistle as loud as you can."

Remembering that warning, Tobias couldn't help but smile. "Wow, was my grandpa right! Grandma CeCe would have tossed that whistle out the fifth-floor window and me right behind it, that's for sure." Looking at the tin box, Tobias thought about that special night his grandpa came into his bedroom and placed it on the wooden crate that sat next to his bed. He opened it and then explained, "You can never go to bed with that whistle around your neck. During the day, it is meant to keep you safe, but at night, it could choke you. So here is a tin box just for you. Toby Boy, I have had this tin box since I was a little boy, and now I am giving it to you. Every night I want you to put this whistle in your special tin box to keep it safe."

Since that night, his tin box had held all of his keepsakes. As a little boy, his cast iron cowboys and Indians had slept in it. Later on, marbles became his treasures. As a boy, all of the letters he had received from home had been protected by this box. As a young man, for three long years, he had stored the ring he had bought for Ruth in his box. But on this special trip, it held all of the precious mementoes of his family. This trip was in honor of Aunt Pearl, but for Tobias, it was about all of them, what they had endured, what they had overcome, and how everything had worked together to make Ms. Pearl the woman she was.

Once on the landing, he gathered up their belongings and made his way into the car to find Ruth. It took a moment for his eyes to adjust to the darkness. The window shades were still down because most of the passengers had been on the train all night and were still sleeping. Most had boarded the train in New Orleans the previous night and were not yet ready to welcome the morning sun.

Ruth had found two seats about midway back. Tobias pushed one or two suitcases over to clear a place for their things, removed his suit coat, folded it neatly, placed it on top of their case and took his seat next to his beautiful wife. Ruth always dressed impeccably but never showy or arrogant. She carried herself with a humble confidence that came from years of focusing on others rather than on herself. They had been married for thirty-two years, but they had never run out of things to discuss. But this morning, their conversation would not have been appreciated by all of the sleeping passengers. Once the conductor had finished punching their tickets, they settled back and tried to relax.

The train began to pick up speed, and the sound of the rhythmic clicking of the tracks carried Tobias back to his very first train ride in 1904. He was a scrawny, seven-year-old boy, afraid of his own shadow, leaving New York City for parts unknown—at least to him.

Tobias had known this train ride would be a sentimental journey. The weeks of preparing his speech and the sound of the conductor's loud whistle coupled with having handled all of the precious items he had packed into his tin box left him very nostalgic. Tobias allowed his feelings to carry him back to the day he had boarded that other train so long ago. He had shared these stories with friends for years, but today he simply wanted to reminisce in silence; reviewing all of the reasons he had for being so proud and thankful he could call himself a member of the Bascom family.

TOBIAS:
My Life in Harlem
1897-1904

CHAPTER 3

Two Train Rides

MY FIRST TRAIN ride happened back in the year 1904. I was seven years old and all alone as I boarded that train car in New York City. The stench of people's clothing that had gone way beyond their cleaning joined with the smells of food prepared with spices unfamiliar to me. These combinations made my already nervous stomach churn even more. I desperately wanted to climb off that train and run back to my grandmother, who was standing right outside the window, watching me take my seat. I wanted to beg her for a second chance. Even at seven, I knew my begging her for a second chance would be futile. She had waited seven long years to get rid of me. In her mind, I embodied every evil thing that had happened to her family. She thought I was cursed, and she was glad to be rid of me. I was being sent away from my home in Harlem, and that was that.

Surprised by the vivid memory of feeling so rejected as a child, he leaned over and kissed Ruth on the cheek. "Honey, I am so glad you are on this train ride with me today."

Ruth smiled and whispered back, "Tobias, we have a long trip ahead of us; try to get some sleep."

He smiled at his wife. He knew he was no longer that lost little boy sitting on that train so many years ago, but this second train ride was beginning to conjure up a storehouse of old memories. These memories were causing his senses to be on the alert. The gentleman sitting right in front of him had obviously been on the train for many days. His hair was greasy, his scraggly gray beard held pieces of bread crumbs, and his yellowed shirt showed rings of body sweat around the tattered rim of his collar. Studying this forlorn man drew Tobias back to one of the loneliest days of his young life—the day he was sent away from his beloved grandfather.

The image of his grandmother's face that day had been etched in his memory. However, fifty years of life had given him the skills to understand and forgive her. Remembering how he felt that day, his mind could not help but think of those first seven years up in Harlem and how they had shaped his life. This train trip was all about family, reviewing what they had experienced, how they had endured, and how their example had taught him how to live a life worth living. Although not all of it was pleasant, he knew it was valuable. Tobias laid his head back against the seat and let his memories overtake him.

Even though my family's history began in Atlanta, Georgia, my story began in Harlem. Grandpa Samuel was twenty years old when he was emancipated in 1865. He struggled for the next twenty-one years, trying to make a living in Atlanta. Once he was sure his sisters, Pearl and Ruby, were safe and settled, he packed up his little family in the summer of 1886 and headed north with the promise of a better life. He was forty-one years old and not afraid of hard work. My mother, his firstborn, was only three years old when the family arrived in Harlem.

The city had begun expanding from lower Manhattan north into Harlem, so plenty of work was available for day-laborers. Construction of the elevated railroad meant Grandpa was able to secure work almost immediately. He did everything from pit digging to form building. Pit digging paid more because it was so dangerous; determined to earn as much money as possible, he always volunteered whenever the need for pit diggers was posted. Many a digger had been buried and suffocated when one of the pits collapsed before the form builders could get in and reinforce the side walls. Because the Irish preferred to stay above ground, Grandpa knew he could always get work if he became the best pit digger in Harlem.

By 1892 most of the pit-digging jobs were gone, and he had to develop other skills if he was going to support his family. Grandpa knew he had to overcome his fear of heights if he was going to have a chance competing for construction work on the Second Avenue Bridge. He had learned to weld in Atlanta, but the only welding jobs offered to blacks were the welding jobs no one else wanted. He was always the first laborer in line every day. Very few men volunteered for the high-rigging work, which required climbing out onto the most dangerous points of the construction and then welding for two to three hours without a break. High winds, rain or ice, Grandpa would be first in line. Years later, he would reminisce about how proud he was to work on one of Theodore Cooper's famous bridges. Before coming to Harlem to begin his work on the Second Avenue Bridge over the Harlem River, Cooper was already famous for the Mississippi River steel arch bridge as well as the 1876 Allegheny River Bridge at Pittsburgh.

During their first winter in Harlem, Grandpa's boy, my Uncle Virgil, was only two years old when he caught the terrible influenza that hit the city that year. Everyone blamed the Irish for bringing it into the neighborhood, but the truth was it didn't matter if you were white, black, Jewish, Irish, or Eastern European. If you caught it, there was no going to a hospital for help. Men with megaphones walked through the neighborhoods, warning people to stay home and ride it out. The elderly and the young were hit the hardest, and they were also the least likely to survive. So it was for Virgil. Grandma did not even go with Grandpa when he carried away his boy's body that night. So many died during that influenza epidemic that the city decided to station body carts around the poor neighborhoods. Most of them could not afford to bury their dead, and the city feared the results of dead bodies stacking up. Although it was hard on Grandpa to let go of his boy, he never blamed himself for Virgil's getting sick and dying. He always said, "Sickness comes to everyone. You just have to accept it."

My family lived on the top floor of a five-story tenement just off Lexington and 116th Street, and life was good for them until the mid-1890s. Our building had been a factory back in the day, but all that remained of the old factory was the large hand-cranked lift that had been used to haul large bales of raw material up to the top floor where workers Carded and spun raw cotton into thread. During the Civil War, the factory was closed and never reopened. Eventually, the property was sold at auction and converted into a tenement building. Grandpa said the owner was a fair man, allowing the tenants to use the lift when moving in or out of his building. Apart from these times, the lift remained padlocked, forcing everyone to use the stairs.

In 1897, Harlem experienced its first of two serious market crashes, and the owner of our building felt the crash. He no longer invested in maintenance, and the neighborhood began to experience a flood of European immigrants. Owners, once careful to maintain a separation of ethnic groups, found themselves willing to rent to anyone with the money to pay their weekly rent. Work became scarce, and the once friendly building became a dangerous place to be. That was the year I came along.

Not accustomed to big city life, Grandma CeCe would let my mother wander around the building unattended—as she had been able to do back home in Georgia. But when Momma was thirteen years old, she was gang-raped in the broken lift by three boys no older than she was. This atrocity almost killed my grandpa. He felt that he had failed his baby girl by not protecting her; then he couldn't even get justice for her. Knowing nothing would be done to those boys, Grandpa wanted to move his family out of the building, but with so few available buildings open to blacks, they were forced to stay put. Two months later, they realized that I was on the way.

Fearing for their safety and feeling powerless, Grandpa ordered my grandmother and momma never to leave the apartment when he was away at work.

My Grandmother CeCe had been a third-generation slave from a small plantation just outside of Decatur, Georgia, and she believed in lots of things. Most were remnants of fables and superstitions handed down through other slaves, but her one driving belief was, "If the whites believe it, then I will not." It did not matter to her how obvious the facts were; she refused to think like whites. Her attitude brings to mind an old idiomatic phrase: ***throwing out the baby with the bath water.*** The trouble was, I was that baby.

According to her beliefs, my life was over before it began. Everything in my grandmother's world convinced her that I was cursed. I was born on July 28, 1897, the day of a partial eclipse. Grandmother CeCe believed the gods were angry, and the eclipse was their warning. It did not matter what the white scientists were saying, she knew better. While everyone else in the city was excited to see this event, Grandmother stayed indoors lest the gods see her and take out their anger on her.

Grandpa Samuel did not have the luxury of staying inside that day. He was a welder on the Second Avenue Bridge and had never missed a day of work. Grandmother warned him he was going to draw too much attention to himself. She believed his working up so high on the bridge during the gods' angry display was just asking for their rage to be poured down on his family. Grandpa went anyway—a decision she would never forget and never forgive.

Not only was I born during the partial eclipse, I had the misfortune, according to my grandmother, of being born on a Wednesday as well. She believed the day you were born destined you. She didn't care where her supposed "truth" originated; if it had been around for years, it must be true. When Grandma was young, she served as a house slave, caring for the youngest children of her master. One of her responsibilities was to memorize nursery rhymes and entertain the little ones. One of these rhymes, which was called "Monday's Child," had been published in 1838 and had quickly become a popular way to teach children the days of the week. The Mother Goose rhyme went like this:

Monday's child is fair of face,
Tuesday's child is full of grace,
Wednesday's child is full of woe,
Thursday's child has far to go,
Friday's child is loving and giving,
Saturday's child works hard for a living,

But the child that is born on the Sabbath day
Is bonny and blithe, and good and gay.

After years of repeating this nursery rhyme, it had become truth to my grandmother. I was born on a Wednesday during a partial eclipse, and I was a child of rape. To my grandmother, I was the embodiment of evil, and she wanted me to die so her gods would stop looking at her family. My mother, who was only fourteen years old at the time of my birth, wanted nothing to do with me either. While the midwife cared for my mother, my grandmother wrapped me in a birthing cloth and carried me up to the roof of our tenement and laid me out to die in full view of her angry gods.

I was left unattended on that roof for several hours, but just as the sun was setting, Grandpa Samuel returned home, found out what Grandma had done and came to my rescue—a routine he would perform many times throughout my life. Although he could not convince my grandmother she was wrong about me, he demanded that I be cared for. Neither my mother nor my grandmother wanted anything to do with me and had not even bothered to name me. Angry at his wife for being so superstitious, at sun-set Grandpa picked me up and returned to the rooftop. In full view of grandmother's angry gods, he shouted to the open sky, "See this child, this beautiful boy? I give him my name, Tobias Samuel Bascom. He is not responsible for how he came to be. He is not evil. He is innocent, and I love him. I am his grandfather, and I will protect this boy. May his days be many and may his heart be strong. May his courage meet all that life will bring to him; may he never live a single day without knowing he is loved."

My grandpa repeated this prayer to the universe many times during my young life. It became our ritual every night when he tucked me into bed. Fifty years have passed since I have heard his booming voice repeat it, but I can close my eyes and still hear his love-filled voice pleading on my behalf. Although my mother and grandmother remained cold toward me during those first seven years of my life, Grandpa Samuel was bigger than life to me. No boy could ever have had a better role model.

While living in Grandpa's house, the subject of slavery was seldom discussed. Once in a while some of the men at the city park would begin to share their stories, but Grandpa would always pull me away and say, "Those are not stories for young ears." I often questioned him about his past, but he would scowl and say, "Life is hard enough worrying about what lies ahead of you, Toby Boy. There is no benefit in reliving the past."

Although I loved him, there was so much about him I did not know. As a young child, I was taught to fear the gods of my grandmother. She blamed me for every bad thing that touched our family, and I believed I had been cursed. Even though my grandfather loved me and did not believe in the gods of my grandmother, neither did he believe in the white man's God. He had been born and reared on the Stewart Plantation in Atlanta, Georgia, and the master told all the slaves that the white man's God demanded absolute obedience from the slaves. When I was a very young boy, this was the only topic which ever caused my grandfather to mention the subject of slavery.

Whenever a street preacher would approach Grandpa Samuel, he would grab hold of my hand tightly and say, "Tobias, he is talking about the white man's God. That god did not care about us so we don't care about him."

Since I loved and respected my grandfather, I did not question his opinion. His opinions were my opinions. Although Grandpa refused to talk about his experiences, he did try to help me understand why my grandmother was the way she was. I was four years old the first time Grandpa told me her story. "Toby Boy, your Grandma CeCe was born into slavery, set free at the age of thirteen, but then she was left on her own, without any family or education. She about starved that first year and did menial labor until she met and married me. She is a hard-working woman, Toby, and she deserves to be respected. Without any education, she has struggled to get by. Her superstitions are her rule-book for life. It is all she knows."

CHAPTER 4

Brother Jubilee Comes A Calling

TOBIAS WAS STARTLED back to the present by the porter's walking through the car announcing the dining car was now open for breakfast. Of course, no one from the Colored Car could actually enter the dining car, but they were able to walk back to the snack counter to purchase food and drink. Ruth bent down and lifted the brown bag of goodies she had prepared for them. Tobias smiled as he studied his wife and thought, "No one can bake lighter-than-air croissants like my Ruth. Before she took that job in the hospital bakery, I didn't even know what a croissant was."

Trying to shake off the memory of his birth and focus on the goodies before him, he took hold of Ruth's hand, bent down close to her and asked a blessing on their breakfast. True to form, Ruth leaned forward and tapped the shoulder of the gentleman sitting in front of them, "Sir, would you like a bite to eat?"

The man's first reaction to being touched was anger, but as he turned and saw Ruth, he quickly smiled and said, "That'd be nice, thanks."

Tobias smiled as he watched Ruth unwrap a freshly baked blueberry muffin and hand it forward. What that gentleman saw in Ruth's face was the same thing Tobias had been seeing in her face since the first day he had met her when he was seven years old—love, compassion, gentleness, and not one stitch of judgment. Tobias smiled again as he thought, "Oh, how I love this woman."

After they finished their breakfast, Ruth asked, "Honey, would you mind trading seats with me? I would like to chat with the woman sitting across the aisle."

Tobias smiled, grabbed his box, and slid over to the window seat. As he stared out at the landscape flying by, he couldn't help but think about his Grandpa Samuel, way back in 1886, taking his family to New York on these same tracks. Oh, the train cars were different, but the open fields could not have been much different for him. Sitting there, Tobias tried to imagine what his grandfather was feeling the day he took this train ride.

Grandpa was a kind, caring, hard-working man, and he was careful not to talk against the woman he loved. Tobias reviewed what he knew about those first two years of his life. He understood that he was never taken out of the apartment because Grandma CeCe believed that taking him outside was daring her gods to show their anger that he was still alive. Thankfully, inside the apartment, Grandma CeCe tried to be kind to him. His momma, on the other hand, would have nothing to do with him. By the time he had turned two, his sixteen-year-old mother had moved out of the apartment. With this thought, Tobias slid back into his past. Once again his mind drifted back in time.

My earliest memories began when I was around three years old. I remember when the weather was good and Grandpa had a day off, he would take me out of the apartment. We would sit on the front stoop, and he would talk with the other men from the building. I remember sitting on his lap with his huge arms around me and the sound of his deep, booming laugh that shook my whole body. I have such sweet feelings attached to this memory. I can close my eyes and remember how it felt when Grandpa would place his large hand on my chest and pull me back against his chest and whisper in my ear, "Toby Boy, you are *my* boy, and I love you."

Grandma and Momma usually just called me "Boy." By the time I was aware of things around me, Momma was seldom there, and when she was, I didn't much like it. She would smell funny and use bad words to Grandma. She seldom came around when Grandpa was home, so Grandma received the brunt of her anger. I was glad that she ignored me. I think she simply pretended I didn't exist.

I was not treated badly; I was simply ignored by everyone except Grandpa. When Grandpa was home, I was on his lap. Until I turned four, he would even eat his dinner with me on his lap. I remember his telling me all about how they built his huge bridge. He would draw pictures of the bridge and show me exactly where he was working. On my fifth birthday, Grandpa took me on the trolley all the way to the Second Avenue Bridge. I remember how proud I felt, seeing that big bridge and knowing my grandpa had helped build it. Once it was built, the construction company kept Grandpa on the payroll as an inspector and spot welder. He pointed out how high up he had to climb in order to make sure the side-strappings were securely in place. "Toby Boy, it takes me one whole year to climb over every inch of that bridge, make my repairs and fill out my reports." Then he would start the same process all over again. On the way back home, we stopped in at the big library, and Grandpa pulled out a big picture book and laid it on a table. He opened it up and showed me pictures of all kinds of bridges. He explained how they were built over fast-moving rivers, and I was so proud of my grandpa.

Every evening Grandpa would work with me on my letters and numbers. He told stories of when he was a young boy, and how his sister, Pearl, had taught him all of the letters and numbers she had learned. At first, he didn't understand why it was so important to Pearl, but she had insisted, so he did it. He said the first word he ever learned how to write was his own name. "Toby Boy," he would say, "it is important to know how to read and write. It will open up doors for you."

I was so proud when someone in the building came knocking on our door, asking my grandpa to read a letter or notice he had received. He was held in high regard, and well I knew it.

Before I came along, our building had been exclusively black. As with most buildings, when housing became more and more scarce, owners began blending different nationalities in the buildings. Even then, they did try to keep us separated by floors. The Jewish families preferred the first-floor units because most of them worked out of their apartments, and customers did not want to walk up three or four flights of stairs to reach their tailor. Since the top floors were the cheapest, we always lived on the top floor. The Irish and the Italians usually kept to themselves, and we were glad. Regardless of your ethnic background, you learned that living in the tenements of New York City meant following one universal rule: "Mind your own business." The police were never interested in what went on inside the tenements, so the renters were on their own. The Irish and the Italians had clubs or large families that would come to their aid, so you learned quickly it was neither wise nor safe to provoke them.

Our building was sandwiched between two larger tenements on either side. By the time I was old enough to walk around with Grandpa, my momma had been gone for almost two years. Grandpa simply called her "Girl." We seldom talked about her because, by Grandpa's own admission, he had not handled my momma's problems well. His guilt for failing to protect my momma drove a wedge between them, and she began to run with a wild crowd. She would not listen to my grandparents—even when they threatened to send her back to Georgia. She seldom came around, and when she did, I didn't like the shouting.

Life in the tenement was full of rules, and Grandpa made sure I knew them. The earliest rule I can remember was, "Mind your own business, boy." On the rare occasions when Grandpa had a day off work, we walked to the park. I remember seeing something happening, and Grandpa Samuel yanked my arm and said, "Mind your own business, boy. You don't see anything, and you don't remember anything." I knew having a "blind eye" bothered Grandpa, but rules were rules.

One day, when I was four, Grandpa and I walked out of the apartment and down the hallway to the sometimes unlocked lift and saw a man stealing our neighbor's tool chest. Grandpa repeated this phrase to me loud enough for the thief to hear. As he pulled the lift gate closed, he bent down and said, "Do you know why I said that so loud, Toby Boy?"

I shook my head and answered, "No."

"Because I needed him to know that you and I were not a threat to him so he would leave us alone. That man lives on the second floor of our building, and he knows he will have those tools sold within the hour. The police won't do anything to him because it is one black man's word against another's. Without the tool chest as evidence, I would just be putting my family in danger."

Even as a small child, I knew this admission hurt Grandpa, but I also knew I was to say nothing. He was a proud man who knew he could not protect his family. Even though I never thought of him as such, oh, how it must have hurt him to look like a coward in my eyes.

After dinner Grandpa would bring out the large tablet and a box of pencils he always kept on the sideboard. I would climb up onto his lap, and we would trace my letters as I called out their names. One night Grandpa forgot his rule about not speaking about the past, and I was certainly not going to remind him. As we traced the letter P, Grandpa said, "P is the first letter of my sister Pearl's name." As he took the pencil and spelled out his sister's name, Grandpa Samuel's eyes kind of glazed over as his mind traveled back in time. "Toby, Pearl and her twin sister, Ruby, are three years younger than I am. When Pearl turned eight, the missus of the house decided that Pearl should learn to read and write. Toby, this was never done. It was actually against the law to teach slaves how to read and write, but Ms. Victoria did not care about laws when they interfered with her plans. Our Momma Hannah was the house cook but she could not read or write, which meant that Ms. Victoria had to sit in the hot kitchen and write out the shopping list for Momma. Ms. Victoria hated this task and her daughter, Miss Elizabeth, refused to do it.

"My sister, Pearl, was sharp as a tack," Grandpa smiled as he said this. "Ms. Victoria always used to say this to our Momma. Pearl loved letters and words and was an eager student, but the tutor Ms. Victoria hired to teach her own children was not so eager to teach a black child. She was hard and mean to my sister, but the pay was good. Besides, Pearl had no choice in the matter."

Grandpa caught himself and realized he had been talking about their time as slaves and abruptly stopped. "Toby, regardless of how it came about, my sister Pearl was a good student and later, she became a good teacher. She was determined that I would also learn how to read and write, and when Ms. Pearl was determined, it was so."

I remember trying to imagine what this Ms. Pearl looked like. Was she big and strong like my grandpa? I knew Grandpa did not have any pictures of his family—at least none that he had ever been willing to share with me. Even as a four-year-old, I knew better than to ask questions. Grandpa never got angry with me; he would simply say, "Maybe some other time, Toby, when you are a little older."

By the time I turned five, I could print all of my letters, and I could count to one hundred. I knew Grandpa was proud of me, and that knowledge made me feel special.

Two weeks after my fifth birthday, Grandpa was injured on the job. For almost a month twice a week, Grandma took the train to see him in the hospital. I was not allowed to go see him, so I was left with a neighbor. I was told he would never walk again. My big, strong Grandpa, who had built the Second Avenue Bridge all by himself, would never walk again. The bridge had been his life. He loved being the inspector-welder. He was now in his early fifties, but he loved his work and was proud of *his* bridge— as he always called it. He had been inspecting way out on the tresses when the weather suddenly shifted, and as he began making his way back, he lost his grip and fell. His safety harness stopped his fall, but the snap broke his back. Grandpa hung there for thirty minutes before the other workers were able to get him down.

Grandpa came home in a wheelchair, a broken man in body and spirit. Grandma said that when his workmates found out he would need a wheelchair, they took up a collection and bought one for him. For the first time in my life, he didn't seem huge to me. While Grandpa was in the hospital, I was supposed to start public school. Grandma had taken a cleaning job in a big building a few blocks away, and Grandpa could not be left alone in the apartment. Since the lift was either padlocked or did not work most of the time, Grandpa was trapped in the apartment, so I stayed with him and didn't start school.

My job was to run down four flights of stairs and up four doors to the storefront market to buy him his cigarettes, bread, cheese—whatever he needed. On the rare occasions when the lift was working and the weather was nice, I would roll Grandpa out of the apartment to the lift. We would take the lift down to the ground floor, and I would push his chair up the street to the park for some fresh air. Those were the days I lived for.

Having never attended school, I didn't miss going. However, Grandpa would tell me that someday, when things were different, I would get to go to school. Right about this time, a new church opened in one of the storefronts right next to our grocery store—three doors down from our tenement. I remember sitting at the kitchen window on a summer night, listening to the beautiful voices of those churchgoers as they sang gospel hymns. I would ask Grandpa if we could go to that church and watch the singers, but Grandpa would always say, "Not for us, Toby Boy, those people are spreading the slave-master's religion."

I did not understand what Grandpa meant by this statement, but I knew it was a settled issue for him. Slavery was a topic my grandpa would never discuss. Although he loved his sisters living in Georgia, Grandpa would never talk about them either. Grandma told me one or two stories but as soon as Grandpa found out, he ordered her to stop. "We live here now. The past is the past, and it is not worth remembering."

Even though I felt like I needed to hate this slave-master's religion, I loved to sit by the open window and listen to the songs they were singing. You could hear the love these people had for this Jesus, and I was curious to know more about Him. However, Grandpa was firm—"No religion in this house"—that is, until the night Brother Jubilee came a calling.

I had just been tucked into bed when a knock at our door changed everything. I crept out of my bed and opened my bedroom door so I could hear what this stranger was saying. I climbed back into bed and listened while Grandpa Samuel argued with this young man who was sitting at our kitchen table, trying to tell Grandpa about a man named Jesus. As the young man talked about all the wonderful things this Jesus had done, I remember wanting to know more about Him and wondered why I had never heard any of this before. Just as the man began telling about the miracles this Jesus had done, Grandpa ordered the man to stop talking about Him. My heart sank. Then I heard Grandpa say, "You are talking about my slave owner's Jesus. Your Jesus did not care about my father when he was sold away from us when I was six years old. He didn't care about my mother or my sisters. Why would I want to come and listen to a slave-owner's religion?"

I had heard Grandpa Samuel say he didn't like the white man's god, but I never knew why. I had heard the angry conversations of others, shouting about how terrible slavery was, and now I heard the terrible pain my grandpa had experienced. Loyal to him, I instantly took his side, deciding I too would not like this Jesus.

The stranger kept talking. "Samuel, Jesus is not the slave-owner's religion. They didn't make Him up. Jesus came to the Jews first—fellow slaves. They were first slaves in Egypt, and then when Jesus came, they were slaves under Rome's control. Samuel, don't you think Jesus understands what it was like to be a slave? Jesus could have come to the power-hungry Egyptians or the powerful Romans, but instead He came to the ones who knew what it was like to live under the thumb of slave-holders."

I heard Grandpa say, "I never knew that. All I was ever told was that this Jesus wanted us to obey our master and be glad and thankful we had food and a roof over our heads. My own mother believed that Master Stewart was like a god to us."

Brother Jubilee answered, "Samuel, people create lots of little gods, but none of them have ever been willing to give his own life to free us— that is what Jesus did. There is more than one kind of slavery. Slavery is when someone else owns you, right? The Bible says we are all slaves to sin, but Jesus came to free us from that slavery. He gave His own life as a ransom for us. He bought us off the slave auction block and wants to set us free. Samuel, don't you want to get to know this Jesus who was willing to be your ransom?"

I remember lying in my bed, crying quietly, "Grandpa, please, please say yes. I want to know this Jesus."

It was quiet for some time before my grandpa answered him. "Brother Jubilee, I think I do want to know more about this Jesus. I've always refused to read the Bible because I thought it was just a slave-owner's book. My grandson has been begging me to come to your church, so I guess we will come and find out about this Jesus who loved all slaves."

CHAPTER 5

❧

Grandpa's Confession

TOBIAS WAS LITERALLY jolted back to the present, as the heavyset man sitting behind him grabbed hold of the seatback in order to hoist himself up. He angrily shouted at his bedraggled wife, "Get up you lazy, good-for-nothing cow. I need to get to the water closet."

No one looked up as the woman quickly got up and cleared a path for this man who evidently was used to getting his way. As she returned to her seat, Tobias tried to make eye contact and give her a smile, but she never looked up. He suspected she had developed a lifelong habit of not making eye contact.

Earlier, Ruth had turned around and offered them both a blueberry muffin. Although the wife had accepted her offer, she had avoided any eye contact and had mumbled a faint, "Thanks."

Tobias studied this man's face as he made his way back to his seat, and he thought to himself, "It's sad how a face can become a road map to years of selfish bad choices. His eyes are hollow and empty, and I suspect the only feeling this man has felt in years is anger."

Realizing that pressing a conversation upon this man would not accomplish any good right then, Tobias continued to look forward and again opened his tin box. He pulled out the envelope that contained the lapel pin that he had been given when he was seven years old. As he removed the pin from its protective envelope, he smiled as he studied the beautiful mother-of-pearl pin with the word "Mother" etched across it and a dainty heart dangling below it.

Holding the pin tightly, Tobias thought about the man who had given it to him the day he was leaving Harlem for good. Brother Jubilee came by and pinned it on his shirt, saying, "Toby Boy, you keep praying for your momma, and no matter what, you keep loving her."

Holding the pin, Tobias could not help but think about how different his life would have been had Brother Jubilee not come a knocking on their door that night. Clasping the pin tightly, he allowed his sweet memories of how Brother Jubilee helped change his momma's life to flood his mind.

For a good year, when the weather was decent and the lift was working, I would roll Grandpa to the storefront church, and Brother Jubilee would tell us all about this wonderful Jesus. The ladies would fix lunch, and then I would sit and watch them practice the beautiful songs that made my insides want to curl up in pure joy.

One afternoon as we were getting ready to return home, Brother Jubilee stopped us to ask Grandpa, "Doesn't Tobias' mother have a name? Samuel, I notice that you always refer to her as 'Girl.'"

I froze in place, wondering how Grandpa was going to react to such a direct question. I had wanted to ask this same question many times, but I was afraid of hearing the answer. To my surprise, I heard his answer: "Brother Jubilee, could you come round to my place tonight? I think you and I need to talk. Tobias goes to bed about seven o'clock. Could you come round about eight?"

Obviously, Grandpa did not want me hearing what he was going to say about my momma, but I was determined to stay awake and listen. That night, while lying in bed, I could smell the fresh coffee Grandpa was brewing. Brother Jubilee was a very young man, but I knew Grandpa respected him. I knew Grandpa was nervous about their private meeting. My eyes started getting heavy, and I was afraid I would fall asleep. I threw back my blanket, took off my socks, and sat on the edge of my bed, waiting. The warmth of my bed was beckoning me, but I fought to stay awake.

Finally, the welcome sound of a gentle knock on the door signaled Brother Jubilee's arrival. I quickly tucked myself back under the covers—in case Grandpa came to check and see if I were asleep. My excitement was so high at this point; sleep was the last thing I worried about. I could hear the kitchen chair scooting back as Brother Jubilee offered to pour the coffee. They kept their voices low, not wanting to disturb my sleep, so I crept out of my bed and sat on the floor as far out into the hallway as I dared go. I could tell they were struggling to carry on small talk, when Brother Jubilee repeated the same question he had asked that morning.

Grandpa's voice was soft and pleading. "I've been thinking about that question all day, Brother Jubilee. I want to be honest, but I don't think I have a simple answer to your question. You see, I failed my girl, Brother Jubilee. I not only failed her, I betrayed her, and my shame is hurting her and killing me."

While sitting on the floor hearing my grandpa talking with so much emotion, I wasn't sure I wanted to hear what was coming. Grandpa was my hero, but now I was going to hear how he had failed my momma and had even betrayed her—was I ready to hear this?

I could hear Brother Jubilee scoot his chair closer to Grandpa's wheelchair as he said, "Samuel, why don't you just start at the beginning?"

"Brother Jubilee, do you remember my telling you that my family were all slaves back in Georgia before the War? I never talk about our life on the plantation. I think it's best to leave the past in the past. But after thinking about your question all day and your sermon last Sunday about the sin of pride, I think my sinful pride has really hurt my little girl."

Brother Jubilee kept quiet, letting Grandpa work through his story without pushing him. I heard Grandpa blow his nose before continuing, "You see, as far back as I can remember, it was my job to look after my mother and sisters. I was so young when Master Stewart sold my daddy away, I can't remember a time when I didn't feel responsible for them. I always worked extra hard, hoping to make myself so valuable to the plantation that Master Stewart wouldn't dare sell me away from Momma and the sisters. Since I never knew how much *enough* was, I fairly killed myself doing a man's labor. Even as a young boy, I knew he could just up and sell me off without a second thought.

"As the years went by and the war talk grew, Master Stewart was having a harder and harder time selling or trading any of us. When I was about thirteen, five or six of his best slaves started talking about running off. They were sure that if they worked together, they could make it North to freedom; they wanted me to go with them. I wanted to, but how could I leave behind my momma and my sisters?

"That next year Master Stewart's daughter got married, and without a thought, he gave away my sister Ruby as a wedding present. My sweet, kind, gentle, little sister Ruby was suddenly gone, and there was nothing I could do about it. Her leaving about drove me crazy, Brother Jubilee. You see, I had no idea what kind of Master Miss Elizabeth's new husband was. Master Stewart was strict, but he prided himself on being a righteous man. To my knowledge, he never touched any of our women. That is not to say he was above using a switch or selling us off like so much extra crop at the end of a harvest, and he didn't beat us without cause. But what was happening to my Ruby? She was so young and defenseless, and I felt truly helpless."

I heard Brother Jubilee whisper, "I am so sorry, Samuel. That must have been terrible."

"Another day I will tell you all about what happened to Ruby, but for now, it is only important that you know it is because of my love for her that I named my little girl, Ruby Girl. Brother Jubilee, I was so full of pride, working so hard to care for my little family. I would see other men messing with other women, drinking their wages, and living a riotous life, and I would feel so superior to them. I had always been the one who took care of everyone I loved—no matter how hard I had to work. Then, one day after being beaten and raped, my Ruby Girl came running into this apartment, and all of those old emotions of feeling helpless when my sister Ruby had been given away simply overtook me. I remembered how frightened I was about what that man might be doing to my sister Ruby, and now all these years later, standing right in front of me, was my own little Ruby Girl, violated at the hands of three boys. I was again helpless to do anything about what happened to her. Once we were freed from slavery,

I swore I would never be helpless again. I would take care of my family, work extra hard to make sure we never went without, and I would make sure my sisters and my family would always be safe; but I couldn't keep that promise, Brother Jubilee."

By now I had crawled all the way to the opening of the kitchen, so I could see Grandpa. I watched his broken spirit confess his deepest hurt. With his face covered in tears for my grandpa, Brother Jubilee knelt down on his knees and lifted Grandpa's face with his hands and pleaded, "Samuel, we live in a fallen world. You could not keep that promise because it was never your promise to make. But there is one promise you should have kept, and that promise was to love your baby girl no matter what—no matter how she lives her life. No matter what, she deserves her daddy to love her. Do you love Ruby Girl, Samuel?"

"Yes, Brother Jubilee, I do. I have let my hurtful pride at not keeping my promise drive her away from me. It wasn't that she was raped or that my Toby Boy came along. I drove her away because every time I looked at her, I saw my failure. My pride was hurt so I made her pay for it."

Brother Jubilee took hold of Grandpa Samuel's shoulders, pushed them back so he sat straight and tall in his wheelchair, and commanded, "Then Samuel, confess this matter to her. Lay down your pride. Ask God for the humility to make no excuses and tell your little girl how much you love her. She needs to hear this from her daddy, and from now on, you call her 'Ruby Girl' as proof that you do not hold her past against her."

As Brother Jubilee continued to talk with Grandpa, I slipped back to my bed, pulled the covers up over my head and thought about my momma. I knew she hated coming here to see me. I always thought it was because of how I had been born. Many times as she was leaving, I would hear her say to Grandma, "Daddy can't stand to look at me, Momma. I know it is because of how Boy was born and now how I am living. Momma, maybe I just shouldn't come around here anymore."

I never understood what they meant by how I was born, but I always knew that whatever it was, it was my fault. Now hearing Grandpa Samuel so heartbroken over how I was born that he had turned against my momma made it even worse. But somehow, hearing Brother Jubilee's voice reading the Bible to my grandpa brought me great comfort that night.

Two days later, Grandpa called me to the kitchen table and said, "Toby Boy, I have sinned against your momma, and I need to find her and ask for her forgiveness. I felt so helpless when she was rap...beaten up. I wasn't there to protect her. I failed her, and since I didn't know what to do, I just shut off my hurt and ignored her."

I finally gathered up the courage to ask, "Grandpa, are you sorry I was born—like my momma is sorry?"

Grandpa's big strong hands lifted me up onto his lap as he began to cry, "Toby Boy, I could never be sorry having you as my little boy. I hate that my Ruby Girl had to be hurt by those bad boys, but that is not your fault. You are too young to understand what any of this means, but one day I will tell you the whole story. Just you know that we all love you, Toby Boy."

Placing me back on the kitchen chair, Grandpa rolled his wheelchair around and drew up right in front of me. "Toby Boy, your momma needs to know that I love her no matter how she is living. Brother Jubilee says God loved us while we were still sinners, and she deserves a daddy who will love her like God loves her."

That afternoon Grandpa put out the word that he wanted to see my momma. Several weeks went by with nothing from her. Every day Grandpa prayed that God would give him the words my momma needed to hear. Apart from the three mornings a week that we went to Bible study, Grandpa sat in his wheelchair by the window, reading the Bible and waiting for his little girl to show up. On the other hand, I was not so sure I wanted her to show up. Their meetings had never gone well, and I knew that she hated the sight of me. She would show up smelling of cheap perfume, spouting ugly words, and wearing lots of makeup. The last few times she smelled like the barroom down the street and looked like someone had been beating on her, but Grandpa wanted to see her so we waited.

The week I turned seven, she came walking in the door with a baseball for me. Tossing it over to me, she said, "What are you now, Toby Boy, seven?"

I hated her calling me that. From my grandpa, "Toby Boy" was a sweet name—but not from her. I was surprised that she even remembered it was my birthday. Before I could even reply, she turned to her daddy and asked, "So I hear you want to see me. Is my momma okay?"

"Your momma is fine," Grandpa responded. "She works too hard, but she is not the reason I wanted to see you, Ruby Girl. Will you sit down for a minute so we can talk?"

I was seven years old and had never heard my grandpa use my momma's real name to her. She had always been just "Girl." I watched as my momma's usually hardened face became very emotional, and I realized this encounter was something huge. Her eyes filled with tears as she pleaded, "I can't stay long, Daddy. People are waiting for me downstairs."

"This won't take long, Ruby Girl. I wanted to tell you how much I love you, little girl. I should have told you that the night you came into this room after being attacked. I should have told you that every morning and every night after that happened. I knew you thought I blamed you for it, but I promise I didn't, Ruby Girl. I blamed me for not protecting you, and I didn't know what to do with the shame I felt for failing you."

My momma sat frozen. None of her usual foul words were thrown around the room that morning. The tears began to flow, and her shoulders quivered as she tried to hold back the torrent of emotion upon hearing her daddy asking for her forgiveness.

For weeks Grandpa talked about what he should say if Momma ever showed up. Should he challenge her lifestyle, pointing out how dangerous it was and how she needed to return home and change? "No," Grandpa said, "She needs to know that her daddy loves her. Only after she knows this can I tell her that God loves her too."

Grandpa kept repeating the words, "Your daddy failed you, Ruby girl. I should have picked you up and told you that what happened was not your fault and that it did not change the fact that I love you."

I watched as years of hardheartedness washed off my momma's face in only a few moments. For the first time in my life, I saw my momma as a little girl who was hearing her daddy tell her he still loved her—no matter what she was doing now. My grandpa's words were reaching her. He had prayed for weeks about what he should say, and his words were perfect.

Momma Ruby didn't stay long. She knew the man who was waiting for her downstairs would not wait very long, and she did not want him coming up looking for her. "Daddy, I have to go, but I will come back. It feels so good hearing you call me Ruby again. You haven't used my name since that terrible day."

"I know, Ruby Girl. I should have, and I am sorry."

Momma Ruby walked over to Grandpa, bent down and kissed his forehead. "I love you too, Daddy. I'll be back."

It didn't even bother me that she forgot to say goodbye to me. All I had to do was look at my grandpa's face to know that this was a good day.

CHAPTER 6

Why I Was Sent Away

TOBIAS LOOKED DOWN at the lapel pin in his hand and thought about the gentleman sitting behind him and wondered, "Did he ever have a momma that he loved? Has he ever heard his daddy say he was sorry for the disappointments in his young life? Has he ever heard his daddy say, 'I love you, son?'"

He placed his pin back into the envelope and replaced it the tin box. He whispered a prayer for the unhappy man sitting behind him and thought, "That could have been me. How easy it would have been to grow up bitter at not having a daddy, having a momma who hated the sight of me, and having a grandma who thought I was cursed. I owe so much to my Grandpa Samuel and to Brother Jubilee. Without them, I might have been every bit as mean and unhappy."

Ruth leaned over and whispered, "Tobias, I am going to the water closet. Can you keep an eye on our things?"

"Of course I will, Ruth," Tobias replied, bringing his mind back to the present. He watched as Ruth made her way forward and smiled to himself. "I wish I could go back in time to little Toby and tell him how great his life is going to turn out."

Studying Ruth, he couldn't help but think, "She is tall and lean with skin the color of deep, rich chocolate, and just as sweet. That lemon yellow suit is my favorite. I don't know how she does it. She can sit in church for hours and stand up and look as neat and tidy as when she first walked into the sanctuary. Even after sitting on this train for almost three hours, she still shows no sign of fatigue."

When Ruth returned to her seat, Tobias stood up, straightened out his rumpled trousers and headed to the water closet. As he returned, he noticed that Ruth was still deep in conversation with the woman across the aisle, so he slipped into his seat, picked up his tin box and returned to his memories.

Tobias rummaged through the box, knowing two special buttons were at the bottom. First, he removed the large wooden button that his grandfather had lovingly painted to look like a wheel. This button represented both the best memory of his childhood as well as the scariest. As he studied the button, his mind traveled back to the day his grandpa had painted it.

Grandpa had now been in the wheelchair for over a year and was never getting out of it. He knew that my life had become rather mundane. Without school, all I had to look forward to was church meetings three mornings a week and the occasional visit from Momma Ruby. She never stayed long, but at least she was coming more often.

One day Grandpa rolled his chair to the coat closet and pulled down his favorite coat—a heavy pea-coat he always wore while working on the bridge. He brought it back to the kitchen table and took a sharp knife from the drawer and began sawing off all of the big wooden buttons. Once they were all off, he ordered, "Toby Boy, get under the sink and pull out one or two of those old newspapers your grandma saves to wrap up the garbage."

I brought them over to the table, and Grandpa began spreading them out. "Now, Toby Boy, get that chair and push it up to the counter. Your grandma has been saving the empty oatmeal boxes. I think there are three of them up there. Get them down without falling and hurting yourself."

As I was doing that, Grandpa rolled over to the cabinet and pulled out several small tin cans of paint and several small brushes. "You know what we are going to do today, Toby? We are going to turn these oatmeal boxes into toys. This one is going to be a freight wagon. This one is going to be a city bus, and holding up the third box, he asked, "What do you want this one to be?"

"A fire truck, Grandpa!" I squealed with delight.

"A fire truck it is, Toby my boy," laughed Grandpa. "First, we need to paint the boxes to look like a bus, a freight truck, and a fire truck. See these buttons? After we paint them, they will look like tires. Once they are all dry, we will put your trucks together, and you can have fun playing with them."

How I loved playing with those trucks! I would slip out of the apartment as soon as Grandpa fell asleep for his afternoon nap. My favorite spot was up on our roof. We lived on the top floor, and the stairwell to the roof was right across from our door. It was much too cold to play up there during the long winter, but the months of spring, summer and fall were great. That summer I found leftover bricks stacked against the transom that lit up the whole stairwell. I began building make-believe roads out of them. I loved to set up my very own city on the roof. I would pretend to be the bus driver picking up passengers or a wagon driver delivering coal, ice, or building supplies to my make-believe buildings. But my favorite was the fire truck. Grandpa glued toothpicks together and made ladders for my truck. I pretended to run for buckets of water whenever my buildings were on fire. I would knock down my pretend buildings and then deliver new bricks and rebuild them. I loved my city.

I always dreaded the sound of Grandpa's calling for me from our living room window that was right below me. His calling meant he was up from his nap, and I would have to leave my city, take my trucks and return to our suffocating apartment. Our building was sandwiched between two ten story tenements, with only a narrow alleyway between our side of the building and the building next door. Very little air came into our windows, but we were constantly hearing angry foreign voices from all of the open windows across from us.

I hated how the old Italian women would stick their heads out their kitchen windows and holler up to someone on the floor above or below and chatter away in a language I could not understand. But that summer my attitude toward them made an abrupt turn. I had been playing with my city for hours, wondering why Grandpa was still asleep, but loving the extra time alone. Suddenly someone grabbed me from behind, put his hand over my mouth and dragged me over to the far side of the transom. Spinning me around, he punched me in the stomach very hard and warned, "Keep quiet and do what I say."

I knew who he was. Now in his early twenties, he lived on the second floor of our building. Grandpa always warned me to steer clear of this one, believing he was one of the three who had raped my mother seven years earlier. I tried to pull out of his grip, hoping to make a run for the stairwell, but he was much too strong for me. I wanted to scream, but he still had his hand over my mouth. I remember thinking to myself, "Who would I scream to? Grandpa is in his wheelchair and cannot make it up the stairs, and everyone else follows the rules—mind your own business. No one will come to help me."

I will never forget the wild look in his eyes as he undid my trousers and shoved them to my feet. He didn't say a word, just dropped his own trousers and then spun me around and bent me over. I could feel his hot breath on the back of my neck—when suddenly a woman from the next building started screaming something in Italian. Practically climbing out her kitchen window and pointing to my rooftop, she struggled for the right English words. "Calvin James, I see what you are doing to that boy." Then in the most beautiful broken English, I heard her threaten, "You leave that boy alone, or I will call the police. I know where you live."

Someone was breaking the rules for me—and I knew what she did was huge. This woman knew what Calvin was trying to do to me. She knew who he was and where he lived. She also knew that he knew where she lived—but that did not stop her. She was trying to save me. She kept screaming Calvin's name until several other women came to their windows and joined her in screaming his name. First one and then all the rest began swirling around their white dishtowels while they screamed his name. Calvin angrily shoved me back against the transom so hard I was afraid I would fall right through it. He pulled up his trousers, gave all the women a foul gesture and took off down the stairwell.

As I got up and began pulling up my trousers, the women began screaming, "Go home, boy. Run to your Nonno; run to your Nonno!"

I didn't even stop to pick up my beloved trucks that day. I ran down the stairs and into my apartment and locked the door behind me. My grandfather took one look at me and knew I was in trouble. I ran to the living room window and pointed to the window where the Italian lady lived. I waved and shouted, "Thank you, Lady."

She waved back and shouted, "Molto bene, molto bene!"

That night I learned three beautiful Italian words that I will never forget. *Nonno* was the Italian word for "grandfather" and *molto bene* meant "very good."

My Grandpa lifted me up onto his lap, and I told him what had just happened as he cradled me until I stopped shaking, "Toby Boy, I am so sorry that happened to you. I am sorry you have to live in this terrible building where people try to do such awful things to little children. I cannot sit by and let the same thing happen to you that happened to my little Ruby. What I wasn't wise enough to do for your momma, I have to do for you. Just like the story of Moses, his mother had to give him away to save him because she loved him, Toby Boy."

"Grandpa, what do you mean 'give him away'? You aren't going to give me away? Who will take care of you?" I began to cry as I promised, "I will never go up on the roof again."

"Toby Boy, I am stuck in this chair. No one is going to do anything about Calvin James. I can't protect you."

Three days later Grandpa sat me down and told me he was sending me to Georgia to live with my great-aunts, his younger sisters. I cried, thinking that just as they had threatened to send my momma back to Georgia when she misbehaved, now I was being punished and sent away from my beloved grandpa. Although it would be years before I fully realized the sacrifice my grandpa was making, I did know he was trying to protect me. "Toby Boy, I am not sending you away because you did anything wrong. I am sending you away to protect you. This is not a safe place for you. Back home in Atlanta, my sisters, Pearl and Ruby, can give you a good home where you will be safe."

"But Grandpa, if it is not safe here, why can't you and grandma come with me?"

"Toby Boy, there is nothing I'd want more, but I have to stay here for your momma Ruby. You know she needs her daddy if we are ever going to get her out of the terrible life she is living. You know she has started coming around, and she is beginning to listen. She isn't there yet, but I am asking God to help me reach your momma. I need to keep you safe, but I also need to know that your momma is safe too. I can't leave this city without my Ruby girl."

The last morning I was in that apartment, Grandpa removed one of the wheels from that fire truck and placed it in my tin box. "Toby, you keep this button as a reminder of two things: first, remember how much I loved my boy; and secondly, remember how God kept you safe up on that roof.

"Toby, my boy, I never told you where this tin box came from, but before you leave, I want you to know how special this box is. When I was about your age, I lost my daddy. I was really upset because my daddy was going to be sold that day. It was 1853, and my momma wanted me to have something to hold onto to remember my daddy. On the center of the table that sat right in the middle of our cabin, something was wrapped in an old burlap sack. As she unwrapped it, she said, "Samuel, I have owned this beautiful tin box since I was seventeen. It was back in 1841when Master Stewart ordered me to get rid of it, but it was so beautiful I just couldn't part with it. I wrapped it in this burlap sack, and I hid it so no one would find it. I had to hide it because, even though the Master never wanted to see it again, I would be punished if he found out that I had it. It has been hidden for twelve years and it must go back into its hiding place; but this time, it will belong to you. It be best you not know where I keep it, for fear you might give it away, but son, it is enough to know it is there and it now belongs to you."

Smiling at me, my grandpa said, "Toby Boy, my momma wanted me to have two things that would always remind me of my momma and daddy. That morning she opened this beautiful tin box, and then she went over to my daddy and tore off a button from his shirt and placed this button in the tin box." Grandpa lifted the old yellowed button that still had the thread attached and kissed it before returning it to the tin box. "Toby Boy, I have taken good care of this box because my momma loved it, and it reminds me of her. I have protected it, and this button, because it is all I have left of my daddy. Now I am adding this button from my pea-coat into this tin box, along with the whistle I gave to you when you were three years old. Each of these things will always remind you how much I love you. Toby, it is now yours—take good care of it. I am giving you this button and this tin box because they are my most precious possessions. I want you to have them."

I tried not to cry that day. I knew it was hard for Grandpa to send me away, and I didn't want to make it worse. As Grandma opened the door and prepared to take me to the train station, Grandpa called out, "Toby Boy, you keep praying for your momma."

As Grandma and I reached the bottom floor of our building, Brother Jubilee was standing there. Grandma ignored him as she always did, but he gave her a polite nod of the head and stooped down in front of me. "Tobias, my boy, I have a gift for you." While pinning it on my shirt, he said, "This lapel pin is to remind you to pray for your momma Ruby. The heart is to remind you to always love your momma, Toby."

I looked over at Grandma CeCe and saw big tears in her eyes. For two years she had refused to talk to or talk about Brother Jubilee, but that day she could not help but love this man who cared so deeply for her lost little girl. Grandma did not believe there was a God who cared about her girl, but she softened at the thought that this man was giving her grandson a gift to remember to pray for her Ruby Girl. Even though she did not believe in the God Brother Jubilee talked about, she was glad that anyone would care to pray for her girl.

Remembering the soft look in his Grandma CeCe's eyes that day brought Tobias back to the present. He opened the tin box, lifted out the envelope containing the lapel pin he had owned for fifty years. He thanked God that Brother Jubilee had come knocking on their door that night. Brother Jubilee had helped Grandpa lay down his pride and reach out to Momma. He lifted the pin to his mouth and said a prayer of thanksgiving for all of the answers to prayer this pin represented in his life. He carefully re-wrapped the pin and returned it to the tin box.

The porter came through the door that separated our car from the cars ahead and loudly announced, "Spartanburg, South Carolina, in ten minutes. Spartanburg in ten minutes. Gather up your belongings and head toward the back of this car. As soon as the train comes to a full stop, I will open the door."

The gentleman sitting in front of Ruth stood up and gathered his things. The navy duffle bag that held all of his worldly belongings looked like it had seen years of travel. Tobias smiled and thought to himself, "That is probably his tin box. He looks several years older than me."

When the gentleman saw Tobias studying his duffle bag, he asked, "You serve in the Navy?"

"No, sir," Tobias replied respectfully. "U.S. Marines, but I was transported to France in 1919 by a Navy ship. Does that count? Where did you serve, sir?"

The smile quickly faded from his face. "It was a long time ago and another life." Obviously trying to change the subject, he turned and smiled at Ruth as he brushed off the blueberry crumbs from his trousers. "Thanks for the baked goods, ma'am. Those were right tasty."

He hoisted his duffle bag over his shoulder and hobbled toward the back door. Tobias studied how he managed his way along the aisle and thought about offering to help him off the train, but seeing how proud a man he was, he thought better of it. Instead, he called back to him, "Thank you for defending our country, sir."

As the gentleman reached the open door, he turned back and smiled, straightened up as much as possible, threw up his arm and gave Tobias a sharp naval salute. Tobias, in return, smiled, stood and returned a salute before the old veteran slipped out the door.

Tobias was still holding his buttons as he retook his seat. He studied them for a moment and thought about what they represented. The tin box and the small button were physical connections to his great-grandparents who had suffered under slavery their entire lives. Great-Grandma Hannah had touched this box with her own hands, and Great-Grandpa Charlie Bascom had buttoned this very button. The large wooden button, which had been turned into a wheel for his fire truck, reminded him that he had enjoyed the love of a grandfather who cared about him. It also reminded him that he had a lifelong debt to pay.

With a full heart, Tobias replaced the buttons in their envelope and returned them to the tin box. He then retrieved the tattered newspaper clipping that was still attached to his grandpa's letter that he had received way back in 1905. "Dear Toby Boy, I saw this in today's paper and thought you would like to see it. I believe the lady in this photograph, who is standing in front of the Italianna Store on the corner of Twelfth and Lexington, is the wonderful lady from the window. I knew you would want to have this. Toby Boy, keep this in your tin box."

That wonderful Italian lady had changed his life that day. Thinking about her, he surmised, "I doubt that she remembers me, but I will never forget her! Once I became a young adult and realized what she had saved me from and how profoundly my life would have changed had she not stopped Calvin James, I vowed to remember her." At the age of eighteen, I came across a Bible verse that talked about sins visiting to the second and third generation. I thought, "If that is true, then it must also be true of blessings." That day I prayed a blessing on that Italian woman, whose name I do not know, but God does. She risked her safety for me, and I asked God to bless her, to bless her children, and to bless her grandchildren. To this day, I remember her gift to me and pray a blessing on those she loves. In this life, I will never know what my prayers might have done for her and her family. I believe that God's mercy has been showered on them, and they are not even aware of why—but God does, and that is enough."

Overtaken with a profound sense of gratitude, Tobias carefully replaced the clipping in the safety of his tin box and rubbed his eyes. Fifty years later, and all of these items meant as much to him now as they did then—probably more because he now knew how big a debt he owed.

TOBIAS:
Atlanta Became My Home
1904-1906

Meeting Ms. Pearl and Ms. Ruby

LOOKING OUT OF the window at the Spartanburg Station, Tobias spotted a white boy about twelve years of age climbing off the train. His car was two or three ahead, and Tobias had a clear view of the platform. As soon as the boy stepped down, an elderly couple made their way toward him. He assumed they were the boy's grandparents. By the change in the boy's body language, he appeared not to know them very well. The grandmother tried to hug him, but the boy pulled away and started walking. He either did not know them, or he didn't want to be there. Either way, he was not happy.

Watching him avoid their touch reminded Tobias of the day he had arrived in Atlanta, Georgia. Watching that young boy walking away with people with whom he was not comfortable brought back many old memories. He was just seven years old and did not know his grandpa's sisters. He remembered feeling every bit as uncomfortable with them as this young lad appeared to be.

Ms. Pearl and Ms. Ruby were standing on the platform waiting for me. I remember how timid I felt walking up to those two ladies that day. How would I have had any idea of exactly how important they would become to me? That day they were simply strangers, holding a sign with my name printed on it. I walked up to them and introduced myself. "Hello, I am Tobias Bascom. You must be Grandpa's sisters."

Ms. Ruby was the first to respond. She looked like a stiff wind could blow her over, but would soon learn she was stronger than she appeared. I tried not to stare as she tossed her withered leg forward, planted it carefully before putting all her weight on it. She could not stand up straight and tall, instead, she would rest her right hand upon her hip, as if trying to keep from toppling over. Every ounce of her seemed fragile and weak – oh how wrong my first impression turned out to be. I would soon come to learn that Ruby was always the first to respond. She pulled off my cap and rubbed my head, a gesture I detested that day, but one I would come to love and have now missed for eight years. Before sending me to his sisters, Grandpa Samuel told me a little about them. Both of my aunts had married in their twenties, but both of them were now single. Aunt Pearl was widowed and had no living children. Ruby was never able to have children. During her marriage, Ruby worked with her husband on tobacco farms all over the Carolinas. Grandpa said she had gotten hurt by horses and never walked straight again. She had to spend months in bed while recuperating, before her husband brought her back to Atlanta. He could no longer care for her and felt she was better off with her sister Pearl. Grandpa promised me that they were good people.

As I climbed down from the train that day, little did I know that I was to become the center of their universe, and they were to become mine. Their house was small and very plain, but I felt right at home. Ms. Pearl was much more reserved than Ms. Ruby. At first, I mistook her reserve as being unfriendly. Where Ruby was quick with affection and encouragement, Pearl was the keeper of the rules. Years later I would realize that Pearl was the one who worried about my safety, always fearing I might overstep my bounds and get into trouble. In the early years, she would instruct me on how to walk around white folks, how I was to keep my head lowered and quickly step off the sidewalk and make a clear path for anyone white. Those rules also extended to anyone of color who had risen to a higher state than us—which included nearly everyone. Pearl was stern in her admonishments, wanting me to understand how very important they were to my survival.

Pearl was also the planner-dreamer of great dreams. I wasn't in her house for one day before she asked, "Toby Boy, did you go to school in Harlem?"

"No, Ms. Pearl. Grandpa Samuel needed me, but he did teach me my numbers and letters and how to print my own name." I remember feeling so proud of myself—for about one whole minute.

Pearl gave me a studied frown before saying, "The world is changing, and you will need to know more than your letters and numbers if you want to be useful."

I do not believe Pearl meant to hurt my feelings; she was so completely focused on preparation and planning that she did not realize she had just stepped all over my young pride. I remember her saying, "Have you ever heard of a man by the name of W.E.B. DuBois?"

I shook my head no, and Pearl began a speech I would hear many, many times during the next ten years of my youth. "He is a black man who earned his Ph.D. from Harvard University back in 1895. We have Spelman College for women right here in Atlanta. It was started back in 1881, but of course, Ruby and I were already too old to attend. Things are changing, Toby Boy, and I want you to be prepared. We have a country school for black children just three blocks from here, and I am going to enroll you for the upcoming school year. Of course, it only goes through sixth grade right now, but every year they hope to add another year of schooling. Women from Spelman are given college credit under the Atlanta Female Baptist Seminary for coming to our rural schoolhouse, so we have some wonderful teachers."

If a seven-year-old can feel the weight of his people on his shoulders, I certainly did. Pearl's dreams and goals for me were more than I could bear that day. Having never attended a single day of school up until then, Pearl now expected me to go to college. I didn't even know what you did in college, but I was certain I did not want to go. I remember climbing into my warm bed that first night, missing my grandpa something awful. Seven-year-olds are not supposed to cry, but that night the tears flowed. My heart ached to feel the touch of Grandpa's big hand on my back. I buried my face in my pillow and let weeks of pent-up emotions loose. I was just about cried out when I felt a hand on my shoulder, and Ruby was kneeling beside my bed, trying to comfort me. "Toby Boy, it is going to get better, I promise. I know you miss your family, and we are still strangers to you, but you must know how much Pearl and I love you already? I know we can't take the place of your grandpa, but if you will just give us a chance, we can also become your family."

That night I realized that Pearl was the dreamer-planner, but Ruby was the consoler, comforter, and encourager. Oh, I didn't yet know those big words like encourager and consoler, but I remember how they felt to my poor lost little soul that night. I loved Ms. Ruby for playing that role in my life. Where Ms. Pearl would become the keeper of all the rules, it would be Ms. Ruby who would hold me steady and comfort my fears and failures. Every night, while tucking me into bed, Ms. Ruby would say, "Toby Boy, God loves you, and so do we. Inside the walls of this house, you are perfect exactly the way you are. Pearl is just trying to prepare you for life beyond the walls of this house. She loves you, Toby, don't ever doubt it. You are the boy neither one of us were able to have ourselves; you are God's gift to both of us."

Those two aunts were as different as night and day, but I came to love them both. We did indeed become a family.

A few days later Pearl walked me to my new school. She stopped at the door and I asked, "Aren't you coming in with me, Ms. Pearl?"

"No, Tobias." Ms. Pearl answered. "I signed you up last week, and Miss Buttons is expecting you. You have a wonderful day today."

Oh, how nervous I was walking into my new school that first day. I did not know where to sit, where to stand, or what to say. All of the other children busied themselves putting their sack lunches on the back table, but I just stood there, afraid to move. One girl smiled at me, but I was certain she was really laughing at how ignorant I was, so I did not smile back at her. I studied my new shoes, hoping I would just fall through the floor and die. Unaware that the teacher had come into the room, I about jumped out of my skin when she placed her hand on my shoulder and said, "You must be Tobias. Your Aunt Pearl told me you would be joining us today."

I turned around and saw my new teacher, Miss Buttons, and I was smitten. She was beautiful. Her teeth were straight and white and filled her huge smile. She was a tiny woman, about the size of Ms. Ruby. Her hair was pulled back and braided, and her skin reminded me of the deep, dark caramel candies Grandpa would bring home to me. I was sure she was just as sweet. I simply stood there staring at her. She walked over to her desk, took out her chalk and wrote her name in large letters on the board. She then placed the chalk on the tray below the board. Only then did she address the class. "Boys and girls, hurry up and take your seats." Her voice made my heart want to sing.

A heavyset boy pushed past me and grabbed my lunch pail out of my hand. I thought he was stealing my lunch, so I grabbed it back and gave him a mean look. He smiled and said, "I was only gunna put your pail on the back table. All the lunches goes there."

I was immediately embarrassed and thanked him. "Sorry, I didn't know. My name is Tobias. I am new here."

"I know. My name is Sulley. Ain't our new teacher a peach?"

"She sure is. I've never had a teacher before. I just moved here."

"I knows; you just said that," Sulley said with a smile. He seemed a nice sort and offered, "Come sits next to me. The teacher has to test you before she puts you in your seat."

"Test me? What kind of test, Sulley?" I've never taken a test before—what is it?" I followed Sulley to the back row and sat quietly, hoping the teacher would not notice me. The whole class stood up, so I did too. Sulley pushed against my arm and nodded his head as if to say, "Do this," then he placed his hand on his chest and so I did as well. The teacher tapped her ruler on her desk, and the whole class began reciting the Pledge of Allegiance. I was thankful Ms. Pearl had gone over this Pledge five or six times the week before school started, so I felt comfortable joining in. As soon as we finished the Pledge, the girl who had smiled at me earlier led the class in a hymn. I did not know the song, so I stood there watching her as she sang it. For the second time that day, I was smitten. My young heart was filled to overflowing, watching her sing the song. Did all of the boys feel this way about this girl? I certainly wasn't going to ask them. I simply kept my feelings to myself and sat back down as soon as it was safe to do so.

I was still staring at the girl and did not notice that my name was being called. Sulley poked me in the side and nodded toward the teacher. Again, she said, "Tobias, while the other children get their papers, pencils, rulers, and glue out of the closet, I need you to come up here so I can test you to see which grade you will be in this year."

Ms. Pearl had warned me that I was behind. I should have started school two years earlier while I was living in Harlem, but here in Atlanta, I was only one year behind; but I was still behind. As I walked forward, I was proud that my grandpa had taught me my letters and numbers and that I could show this beautiful teacher that I could even write my name. I took my seat and waited to show her all I knew. She handed me an oilcloth book and asked me to read the first two pages. I could not. I simply placed the book on her desk, and, mortified beyond words, said, "I don't know how to read yet, Miss Buttons."

She smiled at me with that big beautiful smile, which made my mind go blank, and said, "That is all right, Tobias; you will learn. It is my job to teach you how to read, but I don't believe you are ready for second year just yet. Even though you are already seven, I am going to put you in with the first-year students."

My little seven-year-old pride was crushed—for only about a minute. The class was arranged front to back, first year to the sixth year. Boys were on the left. Girls were on the right. Miss Buttons walked me down to row two, right on the aisle. "This will be your seat all year, Tobias. Now you can go back to the closet and get your paper tablet, pencil, ruler, and bottle of glue. Put them in your desk."

As Miss Buttons returned to her desk, I looked over to see that same pretty girl who had smiled at me and had led the class in the hymn sitting right across the aisle from me. My pride was no longer crushed. I was now a happy boy.

TOBIAS: Atlanta Became My Home 1904-1906

As soon as everyone had their supplies, Miss Buttons gave the first of many speeches that I would hear at the start of all six years of school. "This school provides six years of learning for the boys. Everyone will be given basic reading, writing, mathematics, history and religious instruction. If you boys stay with the program, you will graduate at the age of twelve, prepared to apply for apprentice training in any number of factories in the greater Atlanta area. Girls, if your grades merit, you, however, will be offered scholarships for an additional four years of instruction. This opportunity has been graciously offered to you by the Greater Atlanta Female Baptist Seminary. Upon graduation, you girls will have a certificate in either nursing or teaching."

After the teacher gave this first-day-of-school speech, you would have thought all of the boys would have felt cheated—quite the contrary. Six long years of being cooped up in this one-room schoolhouse, which was unbearably hot in September, May and June, and unbearably cold from November to March, seemed an interminable amount of time to us boys.

Six boys and eight girls comprised the first-year students, and one of those girls was Ruth Naomi Johnson, the girl with whom I was smitten. I learned that she was the daughter of the local Methodist minister. As it turned out, every morning after we saluted the flag, we would open class with a word of prayer and a hymn. Because Ruth sat right across the aisle from me I could hear her clear, beautiful voice sing the daily hymns. I never tired of hearing her sing.

At recess I looked around for Sulley. Not knowing anyone, at least I felt that Sulley would be nice to me. It turned out that we had no sixth year boys at our school because it had not been open long enough to have any boys get that far. Sulley was the oldest boy, and he only was in year four, although, according to his age, he should have already graduated. I found him at the water fountain. It was a hot September day in Atlanta, and as Sulley was a big boy, he sweat a lot. Every recess he headed straight for the water fountain. Once he had his fill, he suggested, "It's too hot to play ball, Tobias. Do you play marbles? You have any marbles, Tobias?" Then he made a funny face and asked, "You have a nickname, Tobias? Your name is for a grown man. My real name is Sullivan Dunbar, but everyone just calls me Sulley."

"People call me Toby."

"Ah, Toby it is then. If you don't have no marbles, I cans borrow you five or six of mine, but I has to get them back. They really belongs to my big brother. He don't play with them no more, but they still is his."

"I don't know how to play marbles, Sulley." Twice in one day I had to admit to someone that I didn't know how to do something—and for the second time, I was told, "That's okay, Toby, I can teach you." I knew Sulley was going to be a good friend.

Sulley led me under a large pecan tree, found a stick and drew a large circle in the dirt and emptied out his pocket into the dirt. He separated out six small marbles and one large one he called a good shooter and shoved them over to me. He told me the rules and suggested I spend that whole recess practicing how to shoot marbles. "Once you get it, we can play a game," Sulley promised without any insult in his voice.

After a week or two, I noticed that none of the other boys were interested in playing marbles with us. One or two made comments to me about staying away from Sulley, but I ignored them. I could not figure out why they disliked Sulley so much. Oh sure, he sweated like a pig, and his clothes did smell. He was never prepared when Miss Buttons called on him to read or recite something in class, and he could always be counted on to ask for handouts. "You gonna eat that?" Sulley always seemed to be hungry, and the other boys were tired of sharing their meager lunches with him. None of us had much, but the one thing we had at my house was plenty of food. After I told Ms. Ruby about Sulley, I started finding an extra sandwich and cookie in my lunch pail every day. I wouldn't even wait for Sulley to come around asking. I just walked up to the table, sat down next to him, and placed the extra sandwich in front of him. It made me feel so good to see him smile as he picked up those sandwiches.

One day Miss Buttons asked me to stay after class. I was certain I was in some kind of trouble, but after she closed the door and took her seat, she smiled at me. At that point, I didn't care; I was just glad to be there with her. "Tobias, I wanted to thank you for being such a good friend to Sulley. I have watched you sharing your lunch with him for weeks now. You are a kind, good boy, Tobias; don't you ever change. This world needs people like you, and I am so proud to have you as one of my students."

Honestly, I don't remember how I got home that day. I am certain I did not walk because my feet were not touching the ground. That day I added one more person to my list of people whom I never wanted to disappoint. I determined to be a sharing, caring, good boy because it felt so wonderful when people about whom I cared noticed.

I did not want to disappoint Ms. Pearl or Ms. Ruby, so I worked hard, trying to catch up with the other students, but if the truth were told, it was because of Miss Buttons and Ruth Naomi Johnson that I worked so hard on my studies. I desperately wanted to impress them both.

CHAPTER 8

Letters From Home

TOBIAS SMILED AT his wife, as he mused. "I am still trying to impress this amazing woman. Other than my Great-Auntie Ruby, I don't believe there is another woman in the whole world that can hold a candle to my Ruth."

Ruth realized that Tobias was no longer deep in thought and turned around, "Tobias, I notice you have been going through your tin box this morning. How are you holding up?"

"It is all good, Ruth. I love thinking about my family."

"I know," Ruth chuckled. "Are you about ready to take a break and have some lunch?"

"I would love some lunch, Ruth, but would you mind if I took a few more minutes to read through my letters? I have not read them for several years, and I would like to have them fresh in my mind before we reach Washington."

"Take your time, Tobias," Ruth replied graciously. "We still have a long, long way to go today, so pushing back our lunch will just make the afternoon seem a little shorter."

Tobias gave her a kiss on the cheek before opening his tin box and removing the letters. He always kept his letters bound together by a tattered red ribbon. They had been kept in the order in which they arrived, and they quickly told the story of those first few years in Harlem without Tobias.

Grandpa Samuel tried to write letters every few months. At first, very little had changed in Harlem. Momma Ruby was still visiting regularly, and that was good. Every letter ended with the same sentence: "Tobias, keep praying for your Momma and your Grandma."

Tobias remembered how Miss Buttons helped him write his first letter to his grandpa because he did not want Ms. Pearl and Ms. Ruby to know that he was talking about them. He wanted his grandpa to know how much he was enjoying hearing all about Grandpa's life as a boy and what a good storyteller his Aunt Ruby was.

As Tobias removed the first letter from its yellowed envelope, a homesick feeling overtook him. He had been with the sisters for two whole months and was really missing his grandpa. As he held this letter, every feeling he had felt all those years ago came flooding back to him. Just as he had done that day, he held up the envelope to his lips and kissed it before opening it.

October 1904
Dear Toby Boy,

I am so glad to hear that you are enjoying the Sisters. I too remember how well Sister Ruby could make a story come alive. But Toby Boy, as you hear about our time as slaves, I want to tell you something. This took me years to understand, and I hope you learn it sooner than I did.

Toby, slavery was a very bad thing, and a lot of white men were really bad and wicked men. For loads of years, I blamed all white men for what was done to my family. Toby Boy, not all whites did those bad things.

I never wanted you to hear these stories, but I was wrong; you need to know. Toby, three black boys raped your momma, but we don't blame all black boys for what happened to Ruby Girl. So don't blame all whites for slavery.

Always stay my beloved boy,

Love,

Grandpa Samuel

As he replaced this letter in its envelope, he thought about Grandma CeCe. She had remained a stubborn, superstitious woman. She wanted nothing to do with Brother Jubilee or his church. She loved both my grandpa and my momma, but she was not going to change. She worked hard and cared for Grandpa. For all of these reasons, no matter her shortcomings, I promised my grandpa I would always honor her memory because Grandpa loved her.

Tobias replaced the first letter and pulled out letter number two. After months of Grandpa's enjoying short visits from Momma Ruby, I finally received this letter from Grandpa Samuel. Rubbing his hand over the second envelope addressed to him, he pondered, "This letter must have been very hard for my grandpa to write. Even all these years later, as I read it, I can feel the tension and fear."

November 1904
To My Dear Toby Boy,

I need you and the Sisters to pray hard for your Momma Ruby. She came by this morning and looked just awful. She had been beaten hard, but she would not talk about it. She did say, "Daddy, I can't keep coming here. The people I work for don't like it."

Toby Boy, Brother Jubilee and I are going to try to see what we can do for Ruby Girl.

PRAY!

Love,

Grandpa Samuel

As Tobias replaced this letter in its envelope, he remembered how long he had to wait for the next letter. Ms. Pearl had written to Grandpa and told him we were all praying, but we heard nothing. He knew his momma was messing with some bad people, but she was still his momma. He also worried about his grandpa. It was hard for his grandfather to get around in his wheelchair, and Tobias had seen one or two of the men who had waited downstairs for Momma when she came to visit.

He thought about the time Grandpa had sent him down to the deli for some items. He knew Grandpa had really only wanted him out of the apartment so he could talk to Momma Ruby alone. As he came down the last flight of stairs, he noticed a large black man leaning against the wall of the entry. His hair was waxed back, and his face showed signs of several cuts that had not healed right. He was missing several teeth, and his clothes were odd. Unlike most men in the neighborhood, his trousers were shiny light-gray, with very large cuffs. His shirt was not tucked into his waistband, but instead, hung down until it almost covered his trouser pockets. Tobias remembered seeing the butt of a knife sticking out of his pocket, and as soon as the man realized that Toby had noticed it, he unfolded his big arms and pulled his shirt down over the knife handle. His glare was menacing, so Toby made his way past him as fast as he could. As soon as he cleared the doorway, he took off running—jumping two steps at a time to get down onto the sidewalk.

Remembering that incident, Tobias knew this was the man who had brought Momma to visit. He also knew this man was probably the one who was responsible for all her bruises. Momma was never allowed to come visit us alone. Either this man or another one like him always came along.

Those men were bad, and they could care less whether or not Grandpa was in a wheelchair; they would really hurt him if he came between them and my momma. As a grown man looking back on those days, Tobias was amazed at how much he really did not know about what was going on back then. Still, at the age of seven, he had understood the danger his family was in and why his grandpa had sent him away. Those weeks of silence had been hard, but the news, when it did come, was even harder. A letter finally arrived, but this one was not from his grandpa, but from Brother Jubilee.

Tobias opened the letter which had arrived so many years ago.

December 1904
Dear Tobias,

Sorry this letter has been so long in coming, but your Grandpa did not want to write again until he had some good news. Some is not good news, but overall it is great news.

After Samuel's last letter to you, he and I decided we would try to get your Momma Ruby away from the bad men who had her. We knew this would be dangerous, but God is for us, so who can stand against us, right?

On Ruby's last visit, she shared that she did want to believe in Jesus and to leave her bad life. Samuel had me come to the apartment and talk with your Momma, and I believed she was sincere. I didn't think she was just using us to get away from these bad men—she wanted to change her whole life. For this, Toby, we are all praising God. Our church has been praying for your Momma for three years.

That day, we decided it was not safe for Ruby to stay in the apartment. These men would come looking for her. We decided to have her stay in the church for several days before finding her a place to live. Toby, those bad men came anyway. They came in the middle of the night, broke in and attacked your grandma as she tried to protect your grandpa. Once they were finished with CeCe, they went after Samuel.

Tobias, your grandpa is now safe, although he spent a week in the hospital because of the beating. But Toby, I am so sorry to tell you that your Grandma CeCe did not make it. They beat her so badly, she never even woke up from the beating. The church was so worried that Ruby would give in and go back with those men, but she didn't, Toby. Your momma is being so strong right now. We are secretly taking her to the hospital to visit her Daddy, and the women in the church are taking care of Ruby.

Tobias, most of our prayers have been answered. We are so sad about CeCe. I just pray that behind her stubbornness, she really listened to Samuel and cried out to God at the very end. We will never know, but God does.

As for Ruby, you would be so proud of her. She and your Grandpa are holding onto each other in their loss and are really talking and planning their future—because Tobias, now your Momma Ruby finally has one.

Brother Jubilee

Oh, how I wanted to get on the train and go back to Harlem that day. I wanted to see for myself what Brother Jubilee was saying, but I couldn't. It was not safe. Ms. Pearl and Ms. Ruby held onto me for days as I cried, screamed, threw tantrums, and then finally allowed the good news to overtake the bad news. Nine-year-olds should not have to face this kind of pain, but many do—so why not me? Slowly, more letters began to arrive monthly, and they were filled with good news. Grandpa was now strong enough to write his own letters to me.

January 1905
Dear Toby Boy,

I know you heard about Grandma CeCe. I am sad and I do miss her, but God has work for me to do. Your momma is now safe, and we are living together in a new place. We are careful not to be out on the streets too much.

Your Momma took over the cleaning job that your Grandma had and is happier than I have ever seen her. While she is working late at night, Brother Jubilee stays with me until it is time for Ruby to walk home. He then leaves me alone just long enough to go get Ruby and bring her back here.

Life is good.

I sure miss my boy! Be sure to write me soon,

Grandpa

June 1905

Dear Toby Boy,

I was so proud to read your letter about passing into second year. I knew you could do it. I'm sorry to hear about your friend Sulley being held back again. Not everyone has great-aunties who can help with homework. You keep being a good friend to him at school.

Ruby Girl is doing great. You should hear her sing. She joined the church choir, and all day long around the apartment she practices her songs. Toby, who would have known your Momma was a songbird?

Brother Jubilee has been a wonderful friend to us. He is helping me teach Ruby Girl how to read and write. One of these days, she will write you a letter with her own hand.

Love,

Grandpa Samuel

P.S. Ruby Girl says hello to you.

September 1905
Dear Toby Boy,

Great news! Your Momma Ruby got baptized last Sunday. Nothing more to say but praise God from whom all blessings flow.

Love,

Grandpa Samuel

October 1905
Dear Toby Boy,

Our captivity is finally over! Brother Jubilee read in the paper that the whole bunch that had your Momma were arrested and found guilty of murdering another girl. They are all going to prison for the rest of their lives. Your Momma is finally safe, and we can go out without fearing she might be taken.
God is good.

Love,

Grandpa Samuel

October 1905
Dear Toby Boy,

It has now been almost a year since we rescued Ruby Girl. I can hardly believe it. Now that you are eight years old, I would love to have a picture of you. I know it is expensive, but Ruby and I have been saving up. We are including five dollars in this letter. Would you please ask the Sisters to take you down and have your picture taken so we can have it to look at?

Love,

Grandpa Samuel

The next letter is so tattered from reading and rereading it that it is in danger of falling apart. Even if it did fall apart, the words are seared into my heart.

November 1905
To My Dear Boy, Tobias,

I have read all your letters to Daddy, and I am so very proud of you, Tobias. I know you never liked it when I called you Toby, so I won't. I don't deserve to, and I know it. Tobias, I am so sorry for not being a good mother to you. I would not blame you if you never wrote me back.

I would understand. I do love you and hope—someday—we can get to know each other.

Love,

Momma Ruby

P.S. Jubilee helped me—but I wrote it.

December 1905
To My Dear Boy, Tobias,

Thank you for your beautiful letter. I feel so unworthy of your forgiveness, but Brother Jubilee says that when we are offered unearned forgiveness, that is exactly how we should feel. Tell your Aunties that I will forever be in their debt for raising my boy into such a wonderful person. I hope that someday we might be able to see each other.

Missing you,

Momma Ruby

January 1906
Dear Toby Boy,

    We got your picture today. Oh, how much you have grown. Your Momma took it to church and showed it to everyone. She is so proud of you, and so am I. Your Momma is happy and doing well. I loved your last letter telling me how the Sisters are telling you all about our life on the plantation. I am glad you know. I am sorry I never told you.

Love,

Grandpa Samuel

I was surprised the day I got this next letter. I was surprised but also happy and gave my blessings.

March 1906

Dear Tobias,

    Greetings from Harlem, this is Brother Jubilee.
    You are only eight years old, but you are Ruby's son. I want you to know that I have witnessed such a change in your momma over the past two years. It has been a change in her character, her heart, and her soul. The Bible teaches us that when God forgives us, it is completely.

He does not hold onto our transgressions; He remembers them no more. We are told to love others just as God does.

Tobias, I believe I can love your Momma Ruby without holding her past life against her. I therefore ask you, her son, for permission to ask your mother's hand in marriage. My plan is to move both your mother and your Grandfather Samuel into my home so I can have the privilege of caring for them both for the rest of our lives.

Tobias, do you give me your blessing?

Brother Jubilee

In July of 1906, I received a large envelope with a picture in it and the following letter. Ms. Ruby found a pretty frame, and we hung the picture above my bed where it remained until I moved out of her house years later. This letter was also added to my tin box.

July 1906
Dear Tobias,

We just received the photos of our wedding and are sending you our favorite one to celebrate your ninth birthday. You can see just how healthy your Grandpa Samuel looks sitting next to your Momma Ruby in her wedding suit. Doesn't she look wonderful?!

We were sorry you could not come up for the wedding, but we certainly understand. We hope to hear from you soon and please know that all our love is with you.

Your Momma is doing very well. She misses you, Tobias. Your picture sits right by our bed, and she prays for you every night. I know you are doing the same for her. Forgiveness is the best gift we can give. It lightens our heart and sets our imprisoned souls free.

Love,

Brother Jubilee and Momma, and Grandpa Samuel

Tobias carefully repositioned the tattered red ribbon around the letters and placed them back into his tin box. He never tired of reading them. Those letters had kept him connected to his family during those first two years in Atlanta. They gave him hope for his momma and helped him understand why his grandpa had to stay behind.

Realizing that he had taken far longer with these keepsakes than he had intended, and needing a break from all this nostalgia, Tobias replaced the photos, put his tin box up on the suitcase shelf above his head and said to Ruth, "Are you ready for lunch? Would you like me to walk down to the lunch counter and get us something?"

"Something cold to drink would be wonderful," Ruth responded. "I already have our lunch ready for us."

"Of course you do. Why am I not surprised?" Tobias stood up, shook his suit trousers loose, bent down and kissed Ruth before he went to the lunch counter.

CHAPTER 9

My Loss of Innocence

AFTER LUNCH, RUTH found another lonely woman in need of company. She took several cookies out of her goodie bag as a way of introduction. No one could say no to one of Ruth's molasses cookies.

Having read his letters and reminiscing about how he had acquired the family photos, Tobias could not help but review what had happened to him as a young boy in Atlanta, while so much was happening in Harlem. Ms. Pearl and Ms. Ruby had made sure his life was routine and peaceful, consisting of eating well, going to school, studying hard, and filling his evenings with exciting stories.

Remembering how wonderful that time was for him, Tobias pulled out the small white button and the marble from his tin box. The white button represented a bittersweet season, while at the same time, the marble represents one of his longest gifts of friendship. Both of these had come to him on the same day. The button reminded him of the beautiful Miss Buttons, and the marble had been a gift from Sulley. Rolling them around in his hand, Tobias slid back into his childhood…back when his life became much too real.

Auntie Ruby cleared the table and washed the dishes while Ms. Pearl helped me with my homework. When homework was finished, Ruby would return to the table with her mending, and Pearl would read the newspaper to us while I played on the floor of the dining room with whatever toy I had conjured up with my imagination.

Once the homework and newspaper reading was finished, Pearl would take out the current novel she was reading to us, and I would be transported to strange and wonderful lands. I spent my evenings living with swashbuckling pirates or with Oliver Twist and the pickpockets on the streets of London. I loved these stories, but the stories I loved the best were the ones the sisters told me about their life with their big brother Samuel. They were careful with their stories. They avoided telling me the whole truth about slavery. As a seven-year-old, they felt I was too young to hear the dark side of their experiences, so they filled my heart with all my grandpa's amazing accomplishments as a young boy.

I learned how my grandpa always watched over them. For the first two years, they shared with this excited young boy about how Grandpa Samuel found the caverns, stocked them with supplies, and kept his sisters hidden and safe during the final months of the Civil War. Stretching my imagination, they took me from there right into the livery where they had lived for the first four years of their newfound freedom. I never tired of hearing their exciting stories.

Auntie Ruby was so good at telling a story, I believe I could smell the fresh hay. I remember the first time she told me about my Great-Grandmother Hannah. Before she started, I pleaded, "Ms. Ruby, could you please wait a minute? I want to get my tin box and put it on the table. Grandpa Samuel said Momma Hannah gave it to him the day your daddy went away. I'd like to look at it while you tell me about her."

Once the tin box was in its place of honor, Ms. Ruby began. "Momma Hannah was born on the Stewart Plantation in 1824. Momma never knew who her daddy was, and then she lost her momma when she was only seven years old. Momma Hannah never even knew her Momma's real name; she only knew her as Momma. Since all of the family records were owned and kept by Master Stewart, our family had no way of knowing where we came from or what our real family name was. For this reason, Momma always insisted that we always use 'Momma Hannah,' as her whole name. It always bothered our momma that she never knew her momma's name."

When I was young, Auntie Ruby glossed over certain details, simply jumping over to the happier facts. "Our momma married Charlie Bascom when she was twenty years old. Charlie worked in the gardens, while Momma managed the kitchen. Young Master Stewart was much nicer than Old Master Stewart, and he allowed Momma and Daddy to live in the cook's cabin out beside the canning shed. One year later, Brother Samuel was born. Three years later in 1849, Pearl and I were born. We were the first set of twins ever to be born on the plantation. Our Daddy Charlie was a slave on the Stewart Plantation for only eight years. We never knew where he came from or where he went after being sold, but we loved him."

At this point in Ms. Ruby's story, she would always reach over and open my tin box, lift out the old, discolored button with the thread still hanging from it and say, "Toby Boy, this is all we have left of our Daddy Charlie. When our momma was saying her goodbyes, she tore it off his shirt as a remembrance. Some people are left mansions, some are left noble titles, but none of that is any more important to those people than this button is to us." Then with a big smile, she would put it up to her lips and kiss it. "This was my daddy's shirt button."

Over that first two years, the tin box and the button became anchors from which all these stories were launched. They were repeated so often, they became emblazoned into my memory, but in September of 1906, everything changed.

❧ The Atlanta Riots of 1906 ❧

For two long and wonderful years I had gotten up every morning, eaten breakfast and headed off to school, but that Monday, September 24, 1906, I was told my school was closed. They were not sure when it would reopen. That whole weekend we sat home, hearing about the terrible riots going on in the business district of Darktown, an area of Atlanta where all the business owners were Negros. Ms. Pearl worked there, and, on Saturday morning, her boss, Mr. Ward, stopped by and warned her to stay home. "The mobs are everywhere, Pearl. They broke out all of my windows and beat old Smithy almost to death when he tried to keep them from torching the place. Pearl, Jackson saw them beating Smithy and tried to rescue him but they shot and killed him."

I knew Jackson was a friend of Ms. Pearl's. He had sat at our table many a night. She dropped into the kitchen chair and lowered her head to the table. Her boss warned all of us to stay inside. "Don't you even think of going to church tomorrow. Most people believe the mobs are going to go after the black churches tomorrow."

I remember how shocked I was, and I blurted out, "Mr. Ward, you mean the mobs are white people? I had just figured they were black men, angry at having to go without."

Mr. Ward then asked me this question: "Toby, why are you surprised the mob is white?"

In my nine-year-old mind, my answer made sense to me. "Mr. Ward, all my life when I lived in Harlem, everything bad that was ever done to me and my family was done to us by black people. I just figured it is the same here."

Mr. Ward turned to Ms. Pearl and said, "Pearl, how are you preparing this boy to live in this world? He needs to know how dangerous it is out there for a black boy, and he can't know it without knowing what his people have gone through. You cannot paint a pretty picture of slavery and send him out there and expect him to know how to act around people who still believe he should be a slave."

That day the stories began to grow up, and so did I. That Sunday we heard that my teacher, Miss Buttons, had been shot trying to defend her father; both had been killed. Reality was hitting me hard. No more sweet stories. That weekend, I lost my innocence. More than two hundred blacks were killed during that four-day riot. Only one white person died, and she died of a heart attack at seeing all the violence.

I am thankful I was told the truth. When I hear comments like, "Most slaves had it pretty good," they do not understand what it was like to live without self-control or self-determination; nor to be treated as if you were inhuman and emotionless. I learned how unjust it was to live under even the kindest of masters. Once I lost my beloved, Miss Buttons, I no longer felt like a child. Reality had knocked on our door and would not be denied entry.

My little boy's heart was crushed. Ms. Pearl cautioned, "Toby, while we are trapped here in this house, Ruby and I need to tell you the whole truth about our lives as slaves. Toby, you can only appreciate how wonderful your grandpa was when you fully understand what those before you went through. We've told you all about when we ran and hid in the caverns, and you love those stories. What we have not told you is that our Momma would not go with us. She wanted us to run and be safe, but she refused to go with us. At the time, Sister and I were fifteen, and Brother Samuel was nineteen. We all knew Sherman's army was coming, and we needed to hide because no one was safe. We didn't understand how Momma could feel so loyal to Ms. Victoria that she would choose her over us. It took us years of thinking about her life before we finally understood why Momma did what she did. Toby, it is important that you know what people experienced back then—so you won't judge them for what they did."

A fast moving southbound train startled Tobias back to the present. Ruth was still deep in conversation with the woman across the aisle so, instead of interrupting them, Tobias lifted his great-grandmother's tin box and silently repeated Ms. Pearl's caution so many years ago: 'Toby, it is important that you know what people experienced back then—so you won't judge them for what they did.'

As a boy, he had struggled when he had learned what Momma Hannah had done. He did not understand it—even when the sisters told him why. Today, thinking about all that 'Little Hannah' had endured, he no longer judged her for her choices.

Today, more than ever, this box represented the best and the worst of his family history. Holding the same tin box that Great-Grandma Hannah once held brought both comfort and real sorrow. Rubbing his fingers across the surface, he could not help but ponder, "Did my great-grandma ever rub her fingers across this surface?"

Momma Hannah was not simply a character in one of Auntie Ruby's great stories. She was as real as this tin box, and I love her because she deserved to be loved. She had a hard life and did the best she could. I am so thankful I was allowed to get to know her through Ms. Ruby's great storytelling. She repeated Momma Hannah's words so smoothly, that even all these years later, I can sit here on this train and imagine myself being in that canning shed with Momma Hannah.

Aunt Ruby always started this story with, "Toby Boy, as children, Samuel, Pearl, and I did not understand our momma. Her blind loyalty to Ms. Victoria, the Master's wife, was always a puzzle to us, and to be honest, it hurt our feelings. It was not until our four months in the cavern that her reasons for being loyal to Ms. Victoria became clear to us. But Toby, even though we understood, it was hard to watch our momma choose Ms. Victoria over her own children.

"Toby, it is not fair to tell you that Momma picked Ms. Victoria over us without telling you why. There is always a 'why' behind every choice we make. Our whys are not always good ones, but we all have a why. When someone's choices hurt our feelings, it helps to look a little deeper and try to understand that person's why."

Ms. Pearl joined in and added, "Toby, sometimes we will never know a person's why. Our momma would never talk about her life. We might have lost her for good, without knowing what she had experienced, had it not been for that canning season the year Sissy and I were six. After that canning season, Momma Hannah refused to speak about the matter again, but at least we finally knew her story."

Aunt Ruby's face would brighten up whenever she talked about her time in the canning shed with her momma. Ms. Ruby would change her voice so it sounded like Momma Hannah whenever she would quote her. I had no trouble believing every word.

"Toby, while we were in the canning shed, Momma said, 'As far as slave owners go, the Stewart family is fair enough. They is known to use a gentle hand with their slaves, but don't you never let down your guard. One slip of the tongue, and you gunna find yous self sold off. Believe me, I know what I is talking about. You best always keep your thoughts to yourself. No storytelling. Ms. Victoria won't care if you is just a child. She won't care that you is just repeating something one of the old slaves told you. You best remember, even if'n those stories are only half true, it is lots worse where Ms. Victoria would be send'n you.' "

Pearl would smile and say, "That is exactly how Momma talked."

Then Ruby would add, "Momma always warned us, 'Now, Young Master Stewart is a kind man—better than his daddy was, but he ain't gunna brook no rebellion. Ms Victoria is always saying she don't trust none of us, so don't you give her no reason to send you away from here.' "

Looking over at her sister, Ruby said, "Remember how hot it was in that shed, Sister?"

Pearl nodded, smiled and said, "But it was worth it, wasn't it, Ruby? If not for that canning season, we might never have learned our momma's story."

"Toby, the only reason our momma told us her story was because it was so hot in that canning shed. She knew Master Stewart would never come close to the shed during canning season. The heat was terrible, and the flies were everywhere. Ms. Victoria would not be caught anywhere near the shed, so Momma felt safe to talk.

"Pearl and I were given the task of water bathing the peaches, pulling off the stems, and making sure no rotten peaches were sent to the hot-water dip. Momma made sure we stayed away from the big copper pots filled with boiling water. As we filled a basket with clean peaches, she would carry the basket over and dump them into the boiling water to release the skin more easily. She would then take a large ladle and scoop out the peaches before they cooked, dip them into ice cold water and give them back to us. Then we would pull off the skin and place them in another pot for Momma to cut and pit. We spent weeks with Momma out in the canning shed during the height of canning season.

"It was hot enough during a Georgia summer, but that shed, with those three big copper pots full of boiling water, represented such hard work. But we loved it, didn't we, Sister? That was the only time we could get Momma to talk."

Pearl sat back and smiled at her sister. "Ruby, you tell Toby Boy this story. You tell it so much better than I do. Besides, when you tell it, I can sit back, close my eyes, and be right back there in the canning shed with our momma."

"Well, it started out plain enough. Momma got the fires started, and the big copper pots had been filled with water when all of a sudden, she said, 'I remember canning with my momma when I was about your age. This shed wasn't here then. Old Master Stewart hated all the flies that came with canning, so he had a shed built out at the far edge of the garden. That shed has been gone a long time, but I still remember.'"

"Toby," Ms. Pearl added, "we were so excited to hear our momma telling her story we did not dare say a word—for fear of stopping her."

HANNAH:
Me and Ms. Victoria
1824-1853

CHAPTER 10

Ms. Victoria's Helper

I WAS BORN to one of the favorite house cooks, but I don't even know her name. I was only seven when she died. All I ever called her was "Momma." I never knew who my daddy was. Old Master Stewart did not believe in letting any of his slaves live under his roof—not even his favorite cooks.

Seems there was a cook from somewhere down in Louisiana, and she up and poisoned the whole family for selling off her children. I was only three years old, but I became the Master's taster. Old Master Stewart would not touch a bite of food until I took a bite first. I had to take a bite of everything that was served at the family table while standing right in front of old Master Stewart. Didn't matter if I liked it or not; I took a bite, and I swallered. He was sure my momma would not poison me—at least that was what he counted on. This went on for three years—every single meal. I swallered some right nasty stuff back then.

I got two canning seasons in with my own momma before she died. Up until then, Momma and I had the cook's cabin all by ourselves. Old Master Stewart was so afraid of catching some sickness from the slaves, we were kept away from the field workers.

I was seven when my Momma died. I don't know what she died of; she just died. But once she did, old Master Stewart just sent me down to live in the slave's quarters with the older women. I was too young to work in his kitchen without my momma, so I was sent out into the fields for two long years, working beside the older women. I hated that work, and I hated the field cabins, but what was I to do?

It was really dirty in the field cabins, and the old women were worn out and mean. I had been accustomed to clean clothes and good food, but out there you fought for every single scrap. I stayed out in the field sheds for two long years. About the time I turned nine, Master Stewart brought home his cousin's daughter, Victoria, who was about eight years old. Her parents had died in a smallpox epidemic in Charleston, so he went and got Victoria. One day, old Master Stewart walked out into the field, pointed at me, and said, "Go clean yourself up, Hannah. From now on you will live in the cook's cabin with Molly because I won't have a dirty girl walking around in my house. The Missus has some new clothes for you, and, from now on, you will be Victoria's helper. You are to do everything she tells you to do or else you will find yourself right back here in the fields. You understand?"

I was so happy. No more field work! Clean clothes and good food, and all I had to do was keep Miss Victoria happy. Life was good again. I learned all kinds of games, but I always had to let Ms. Victoria win. I learned how to braid her hair and how to keep her clothes in order. It was my job to listen to her constant prattling all day long. As a young girl, Ms. Victoria was a spoiled, tantrum-throwing brat, but it was better than the fields. I was to walk beside Ms. Victoria when she took her pony out for a walk, making sure to have plenty of fresh water whenever Ms. Victoria wanted any. For four long years I was in and out of the main house from sunup to sundown. The most serious rule old Master Stewart had was: "Once the sun goes down, all slaves must be out of the house, and the doors are to be locked." Old Master Stewart never trusted any slave.

My life was good until the day I got too comfortable and forgot my place. Ms. Victoria had insisted we play a game that day, and Ms. Victoria thought I had cheated. Angry at being accused of cheating— especially when I always let her win—made me mad, and I defended myself and yelled back at Ms. Victoria. She took my outburst well, but just outside the bedroom door, Old Master Stewart heard me yelling and came in, snatched me up, and dragged me right out to the field house. I was thirteen years old, and it didn't matter that I had been good for four long years.

HANNAH: Me and Ms. Victoria 1824-1853

Old Master Stewart did not trust his slaves—especially anyone show-ing anger, so I was banished from the house. The stories I heard from the field slaves scared me something awful. The slaves who had been traded in would talk about how small our plantation was compared to others. They said most were many times larger, but old Master Stewart was known as a dabbler. When I asked what that was, one old woman pulled me aside and asked, "How old are you girl?"

When I told her I was thirteen years, the old woman made a face and barked, "And you don't know what a dabbler is? Where you been, girl?"

That night I learned that a dabbler is like an old horse trader—only he buys, sells, trades, and breeds slaves to make money. Some of the men who had come from the auction house in town said they heard the other owners giving old Master Stewart a hard time. They felt cheated because Master Stewart would hear about an owner's having money trouble and get to him before he came to the auction. Master Stewart would choose the man's best slaves and buy them low, but the owner saved himself the auction fee. Master Stewart kept them for a while and then sold them high to make a lot of money.

That was why Master Stewart was so afraid of one of his slaves start-ing a rebellion. The slaves never grew up on his plantation, so he couldn't trust them. He would get rid of someone at a whim; but the truth be told, he didn't trust any of us—born here or not. We all had to be so careful not to talk in the house. I always feared I might be traded away if Ms. Victoria heard me complaining.

It is never safe when you is a slave, and I hated living out in the field cabins. You can't go trusting nobody. Every night, all they did in the eve-nings was tell stories about what it was like on other plantations. They would tell about beatings, hangings, and masters who would violate the women—both young and old. I wanted to hate old Master Stewart for throwing me out of the house and into that hellhole, but then, when I heard how so many other slaves were treated, I was confused. Here I was in this terrible place—but still feeling thankful it wasn't as bad as it could have been. I thought I was locked out of the main house forever.

I was thirteen when I forgot myself for a moment and was tossed into that hellhole. "One more year," the old woman would snarl at me as she pointed her gnarly finger in my face. "One more year and old Master Stewart is going to tag you; just you wait. You will wear a badge on your skirt that tells all the breeding slaves that you are free for the taking and don't you dare refuse them. Old Master Stewart will haul you off to the auction house that very day. Then you'll know what it's like out here, you soft little kitchen girl; just you wait and see."

That mean old slave woman enjoyed telling me all about dabblers. She wanted me to be scared as she told me what old Master Stewart did for a living. Her toothless grin reminded me of the same look the old hunting dog gave when the cook tossed a soup bone out in the yard. No one got near that dog when he was enjoying that bone—and that old woman was enjoying puttn me in my place. "Old Master Stewart is a dabbler. He runs his business with only two goals: keep him and his family safe, and build his stock—that be us slaves."

Old Master Stewart had very few rules: 1) Don't couple with non-childbearing women, 2) Don't couple with a pregnant woman, 3) Don't damage my inventory, 4) Girls are to be tagged at age fourteen, and 5) Order the girls not to refuse.

I already knew all of these rules. I had seen plenty of girls "taken" as they called it. Of course, no love was talked about. These men were not gentle. They didn't care about the girls. These men knew they would be bred and traded off well before any baby would take its first breath, so who cares? I knew that was how I had come to be, and I hated the idea—just like my momma hated it. She wanted and deserved to experience love and caring. But without any choices, that was never going to be. I knew that my tagging was coming soon.

I spent that whole year working in the fields and watching the tagged girls being taken. Just before turning fourteen, I was called back up to the main house. As I walked up to the back door, I was sure it my tagging time and I felt powerless to do anything about it, but instead, I was given a job in the kitchen.

Always fearful of catching some illness from the dirty slave quarters, old Master Stewart kept the house slaves in cleaner quarters closer to the house, and they were also off limits to the men. It took some days before it sank in that I was now safe! If'n I kept my tongue, I was never going to be tagged.

I had thought I had been banished from the house forever, but Old Master Stewart gave me a second chance. I didn't know why I got a second chance, but I was never going to do anything that would send me back into that hellhole—not if I could help it. Then one day while washing the breakfast dishes, Ms. Victoria slipped into the kitchen and told me she had pleaded with old Master Stewart to give me another chance. After months out in the fields as punishment, he had relented and had allowed me back into the house, but not as a helper to Victoria. I was to begin my training in the kitchen. I knew I owed this change of station to Ms. Victoria, and I loved her for it. I was going to spend the rest of my life showing my loyalty to Ms. Victoria. I knew that Ms. Victoria had saved me. Ms. Victoria's happiness was all that stood between me and that hellhole in the field house.

For the next two years, from ages fourteen to sixteen, I set about learning how to run the kitchen. When Ms. Victoria turned sixteen, she married the young Master Stewart. For the next year, life was crazy around the house. Old Master Stewart took ill and spent months in his bed. His wife had passed away just weeks after the wedding, and the old Master simply stopped caring about anything. Under these circumstances, the young Master began taking over.

Everything was about to change in the house, even for me. I remember the day I got my hands on the tin box. It was three weeks after Ms. Victoria's wedding, and old Mrs. Stewart had just passed on. She had been sick unto death for many months, and we all knew she had simply held on so she could see her boy married. The doctor had tried every powder, potion, ointment, cream, and sedative known at the time, but nothing worked.

In desperation, young Master Stewart had seen an ad advertising Europe's most advanced medicinal cures in one of his fancy magazines, and he had promptly sent away for it. I remember the day it arrived, and Master Stewart's unwrapping the package. They were all excited to see what was inside the box, but I couldn't take my eyes off the pretty tin box, which was covered in red enamel with fake silver decorations and a beautiful latch. Although the tin box was fancy, nothing inside the box had proven helpful. Even Europe's most advanced medical cures brought his mother no relief.

That morning Ms. Victoria came into the kitchen as I was finishing up with the dishes and asked me to follow her upstairs. I had not been up those stairs since I was thirteen years old and had never been in the Master's bedroom. She explained that old Master Stewart had not slept in the room for almost a year. Once his wife had taken sick, he had moved into another bedroom. Ms. Victoria had joked, "He said it was to allow her more room and comfort, but we all know how afraid he is of catching some disease—even from his wife. Now that she is gone, he refuses to return to his bedroom."

I wondered why Ms. Victoria was telling me all of this, but then I realized she was simply prattling on as she always had as a child. She was not really talking to me; rather, she was expressing her nervous excitement at getting to move into the biggest bedroom in the house. She needed me to help clear out every reminder of the old mistress before young Master Stewart returned home from a business trip.

First, we emptied out the chifferobe of all his mother's dresses and shoes. Then we quickly emptied out the large burl wood dresser that had always been his mother's most prized possession. She and old Master Stewart had bought it in Europe while on their wedding trip. Ms. Victoria smiled as she rubbed witch hazel oil over it and said, "Just think, Hannah, this was out of some castle in Europe, and now it belongs to me."

I was not impressed—just good and tired of all the trips up and down the stairs carrying piles of clothes to the pantry. Most of them, which were too worn out for her taste, were considered too fancy for any of us slaves.

Ms. Victoria decided to sell them to the rag man the next time he stopped by.

As we were finishing the task, young Master Stewart returned home. He climbed the stairs, heard his wife talking and came in to see her progress. As he walked around the room for a moment, he said, "Good work, Victoria. Even her smell is gone. I guess it would be okay for us to move in here."

Ms. Victoria squealed with delight, until her husband froze in his steps. Turning toward the fancy European tin box that was still sitting on his mother's side table, he pointed at it and said to me, "Hannah, get rid of that box! I never want to see it again. If that company had spent half as much time making sure the cures were as nice as that box, maybe my mother might have survived."

That was the day I took ownership of the fancy tin box. Well, not actually ownership. Master Stewart wanted it gone to where he would never see it again. I could have sold it to the tinker who came by to buy and sell things, or I could have tossed it in the rubbish pile. Young Master Stewart would not have cared; but no slave of his dared to claim ownership of anything he owned—even things he wanted gone.

I took it down into the root cellar and tightly wrapped it in a burlap sack so it would not get scratched. A casual glance at the bundle would not give away the fact that I had not gotten rid of it. For years, that tin box was my happy little secret. I was a slave, but I owned something fancy and beautiful! Even though I never dared unwrap it and look at it, just knowing I owned it always brought a smile on my face.

As soon as the Old Master passed, Young Master got busy making changes. The first thing he did was to hire a crew to build on a wing to the main house and a new canning shed. Young Master Stewart had little interest in his father's business. While serving his breakfast, I heard him tell Ms. Victoria, "Being a dabbler turns my stomach. Instead of running this place the way my daddy did, I am looking into expanding the orchards and the vegetable gardens. Not needing as many slaves as my daddy tended to keep around, I will weed through the group, find those who had experience in gardening and begin selling off the rest. Since I will not be breeding any longer, more than half of the females will be taken to auction. I can't see any sense in feeding unproductive help."

I remember standing at the pantry window watching them load the field women on the wagons to take them to auction. Again, I owed Ms. Victoria for me not being on one of those wagons.

The old master died before his first and only grandson, Charles, came into this world. Two years later, Ms. Victoria had a girl, and they named her Elizabeth, and life was happy.

CHAPTER 11

How I Married Charlie

As Tobias remembered Hannah's story about Charlie, an old warning from Auntie Ruby rose up in his soul, "Toby Boy, don't you get overtaken in bitterness when you think of my daddy. Bitterness is a fruit that kills all other taste. When my daddy was sold off, I almost lost all of my memories of the precious days I had with him because all I could remember was how I felt the day he was hauled away."

Smiling out the train window, Tobias chuckled to himself, "Oh, Auntie Ruby, you knew me really well. You knew I would struggle with the injustice of it all, and I would miss the sweetness if I wasn't careful."

With this warning securely planted in his heart, Tobias allowed himself to return to Great-Grandma Hannah's story about marrying Daddy Charlie.

While Ms. Victoria was going over the menu for the week, she up and said, "Hannah, don't you want children? It is such a wonderful feeling to hold your own child."

I was now twenty, but wasn't ready to start messing with no men. Because the male slaves who survived the auction house were no longer traded in and out, I had started to notice one or two of the younger ones, but I kept my distance. Old Master Stewart was long dead, but he still scared me. All I dared say to Ms. Victoria was, "I wouldn't mind having a baby."

The next thing I knew, Ms. Victoria had up and picked out a husband for me. I guess Ms. Victoria figured any old healthy buck would do, 'cuz theys all thinks black slaves don't care about love like white folk does.

The next day Ms. Victoria brings Charlie Bascom up to the kitchen, shows him to me, and that was that. We was given the old cook's quarters that was at the far edge of the garden. Young Master Stewart moved it there to make room for the new wing, and ten months later Tobias was born. The year was 1845.

Charlie was a nice enough man. He was kind and never hurt me; I just didn't love him. But I did like him right enough.

Three years later, while I was carrying the girls, young Master Stewart made a deal with one of the large plantation owners. He traded five of his less productive slaves for two slaves who were well-trained in gardening. When they were delivered and young Master Stewart was recording them into his ledger book that he kept in his desk, he called me into his office. "Hannah, I have just made a trade for two very good gardeners. The trouble is, one of them is named Tobias. He is a fully grown man, and I can't change his name now, so I need you to change your Tobias' name. It is too confusing to have two with the same name."

I dared not argue with Master Stewart, but we had called my boy, Tobias, for three whole years, and Master Stewart wanted me to think up a name right then and there so he could change it in his slave's ledger—just like that. That day I added a middle name—something most slaves never had. I decided upon the name "Samuel," and young Master Stewart looked up where he had added Tobias to the ledger the day he was born and noted, "From today on, Tobias Bascom will henceforth be known as Samuel." Five months later, my Pearl and Ruby came along and always knew him as their brother Samuel.

For six years me and Charlie was allowed to live in the cook's cabin as a family. Daddy Charlie, as I called him, worked out in the orchard and garden all day long. Once Samuel turned four, he would go along and help wherever he could. Everyone knew things were changing around the country; even the field slaves had their own way of finding out things. I was very careful not to talk out of turn for fear of being overheard, but in the safety of our cabin, Charlie and me knew some bad times was coming.

Samuel was only five, but he overheard me and his daddy arguing about the threat of war. Daddy Charlie was all for it, believing that anything that would bring us freedom could not be bad. I did not agree with him. I was set on remaining true and loyal to Ms. Victoria. Every day I could see that Ms. Victoria was worried that she might lose everything. Ms. Victoria's being in such a state was upsetting to me.

Ms. Victoria would tell me how much she feared some of the things the government was doing. The Compromise of 1850 was worrying all of the slave owners. They knew things were moving quickly and talk of seceding from the Union could only mean that war was inevitable.

Ms. Victoria did not even think how I might be frightened by this news. I was just "Hannah" to her. I think Ms. Victoria was so afraid she was going to lose everything, she did what she always did, turn to me, her trusted helper since she came to the plantation at the age of eight. I don't think she was even capable of looking at me like another woman; I was simply Hannah.

Ms. Victoria told me that Master Stewart and other slave owners were beginning to have meetings to warn of new laws coming along and what they should do to protect themselves. The owners knew that the time was quickly coming when no one would be able to sell—even their best and strongest slaves.

One night Master Stewart came home from one of these meetings, having decided that his most valuable stock—every male under the age of thirty-five—must go to auction. I had seen his buggy coming up the drive and had prepared a light snack for him. I tray'd it up and started heading for his library, but hearing Ms. Victoria's voice arguing with the Master, I froze just outside the library door. Because of her fondness for me and the twins, Ms. Victoria questioned Master Stewart about my Charlie.

"He must go, Victoria," he said with an uncommonly harsh voice. He never raised his voice to her, until that night. "Victoria, he is too valuable to keep. I have already sold many of my daddy's slaves, but now that we are being pressed by all of these new laws, I need to sell off the most valuable ones while I still can. Victoria, we might be able to force a compromise with the North, but I doubt it. You and I cannot sustain our lifestyle if war breaks out, and we don't know when that will happen. I need to prepare for it. Right now, because I restructured this plantation, we are sitting pretty. We raise fruits and vegetables—not cotton. Embargos are killing the other plantation owners, but everyone needs fruits and vegetables. I don't need young, strong slaves for this type of work."

"But what about Hannah and the girls?" "Victoria, we can bring Hannah and the twins into the house. We can move the dry storage room out to the old canning shed, and I will build a smoked meat house next to it. That will free up the two rooms beyond the new kitchen. Hannah and the girls can have those two rooms. Will that make you happy? But her boy Samuel cannot come in. He has to live with the men. Samuel is nine years old and can do a hard day's labor all by himself. I couldn't get much for him anyway. This way, everybody wins."

I quietly returned to the kitchen, put down the tray, and headed out to our cabin. Charlie had all three of our children tucked into bed and was waiting up for me. At first I tried not to tell him what I had overheard, but he could see I was holding back something. After some poke'n and prodd'n, I finally told him what Master Stewart was planning. "Right, everybody wins? What are we supposed to tell Samuel and the girls? Charlie, I never wanted a family because I didn't want this kind of pain. But now, after living as a family for eight years, I realize that I love you and you are a good daddy, and now my children are going to feel the pain of losing their daddy."

Trying to keep me calm, Charlie asked, "Did he say how soon this is going to happen?"

"Right away, I think. Master Stewart wants to beat the other owners to auction so he can get top money. As I was backing away from the library door, I heard him tell Ms. Victoria, 'I stopped by the photographer before coming home. He agreed to be here tomorrow to take pictures of every slave I intend to sell. He promised me he would have the slave bulletins ready by the week's end.' "

Standing up with a steeled, measured resolved, Charlie announced, "Then Hannah, we only have a few days. We need to tell our children what is going to happen. We need to prepare them so they will keep their emotions under control. I can't let my boy be blindsided. I know my boy. Samuel will not be able to stand there quietly and let them shackle me and load me onto that wagon, without us talking to him first."

"Charlie, our Samuel is a good boy and he will do whatever you tell him to. Little Ruby is my shadow. With her shy little ways, she would not think of going against what we tell her. It is Pearl that I am most worried about. She is only five years old, but that girl is already full of her own opinions and has a hard time letting things just be. She is stubborn, will-ful, and has a mind of her own. She is not going to stand by and let her daddy be hauled away without a fight."

"Hannah, it is our job to get her ready. We cannot stop what is about to happen, but we must protect our children and keep them with their momma."

That was the night I realized that loving people only brings me pain. I can't do nothing about nothing, except try to make sure I protect me and my children from getting sold off. I tucked my love for Charlie deep down inside of me so I could survive his leaving. Then I pledged to myself, "You do everything in your power to keep Ms. Victoria happy so she will continue to fight for you and your children. That is your only way out of all this."

The next day, I watched from the kitchen window as the photographer positioned Charlie beside the canning shed and took his picture. Charlie knew what this meant but he just stood where he was told and then walked back out to the orchard as if it was just another day.

I tried to stay busy so I would not get myself so riled up that I could not put on my slave-face. I had practiced that face for years, and it had served me well. It was getting towards mid-day and I needed to get lunch on the table. Ms Victoria had come through the kitchen around ten o'clock to inform me that the photographer would be joining them for lunch. Unaware that I knew what was going on, Ms. Victoria offered, "Hannah, Mr. Saint John is a wonderful photographer. He has taken all of our family photos. He is especially good with children."

I wondered where she was going with this, when suddenly she stopped in midsentence, as if just getting an idea, and said, "Hannah, you don't have a picture of your children, do you? Would you like Mr. Saint John to take Samuel, Pearl, and Ruby's picture before he leaves today? That way you will always remember what they looked like as small children."

Terror ran through me at the idea of my children getting their picture took. Slave's pictures meant they were being sold. My face must have given me away because Ms. Victoria grabbed my arm and said, "Hannah, you know how much I care for your children. I just wanted to do this as a gift for you, really. I have gathered up some old, but very nice, clothes that my Charles and Elizabeth used to wear. While we are having lunch, you can clean up the children and get them all dressed up. Then, just before Mr. Saint John packs up his gear, I will ask him to take the children's photo. He would not think of refusing my request."

I agreed—what else could I do? But I had another reason for agreeing. Not knowing it would take too many days to get the picture back, I was hoping I might have it in time to give Charlie a picture of his children. I wanted him to have this to remember us, so I set aside the terror of seeing my children get their picture taken and thought about Charlie.

My Samuel hated that getup. Young Master Charles' fancy Sunday clothes had been stored in the upstairs trunk for more than ten years and they smelled funny. How my Samuel hated that blue velvet suit with short pants and stiff white collar around his neck, but he always did as I said.

Pearl and Ruby loved the dresses Ms. Victoria picked out for them. They had never had such lovely clothes and Ruby spun around the kitchen feeling like a little queen that day. She squealed in delight, 'Momma, do we get to keep these pretty dresses? Pearl, always much more in control, kept questioning why? 'Momma, why are we getting dressed up? Momma, why are we getting our picture took? Momma, why is today different than every other day?'

Pearl was not built to be a slave. That girl always had too many 'whys' in her head, and asking 'why' will only get you into trouble.

Think'n back, I never did get that picture. It didn't come in time to give it to Charlie and then I just forgot about it. Charlie was gone and life just went on. I put my slave-face back on and buried my loneliness for Charlie way down deep inside of me—and just kept going. That is what a slave does, if they want to survive.

TOBIAS:
My Link To My Past
1951-1954

12. Putting Faces To The Names

CHAPTER 12

❧

Putting Faces to The Names

REMEMBERING ALL THE terrible things little Hannah went through has always been difficult. Sitting here on the train all these years later, I can almost hear Ms. Pearl's words of caution so long ago. Although hard to hear, Hannah's story taught me a valuable lesson. Today, I want my Great-Grandma Hannah with me as I travel back in time and revisit these stories. I have always had her tin box, but recently, thanks to a timely newspaper article in the *Atlanta Herald*, I now possess three of my most precious gifts.

During my youth, when the Sisters told me all about life on the plantation and Momma Hannah, I had to imagine what she looked like because even the sisters did not have a photo of their momma or the plantation. There never were any photos of Momma Hannah, Samuel, or the sisters because slaves did not have cameras or the necessary funds to have their photos taken. Growing up, the only photo Grandpa Samuel ever had was his wedding photo.

Years later in the early 1920s, we had read with interest that the old plantation had finally been sold to some investors. We were all happy that the place no longer belonged to the Stewart family. The old place had been ransacked, boarded up, and left in ruins for more than sixty years. The newspaper article reported that some investors planned to gut the place and turn it into a grand hotel. However, before the major demolition could begin, the crash of 1929 hit; the place was boarded up again for another twenty years.

In 1948 another investment group purchased the plantation and spent three long years turning it into a fully restored antebellum bed-and-breakfast resort. While doing the restorations, the new investors were given all of the old slave documents, photos and ledgers that had been held by the Stewart family. In 1951 while planning their grand opening, the local newspaper featured several articles about how these old documents were being displayed around the main house.

Knowing a black man would not be welcomed through the front doors of this fancy new resort, I almost talked myself out of writing a letter, explaining who I was and how I was connected to the Stewart family. Ruth kept after me to write that letter, and yet again, I owe one of my greatest gifts to her.

I asked if I might be allowed to come and look at the documents while the resort was still closed to the public. I did not hold out much hope for an answer, so I was quite surprised when Ruth and I received a gracious invitation to stop by the plantation a day or two before the grand opening.

Sitting on this train, bound for such an honorable event, Tobias could not help but let his mind drift back to three years earlier, on the day when he and Ruth had walked up the paved walkway to the grand front door of the former Stewart Plantation. He knew that he and Ruth would never be allowed to walk through those doors once they were opened to the public—at least not in his lifetime.

Standing nervously at the grand walkway that lead to the front steps, Tobias suspected his Great-Grandma Hannah had never been allowed to walk on this pathway, or walk through those front doors. A strange feeling came over him as he approached the house. He *knew* this house even though he had never before been here because he had spent many an evening walking through it via the great storytelling talent of his Great-Auntie Ruby.

"Ruth, I wish Aunt Ruby could have lived to see this day."

Ruth did not agree with his desire. "Tobias, I don't believe Ruby's returning here would be as special to her as it is to you. Her memories were not as sweet as yours are."

As they climbed the entry steps, a gentleman opened the door and invited them to come in. As they walked around, Tobias' mind could hear Ms. Ruby and Ms. Pearl describing each room to him. He wanted to run into the kitchen where Momma Hannah had spent her life, then into the pantry where Pearl sat listening to the school lessons, and he wanted to climb down into the secret cellar where Momma Hannah and Pearl had hidden the canned food. He whispered to Ruth, "I wonder if these men even know about the secret cellar?"

Upon walking into old Master Stewart's office, which had been converted into an intimate dining room, Tobias was not prepared for what he saw. The investors had gone through old Master Stewart's papers and discovered that he had truly conducted his business well. Unlike most sellers, Old Master Stewart always hired a photographer to come to the plantation and take photos of the slaves he was planning to sell. Each photo was printed on a Slave's Bulletin, listing the slave's age, his overall health, his abilities, and the price he wanted for him. At first Tobias thought he might find a photo of his Great-Grandpa Charlie Bascom, but then he noticed the dates were all 1828. He knew that would have been too early for Charlie.

Although disappointed, he continued to flip through the bulletins because these men deserved to be remembered. At the very bottom of this stack of bulletins was a single photo of a little girl sitting on the top step of the old kitchen door. Tobias noticed a caption scribbled below the photo that read: Little Hannah, age 5, Kitchen Helper, 1829.

Tobias stood looking at the photo with tears streaming down his face. He was seeing the sweet little face of his great-grandmother Hannah when she was only five years old. Whispering to Ruth, he lamented, "Oh, how much my Grandpa Samuel and the Sisters would have loved to have seen this photo of their momma."

The gentleman standing by the doorway could see Tobias' reaction and came over. "Is there something wrong?"

"No, sir," Tobias quickly answered. "See this photo of the little girl, Hannah? She was my great-grandmother."

"Are you sure?" the gentleman asked in amazement. "We have been trying to do research about everyone who ever lived on this plantation, but after the Civil War, everyone had scattered. These people are long since dead, and we have no idea how to contact their families."

"Well, sir," Tobias said with great pride, "I lived with her son, my grandpa Samuel until I was seven. He was born and reared as a slave on this plantation. At seven, I was sent to live with his sisters, Pearl and Ruby, who were also born on this plantation."

With an urgent, but excited, tone in his voice, the gentleman said, "Wait right here, Tobias."

A few minutes later, the gentleman returned with a file dated 1853. "Tobias, I have spent the past three years archiving every photo, legal document, slave ledger, and Slave Auction Bulletin the Stewart Family had in their possession. Most of them were incomplete, and because the Stewarts tended to rename their slaves and often reused names, I could not do anything but put them in some kind of date order. The name Hannah seemed to be a name Old Master Stewart liked, so when I saw this picture in the file, I could not assume it had anything to do with the photo of Little Hannah from 1828. But you mentioned that your great-grandmother Hannah had three children by the names of Samuel, Pearl, and Ruby, correct?"

"Yes, sir," confirmed Tobias with so much emotion he could hardly contain himself.

"Tobias, in 1853, twenty-five years after little Hannah's photo was taken, young Master Stewart ordered several Slave Auction Bulletins printed. Talk of war was making it difficult to sell slaves, not knowing if their purchases could remain secure." Then opening the file, the gentleman handed Tobias a bulletin, "Might these be Hannah's children?"

Tobias took hold of the bulletin, and there was Grandpa Samuel standing beside his sisters, Pearl and Ruby. By the date, it must have been about the time Great-Grandpa Charlie had been sold. Tobias fought back tears as he confirmed the man's belief. "Yes, these are Hannah's children—my Grandpa Samuel, and his twin sisters, Pearl and Ruby. Pearl is standing, and Ruby is sitting."

Once Tobias had indeed established the identities of those in the photo, the gentleman handed him the original photo from which the Auction Bulletin had been created. "Turn it over, Tobias, and read what is written on the back."

Tobias turned it over and in a clear hand it said, "Photo ordered by Mrs. Victoria Stewart as a gift to Hannah, the cook, for selling Charlie Bascom. At the bottom of the photo was a second note: Auction Bulletin of children ordered by Master Stewart."

As Tobias and Ruth studied the photo, the gentleman again opened the file and pulled out a second auction bulletin. "Using the year 1853, I went through all the Stewart records to find an Auction Bulletin for any slave by the name of Charlie Bascom, and I found this."

Unable to contain her emotions, Ruth cried out, "Oh, Tobias, I wish Pearl and Ruby could have seen this."

Tobias dared not respond. Gripped with emotion, he studied the photo of his great-grandfather Charlie and carefully read the history that accompanied so many of these seller's bulletins.

Charlie Bascom is thirty-three years old, in good health, and a good strong worker. He was born in 1820 on the Bascom Plantation in Monroe, Louisiana, to a healthy twenty-seven-year-old female purchased in 1798 from a ship transport from Upper Guinea. His birth papers note that the mother was from the Yoruba people. Master Bascom trained this slave to do orchard keeping; however, this slave is a fast learner and can be used for nearly any type of heavy labor. Being of sound body, this slave has never been beaten for running away or causing problems. Having purchased him directly from his original owner, this seller can attest to this slave's background and merit. Asking $4,500.

Tobias stared at the information provided about his great-grandfather's lineage—the Yoruba people of Upper Guinea, and the name of the Bascom Plantation. After all these years, on one single sheet of paper, he now knew where his name came from and where his great-grandpa came from and what he looked like.

As Tobias stared into the eyes of his grandpa's daddy, he knew he had to do something to get this man to give these photos to him. "Sir, did you know that there is a secret cellar under the floor of the back room—right beyond the kitchen?"

Surprised, the curator asked, "Really? Would you be willing to show it to me?"

Tobias smiled. "Sir, this is the first time I have been inside this house, but my Great-Auntie Ruby was a great storyteller and included many details. I believe I know exactly where to find it."

"Then let's go," encouraged the gentleman.

Tobias was excited to learn that the secret cellar was news to this gentleman, and he was happy to see that the investors had left the room as they had found it. In their desire to maintain as much authenticity as possible, they had not gutted this backroom. They simply cleaned it up and placed a sign at the door, "House-slaves quarters."

Tobias walked in and stopped for a moment as he thought, "I knew the people who lived in here." Then he quickly requested, "Sir, if you would take the end of the bed, I will take the top and we can move the bed across the room."

As they did so, Tobias could almost feel Ms. Pearl and Momma Hannah doing this same thing so many years earlier. Once the bed was moved, Tobias put his finger in the small hole in the floor and lifted the hidden hatch. Even though the curator was wearing his suit, he quickly laid down on the floor so he could look around the hidden cellar. "We had absolutely no idea this room was here. Do you happen to know what they used it for?"

"Yes, sir," Tobias smiled. "I know a great story about this secret cellar. By the way, do you know about the caverns?"

"What caverns?"

Tobias grinned like a Cheshire cat. He knew he had a bargaining chip that just might secure those family photos for him. "Sir, if you would be willing to give me those three photographs of my family members, I will tell you everything I know about this plantation."

As he stretched out his hand, the curator smiled. "You have a deal."

Over the next few months, Tobias kept his promise and did tell the curator all about the Bascoms' family stories; in turn, he was given the photos he had requested.

Lifting out the envelope from the tin box, Tobias remembered how very selective he had been about which stories he had planned to share with that curator. Although that gentleman was appreciative and gracious, he was not interested in a slave's point of view. But today, while on this train ride to Washington, Tobias intended to review every last detail of the accounts he had been told. This time though, instead of having to imagine what each person looked like, he now had real images so he could easily put a face to all of the stories.

One by one, the photos were lifted out of the envelope; Great-Grandma Hannah at the age of four, Great-Grandpa Charlie, Grandpa Samuel, Great-Auntie Pearl, and Great-Auntie Ruby.

Tobias smiled as he held these photos and allowed his mind to return to their hiding place during the Atlanta riots, when the sisters told him what it was like after their daddy was taken away.

Little Hanna age 5
Kitchen Helper 1829

THE SISTERS:
Life Without our Daddy
1853-1865

CHAPTER 13

Pearl Remembers When our Daddy was Sold

SISTER AND I were only five years old, but I still remember that night in the old cabin. Momma sat us down and told us that Master Stewart was sending our daddy away. She would not even allow us to cry. She said, "You must not betray yourself, Pearl. You keep your feelings hidden, or Ms. Victoria will send you away too. You watch your face; don't you show any attitude at all. Pearl, you hear me?"

Momma always worried about me. Ruby was so shy she naturally kept her thoughts to herself, but for me…it was so hard to act like nothing was wrong. Our world was falling apart, and we were not allowed to show our feelings. I believe that is why I have such a hard time letting people see how I feel. It was so dangerous back then, and I dared not give in—even as a five-year-old. No child should have to fear betraying her feelings.

Master Stewart and Ms. Victoria were not aware that they had been overheard, nor did they feel remotely accountable to tell Momma their plans. But we knew Daddy was going to be hauled away in two days, and we were to act like nothing was wrong.

Very early that terrible morning, we all got up and said our good-byes. Daddy Charlie gave each of us a hug and wiped away our tears. Even brother Samuel cried. That was when Momma pulled something wrapped in a filthy old burlap sack from under the bed. She carefully unwrapped it and held up the prettiest box we had ever seen. She proudly held it high for all of us to behold. Momma turned to Samuel and said, "Wipe your tears,

Samuel. This has been my box for many, many years. I have kept it hidden so it would not be taken away from me, but today, I am giving it to you."

Momma then went over to Daddy and twisted a button off his shirt. She shoved that button into Brother's hand and said, "Samuel, you hold tight to that button today. It is all you will ever have of your daddy's—but it is more than most of us will ever have. It is your reminder that you did have a daddy and that he loved you with all his heart."

To this day, I remember how Samuel held onto that button that day. I thought he was going to crush it into dust, he held it so tightly. I also remember how hard it was for Momma to get it away from Samuel that night. She told him that she needed to put his button into the tin box so he would not lose it. Then she told him that she would return the box to her hiding place to keep it safe. Brother argued with Momma. He did not want to let go of his button, but Momma won out in the end.

That morning, Daddy was hauled off to the auction house, and we never saw him or heard from him again. The only good thing was the four of us were still safe—at least for the moment. Ruby and I were five when our daddy was sold away. As we were preparing to serve the dinner that night, Momma warned us again about showing any feelings. Momma kept a fairly close rope around us so she could stop anything before it started. Weeks passed before Momma relaxed and let me move about the house without her.

It took me more than a few weeks to fully swallow my anger at losing my daddy, but I did get to the place where I could move on. To tell you the truth, I really don't believe I ever really got past that experience, but life does go on; and so did I.

Right after sending our daddy away, Momma, Sissy and I were moved into the main house and for the next two years, we only saw Samuel on Sunday afternoons. He was never allowed inside of the main house, but he was allowed to sit on the kitchen steps and visit with Momma, Sissy, and me for a few hours once a week. Sissy and I had to be very careful what we said or Momma would send us to our room, and we would miss our time with our brother.

By the time Sissy and I were eight, Master Stewart was also getting tired of having to listen to his children's lessons being conducted in the dining room. He would come home from one of his political meetings so riled up he had no patience for their chatter. He wanted the schoolroom moved out of the main house, so the large keeping room that separated the new wing from the main house was divided into two rooms. One side was to be used as a classroom for Master Charles and Miss Elizabeth, and the room next to the kitchen became the dry goods room.

By the time we were six, Momma had trained us both to do simple tasks around the kitchen and keeping room. My favorite task was measuring out dry goods for Mother—not because I cared about baking, but because I could sit quietly by the keeping door and hear the tutor in the next room teaching Master Charles and Miss Elizabeth. Master Charles was almost finished with school and hated every minute he had to sit in there with the tutor. I'd hear him complain, saying there was no reason he needed to know all this stuff. His daddy had already purchased his land, and he would be rich like his daddy very soon and wanted to get on with it.

Miss Elizabeth complained less but never seemed to do well with her assignments. She was only a few years older than Ruby and me, but at the age of fourteen, she was already talking about when she was going to get married. She intended to marry as soon as she turned sixteen and could not be bothered with spelling. I, on the other hand, drank up the tutor's lessons. I wanted to know everything all at once. One day Momma came to me and said that Ms. Victoria had taken a liking to me; and when Sister and I turned seven, Ms. Victoria intended that I should learn how to read, write and add sums so I could take over the household accounts someday. I remember feeling very proud and excited until Mother sadly added, "But Ruby is going to start training as a domestic."

It took me years before I understood why Ms. Victoria had made this decision. Ruby was sweet, kind and helpful, but quite shy. I, on the other hand, was more outgoing and bristled at the bridle. Mother used to say that Ruby was always going to get along, but she worried that I would never learn to cuff my mouth. I had definite opinions, and I had a hard time hiding them—a dangerous weakness for any slave. I believe Ms. Victoria took my outgoingness as being smarter than Ms. Ruby. That is not true. Ruby is every bit as smart as I am; she is just shy and willing to accept things without bristling. Ms. Victoria took her shy nature as being backward.

For several years Ruby was instructed in everything she needed to know about cleaning a large house, doing laundry and mending and anything else Miss Elizabeth ordered her to do. During this same time, I was allowed to work in the kitchen with Momma every morning until it was time for my schooling. Master Charles had just recently moved out on his own, and Elizabeth was almost finished with her schooling. All afternoon the tutor began the work of educating me. Although I loved to learn, this woman made it very clear that she did not approve of teaching slave children, but I guess the money was good. There never was any love lost between the two of us, but I did learn how to read—which was all I cared about.

When we turned nine, Miss Elizabeth married her second cousin who was much older than she was, and Master Stewart gave Ruby to her as one of her wedding gifts. She was to be Ms. Elizabeth's downstairs domestic. Her home was only five miles away but might as well have been five hundred. Mother and I were both sure we would never see our Ruby ever again.

Plantation life was really getting hard. For several years before the war actually began, tensions ran high in the house because Master Stewart was unable to sell or trade slaves. It seemed that all of his fellow owners were afraid the upcoming war might go badly. Therefore, they did not want to invest in labor, only to have it taken away from them. Even though there was tension in the house, we felt good. We thought we were finally safe from trades; we simply hadn't counted on his giving us away as gifts.

I get angry when people say that slaves had it pretty good. We did have it better than anyone we knew, but having my sister packed up and sent off when we were just nine, believing I would never see her again, is a pain I cannot even begin to express. I remember the night before Ruby was to be shipped off. Momma was upset about losing our Ruby, but she could not express her feelings. She took us out to the canning shed and sat us down, and with tears in her eyes, she warned, "What I is gonna say to you girls is very bad."

I remember the look on my sister's face when she learned she was being sent away. We had just turned nine, but Ruby sat there—quiet as a mouse, no tears, no tantrum, nothing. I, on the other hand, was beside myself. None of Momma's warnings could make me hold back my tears. I hated Ms. Victoria! I knew this was her doing, and I hated her for it.

Momma was so worried that I would not hold my tongue that night that she made me promise her by saying, "Pearl, I lost Charlie and now my Ruby. Don't you never make me lose you too! I woulds just lay down and die if you did."

When I saw my momma so broken, I hugged Momma's neck and gave her my promise to obey. We both served the dinner meal that night, and Ms. Victoria acted as if separating families was the most common occurrence in the world. After all, her daughter needed some extra house help, and Ruby was certainly old enough to be a real help. That was the night I realized that, although this woman had cared about us, we were nothing to her but useful tools to be exchanged at her whim without the least bit of thought.

Ruby was sent away in 1858, and the actual war, as we know now, was not going to start for three whole years. Even before the war became official, life was becoming difficult. Supplies were short, Master Stewart was often gone on political business, and Ms. Victoria refused to talk to, let alone manage, any of the field slaves.

Master Stewart knew he could not leave the plantation in her hands, so he made arrangements to have a man named Brown come to the house for an interview. Mr. Brown was from North Carolina, and he had lots of experience managing plantations—at least that is what he told the master. With the master frequently gone and her children both gone, Ms. Victoria had no interest in staying home. Ms. Elizabeth lived only five miles away, and Ms. Victoria took to spending long periods of time at her daughter's place, leaving Mr. Brown in charge of everything. We soon learned exactly how he intended to keep the slaves in line.

Brother Samuel and the others worked hard, keeping the gardens going. From sunup to sundown, the new manager, Mr. Brown, had all of the men working the garden. Samuel was fourteen when Mr. Brown showed up. As soon as Master Stewart rode off, the whip came out. For three long months, Samuel toiled all day long in the Georgia heat without water—simply because it pleased Mr. Brown to make them work without water. Several of the older men could not take it. Remember, Master Stewart had long since sold all of the men under thirty-five, so it was Samuel and seven or eight worn-out slaves carrying the load. Brown began taking a liking to using the whip—especially on Samuel. I don't think he worried much about the old men. He used Samuel as an example to keep the rest in line.

Because all of the embargoes intended to break the resolve of the South, meat was in short supply. Even the wealthy whites could not use their money to bribe their way into portions of meat; meat bribery came with very harsh penalties. With no meat, all we had to look forward to after a long day of hard work was boiled vegetables. Once in a while Mr. Brown caught himself a rabbit, but he never shared it—not even with Ms. Victoria when she would come back to check on the plantation.

Eventually, Master Stewart came back for a short visit. His political business was keeping him away more than he thought, and he was glad that Ms. Victoria was with their daughter. He did not know how long it would be before he could come back, so he spent several days boarding up the upstairs windows. He walked the land with Mr. Brown, looked in on the slaves and was shocked to see their condition. Brown told him a lie about how all of them had tried to run off, so naturally, he had punished them.

Samuel told me he didn't think Master Stewart believed his story, but he only told Mr. Brown to use a lighter hand on such old men and walked back into the main house. Master Stewart was in his study when Momma brought him some cold water and a plate of canned peaches she had tucked away.

I was in the next room cleaning when I heard Master Stewart tell Momma, "I know that man has taken the whip to your Samuel, Hannah. What did Samuel do to deserve a whipping?"

I cautiously peeked around the corner and saw Momma look Master Stewart right in the eyes and say, "You know my Samuel is a loyal boy to you, Master Stewart. You can trust him. I don't think you can trust that Mr. Brown."

Master Stewart stood up, and I was afraid he was going to hurt my momma for talking so straight to him. Instead, he walked over to the window that looked out over the garden. He stood there for a long time before turning back to Momma and saying, "I'm going to take that whip away from him. I think he likes it a little too much. I am going to give Mr. Brown three more weeks to show me he can run this place for me. I am going to give you this money packet. It is Brown's wages. I don't dare hand it over to him right now. I think he will just take off with it. I haven't yet paid him for the three months he has already managed. I think I can be back here in three weeks, and I will decide then if I am going to keep him on. I'm giving it to you, Hannah, because I can tell that Mr. Brown has been through my office. You put it somewhere safe for me. I trust you, Hannah. Do not disappoint Ms. Victoria."

As it turned out, Master Stewart was not able to return in three weeks like he had intended. Every able-bodied white man had been called into service. Master Stewart thought he had more time, but a war was being planned. Mr. Brown was tired of waiting for his pay, and the new Confederate Army was paying men a conscript for signing up. Momma knew if she handed over that pay sack, Mr. Brown would stick around. So she just played dumb, and we watched that man pack his satchel, go into Master Stewart's office, take several items that would be easy to sell in town and off he went.

Once he was gone, only us slaves were left, so we did what we always did; we ran the plantation until Ms. Victoria, Ms Elizabeth, and Sissy came back home; but since it is her story, she needs to tell it.

CHAPTER 14

Ruby Remembers Life with Ms. Elizabeth

IT WAS DAY three of the Atlanta riots, and with the need to keep my nine-year-old mind off of what was going on in town, Ms. Pearl and Ms. Ruby continued their stories about their lives as slaves. After breakfast, while still hiding in the back bedroom, Ms. Ruby leaned against her bed, tucked her good leg under her bad one and began.

I was nine years old when I was ordered to climb into the back of the wagon old Master Stewart had used to haul his slaves to auction. As I waited to be loaded onto the wagon, I remembered the day our daddy had climbed up onto that very wagon, had the shackles locked around his ankles, and off he went—never to be heard from again. I still remember that day. Ms. Victoria allowed my momma to stand at the window in Master Stewart's library, but only if Momma promised not to make a fuss. Momma had one hand on my shoulder and her other hand on Pearl's. I wanted to tap on the glass so Daddy would look up at us, but Momma shook my shoulder and said, "Be quiet, Ruby; he knows we are here."

Only after Master Stewart slapped the reins, and the horses began pulling the wagon up the long drive did our daddy look back at us. He was shackled hand and foot so he could not wave goodbye, but I will always remember his big smiling face with tears streaming down his cheeks. Momma just stood there still as a statue. I wanted to scream but knew that would never be allowed. I dared not look over at Pearl. I knew if I did, I would not be able to hold back the tears. Little children should never be ordered to hold back their tears because doing so changes who they are.

Remembering the morning I had said goodbye to my daddy, I asked Momma and Pearl to stand at that very same window when the wagon hauled me away, so I could look back and smile at them just as my daddy had.

Ms. Victoria refused to ride on the wagon with Master Stewart that day; instead, she climbed into the family buggy, pulling her huge skirt in just before Elmer, Master's driver, closed the door behind her. Ms. Victoria stuck her head out the window and yelled to Master Stewart, "I am not going to eat your wagon dust all the way to Elizabeth's place. Let Elmer take the lead." Elmer quickly climbed up into the driver's seat and gave the horse a quick snap of the whip. Ms. Victoria sat back and rearranged her skirt for the long, dusty ride to her daughter's new house.

I was surprised when Master Stewart climbed up onto the wagon seat. He had not come back and shackled me to the wagon. At first I thought he had simply forgotten, but I soon realized that he was not worried about my jumping out and running. I was little, and I was scared to death of Barkley, Master Stewart's bloodhound. Barkley was always at Master Stewart's side. The wagon bed had a set of stairs that could be leaned against the back, so it was easier for the slaves to climb up while shackled. Old Barkley was used to climbing up the stairs, then squeezing past the slaves to make his way up to the front. He would get down on his belly and scoot under the seat and then climb up and sit proudly beside his master. Barkley knew his job was tracking runaways, and so did all the slaves. Every so often, Barkley looked back to make sure I was still sitting exactly where I was supposed to be sitting.

Even though I was not shackled like my daddy was, I dared not wave my arms around for fear of Barkley's taking that as some kind of attack. I slowly turned my head back toward the house, and I could see Momma and Pearl standing at the window. Pearl placed her hand up against the glass as if to say, "Goodbye, Ruby." As the wagon reached the end of the long driveway, I spotted my big brother Samuel's standing at attention in the front field. He did not wave or draw any attention to himself; he simply stood at attention and watched me pass by and kept his eyes on me until we were far enough down the road that I could no longer make out his face. Only then did I turn around and check on Barkley. Sure enough, Barkley was still staring at me. I settled back against the side of the wagon and tried to pull my dress collar up over my face to shelter me from the dust the horses were kicking up.

The dust was just awful. Ms. Victoria was anxious to see her daughter. Miss Elizabeth was just recently home from her wedding trip, so Ms. Victoria ordered Elmer to speed up the buggy. She did not care that the increase of speed meant lots more dust for those following right behind her. Neither did she care that increasing the wagon's speed meant a much rougher ride for those sitting on the bare wagon bed—namely me.

It was well into the afternoon when we pulled off the road and stopped in front of Miss Elizabeth's new place. She and her new husband, Mr. Tulley, had seen us coming up the road and were standing on their front porch, waiting to greet her momma and daddy. I remained seated with Barkley staring down at me while they visited for several minutes. Finally, Miss Elizabeth suggested they take their visit into the house, and Master Stewart slapped his hand against his thigh, signaling Barkley to jump down off the wagon. Barkley lit off the wagon immediately and made his way onto the porch. Master commanded Barkley to sit on the porch and asked Elizabeth's new husband, "Do you have some water for my dog? He has been eating Ms. Stewart's dust the whole five miles."

Mr. Tulley quickly ordered his slave standing at the door to get the dog a fresh bowl of water while Mr. Tulley escorted his visitors into the house. I, on the other hand, remained seated in the wagon in the full sun because I had not been ordered out of the wagon. Besides that, Barkley was still staring at me.

Finally, the same slave who had brought Barkley his water came back out and ordered me to follow him. Barkley sat up as I climbed down out of the wagon, but he did not move. Only then did I see Master Stewart standing at the window. I heard a tap, and Barkley turned to see where the tap was coming from. Master Stewart pushed his hand down, commanding Barkley to lie back down.

Relieved, I made my way to the back of the house and quickly caught up with the other slave. I desperately wanted a drink of water but did not dare open my mouth. Momma had warned me to remember my place. "Ruby, until you know your way around that new place, you keep your wits about you. You make one of Master Tulley's slaves mad at you, and they can make your life hell. Every one of them is scared of new slaves coming in. They won't trust you, so you give them no reason to worry. You understand me?"

You would think that all the slaves would have helped each other. We were all in the same situation, but I quickly learned why it was not so. I was given my job to do, told where I was to sleep, and ordered not to make any trouble. One week later, Master Tully bought six new slaves from the auction house for Ms. Elizabeth. He had been married before, and his first wife had trouble having children. According to the cook, she had lost three in three years before dying with the last one. After that, the Master sold off all but three of the house slaves and lived like a bachelor for about eight years before deciding to try again. Mr. Tully was almost twenty years Ms. Elizabeth's senior, and he wanted to make her happy and impress her. Happy, for Miss Elizabeth, was having as many servants as her mother had, so off to the auction he went.

We all waited to see just who he would bring back. The cook lamented, "It is dangerous to bring in six at once. We can't control that many all at the same time." I didn't understand what she meant because in my whole life at home, we had never had a new slave in the house, but I soon learned.

Clifford was the head slave, and he took his job very seriously. He lined all six up in a row and gave them the same talk he had given me on my first day. I watched as five of them nodded their heads in agreement, but one of them stood there filled with anger. We all knew she was going to be trouble. Clifford stood right in front of her as he shoved his finger right into her chest and said, "You think you going to make trouble here? I don't care where you been or what's happened to you. You get that look off your face, and you do what you are told to do. You hear me?"

That girl named Tyri simply stared back at him. I remember thinking, "She is going to get in trouble." What I didn't yet understand was the way Mr. Clifford got his way when one slave misbehaved, we all paid. It was his way of breaking someone. He was not about to lose his position in the house because he could not control his help. I learned very early on that Mr. Clifford was someone I needed to fear. He had lots of power, and he used it that first day. Standing right in front of Tyri, he ordered, "Since Tyri thinks she can stand here in my kitchen and sulk at me, none of you gets supper tonight. You can all thank Tyri for that."

I would not have liked to be Tyri that night. We all worked hard all day—every day. Going without supper meant a long night of pain, and Tyri was going to feel every bit of it from the older slaves who were being punished because of her. I just climbed into my bed and tried to sleep. My momma's warning to me to keep to myself and stay out of trouble was good advice that night. I pulled the cover up over my head and heard the others pounding on Tyri for a long time.

The next morning when Mr. Clifford made us all stand at attention in the kitchen before getting our breakfast, Tyri could hardly stand up straight. She no longer had that look of rebellion on her face. Lesson meted out and learned; breakfast was served.

I quickly got into my routine. I did my job and stayed to myself. Soon we learned that Miss Elizabeth was going to have a baby. We didn't learn it until she was well on her way, and no one could miss the fact by looking at her. When she was far enough along to make Master Tulley relax, he gave us all a big party—not the field hands—only the house slaves. We were given one afternoon off and all the treats we could eat. Some of us ate more sweets than we had ever had and I got sick, but it was worth it. That evening Master Tulley stood on his front porch and told us he was going to have a pig feast for us one week after this baby arrived. Two months later, young Master David was born, and Master Tully kept his promise.

One year later baby Charlotte arrived, but there were no treats or afternoons off. Talk of war was all around, and no one was feeling festive. Miss Charlotte was not yet one when Master Tulley was called up for duty.

Everyone knew it would only be a matter of time before all able-bodied white men would be called up. Fearing being in the house without her husband, Miss Elizabeth sent for her mother. Only after Ms. Victoria's arrival did I learn that Master Stewart had also been called into service to protect the South. I was not told; I overheard them talking. I so wanted to ask about Momma, Samuel, and Sister, but I knew better. For months Ms. Victoria stayed with us, seldom taking a day away to check on things at home. I tried to read her face whenever she returned, but Ms. Victoria was hard to read.

During all these months without Master Tulley around, most of the younger slaves had run off. Some were brought back by marauders. These men expected to get paid for returning runaways, but Ms. Elizabeth had no money to pay them. After ransacking the house for supplies, these men would take the runaways with them, hoping to sell them to another plantation. Someone was always willing to buy—if the price was right.

Ms. Elizabeth began to fear the marauders as much as the slaves. She had heard that sometimes they took their pay in services. This news scared them to death. Both of these women were beautiful, and both were used to being treated well. Finally, Ms. Elizabeth made the decision to take her children and her momma and return home. The Stewart house was much further off the main road, and she believed they would be safer there. The night before they were to leave, she had two wagons loaded with her favorite furniture pieces, as well as all of the remaining supplies. Only then did she tell us her intentions. She wrote hasty notes of emancipation for the remaining slaves—all except me. I was going back home with them—but not because they cared that I might again see my family. My job was to care for young Master David and Miss Charlotte. That day I didn't care why; I was just happy to be going back home.

The next morning Ms. Elizabeth handed out the emancipation letters, full-well knowing that the marauders would not care about a silly letter written and signed by a woman. She sent them off with not so much as a pitcher of water or a sack of food, but off they ran, feeling free for as long as it lasted.

Ms. Victoria had spent the first year and a half of the war at her daughter's house. Master Stewart had been called up for duty, and she did not want to stay home alone. Soon after, Master Tulley was also called up for service. At first, the women did fairly well at Ms. Elizabeth's because Master Tulley had a good strong manager running the place. Tulley thought they would be okay because his manager, Scotty McBride, was from Scotland. Being a foreigner and blind in one eye, he would not be pressed into service. But as the situation became more and more unstable, McBride decided he would be better off heading out West. After all, he did not have a dog in this fight, so why should he suffer to keep these women safe? Once he was gone, Ms. Elizabeth began to fall apart, so they decided to go back home to the plantation.

I was twelve years old when we headed back, and I just hoped my momma, my brother and my sister would still be there.

Tobias smiled as he sat on the train, remembering how great a storyteller his Auntie Ruby was. Even all of these years later, he was tempted to ask the same question his young heart asked that terrible day they were in hiding, and he had heard this same story.

"Were they, Ms. Ruby? Was Grandpa Samuel still there when you got there?"

"Yes, they were, Toby, but that story must wait until tomorrow. It is time for bed."

"Ms. Ruby, you were sent away from your momma—just like I was sent away from my grandpa. I guess that is why you understood how I felt that first night I got here. You understand what it feels like to be alone."

CHAPTER 15

Pearl Remembers Back at the Stewart Plantation

AFTER BREAKFAST ON the fourth day of the riots, Ms. Pearl continued the story.

The story was different at the Stewart Plantation. Once we got rid of Mr. Brown, Samuel brought all of the remaining slaves to the big tree at the end of the garden. He hauled four buckets of cold water, gave each slave his own jar of cool canned peaches, and Momma brought out a roasted potato for each one. Momma warned us not to tell the other slaves that we had more. She explained, "They will eat until they can't eat no more. Best if they think this was the last of it, Samuel."

After we were all fed, Samuel explained his plan. "Old Luther and I will go out early every morning and see if we can catch either a few rabbits or fish. We all have to be careful. Marauders are everywhere. With most of the owners gone to war, lots of slaves are on the run. The marauders have been hired by the wealthiest owners to catch runaway slaves and bring them in. These owners are hoping the war will be short, so they hope to double their investment."

Samuel also warned, "We need to work this place as if a white man is running it. If we don't, these marauders will take all of us and sell us for whatever they can get, and we will be the worse for it. We also need to find a safe place to store the crops that will keep. We have had three different groups of marauders come through, and they took everything with them. We will not make it if we don't protect what is ours. I don't think they are interested in going into the garden and picking their own supply. They only want to take our supplies. The twenty of us will need to work together."

I was so proud of my big brother. After everyone else went back to the field cabins, Samuel stayed and talked with Momma and me. "Okay, Momma, where did you get all those peaches? The war has been going on for three years, and one year has passed since any peaches have been canned. Supplies have been so low, every peach that was picked was eaten."

Momma and I smiled at him, and Momma said proudly, "Come with us, Samuel. Before the new kitchen wing was added to the house, do you remember the root cellar that was just outside the back door? Master Stewart had a new cellar dug out by the new canning shed. The old cellar was covered over by the new addition, but they put a trap door in the new dry goods room; that was the room that became my bedroom. The trap door is under my bed. During every canning season, Pearl and I would take as many jars of canned green beans, corn, squash, and peaches—whatever we were canning, and we slipped down into our dry cellar and stored them away. We have been doing this for three years. I found out that if we stacked them upside down, the jars would not dry out the seals. If we packed them in hay to keep them really cool, they last a long time. I'm sorry there is no meat, but at least we will not starve."

For the rest of the war, we got by. We all got sick of having only vegetables to eat, but Samuel was a good rabbit hunter. Once or twice a week, we added rabbit to our stew. We were determined to keep our storehouse a secret from everyone.

One day, we got word that Ms. Victoria and Ms. Elizabeth were coming back home. Ms. Elizabeth's home was right on the main road, and they no longer felt safe. We were ordered to remove all the boards from the upstairs windows and get the house cleaned.

I was really angry with Momma that day. Momma was so happy that Ms. Victoria was coming home. I just did not understand her. Ms. Victoria had gone off without a single care about any of us. For all she knew, we were all dead of starvation—or worse. Then, I thought that maybe Momma was happy because Ruby was coming home, so I asked her. No, she hadn't even thought about that. I stood there staring at Momma, trying to understand why she was so loyal to someone who did not care about her.

Samuel and I warned Momma not to tell Ms. Victoria about our secret cellar. We knew we couldn't trust Momma if Ms. Victoria returned home hungry. Momma would do whatever was best for Ms. Victoria and her children, and now that we would have five more mouths to feed, it was a real burden on Brother Samuel. Although we worried about Momma's telling our secret, she remained quiet.

As the garden began producing an overabundance of food, Momma fired up the canning shed and began collecting jars, getting them washed and ready. As long as Brother Samuel could keep food on the table, we were certain our secret would be safe. We divided the canned goods in two batches; half went to the dry goods shelves in the kitchen where everyone could see them. We all worried about marauders taking our supplies, but we needed to have a cover for the real supplies going down into our secret cellar. After a few weeks of everyone's getting used to seeing us carrying the finished jars into the kitchen, they stopped watching us so closely.

Ruby's pride at what her momma and sister had accomplished bubbled over. "Let me tell this part, Pearl. All day long Momma and Pearl worked in the hot canning shed. I would join them whenever young Master David and Miss. Charlotte were either sleeping or off walking with their mother. I would fill a basket with as many jars as I could carry, make my way to the kitchen and stack half the jars on the shelf before slipping into Momma's bedroom and pushing the remaining jars far under her bed. We did not dare open the old root cellar door during the day for fear of being seen. Late at night, when we were sure everyone was fast asleep, Pearl, Momma, and I would pick up Momma's bed and move it to the other side, pull up the trap door and Pearl would climb down into the cellar. Momma would hand the jars down, reminding Pearl to stack them upside down so they would last longer, and then pack them with hay. My job was to stand guard. In order to use up the older stock, we would always replace the newly canned jars from the kitchen with the older ones in the cellar. Pearl would pack them carefully before climbing back up into Momma's bedroom. Only after we replaced everything just the way it had been did the three of us go to bed.

Taking back the story, Pearl continued. "Once we were in bed, I rolled over and told Sister my secret. Ruby, I found Samuel's tin box. Momma has it hiding it down in the cellar. I was moving jars around, trying to make room for tomorrow's batch, when my foot hit the edge of an old piece of shed planking. I carefully picked it up and saw the tin box still wrapped in that old burlap sack. The sack is so old, just touching it made it fall into dust. I quickly replaced the wood plank and returned to my job."

I wanted to tell Brother I found it, but Sister said we must not let Momma know I saw it or she might find another hiding place and then we might never find it again." With a twinkle in her eye, Pearl added, "That night Sister and I agreed to keep it our little secret."

About the time the garden was slowing down, the orchards were ready to pick. Samuel and the other men picked peaches, pears, plums, and even pecans. We had not had flour or sugar for months, but when Ms. Elizabeth returned, she brought two big bags of each. The sugar was set aside to help with the canning. Momma would cut and stew all the fruit, adding just enough sugar to preserve it, load up the jars and water bath them. Each evening, she would take just enough flour to make biscuits. Everyone was given half a biscuit, with a ladle of whatever fruit stew she was canning that day. We did not have enough flour to make bread. It would have gone too quickly, but no one complained. Everyone was quiet as they ate their biscuit and fruit; even young Master David and Miss. Charlotte.

Life went on like this for a long time. Ms. Victoria seldom received letters from Master Stewart, but when she did, she took to her bed for days. During these spells we worried about Momma's telling our secret. Momma would do anything to cheer up Ms. Victoria. Thankfully, she never did, which amazed us all.

Ms. Elizabeth, on the other hand, became more and more demanding. She stormed around the house, shouting orders and throwing tantrums as if she was the only one going without. Even her children were not spared her wrath when she was in one of her moods. Ruby tried her best to keep Ms. Elizabeth calm and happy, but her attempts seldom worked.

One day, as Ms. Elizabeth descended the stairs, her hair completely undone and her dress unbuttoned, she began screaming for Ruby to come to her aid. "Ruby! Ruby, where are you? Why is the button missing on this dress? Ruby, where is my button box?"

As Ruby made her way to the front hall, Ms. Elizabeth let lose all her pent-up anger at going without for so many years. Hearing her screaming at Ruby the way she was, I quickly made my way to the front hall to see if I could do anything to protect my sister. Just as I reached the hallway, Ms. Elizabeth began crying and crumpled to the floor. I had feared she might slap Ruby and did not know what I would do, but I knew I was going to do something awful. Instead, I saw my sister bending over her, caressing her wild hair, and speaking softly to her. It was so like Ruby to do this, yet her nurturing this selfish woman made me mad. As Ruby gently helped her up and then helped her back to her room, I knew I had to go for a walk. I was right on the verge of throwing my own tantrum, but, oh, how our Momma would have come undone if I had.

Ms. Victoria stayed to her room most of the time. Not even her grand-child could get a rise out of her. Many a day, she would call for Momma and ask her to sit with her in her bedroom, and she would talk about their time as children together. Of course, her memories were quite different from those of our Momma's, but talking about those days brought com-fort to her, so Momma smiled and nodded, "Yes," to all of Ms. Victoria's questions.

Once or twice, we were awakened to Ms. Victoria's wandering around in the kitchen. Momma would talk gently to her and get her back to bed, but we all knew she was beginning to lose her proper mind. She always recognized Momma, but at times, she did not even recognize her own daughter. Fearing she might do something awful like setting the house on fire, Momma took the mat off one of the beds upstairs and would place it in front of the bedroom door and sleep there. At least everyone else in the house would finally get some sleep.

Late in the fall of 1863, Ms. Elizabeth got word that her father had been injured and was recuperating in a field hospital somewhere in South Carolina. Knowing her momma would not survive this news, she ordered all of us to keep quiet. Two months later, she got word that her own husband had been wounded and had lost a leg, but he would survive if they could keep infection from taking over. She did not handle this news well at all. Ruby tried to keep the children out of the house so they would not hear their mother's screaming tantrums about having a one-legged husband. She was not yet twenty-five, and she felt her life was now over. None of us heard a word from her about how her poor husband must be feeling; it was all about her and how the children needed to be spared. Hopefully, as time passed, maybe she would come to her senses and curb her tongue in front of her children.

By the spring of 1864, the war had been going on for three long years. Everyone was getting tired of meatless stew, no butter, no bread, no coffee; it had been a long three years. We began hearing from people who were traveling the road that Sherman's Army was heading for Atlanta, and the soldiers were burning everything in their path. Black, white, young and old—no one was safe. At this precarious time, Brother Samuel came up with his plan.

One night Samuel woke Sissy and me in the middle of the night. I opened our window and Samuel said, "Don't wake up Momma. Get dressed and meet me in the canning shed. We need to talk."

Sissy and I hurried, being careful not to make any noise. Daring not to walk through the kitchen, we carefully climbed out of the window and made our way to the canning shed. Sister and I were both excited and scared as we climbed out of our bedroom window and headed toward the shed. We had never been outside after dark without Momma, and if she caught us, she would tan our hide.

Brother was there waiting for us. Once the door was closed, he began. "You cannot tell any of what I am going to say to Momma. When we are ready to carry out my plan, we will tell her—not until. We all know what is coming. General Sherman's Army is only a few months away. They are burning everything, and no one is safe. We cannot stay here. I think my plan can work, but only if we are very careful."

That night, Brother told about Old Matthew, one of the slaves who worked with Brother Samuel back when Master Stewart still managed the plantation. They were working the land way out beyond the far orchard and sometimes, he and Brother would slip away to wander around the rock outcroppings and gullies, looking for fresh water or a stray rabbit. In the deepest gully, they came across a cavern. The opening was so covered in brush, Brother said they almost walked right by it. They decided to go in and look around. They walked very carefully, fearing the floor might open up and swallow them alive. They hugged the wall as they made their way to the back of the cavern. They found the cave was dry, clean, and cool.

Brother said they explored the cavern several times the summer he was twelve. They worked fast collecting the ripe fruit, hoping desperately the Master would leave them alone again. Old Matthew had this strange look on his face as he took the wooden box of plums over to the wagon and stacked it carefully. Once the box was in place, he walked back to Brother as if he did not have a care in the world. They continued gathering plums, hoping Master Stewart would tire of sitting atop his horse in the hot Georgia sun. Sure enough, he turned the horse around two times as he tried to decide if it was wise to head back to the main house for lunch. After yelling at the slaves to take a short break, off he headed for the cool of his house and a bite to eat.

Old Matthew and Brother waited until all the others were resting near the buckets of water. When they were sure none of them were looking around, they grabbed a handful of plums and took off for their cavern. Brother said they ate their fill and took a short nap in the coolness of the cavern. They did this several times, always making sure they wiped away their tracks with a broken bush limb so no one would find their cavern.

After a few days they decided if there was one cavern, maybe there were others, so they began looking. Sure enough, they found two more.

The second cavern turned out to be like the first. Eventually, they found a third opening in the outcroppings. When they entered, Brother said they could tell it was not a dry cavern because they could smell the water. As they carefully made their way into the darkness, clinging to the walls and watching where they put their feet, they found cold, fresh water in the very back of this deep cavern. Old Matthew swore Brother to keep their find a secret. They were sure Master Stewart did not know about these caverns. Brother said that Matthew got down on his belly and drank his fill of the cold, fresh water. He rolled over, smiled and declared, "While you and me is in this cavern, Samuel, we be free men. Us owns this place. It belongs to us. Out there, us be slaves, but in here us be the masters. Don't never tell nobody bout this place. As long as us is the only ones knows, it belongs to us."

Brother told us that a few months later old Matthew got a sore on his leg that would not heal. A few days later, he was dead. That night in the shed, Brother said, "I am the only one who knows about those caverns. I think we can hide out there for months without getting caught. The four of us cannot make it all the way North without getting caught. I can haul supplies out there every night until we think we have enough for many months. We will have all the fresh water we would ever need. We can live and sleep in the dry caverns, and I can take a bucket and slip over to the wet cavern whenever we are running low of water. If we are careful, I am sure we will be safe there."

CHAPTER 16

Ruby Remembers Hiding in the Caverns

TOBIAS SMILED, REMEMBERING how proud Aunt Pearl always was telling how smart my Grandpa Samuel was, but it was Aunt Ruby who always told me about the caverns. When she told the story, nine-year-old Toby Boy was right there with them; and now, grown-up Tobias was drawn back in time and heading for the caverns right behind Ms. Ruby.

We knew we did not have much time to prepare—maybe a week or so. Every night, Brother gathered up two burlap sacks, one filled with hay, one filled with root vegetables. Some nights he would make two or three trips. He began gathering up things he knew we would need. One night he took three wooden buckets out of the shed and carried them to the cavern. Another night he pulled out the large pickle barrel that sat in the tool shed, filled it with jars from our cellar and packed them in with hay. He strapped it on his back and carried it all the way there without any help.

Pearl and I began taking items from the kitchen. We would need a sharp knife, several kitchen towels, and any spices that might make the vegetables tolerable. We made sure Momma didn't notice they were gone. We would carry them out to the canning shed and hide them there for Samuel. Though Brother was sure we would not be able to have a fire for fear of someone seeing the smoke, we still packed several pieces of flint—just in case.

Samuel made many trips out to the caverns with jars and jars of fruits and vegetables. We always feared some marauders would catch him. The fact that he never left the plantation would not have mattered. The marauders didn't care about land markers. Knowing that a black boy out at night was fair game, Samuel was always extremely careful.

When Samuel was sure we had almost everything we needed, he told Momma the plan. He did not tell her about the caverns for fear of her telling Ms. Victoria. He simply stated, "Momma, I think it is time for us four to go. The Union Army is coming, and you know what they will do to Pearl and Ruby. I have to get them to safety. Momma, if we can take some of the jars from our secret cellar, we can leave all the rest for Ms. Victoria, Ms. Elizabeth, and her children. That way you can be sure they won't starve. We will share it with them, Momma."

Samuel thought this approach might help. If we were willing to share the root cellar and actually show Ms. Victoria she had a good hiding place for her family, maybe Momma would be willing to come with us. He was wrong.

I remember asking Brother, "Why can't we all just hide down in the root cellar?"

Brother said it was not big enough for all of us, but the four of them would do just fine. But Momma said she needed to stay with Ms. Victoria. Oh, she wanted us to go, and she was willing to give us as many jars as Brother could carry. She even found several baskets and packed them with jars so Samuel could do two baskets at a time. The last several burlap sacks were filled with extra clothes, blankets, tin cups, and plates.

When we were sure we were ready, we asked Momma one more time, but the answer was still, "No, you children go and be safe. I will stay here and help Ms. Victoria. We will keep a watch for the Army, and I will get them down into the cellar. We will be safe."

Momma had lived in that house her whole life, attending to Ms. Victoria since she was eight. She would not leave. Samuel, determined to get us into hiding and protect us with his own life, told us we had to run. For several weeks he had set aside apples, carrots, potatoes, and turnips, hauling bags of these supplies out to the dry cavern. He packed them in hay to keep the critters out of them. He also held back one fish every time he went fishing, skinning it, salting it, and laid it out to dry like the old timer Ben showed him. Sister and I hated that dry fish, but we learned to eat it. It's amazing what you will eat when you are hungry enough.

Just before we were set to run, Samuel did one last midnight trip. He returned to the cavern, set up the large pickle barrel deep in the dry cavern, then took the buckets and made many trips from the wet cavern, drawing water and carrying the heavy buckets back to the pickle barrel. He repeated this until the barrel was full. He knew every time he would have to leave the dry cavern to go get water for us, he would be putting us in danger of discovery. He wanted our first few days to be as safe as possible. Brother had thought of everything.

We were now ready to run. Brother told us not to tell Momma the actual night we were leaving. That night we kissed our momma goodnight, slipped into bed with three layers of clothes on our backs and waited for our big brother to come to our window. We were both excited and scared, but we trusted our big brother. As we made our way across the fields, Pearl and I were taking our first steps toward freedom. Although we were both frightened at getting caught, we had our brother leading the way. It is always a little easier when someone who has already walked that path leads the way.

As long as we were careful, Samuel felt we had about three months-worth of supplies. Once we entered the dry cavern, we were never to come out again until we were sure it was safe. Of course once every few days, when he felt it was safe, he would slip over to the wet cavern and bring back two buckets of fresh, clean, cold water for us. We did not dare light a fire because the smoke would not only drive us out of the dry cavern, it would tell the army where we were. We could not eat raw potatoes or turnips, and we were sick of apples and carrots. Brother was concerned that we were going through the jars of fruit too quickly.

One day, Samuel explored the wet cavern, which was much deeper than our dry cavern. He came back quite excited; sure he could light a fire deep in the cavern, beyond the pool of fresh water. He thought if we packed the cast-iron pot with food and buried it under the fire, surrounding it with rocks, we just might get away with it. Sister and I packed the pot with potatoes, carrots, turnips, and apples. Brother believed it would be so deep in the cavern that no one would see the smoke. Several times a week we dined like kings, and no one ever saw any smoke or smelled the fire.

Although the fire never gave us away, we did almost get caught. During the day we would take an apple or a few carrots and sit right by the cavern opening in order to get some fresh air. We knew better than to speak above a whisper, unsure if someone might be approaching us from behind. We would lie on our tummies, munch on our food and listen for sounds that did not belong there.

One day Brother slapped my leg and signaled us both to quickly and quietly make our way back into the deepest part of the cavern. We had practiced this many times and thought he was simply doing another drill. Brother would usually whisper as we made our way to our assigned spots, "Quiet feet, remember?" This day he just kept shoving us, whispering for us to keep very quiet. Once I was tucked in my spot, Brother covered me with hay so a casual glance would not give me away. Then Pearl slid into her low-hanging crack, tucking her long legs as tight against the back wall as she could, and he covered her up, and then pulled the hay up against himself once he was sure we were safe. But this time it was different. Samuel warned us not to move a muscle until he said it was safe. Off in the distance, we could hear men talking. As their voices got louder, every part of me wanted to run—but where? The hollow echo of their voices told us they were in our cavern, and we remained very still. I was certain they could hear my heart beating. We heard footsteps working their way deeper into the cavern, and we were certain we would be discovered. The men, unaccustomed to the dark, were having a hard time seeing, when a loud shout came from far away, "We found fresh water over here."

All of the men scrambled out of our dry cavern and headed for the fresh water. Brother tapped at Pearl's foot and whispered, "Stay put; they might come back here." We remained hidden under the hay until well after dark, afraid we might walk into a trap if we moved. Finally, Brother quietly crept toward the mouth of the cavern and listened for anything that might give away someone's lying in wait for us. When he finally felt it was safe, he crept outside and scouted the area, expecting to see the smoke from a campsite off in the distance. He soon returned to our cavern with news that the patrol must have enjoyed their fill of fresh water, filled their canteens and moved on.

As we stood at the opening of the cavern with the moonlight shinning in, Samuel spotted a half-eaten apple that I had set aside that day. He could also see exactly where each of us had rested all afternoon while enjoying the fresh air. If those patrollers had been the least bit observant, we would have been captured or even died that afternoon. As a result of our nearly being discovered, he came up with a safety plan. We were no longer allowed to eat at the mouth of the cavern. We were to bury our daily garbage deep in the cavern after every meal, and we were to use a broom made of brush to hide our footprints and not leave a flattened area where we had rested at the mouth of the cavern. About two weeks passed before Brother felt safe building a roasting fire in the wet cavern. For two weeks, all we had to eat was raw, cold carrots, apples, canned fruits and vegetables. Whenever Pearl or I complained, Brother would remind us how it felt having the patroller standing just a few feet away from us. We would both just quietly begin gnawing on a raw carrot.

We hid in that cavern for almost four months. If it hadn't been for Brother, I don't believe we would have made it through the war. We all worried about Momma. We wondered if she had enough to eat back at the house, and although none of us said it, we all worried if she was still alive. One night Brother said he was going to return to the big house and check it out. Pearl and I were to stay deep in the cavern until he returned. That was a very long night for us.

Right at dawn, we heard footsteps in the darkness and wanted to scream, when we heard Brother call out, "Sisters, you can come out; it is safe." Those were beautiful words coming out of Brother's mouth.

Samuel told us he had run into one of Ms. Elizabeth's slaves just walking down the road looking for something to eat. Samuel gave the frightened old man the lunch we had packed for his trip. While the old man enjoyed his first food in days, Brother learned that the war was not yet over, but the real danger in Atlanta was over. Sherman's Army had burned just about everything in Atlanta and had moved on toward Savannah in December of 1864, leaving only a small command to maintain control of Atlanta. They were ordered to keep the peace and let the people go about their lives as long as they behaved.

Our first question to Brother was, "Is Momma all right?"

The look of pain on his face when he had to tell us everything was gone—including our momma—is a pain I will always remember. Brother said the barn and all the outbuildings had been burned to the ground. The main house had been torn-up something awful. All of the windows had been broken, big holes had been kicked in all of the walls, the furniture had been dragged outside and used for a bonfire of some sort. Not a stitch of food was left in the house or in the garden—not even in the root cellar. Even the well had been busted up and destroyed. Nothing was left to go back to.

The porter's loud announcement brought Tobias back to the present. "Charlotte, North Carolina, in ten minutes; Charlotte, North Carolina, in ten minutes. This will be a thirty-minute stop, so if you are planning on stretching your legs, be sure to have your ticket stubs on you. You will not be allowed back on without them."

Tobias looked around to see where Ruth had been all this time. She was still deep in conversation. They had now been on the train for six hours, and Tobias needed to stretch his legs. He secured all of their belongings and made his way back to where Ruth was sitting. "Pardon the interruption, but Ruth, would you like to stretch your legs before the train takes off again?"

Ruth quickly answered, "Yes that would be so nice." Turning back to the woman, she asked, "You are traveling up to Culpeper, Virginia, correct? I'll be right back. I would like to hear the rest of your story."

The Five Points Station at Charlotte, North Carolina, was lovely. They kept their eye on the time, but the two of them wanted to walk the platform to drive the knots out of their legs. Neither was used to sitting so long and knew they had another five hours before reaching Lynchburg, Virginia, where they were scheduled to have a one-hour dinner stop.

At the far end of the platform was a fruit stand. Ruth picked out three oranges, three apples, and two bananas. After paying for them, Tobias asked, "Why so much fruit, Ruth?"

"Did you see the two little children sitting behind that woman I was talking to? Those are her grandchildren, and apart from those two molasses cookies I gave them, I don't think they have eaten anything else since we boarded the train in Atlanta."

It was so like Ruth to pay attention to such matters. Tobias asked, "Ruth, do you think that woman would be offended if we went inside the station and bought two bottles of cold milk for the children? They have orange and grape Nehi soda at the snack counter, but cold milk might be better for them."

"She might be offended at first, but those children look hungry. I still have three more cookies in my bag. You wouldn't mind going without your evening snack, would you?"

Putting his arm around her waist, he teased, "Do you even need to ask?"

They were the last ones to re-board the train. Ruth stopped at their seats, collected the cookies and returned to visit with the woman. Tobias knew Ruth would be able to share that food without offending the woman—because that was what Ruth did best.

SECTION SEVEN

---✦---

THE SISTERS:
Learning To Live Free
1865-1904

CHAPTER 17

---✤---

Ruby Remembers
Life Above the Livery

As THE TRAIN pulled out of Five Points Station, Tobias knew he had five more hours of sitting to endure before their dinner stop. He thought about what his grandpa had done to keep his great-aunties safe in those caverns and how hearing that story had helped his young, frightened heart get through the worst of the Atlanta riots when he was only nine years old. Ms. Ruby told that story on the Tuesday of the riots. As it turned out, that was the last full day of rioting, but we did not yet know this. The large masses of rioters had finally been disbursed, but it still was not safe to move about. The riots had forced them into hiding; but in order to keep my mind occupied, the Sisters continued with the history of their family.

That Wednesday morning, Mr. Ward slipped in our back door for a quick bite to eat and give us an update on the situation. Miss Buttons was to be buried that afternoon, but it was not a good idea to attend. Everyone was still fearful of attacks, and a large group of blacks at a funeral was simply asking for trouble. To comfort my broken heart, Ms. Pearl offered, "Toby, once it is safe, we will go place flowers on Miss Button's grave."

I remember asking Mr. Ward, "Why are those people doing these terrible things?"

I remember what he said that morning, but it took me years to fully understand his answer, which made no sense to me then or now. "Toby, lots of white people don't mind us doing well—as long as we stay to ourselves, keep out of their way, and stay out of trouble. Most don't even mind that we are building businesses and improving our lot in life. After the war, Atlanta had to rebuild, and us blacks got a chance to build along with it. With the help of some wealthy whites from up North, the Baptist Seminary has been educating our children and teaching our adults how to be self-sufficient."

"But Mr. Ward, that's good. Why are all the white people angry?"

"Not all white people are angry, Toby—just those white folks who are not doing as well. They are struggling to get by after the war, and they hate to see any blacks doing better than themselves. They still think we all should be back on the plantation, under some white man's thumb. They think we are too ignorant to be trusted with self-will and self-determination, and they want to believe we are not capable of self-control. Toby, they are scared to death that we will show they are wrong about us. They have always felt superior to us—even the least of them to the best of us. I sure hope someday, boys like you, Toby, will get the chance to be all you can be without worrying about someone coming after you for being uppity."

Mr. Ward scowled and then added, "Toby, I have come to hate that word 'uppity.' We have every right to carve out a good life for ourselves and our family without somebody trying to put limits on us—just because they think we have no right to dream big dreams."

After breakfast, Mr. Ward slipped out the back door, and Ms. Pearl decided we no longer needed to sit on Ruby's bedroom floor. We cleared the breakfast dishes and returned to the table where Ms. Ruby returned to the story about how they ended up living in the livery.

At first Samuel did not want to take us back to the house, but Pearl and I begged him. I think we both believed that if we both yelled loud enough, Momma would come out of hiding. Of course, she didn't. Walking through that big empty house all busted up and smelling awful, made us want to cry. The Army men had not only broken all of the windows, they had torn the doors off their hinges and had also kicked or knocked big holes in most of the walls. In utter disrespect, they even used it as a water closet.

Pearl and I wanted to clean it up and stay there, hoping Momma would return, but Samuel said, "No, there is nothing here for us, Sisters."

We were just about to leave, when suddenly, Pearl took off running. Brother and I followed her, shouting, "Where are you going, Pearl?"

We caught up with her as she was trying to move momma's bed. "Brother, take the foot and help me move the bed."

"Pearl, I already checked the secret cellar. All the food is gone. I put the bed back after I checked it out because I knew Momma would have wanted me to."

"Brother, please!" The sound of Pearl pleading brought tears to my eyes, and I grabbed the bed and said, "Brother, just do it."

The hatch was barely out of the way before Pearl was climbing down into the cellar, making her way to the far back corner. "It is still here, Sister," came Pearl's call of relief. When she reached the ladder, she lifted Samuel's tin box up into the opening. "Brother, Momma hid this back in the far corner of the cellar. I found it several years ago but did not tell Momma."

Brother sat down on Momma's bed and unwrapped the tin box, then opened it and took out his daddy's button. With big tears welling up in his eyes, Brother said, "I thought this was gone for good." Wiping his eyes, Brother regained his composure and announced, "We need to make our way into Atlanta and start looking for our Momma." He then explained, "It was dark the other night when I came here, but just now, I walked all around the yard and cannot find a fresh grave. Those men would not have taken our momma. They might have taken Ms. Carolyn and Ms. Victoria, but what would they have wanted with Momma? If they shot her, I think they would have left her where she fell. If they buried her, they would not have dragged her very far. So I don't think Momma is dead. Maybe Ms.Carolyn and Ms. Victoria left here after we ran away, and they took Momma with them. Maybe they are all in a house in town, waiting for this war to end."

Pearl, always the practical one, said, "But Brother, we cannot carry this tin box around looking for Momma. Someone will accuse us of stealing it. Maybe we should hide it back in the cellar until we find Momma."

We all agreed it was best to hide the tin box so Pearl climbed back down into the cellar and replaced the box in its safe hiding place, and then we made our way into town, hoping we might find Ms. Victoria because that was where our momma would be. We spent the next five months walking the streets, asking people if they had seen the Stewart family, but no one had. Brother picked up lots of day-labor jobs since all the able-bodied men were fighting the war. Samuel did lots of work for a man who owned a business, and he allowed us to sleep above his livery instead of paying Samuel for his labor.

Pearl and I would knock on back doors asking if anyone needed any work done. We usually came back to the livery empty-handed, but every few days someone would give us a little food in exchange for a whole day of labor. Brother worked from sunup to sundown and kept food in our belly and a roof over our heads—even if our beds were made of hay.

In April of 1865 when the news finally came that the war was over, Samuel said, "We need to go back home and wait for the Stewart family to return."

Pearl and I didn't want to leave the livery. It had become home to us, and we remembered what the Stewart place had looked like and, even more, how it had smelled. It had not been burned to the ground like most of Atlanta, but it had been left in ruins. We finally talked Brother into taking a note to the house and nailing it on the wall in the entryway. We would tell the Stewarts where we were and ask if our momma was with them. We also agreed it was now safe to bring the tin box back to the livery. Three weeks after the war ended, Samuel made the long trek out to the Stewart place, retrieved his tin box, and hung my note in plain sight.

Four months passed before we heard from Ms. Elizabeth. She was in town, waiting for her crippled husband to return home from the war. He had lost a leg in the battle of Allatoona Pass in October of 1864 and was finally coming home. Because of his wounds and age, her father, Master Stewart, who had been seriously wounded defending Savannah, had apparently been allowed to make his way home as soon as peace was declared. She said it was only a few days earlier that he felt strong enough to go see his house. He saw our note and sent her to come get us. She said they had been living at her home for the past several months.

Ms. Elizabeth had two reasons to stop by the livery that day—one was to tell us our momma had died about a month after we ran off. Apparently, Ms. Victoria threw a tantrum after we left, and our Momma had tried to calm her down by showing her the root cellar. Ms. Victoria refused to climb down into it. Ms. Elizabeth, seeing her mother in such a state, ordered the remaining slaves to bring up all of the remaining jars and load them in the wagons. She then took her children, her mother, and our momma, back to her home. They were not even in the house when Sherman's Army ransacked it. Ms. Elizabeth told us that her mother got very sick and would not be comforted. When the army troop arrived at Ms. Elizabeth's house, Ms. Victoria stood on the front porch and screamed at the men so defiantly they did not know what to do. She was so out of her mind, screaming nonsense, they simply remounted their horses and rode off.

Ms. Elizabeth said our momma tried everything, but Ms. Victoria would not yield. She walked the house all night long, calling for Master Stewart to come get her. Finally, one night while in a rage, Ms. Victoria fell down the stairs and passed. Ms. Elizabeth then added, "Your momma and I went out into my garden and dug Mother's grave. We rolled Mother's body onto a blanket, and the two of us dragged her body outside and buried her." With more compassion than I had ever seen out of Ms. Elizabeth, she added, "I think that was just too much for your momma. Her spirit was broken, and she just sat in the kitchen all day, looking out into the garden. I truly believe Hannah loved my mother. About that time my daddy returned home to his plantation, saw the devastation the army had done to his place, and came here, hoping to find my mother. Instead, he learned she was dead. A few days later, your momma died. Daddy buried her out in the garden a few feet away from Mother. Daddy said to tell you that it would be all right if you three wanted to come out and lay flowers on her grave."

So our momma was dead. At least we knew where she was, and that knowledge felt good. It didn't hit us right away that we were never going to see her ever again, but at least we had each other. Brother, Sister, and I knew we would be fine once Ms. Elizabeth would take her leave so the three of us could cry for Momma.

The second and most urgent reason for Ms. Elizabeth's coming out of her way to visit us was to invite us out to her place to set a marker on our momma's grave and to have a conversation with her daddy, Master Stewart. Almost a month had passed before the three of us were able to make our way out to Ms. Elizabeth's place. For weeks Brother Samuel bent and welded the most beautiful grave marker for our momma's grave, making sure it was sturdy enough to hold up for years to come. It took us five hours to make the emotional trek, but we all wanted to say a proper goodbye to Momma.

Master Stewart sat on the front porch while we stood beside Momma's grave. Sister and I cried quietly as Samuel pounded the beautiful iron marker in place. Knowing we had another five-hour walk back to town, we walked up to the well to fill our water jug and say our goodbyes to the family. As we reached the front step, Master Stewart stood up, steadied himself with a cane and approached us. "Hello, Samuel, good to see you and the sisters are still together. As you can see, I am not able to get around much anymore, and my son-in-law is faring little better. I would like for you and the sisters to come here and live and help us out."

Brother just stood there for a moment staring up at Master Stewart, a broken man who had lost the war. Not only had he been grievously wounded, he had come home to find he had lost his wife and his wealth, and his home was in ruins. Yet he spoke to Brother as if he still owned the world! Master Stewart could see that Samuel was resisting the idea, and he said, "Didn't I treat you fair, Samuel? You never got beaten—at least not by my hand, did you?"

Finally Brother straightened his back and said, "No, sir, Master Stewart, you are right there, but you gave our Ruby away like she was an extra pair of shoes you had laying around the house. If the three of us is ever to truly be free, we have to earn our own way and never call another man Master ever again."

Master Stewart pleaded, "I would pay you a wage, Samuel. You and your sisters would have a clean place to live, food to eat, and be treated fairly, I promise you that."

"No, sir, Master…Mr. Stewart, because in my head, you would always be Master Stewart, and I believe in your head, I would always just be your slave. Our momma loved Ms. Victoria her whole life, but the sisters and me don't owe you nothin', Mr. Stewart. We only came to put a marker on our momma's grave, and we will be going."

Sister and I knew Brother was right. Oh, we didn't believe it at first. All the way back to town, we argued with Brother. We reminded him that we would not have to live in a livery, sleep on hay, or beg for work. We did not understand why Samuel would not think about working for Mr. Stewart.

When we got back to town, Samuel sat us down in the hay loft. "Listen, Sisters, we have lived our whole life as slaves. We don't know how to live as free people—yet. We need to stand on our own, work hard, earn our own way, and finally learn to make choices for ourselves. We will never truly be free until we learn this. Mr. Stewart just wants an easy way out of his problems. He wants us to go back to how it was because it is easier for him. While living here above the livery, I have worked for lots of different men. I am willing to do lots of things I don't like to do. I work for small wages, but it is my choice. I will be a man doing it—not a slave who was born under his roof. Yes, it will be hard, but it will be worth the struggle, Sisters."

Pulling out of the story, Tobias thought about how the Sisters got so serious each time they shared this story with him. As a boy, he didn't really understand it. Giving up a warm bed and the promise of hot food seemed like a fair trade, but then he remembered the Sister's warning to him.

"This is why it's important that you know about your family, Tobias. You need to know where you come from and what it cost those who went before you so you could have the life you now have. Most folks look at us blacks and think we're not good for nothing except backbreaking labor.

Nothing is wrong with doing backbreaking labor. Your grandpa kept a roof over our heads and food on the table doing anything offered to him. He never let his pride get in the way of making sure Pearl and I were taken care of. But Toby, your grandpa was always trying to learn new skills. He was determined to improve himself so no man would ever own him again. With this warning fresh in his mind, Tobias escaped back in time to a part of Ruby's story that always filled his heart with pride.

After a hard day of work, Brother would come back to the livery just about sundown, eat a bite, and then sit with Pearl while she taught him how to read and write. In order to learn new skills, Brother knew he needed to be able to read. I remember so many nights as Pearl and I fell dead-tired onto our beds, hearing Samuel repeating the new words Pearl was going to test him on. The soft sound of Brother's voice confidently spelling out his words in the dark brought great comfort to me.

We lived above the livery for almost four years. Housing was scarce in Atlanta, and even if we could have found a place, we couldn't have afforded to pay rent. The livery owner traded use of the loft for keeping the stalls clean, the horses watered and walked, and Brother learned how to shoe horses just so the livery owner would keep us on. There was a 'johnny' out back, and we hauled fresh water from the pump by the livery office so we were doing better than some. Of course, with all of the hay in the livery, we were not allowed to cook, but twice a week Pearl and I cleaned the owner's whole house and did his laundry. In exchange, we were allowed to use his stove. Once a month, Brother would pay the livery owner two-bits for new hay; that way our beds were always clean and fresh.

The four years above the livery were difficult ones. Whenever Pearl or I were tempted to complain, Brother Samuel would remind us just how good we had it.

Pearl would be the first to tell you that she has never been good at suffering silently. To this day, I do not know how she managed all those years as a slave. Slaves were not allowed to express their opinions, and she had plenty of opinions. I think of how much Momma had to stuff down and hide, always fearing banishment and knowing tagging was just outside the kitchen door if she failed to keep her thoughts to herself. Thankfully, by the time Pearl and I were old enough to hear Momma's story, tagging, at least on our plantation, was a thing of the past. But Momma always reminded us that trading or selling was still a possibility, and other plantations could be much, much worse.

While sitting on the train, Tobias couldn't help but think about how emotional his aunts were when they were telling him that story. Reminiscing made him think about sweet little Hannah. He thought about five-year-olds these days—so full of energy. Tobias wondered what Hannah's momma had to do to keep a tight rein on her little Hannah? After all, every little child—black or white—is born with an imagination, and they all dream big dreams. What must her momma have done to her in order to kill her imagination and stop her from dreaming? Parts of slavery have remained in the shadows because the whippings, hangings, and demanding labor is such an easy picture to paint for people. But when you have to destroy a child's will in order to keep that child safe, how do you fix that broken will once freedom is achieved? Once their spirit and will have been broken, only God can put them back together. For so many, breaking free went way beyond the physical. They needed to learn how to hope and dream before they could ever even begin to feel free.

So it was for all those years above the livery for Grandpa Samuel and his sisters. They struggled to learn that it was all right to dream, to plan and to share their innermost thoughts without the fear of that unbearable feeling of dread overwhelming them. So many displaced people, both black and white, were wandering the city looking for work and looking for lodging at the end of the war. Blacks who had been released from slavery, but who had not yet been released from its effects, had no idea how to manage. They had never made a decision on their own in their life; now their life depended on their making the right decision. Many crumbled under the weight of their own responsibility. Many surrendered to former masters and became sharecroppers because that was the only life they knew or understood. Many surrendered because starvation required it. Ill-prepared for life outside the plantation, former slaves either returned or they died. Most whites misread these actions, believing the slaves were happier with the old ways. These choices thereby reinforced their opinions of blacks as being worthy of nothing more than being managed.

Young Samuel understood this and warned his sisters, "Never surrender. Never give up your right to choose your own path. Never give away your self-determination for a crust of bread or a soft place to lay your weary bones. I, for one, would rather starve than surrender. I will die a free man before I will surrender and live as a slave ever again."

CHAPTER 18

Pearl Remembers Freedom Has A Price Tag

WHILE LOOKING OUT of the window on the train, Tobias was filled with admiration for his grandfather. What courage it took for him to stand his ground! He had worked hard all of his life and had tried to do right by his family; as did his sisters. Even while the three of them struggled to get by, they never walked away from an opportunity to help others. Reviewing all of these wonderful family stories, Tobias never tired of replaying them in his head. Soon he was back in the past, reliving one of the Pearl's stories about their life of freedom.

By the time we were ready to move out of the livery, Brother was twenty-four, and Ruby and I were twenty. I found a job in the office of a black-owned welding shop. The boss wanted someone who could put nice ads in the newspaper for him, write his business letters and pay his bills. I loved the office work, and old Mr. Washington made it clear to everyone that I was off-limits.

Mr. Washington had a daughter who was several years older than us, but she never left their house. Well before the war, she and her mother had been caught by patrollers while trying to run. She was only eleven when the squad caught them just as they had crossed over the South Carolina border. Estée was tied up against a tree and had the bottoms of her feet whipped for running, then she had to sit and watch while the patrollers

159

repeatedly violated her mother. Three days had passed before the patrollers returned Estée and her mother back to the farm and collected their bounty.

Estée got by with one more really bad whipping, but her mother did not fare so well. Wanting to make her an example to the others, the owner ordered her tied to the barn door, broke one of her legs and ordered everyone to leave her there until she could walk away from the barn on her own. Estée was allowed to bring her food and water once a day, but she was forbidden to stay and talk. Mr. Washington had made his escape several years earlier and had been working in the Baltimore shipyards. Once the war was over, he made his way back to Atlanta where he found Estée and her mother still living on the farm.

Now an experienced welder, Mr. Washington opened his own shop and started building his welding business. His wife would only live a few more years, so by the time we met them, it was just Mr. Washington and Estée. I had only been working for Mr. Washington for a short time before he asked me, "Would you mind taking this over to my house, Pearl? Estée won't come out of the house these days, and I was careless the other day. I knew we were getting low on supplies, but I didn't want to go back out to the store. This morning I left Estée alone in the house without food enough to make tonight's dinner. I know it is not your job, but I sure would be thankful."

That was the day I met Estée Washington. I must have knocked on that door for five minutes before she opened it barely a crack. Seeing the fear in her eyes made me want to cry, and I felt immediately drawn to her. I told her that her daddy had sent me there with supplies, and I offered to help her get her dinner started.

Estée slowly opened the door, making sure she kept the door between herself and me. I found my way to the kitchen table, set down the bag and began to unload it. I tried to start up a conversation, but no matter what I said she made no comment, no response. I tried very hard to speak calmly to Estée, hoping to draw her out of that invisible shell she had all around herself. On purpose, I pulled out the wrong pan for doing sausage, and sure enough, Estée could not stop herself from running into her kitchen to correct my mistake. She didn't say a word, simply bent down, pulled out the cast iron pan and switched it with the copper pot I had taken out. I just smiled at her.

Once we had the dinner well in hand, I asked, "Estée, I think you and my sister, Ruby, would get along wonderfully. She is sweet, calm, and is not as pushy as I can be. Would you like me to bring Ruby by after work on Saturday? I only work until one o'clock, and we could help you make your daddy's dinner while we visit." Estée remained silent for several minutes. I made my way to the front door, assuming I would never be invited back. Just as I reached for the door knob, I heard a soft, squeaky, high-pitched voice say, "I'd like that."

I turned around and smiled at Estée. I knew this reply had taken all of her strength, and I did not intend to push her anymore that day. I winked at her, nodded my head, and closed the door behind me.

When I told Ruby about my plan for us to visit Estée, my gentle sister came up with a wonderful idea. "Pearl, if it took so much for Estée to say three words to you, I think we need to do something that will take the pressure of talking off of Estée until she gets comfortable with us. Why don't you bring the new book Brother just bought for us? If we just sit with her and you read to us, Estée might enjoy her time with us. It might help."

I remember staring at Sissy. "You are amazing, Ruby. I would have talked at her until she caved in. I would have asked her questions and pushed her to answer me. You, on the other hand, really thought about her. You listened to my story about Estée, and you came up with a safe way to be with her—not for us—but for Estée."

Praise always embarrassed Ruby, but she knew how to get close to Estée. The year was 1869, and Brother had been working steady for four long years at this point. Brother would often surprise us by stopping by the used book cart downtown and buy us a book. Our newest used book, *The Count of Monte Cristo*, was a tale of love, friendship, betrayal, riches, and revenge. Of course, Brother could not afford anything as fancy or expensive as a first edition, but that did not matter to us. This book was worn and well-used, having been printed in London in 1859. It was almost worn out when we received it, but we still loved it.

That first Saturday with Estée, we took our time getting the dinner ready for the stove. Then I opened the book and began our adventure. I was not three pages into it before we all knew we had wasted precious time fussing with that dinner. We spent the next few Saturday afternoons quickly preparing the Washington dinner and getting it on the stove so we could take our glasses of cold water and get lost in the life of Edmond Dantès.

Estée sat quietly for several Saturdays. We could see she was right there with us, and her eyes blazed with excitement or fear as Edmond's story unfolded. She did not make a comment until Edmond escaped from his terrible prison and came up for air on the faraway beach. I had been reading with the same excitement the story demanded, and when the story reached a resting place, so did I. Then we heard Estée's first comment: "I am so happy Edmond found his way out of Chateau d'If."

Being the pushy person I am, I jumped in and began talking about the guards, the priest, and the thrill of the escape, when I noticed Ruby's face. She gave me such a disappointed look that I instantly knew what I had done. I had stomped all over Estée's first comment just so I could share my thoughts. Ruby was so wise. I sat back and allowed the quiet of the room to overtake us. We all wanted to enjoy the thrill of Edmond's escape before moving forward. I watched Ruby studying Estée. I dared not open the book before Ruby thought it was time. Finally, with a soft and gentle voice, Ruby asked, "Estée, it feels good to see Edmond get free, doesn't it?"

Estée was silent for a long time before sharing, "Yes it does, but Ruby, I feel like I am still in Chateau d'If. Oh, I'm not beaten anymore, but I am still there."

Ruby did not say a word. In her wisdom, she allowed Estée to voice her feelings in her own time. We could both see that Estée was deep in thought; we just were not sure if she would say her thoughts out loud. Ruby was so much better at being still and patient than I was. But then came, "I hate that I am like Edmond when he first arrived at the prison. Until he met the priest, he just wanted to die in his misery."

Suddenly, I knew what to say. I looked over at Ruby, smiled, then suggested, "Estée, then you be my Edmond, and I will be your priest. Oh, I can't teach you how to wield a sword, but I can teach you how to read and write. Estée, once you know how to read, you can escape your Chateau d'If whenever you want to by picking up a book. Just like Edmond had to prepare for his freedom, so must you. Are you willing to work with me?"

"Oh, Pearl," Estée responded with such hope, "do you think I could?"

Being careful not to push Estée too far, I smiled and said, "Just like Edmond, we aren't going anywhere, and we have nothing but time. It took Edmond many years, and it will take you many years. But Estée, just like the priest said to Edmond, I am saying to you—you can either rot away here in your prison or you can use the time to improve yourself. Time is life; how are you going to use it?"

Estée took her first step of courage that day. She decided she was going to learn how to read, and she was going to let me be her teacher. Once Mr. Washington learned that I was going to teach Estée how to read, he changed my work schedule. For three mornings a week, I was to report to his house for one hour of teaching, and I was no longer scheduled to work at the office on Saturdays. While Ruby finished up her laundry business by noon on Saturdays, Estée and I did school, then we all had a quick bite to eat, got dinner on the stove and spent the afternoon and evening reading together.

Over the next year we reread that book twice before moving on to other books. We three talked about Edmond's feelings of revenge—a feeling we all knew quite well. We felt safe to explore our own feelings in the life of someone who lived so far away from us and so many years before our own experiences. We all wished we could wield a sword like Edmond, never to be weak and vulnerable again, but that was never to be. After reading the book twice, we struggled with the book's ending. Edmond did get to see those who betrayed him punished. He lived out his life with the ones he loved, but he did learn the lesson that revenge would destroy him. We did not understand it, but we loved it.

Two or three books later, Mr. Washington told us the house next door to him was available. Samuel did not believe we could afford it and refused to go look at it. Mr. Washington came by the livery to talk with Brother. "Samuel, I own that house. I bought it two years ago. My Estée is so fragile I was afraid of who might move in. I want you, Pearl and Ruby to live in it. Estée needs to have Ruby and Pearl close by. She is actually starting to come out of her shell. I will make you a deal, Samuel. Pearl is due a raise, and I will help Ruby get new laundry customers. I only ask that Ruby keep Estée company during the day, and I will pay her."

Brother Samuel finally agreed to the deal, and Ruby was allowed to come and go as long as she never left Estée for more than two hours. She developed a regular routine. Mr. Washington took parts from an old hay cart and welded a small frame with better wheels to it. He then made a wooden box and fixed it to the frame. Ruby was able to pull that cart all over the area, picking up laundry and mending from customers. She could fill that cart and return home well within the two-hour limit. Sometimes Estée would venture out as far as the shade tree in her back yard and sit and chat with Ruby as she worked the wash tub and hand-cranked ringer Mr. Washington had made for her. They would stop and have a cool drink of water and visit once the wash was on the line, but if ever anyone walked behind the back fence, Estée would fly back into the house and stay there for days.

Whenever Mr. Washington could, he would buy a book off the used bookseller's cart that came around about twice a month. He would ask me to show him which ones I thought would interest Estée. Some were children's books that Estée could now read, while others were books that I would read aloud to us. Our very favorite book turned out to be *Little Women*, and Estée made me read it three times. Estée always thought of herself as Beth, the fragile one, and she would tease me and call me Jo. Estée loved my strength and fearlessness—so opposite her own fearful nature. Ruby, on the other hand, wished to become Meg. Just like Meg in the story, she longed desperately to marry a Mr. Brooke, keep his house and have her own twins, just like Meg and our own Momma. She was going to name them Demi and Daisy just like Meg did and live happily ever after.

Estée never truly escaped her Chateau d'If. She did, however, learn how to read and began many an adventure on her own in the world of books. She often said that while lost in one of her stories, she truly felt free. We three had many years together and remained friends until the day she died. To the last, her greatest treasure was that first book, *The Count of Monte Cristo.*

Tobias stopped here and took this book out of the tin box. He was seven when Aunt Pearl had read this book to him. He gently caressed the cover, knowing his Grandpa Samuel had purchased it for Auntie Pearl. This book had been read to dozens of people, and that sweet, broken bird, Ms. Estée, had loved this very book. Holding it always made him feel connected to Estée—even though they had never met.

Placing the book back inside the tin box, he could not help but think about all of the hard work his grandpa had to do in order to purchase this book for his sisters. As he closed the tin, he smiled, remembering how loyal Ms. Pearl always was toward her big brother and how well-deserved that loyalty was. With a thankful heart, Tobias returned to Aunt Pearl's story.

Brother Samuel struggled to find work. Between his regular jobs, Brother would help Mr. Washington in exchange for welding lessons. It took him almost a year to save up enough money to buy his used welding helmet and gloves before Mr. Washington would start the lessons. Brother took to welding, but there wasn't enough work for two full-time welders at the shop, so he kept doing backbreaking day-labor jobs and practiced his welding on anything he could find. He would spend his Sunday afternoons digging through people's dump-piles looking for anything he could fix by welding it back together. After a while Samuel became fairly good at seeing the value of broken items, picking them up, welding them and selling them back to the very people who had tossed them out. Word got round that he could fix things, and people started looking him up instead of tossing out something that had broken.

Brother always had a project going. He loved welding more than anything, but being practical, he knew that any job that put cash in our money jar was good work. He would get up early every Saturday morning and make his way down to the railroad yards in hopes of getting pick-up work. He never minded the grueling labor of the railroad yards—after all, he was young and strong. Although he tried to downplay his concerns, Brother knew that standing among the labor force at the entrance of the railroad yards was a dangerous place for him. Jobs were scarce, men were hungry, and lines were quickly drawn. A black man who did not keep his wits about himself could easily become the scapegoat of someone's anger and frustration. Atlanta was struggling to hold on, and the white men of the city were not used to hard labor. On more than one occasion, Brother had been selected instead of a white man. The yard boss knew Samuel would give a whole day's labor without complaining, but Samuel's character meant nothing to the white men who were turned away without work that day.

Several times, as he made his way forward to get his assigned boxcar orders, he had gotten a swift kick in the shins or a punch in the back. One time he even had a knife drawn against him. Brother knew these men were scared and hungry, but the real truth was that they were not used to being ousted by a black man. The hardest Saturdays were the ones when he found himself partnered with someone who did not appreciate working alongside of him. He not only had to work twice as hard, he had to make sure he never allowed himself to get caught toward the back of the boxcar. He had learned that lesson the hard way.

One Saturday he was busy pulling down large wooden crates that had been stacked three high toward the front of the boxcar. He would strap a leather loop around the crate, toss the strap end over the steel harness that lined the ceiling of the boxcar and use all of his own weight to lift the heavy crate while trying to swing it free of the stack so he could guide it down to the floor of the car. That day he was busy bringing down one of these crates when someone climbed into the boxcar right when he had the crate fully suspended. Without warning, the man grabbed a crowbar and hit Brother right across his lower back. Losing his grip, Samuel let go of the leather strap, causing the crate to crash to the ground. By the time the yard boss got to the boxcar, his assailant was long gone, leaving Brother to pay the losses from his day's wage.

This harassment went on for months, but every Saturday Brother was back at the railroad yards ready to work. Within a few months, his hands became strong and sinewy. His youthful frame had filled out, and his arms showed the result of months of hard labor. The men began to cut a clear path for this strong young man who stayed to himself, did his work and went right home at the end of the day.

Samuel would seldom talk about what went on during the day. He said, "It is hard enough living it; I don't want to come back here and live it again in the telling."

But on the days when he got hurt, he would have no choice. Ruby and I would not be set aside. We would badger Samuel until he told us what had really happened. Brother said, "There is nothing I can do about some things. No one cares if a black man is tossed around, but you let that same black man defend himself, and there is sure to be a hanging. It ain't fair, but that is the price tag for working side by side with these white folks."

I remember arguing with Brother, "Is there no one you can tell? That boss picks you to work. Doesn't he care if you get hurt and can't work?"

Always the most level-headed of the three of us, Brother said, "Pearl, what do you think he can do? You think he is going to side with a black man against his own? He really tries to keep me away from the four worst ones. Most of the white men are only interested in getting a day's wage for a day's work. They don't mind sharing a boxcar with me because I work hard and do more than my share. When Boss puts me with one of them, I know I am going to have a good day. When he has to put me with one of the bad ones, I try to keep a safe distance between us. They don't feel safe coming directly at me, and I don't dare fight them. Even if I would win, I would lose. It is hard work for fair pay. I need to be careful and watch those four. What else can I do?"

I remember screaming at Brother, "Samuel, it is not fair!"

I remember Brother's response to me, as if it was yesterday. "When has life ever been fair, Pearl? I still won't surrender. These four men are not going to rule over me. Sure, I have to be careful around them. I can't let them get me so mad that I get myself hung. I am going to get back in that line every morning, do my work, be smart about where I am and where they are, do my job and bring home my wages. I will keep learning how to read and write so someday I can pick my work. That someday is not tomorrow; but someday."

CHAPTER 19

Ruby Remembers
How Love Changed Things

LOOKING OUT THE window of this northbound train, Tobias struggled with the same frustration he had felt the first time he had heard Aunt Pearl's story, but just as quickly he remembered Auntie Ruby's warning, "Don't you hold onto bitterness, Toby! Never let bitterness rob you of your memories. My big brother, Samuel, was so much more than those injustices. He was the best brother Pearl and I could ever have, so today, let's leave all the injustices aside and focus on some wonderful memories."

Remembering her warning, Tobias returned to one of his favorite stories—how love came into his family. Ruby was the one who always told this story, because, as she put it, "I was the brave one, Toby. Can you imagine that?"

Tobias smiled as he returned to that memory, "Yes, Ms. Ruby, I can truly imagine just how brave you were."

But the real truth why Aunt Ruby always wanted to tell me this story was because Aunt Pearl never like my Grandma CeCe and could let her temper get the better of her in the telling of it. Aunt Ruby knew that I would side with my Aunt Pearl; so instead, she would tell it and try to help me understand my Grandma CeCe's reasons for being who she was.

The year was 1875. The business owners in Darktown began to organize social gatherings. It had been ten full years of freedom, and everyone wanted to celebrate. We had spent the first four years of our freedom living above the livery, and the next six, feeling the pride of renting our own house. We worked hard and lived day to day. None of us ever talked about marriage or moving out. If Brother thought about such things, he never shared it with us. Pearl and I were now twenty-six years old, and although we were happy, I was not content. I wanted to experience love, children, and all the things any young woman desires. We had spent six long years focused on Estée, but as thrilling as it was to see her beginning to blossom, I longed for more.

Samuel and Pearl were in no hurry to marry, but I was. I begged Brother and Sister to come with me to the Greeting Parlor, which had been opened that winter by the black business owners of Darktown. They believed they would have a better stock of employees if they were married and settled. They advertised the Greeting Parlor as a place for black people to meet, chat, get to know each other and hopefully meet someone else with the same intention—marriage. Because Brother and Sister were not interested in going, I went alone to the Greeting Parlor. After several failed suitors, I asked if I could invite Arthur Beachum to Sunday dinner. Pearl liked him right away. Arthur held down a steady job, had big plans for his future, and treated me well—everything Pearl respected.

Seeing me so very happy with Arthur, Pearl began to rethink her position. I no longer went to the Greeting Parlor since me and Arthur were now walking out together. Pearl wished she had not made her decision so hastily. Now, like me, she would have to walk into the Greeting Parlor all alone. She knew the kind of man for whom she was looking—someone just like Samuel who was hard-working, loyal, ambitious, and clean. Pearl went about it much like she saw Mr. Washington go after a new employee. She scared off most of the suitors right away, not realizing how aggressive she was being.

Pearl was like bull in a china shop at the Greeting Parlor. She scared off lots of good men, but then she took Mr. Washington's advice and did what she thought I had always done best—let the man talk. She decided to give it a try, and men began to respond to her. Of course, she always joked, "I couldn't act just like Ruby, but I did tone it down, a little. I looked around, found a decent-looking man and went after him."

Pearl had never been the romantic type, unlike me. As long as the man was well-mannered, hard-working, and was willing to improve himself, that was all she wanted. Joseph Lagolaei possessed all of these attributes; he simply did not realize how determined Pearl could be. For several weeks they sat together talking. She did her best not to pressure Joseph, and her plan was working. He finally asked, "Would you like to go out walking with me?"

Joseph had now declared himself, and Pearl was happy. She invited him to Sunday dinner, and he accepted. She was sure Samuel would like him. One month later, the Darktown owners' celebration party was on. Both Pearl and I had suitors, but Samuel only planned to tag along.

Joseph and Arthur were getting along well, and we were happy being on their arms. There was ample food, thanks to the generosity of the business owners and the local black churches. Several bands were playing, and people were dancing and having a great time. Everyone enjoyed themselves well into the night, and we came home exhausted, but happy.

The next morning I was the first to broach the subject. "Did you notice the young woman that Brother was sitting with last night? He seemed quite taken by her. I had even noticed that Samuel was actually smiling." Pearl had not notice her. I guess she was having too much fun with Joseph to pay attention.

I don't think that was the first time Brother had talked to that girl. He seemed too comfortable with her for last night to be the first time. I thought her name was CeCe, but I didn't get a chance to speak with her that night because I did not want Brother to feel like I was meddling in his business. Pearl and I realized that Samuel was almost thirty years old and had not even talked about stepping out with anyone. We wondered if Brother was afraid to step out with someone because of us. We knew he felt responsible for taking care of us.

Pearl and I agreed that we needed to put a plan together, but Pearl being Pearl, she wanted to get things done. She wanted to invite CeCe over for lunch, but I put a stop to that idea by warning Pearl, "Samuel would not appreciate our taking over his life. Brother has taken care of us for fifteen years. You have a good job, and I have enough customers now that we could manage on our own. We both have suitors, and I don't want Brother to feel like he cannot move out on his own because of us."

"But, Ruby," Pearl protested, "If one of us gets married, what will the other one do? I'm not so certain that Joseph is going to ask me to marry him any time soon. You and I have only been walking out with Arthur and Joseph for a few weeks. It's too soon to be thinking of marriage."

I smiled and announced, "Well, Arthur and I have been talking about marriage."

Shocked, Pearl gasped, "Ruby, you need to go slowly! You don't know Arthur that well yet."

I knew Pearl was right, but I was twenty-five, and I wanted to start a family. I did not argue with Pearl, I simply remained quiet—but still quite determined. Seeing my dejected look made Pearl realize she had again stomped on my dreams. "Ruby, I don't want you to turn down the chance of marriage because you feel you must stay here to help me out. I want you to be able to dream of a future with Arthur. I want to be able to make plans with Joseph without having to worry about you or Brother. Saying that, I'm sure Brother will have thought of this too."

We agreed that if we ever want to give Brother his freedom, first we each needed to have our life safely planned out. Since we both had a beau, we could get married so Brother would feel free to do the same. It was the only way we could convince him that it was all right for him to move forward with his life.

We didn't know that Brother was even thinking in terms of marriage. We didn't know anything about this CeCe. We were running way ahead of ourselves. What we did know was that we would have to do something in order to give Brother permission; he will never do it on his own, and keeping him here would be so selfish of us. Pearl offered to ask Mr. Washington if he knew anything about this CeCe. He was meeting and greeting everyone at the celebration. She thought if we could find out where she lives, we could call on her.

"Pearl," I cautioned, "I don't think we should do that. What if Brother does not like her well enough and gets angry at us for meddling? Maybe we simply need to talk to Brother. We need to be honest with him and tell him what we have talked about. If he feels like he is standing in our way because we are worried about him, maybe he will see things differently, and I should be the one to open the conversation. Pearl, you tend to be too abrupt, whereas I can usually slide into a topic with Brother without making him want to run."

After an hour of Brother's denying any interest in CeCe, he finally realized we were not convinced by his arguments, confessed that he did like CeCe. He thought she was a nice person, but she has lived a very hard life. He assured us that he was not ready to think of marriage, but he would like to get to know her better. I suggested, "Why don't you invite her over for a Sunday dinner? That way Pearl and I could get to know her and you could spend more time with her."

Just to clarify what he was agreeing to, I asked, "Samuel, do you want CeCe here alone, or can Arthur and Joseph come to dinner also?"

Brother smiled. "Let's invite all three of them." The plan was set and Brother wasted no time inviting CeCe to Sunday dinner. They both knew this invitation represented more than just a Sunday dinner. Samuel was asking to walk out with her and was bringing her home to meet the family.

✢ Sunday Dinner with CeCe ✢

Arthur and Joseph had been to dinner several times already, and the conversations were always pleasant. Joseph was easy and quiet, willing to listen to others, whereas Arthur was filled with plans for his future. But the first dinner with CeCe was quite different. CeCe had no problem giving her opinions or telling her story. Poor Joseph, who, in trying to be friendly, asked an innocent enough question, "CeCe, what is your name?"

CeCe glared at him as she replied, "It is CeCe."

Joseph had no way of knowing his was stepping into a firestorm when he clarified, "I know that, but what is your last name?"

Samuel tried to change the subject, but CeCe would not be redirected. "Joseph, I will never use, or even say, that name ever again. My momma named me CeCe, but the Master gave my momma her last name, and I do not want anything to do with him ever again. I don't need a last name to get by. I would think the rest of you would think twice before using those names that were put on you by whites."

Samuel again stepped in and tried to soften the moment. "CeCe, I get what you are saying, but for some of us, there is another side. Take the Sisters and me, for example. Yes, our daddy was given the name Bascom by the first owner who bought him at auction, but we loved our daddy. He was good and kind to us. If I did as you say, I feel I would be throwing away my daddy—not the Master who named him. I am proud to have my daddy's name."

CeCe softened—but only a little. "Samuel, not all of us were lucky enough to know our daddy, so that is not my problem. I've been on my own since I was eight years old. My mother was sold away, and I was put to work as the nanny for her Master, just outside of Decatur, Georgia. I was thirteen when the Civil War ended, and I was turned out on the street without money, family, education or help."

Over several Sunday dinners, we learned that CeCe did not talk about her first three years of freedom. I suspected CeCe had been forced into something she was not proud of. Eventually, she found work cleaning floors at a big hospital in Montgomery. It was obvious to both of us that CeCe was a survivor. We could also tell that CeCe had strong opinions and was not afraid to voice them. Although both of us appreciated what CeCe had endured, we worried about Samuel. CeCe had a strong personality; yet she was also a broken, lost, little girl. Pearl was convinced that Samuel was drawn to this brokenness of CeCe. He ignored how she would hatefully argue with all of us when she was challenged about her opinions. Pearl felt like she would go crazy when she would try to tell CeCe that things were not always the way she looked at them. CeCe would simply shake her head and say, "You can think that if you want to Pearl, but I never will."

Every Sunday afternoon for the next year, nothing changed. CeCe was nothing, if not consistent. She had no interest in learning anything new. She had no interest in rethinking her opinions. She had no interest in changing anything.

Many a Sunday, Pearl and Joseph left the house so she would not say what she was thinking. Neither of us wanted to put Brother Samuel in the middle. He had always sacrificed for us, and we wanted him to have a chance at love; we just did not think CeCe was the right one. The truth was, Brother Samuel was well aware of how stubborn CeCe was, but it was clear to us that he had no intention of walking away from her. Brother Samuel was free to choose the woman he loves. We had done our best to help him see what we saw, but once he made up his mind, we had to accept CeCe as one of our own—for our brother's sake.

CHAPTER 20

Joseph
Tells His Story

BEFORE ANY OF the three couples dared speak of marriage, they spent many a Sunday dinner sharing their stories together. Estée especially loved hearing everyone's story. As they learned what each other had survived, their deep friendships became unbreakable bonds. One Sunday even shy little Estée shared her painful story. When she finished, she added, "It feels good to tell my story to people who have shared their painful stories. I don't feel like you are judging me because you understand my pain."

Joseph, on the other hand, seldom volunteered information about his past, but Samuel could see his sister Pearl was growing rather attached to him, which concerned him. As a young boy, I loved hearing Joseph's story, which was one of my most requested stories. I heard it so often, I felt as if I was sitting at that dinner table listening to Joseph himself tell his story to me.

During one Sunday dinner, the question was finally posed: "So, Joseph, why don't you tell us your story?"

Unaccustomed to being the center of attention, Joseph was noticeably uncomfortable. Pearl spoke up, "I don't think it is fair to put him on the spot like this. Joseph, is there anything in your past that Samuel should be concerned about?"

Joseph quickly responded, "No. I'm not hiding anything. I just have a hard time talking about such difficult matters. My emotions might get the better of me, and I don't want to break down in front of all of you."

Aunt Ruby, always the kind and caring one, offered, "Joseph, who better to break down in front of than those who understand your pain. We all have endured a terrible childhood, and we would not judge you."

✤ Thus Began Joseph's Story ✤

It's just that my story is quite different than the rest of you. You see, I was not born a slave like the rest of you were. I remember a time when I had a daddy, a mother, and sisters, and we lived with others who spoke our language. I think I was born around 1840 in a small village. I don't remember its name because I was only four when my momma and I were captured. I remember being chained to my momma, which meant she couldn't run. Our kidnappers walked us for days, screaming and yelling at us to keep going. We got very little to eat or drink until we reached a place where we could smell the sea air. We were pushed into a large pen that held many people. I remember how hot it was with no shade to break the midday sun. Those were terrible days. My momma cried all of the time. I had three older sisters at home and a daddy who was a good hunter, so we never went without meat. I couldn't understand what was happening to us and wondered when we would be able to go back home. Momma became so sick, and no one would help her.

Finally, we were pulled out of the holding pen and forced onto a large ship. I had never seen a ship before, and the movement and smell made me as sick as Momma. Because I was so little, I was kept with the women. We stood on deck and watched as they drove the men down deep into the hold and chained their legs together. The sound of those men crying is a sound I never want to ever hear again. Finally, the women were led to the forward part of the ship and were forced to climb down into another large room down deep inside the ship. I was chained between my momma and another woman I did not know. Neither could I understand anything this woman was saying. We were told nothing; the large hatch was closed, and we were left in the dark to wonder what about our future.

We remained many days in the belly of that ship, and the ship's movements caused everyone to be very sick. Unable to move around, people would vomit, splashing onto those who were chained close. Even if I were able to hold my stomach down, the smell around me was almost more than I could bear. We were fed once a day, without benefit of cleaning off our faces first. For many days my momma would refuse to eat, knowing it would just come back up. Eventually, we became accustomed to the movement of the ship and started eating. Those who did not, died.

The ship's movements were sometimes violent, which caused much sickness. With so much sickness, many lives were lost during those terrible days. Every two days, men would come down and check on us, unchain those who had died and drag their bodies up the stairs. We did not know where they were taken, but we were glad to have them out of our presence.

Though I didn't understand, my momma was with child when we were captured. I was so little; all I cared about was what was going to happen to me. One day, while the hatch was open, I remember seeing my momma's face all gripped in pain. The baby was coming, and Momma could not move her legs without causing pain to the woman beside her. The hatch was open because it was time to drag out the dead bodies. One of these men stopped and undid Momma's chains. He said nothing, just slapped her leg and lifted it free. He pointed to her stomach and put up two fingers, as if to say she had two days to get that baby out before the next men would make their way down to check on dead bodies.

That night my baby sister came into this terrible world. Momma said it was not time, but the baby was alive. Momma had nothing in which to wrap her, so she tore off part of her skirt and wrapped the baby in it and held her close. Two days later, the "body men," as we had begun to call them, came down the stairs. The man who had unchained Momma came to check on her. Seeing the baby in her arms, he quickly replaced her chains before the others could see what he had done. We stayed like this for three more body checks. Momma tried to feed the baby, but she was so sick there was nothing for the baby. Hungry, my sister cried all day long.

On the third body check, one of the really mean body men snatched the baby out of my Momma's arms and tossed her up to another man standing at the open hatch. By now, we were sure the dead bodies were being tossed out into the sea, and Momma feared the same was going to happen to my sister. We never saw her ever again. Many days later, we were all unchained long enough to climb the ladder and stand on deck. The brightness of the sun was painful, but we were all thankful to be out of that terrible place.

We were pushed into another pen on shore and waited for auction day. I learned later that small children were not easily sold. The buyers knew they would have to wait a long time before they would recoup their investment. Consequently, I was again chained to my momma, and we were sold as a pair. Hopefully, someone among the buyers would be glad to get two for one, but that day no one was willing to buy a sick woman with a small child. The body men pushed us off the auction block and returned us to the pen. Several days later we were put on a smaller ship and taken several days away from that place called Savannah to a new port called New Orleans. Most of the men had been sold at that first port, so only women and children were on this ship. We were thankful that journey was not as long as the first, and we all made it there alive. We were also fed better and more often. I learned later that they were trying to fatten us up for a better price. We didn't care why; we were just thankful for good food.

I think I was five when we arrived at Port of Orleans. Again I was chained to my momma, and we were to be sold as a pair. This time the sold hammer came down, and we were quickly shoved off the auction block onto a waiting wagon. Momma and I clung to each other in this strange place where people talked funny and smelled funny. Very late that night, we finally stopped at what turned out to be our haven. I remember the man and woman who were standing on their porch as we pulled up. The first thing he ordered was, "Frenchie, take off those chains."

Of course, I didn't understand what he was saying, but I loved what happened next. The chains were removed, and both Momma and me were given hot water and rags. Then the woman brought out clean clothes for both of us. Once dressed, the woman pushed Momma onto a chair and put salve on the open wounds left on her legs by the chains.

It took us many months to learn the funny language they called Creole. Our buyer's name was Pierre Lagolaei, and his wife's name was Claudine. They decided to name my momma, Caramel, because of the color of her skin. I was to be called Joseph.

CeCe could hold her tongue no longer. "And you still go by Joseph Lagolaei? How could you? Don't you hate hearing that name, knowing who gave it to you?"

Everyone at the table remained quiet. CeCe could get enraged very quickly, and no one wanted to make this situation worse for Joseph. He finally addressed her challenge, "I was only four when I was captured. The only name I had known before was Kabiite."

CeCe jumped on this admission. "Then why don't you call yourself Kabiite?"

Joseph smiled. "Because, CeCe, it means 'sweetheart' in my momma's language. Besides, if I would change my name now, I wouldn't know what to call myself. I don't know my family name. My momma is called Caramel Lagolaei, and they were good to us."

"Good to you? Really, Joseph? They bought you and used you."

"No, not really, CeCe. Just as not all slaves were good and fair, not all slave owners were cruel and heartless."

Having silenced CeCe, Joseph continued. My owners were an older couple, who were afraid of strong-bodied Negro men. They needed help, and they gave Momma and me a good place to live. Ms. Claudine had been a famous cook in N'Oeleans but had suffered a terrible accident. She had been burned something awful. Her scars were many, and she did not like to go out in public because people would stare at her. Momma became her cook. Ms. Claudine was so fearful of the stove, she gave my mother instructions from across the room. Momma was allowed to walk into town and do all the marketing for Ms. Claudine. She taught my momma all her secret recipes, and the two became very close. As long as Momma behaved, I could stay.

By the time I was twelve, I knew how to hunt and fish the swamps; Mother could fix anything I caught. Life was good, and I had free run of the area. Two old French fishermen took a liking to me, and they would take me out on their boats as long as I gutted and cleaned all their catch as well as my own. I had long seasons where I actually forgot I was still a slave, but that ended abruptly when I was fifteen.

Old Master Lagolaei took sick so Ms. Claudine sent for their son, who had not come home once in the nine years I was there. The year was 1856 when the Master passed. His son wasted no time selling the farm and selling us. He planned to take his mother back to Baton Rouge with him, so he had no use for another cook or for a fifteen-year-old 'buck,' as he called me. Mother and I had not felt chains in nine years, but you never forget it. Ms. Claudine protested, but her son would not listen. "Mother," he said with terrible disrespect, "you did them no favor treating them as whites. If I were to bring them to auction unchained, no one would buy them. The buyers want well-trained help who know their place."

Master Walter had no interest in auctioning us off together because you get more when the slaves are unencumbered. Mother's sale placard listed all the foods she could cook and was bought up quickly. I didn't even get to say goodbye. She was pushed off the auction block onto a flatbed wagon and was immediately gone. I was so upset I didn't look around when I was shoved up the steps to the auction block. I heard lots of yelling in French and broken English. When the yelling stopped, I was shoved toward the loading ramp. Not until I was sitting on the flatbed wagon did I look up to see my old friends, Phillip and Frenchie, smiling at me. "You are gunna have to gut lots of fish to pay us back."

I had been fishing with Phillip and Frenchie for nine years, and I loved these men who had been friends of Master Lagolaei. I had spent many a day out on their boat they affectionately called *The Swamp Lady*. "How much did you pay for me, Master Phillip?" Then fearing another surprise, I asked, "How old are you, Master Phillip, and do you have a son somewhere?"

I remember his words to me as if it was just yesterday. "First off, Joseph, it's just *Phillip* like it always has been between us. I'm your captain now—not your Master, and no, I don't have a son. Don't you worry about my age; you just do all the heavy lifting on *The Swamp Lady*, and I will live a long, long time. As for money, I laid out $900 for your freedom. You being fifteen, with all your manhood out in front of you, should have fetched a pretty penny more, but I know things about young Walter Lagolaei, and we struck a deal."

"What kind of a deal?" I asked."

Frenchie smiled, "It helps that Phillip here knew of some trouble young Mr. Lagolaei had before moving up to Baton Rouge. Walter was more than happy to make a quick deal to ensure his past remained so. Besides, Walter was only interested in a quick sale."

As we headed for *The Swamp Lady*, Captain Phillip said, "Joseph, I am going to give you your papers as soon as we get home. I expect you to work with me for four seasons to square your debt to me, but you will do it as a freed man."

It was 1856, and I was seventeen years old when I became a freed man, thanks to these two old fishing mates. Once this fact sunk in and I had thanked them as only a freed man could, I asked, "Captain, do you know who bought my momma?"

"Yes, I do," responded Captain Phillip. "It was Mr. Charles Montgomery's right-hand man. Montgomery is the man we sell most of our good catches to down at the docks. He owns three big hotels and two of the finest restaurants in N'Orleans. Joseph, I think he bid on your momma because her placard boasted she is a great Cajun cook. Old Mrs. Lagolaei was well-known for her recipes, and Mr. Montgomery tried to get her to sell them to him for years. He knows your momma knows all of the Old Lady's recipes. If your momma plays her hand well, she will be okay."

For several years, we fished our hearts out. We were a small vessel, but Phillip knew the waters better than anyone. We would be the first to set out in the morning and the first to return with a full hull. Because there were only three to share the profits, we did quite well. Talk of the War Between the States began to make its way down to the fishing waters of New Orleans. Speculators began buying up catches before they were caught—just to ensure they would not be outbid. Food supplies were getting short, and everyone was feeling the pinch. Phillip worked out a deal with Mr. Montgomery so we no longer sold our fish at the dock, which saved both of us money.

The dock patrol had begun to set a huge levy on every catch. These levy fees became arbitrary, and everyone learned that you either paid a bribe or you paid a levy. Either way, you were going to pay. The city levy was a reasonable fee imposed to help the city maintain the docks, but it had been years since any fisherman had been charged that fee. Levy men were appointed by the city council. In order to get a levy man's post, you had to buy your way in. Levy men ruled the docks, and anyone who went against them took his life in his hands.

We would fish from before dawn and have a full catch by eight o'clock. As we came into port, we would slide along the far side, carefully avoiding the levy tugs. The arbitrary levy fees were outrageous, but the levy tugs bit into the fishermen's profit even more because they were the ones who put you in line. If you did not grease their palms, you would find yourself at the back of the line. After twelve o'clock your catch would only fetch half-price, plus the dock levy was usually twice the price. Many a day a fisherman could work eight to ten hours and barely make the levy fees.

Because *The Swamp Lady* was small, Phillip found if we entered the port shortly before eight o'clock and got past the third post before the levy tugs left the dock, we could slip by unseen and make our way all the way up to Montgomery's warehouse at Canal Boulevard. His men would see us coming and open their docking doors so we could float unnoticed right into his warehouse. Montgomery was always thrilled with our catch because it was half the price and twice as fresh.

We got away with this tactic for almost two years. I had paid off Phillip and was putting money aside every week. Phillip even worked out a deal with Montgomery so that once a week after offloading our catch, he would allow us to tie off the boat and walk up to the back of his restaurant and see Momma. I was surprised at how good she looked. She was healthy and happy and was treated very well. I could see that Phillip liked my momma.

Many a Frenchman had taken a Negro as his wife in New Orleans, but Momma was not free to marry and too old for childbearing. She was still a slave, and Phillip could not afford the price of an excellent cook.

In 1862, well before the Civil War came to an end, Louisiana surrendered to the North. Union ships had stormed into the Gulf in order to cut off the South's supply lines. As far as Louisiana slaves were concerned, the war was over, and they were all emancipated, including Caramel. Mr. Montgomery quickly offered her a fair wage to stay on as his Cajun cook, and she accepted. One month later, Phillip asked her to marry him. The ceremony was nothing fancy—just two minutes in front of the magistrate, a lunch of shrimp and grits, and everyone returned to work.

Phillip, Frenchie and I continued fishing, but the levy men were now on to us. We had several catches dumped overboard and were beaten several times, but Phillip was determined not to pay the levy. We were warned that we might find our boat burned and sunk if we continued. With that threat, Montgomery feared the levy men might burn down his wharf house so we began offloading further upstream, and Montgomery's men would wagon it down to his restaurant.

Phillip and my momma found a little place two streets behind the restaurant, and Frenchie and I slept on the boat so we could be sure to keep it from burning. We lived like this for five years before Phillip was summoned to the dock master's office. At first he thought they were going to fine him for past levy taxes, but it turned out to be much worse.

When Walter Lagolaei sold the farm, Momma and me, he had hurriedly packed all of his father's papers and returned to Baton Rouge. He didn't go through his father's papers until after his mother passed. He was standing in the dock master's office when Phillip entered. Walter handed him an old document he had found among his father's papers. Phillip saw that it was a promissory note for *The Swamp Lady*. Phillip explained, "I paid off that note years ago but never thought to ask for the note. Old Mr. Lagolaei was a friend and knew the note had been satisfied."

Walter did not budge. "I hold the note. If you had paid my daddy, you would hold this note. It is now due and payable, or I take the boat."

The dock master, no friend of Phillip's, stood there with a satisfied smile. "Do you have the funds to pay off the note?" he asked in a syrupy voice.

"You know I don't. This isn't fair."

"Then you are to surrender *The Swamp Lady* to Mr. Lagolaei here, immediately."

If we would have known what Walter was going to do, we could have taken *The Swamp Lady* way upstream and hidden her deep in the swamp, but the dock master and Walter were ready. Levy men were boarding her before Phillip could act. They started tossing all of our personal belongings off the boat. I was given only a few minutes to gather my things before they tied a tow line and began hauling away *The Swamp Lady*. We then learned that Walter had sold her to the dock master for half the note price and was out of town that very day.

Without a boat and with none of the other boats daring to hire us on, we were through. Phillip found work in Montgomery's warehouse, but I could not find any work and having no place to sleep, I quickly ran through most of my savings. I hit the road and headed north. It took me three years to get to Atlanta, but I finally made it. I found work and started saving what I could. After years of working all of the time, I heard of the Greeting Parlor and decided to try it. That is where I met Pearl.

CHAPTER 21

✠

Pearl Remembers My Life With Joseph

PEARL AND JOSEPH'S story revealed exactly how strong my Auntie Pearl was. At first glance, she might seem hard and stringent, and at times, she could be. I am always reminded of Auntie Ruby's warning, "Tobias, pay attention to the whys before you go judging another person. In their whys, your compassion will be found."

Within a month of Ruby's marriage to Arthur, both Pearl and Samuel also married. Knowing that Pearl needed to remain close to Estée, Samuel and CeCe found a place closer to his work. Although Samuel struggled with CeCe's superstitions, he loved her and worked hard to give her a steady life.

On the other hand, by my Auntie Pearl's own admission, she was a driven woman. She lived in a society that did not believe a black person— let alone a black woman—could accomplish anything. She never asked of others what she herself was not willing to do. It was her honest belief that, once given her freedom, she was going to strive for the best life of freedom she could have, and nothing less was ever good enough. Then she learned that love required her to temper her drive. I loved Pearl's honesty.

✠ Our Life ✠

Joseph was a good man. He treated me well—better than I did him. I have always been a driven person, and my desire to improve myself has always overflowed onto those closest to me. My motives have been good; however, my actions can and have hurt those I cared for the most. I don't know why I can never be satisfied with someone's best efforts. I push them, believing I can get even more out of them. I did this to Joseph, the man I loved and the best man I ever knew besides my brother, but that fact did not keep me from pushing. He worked hard and brought home his pay every day, but I knew there had to be better work and better pay out there. I was never satisfied, and I let him know it.

During the first two years of our marriage, I tried to teach Joseph how to read, but he had no interest in learning. He felt he was too old and set in his ways. The truth was, he came home so bone-tired every night he had nothing left to give. It wasn't enough that Joseph had given up his first love—fishing—to do backbreaking labor. I always wanted more from him; that is, until our baby girl was born.

We were so excited when we learned a baby was on the way. We fixed up Ruby's old room, and there was nothing Joseph would not do for me. We thought the baby would arrive near Thanksgiving, but a full two months early, I took to my bed, knowing something was terribly wrong. Joseph ran for the old midwife while Estée sat by my side. We all knew the baby was coming too soon.

We named her Caramel Hannah, after both of our mommas. She came into this world without a sound, save the pleas for mercy from her daddy. The midwife handed little Caramel into her daddy's waiting arms, and I saw the most tender of moments shared between my husband and his child. Joseph stood by the window so he could see her little face as the sun rose that morning. His sweet French accent became even thicker when filled with emotion. He caressed her little face, committing to memory every part of her as he sang a song I had never heard.

After the midwife finished with me, she bent down and whispered, "I need to take the baby from him now. Can you help me talk him into handing her over?"

Ignorant of what was really going on, I asked, "Do we need to send Joseph out to get a doctor?"

The midwife, realizing I did not understand, said gently, "No, Pearl, your baby came out dead. Joseph has been singing and talking to her as if she could hear him. I am afraid to ask him to hand her over for fear of his coming undone when he realizes she's gone."

I immediately ordered the midwife and Estée out of our room. "Leave us alone with our girl."

Estée knew exactly what I wanted and took the midwife's arm and led her into the kitchen. Once we were alone, I asked, "Joseph, bring our daughter over here so we can both say goodbye to her."

He laid our little girl down beside me and unwrapped her tiny body so we could both see her fingers and toes. I traced my finger across her little mouth and chin, while Joseph took her little foot, bent down and kissed it ever so gently. "We must say goodbye to her, Pearl."

"So you know she is dead, Joseph?" Relieved that I did not have to tell him, I asked, "What were you singing to her, Joseph?"

"It was a song in my native tongue that my momma sang to me and to my sisters when we were little. She sang it to the baby born on the slave ship before she was tossed overboard. Pearl, at least you and I will not know that pain. We shall bury her properly with a headstone that says she was loved by her momma and dada."

That morning I vowed never to push Joseph ever again. How could I do anything but love this kind, caring man? Two days later we put Baby Caramel to rest. For the next three years, we were exceptionally happy. I kept my vow and found myself unusually content, except that we wanted another child. I was now in my mid-thirties and seemed to be one of those who struggled with carrying a baby. Several times we were sure I was with child but after a month or so, there was no baby. Joseph, true to his nature, never chided me or showed his disappointment. I knew how badly he wanted a child. I saw the desire in his face the morning he had held Baby Caramel, but he never blamed me. Oh, how I loved that man!

I was thirty-eight the day the men came to my workplace to get me. No one would tell me what was going on; they simply said, "Gather up your things and come with us." They took me to a filthy makeshift, back-alley clinic—the only place Negroes were taken for medical care. Few ever walked out of these clinics, and my Joseph was in there. The wagon stopped at the street, and I was ordered to walk down the narrow alley and take the second door on the right. As I made my way to the door, the smells that assailed my nostrils were unbearable. Right across from the clinic door was the entrance to a back-alley butchery. Hindquarters of beef were hanging from hooks, waiting to be cut up. An old lady was sitting on a wooden box, plucking dead chickens, and a great amount of wretched feathers, mixed with animal blood, covered the alley walkway. As I reached the clinic door, I was attacked by a swarm of flies that had obviously declared that alleyway as their possession.

It took my eyes a minute to adjust to the darkness of the room. A woman was sitting at a desk, but she did not look up when I approached. She simply asked, "Who are you here to see?"

"I believe my husband was brought here," I said, still praying that a big mistake had been made.

Without looking up, the woman asked, "What is the name?"

"Lagolaei, Joseph Lagolaei, and I am his wife, Pearl."

The woman looked up with dead, cold eyes and said, "We have a Joe Leggs here. How do you spell your husband's name?"

Shock set in as I heard the name *Joe Leggs*, and I hurriedly explained, "That is what Joseph's boss calls him. He cannot pronounce *Lagolaei*, so he just calls him *Joe Leggs*. That is my husband. Can I please see him? Is he hurt? Why is he here?" Even as I asked the questions, I could feel myself coming apart. I really did not want any of my questions answered because I was afraid to hear them.

I spelled our name for the woman, and then I was led down a dimly lit hallway through two sets of large doors that had muffled the sounds that were coming from behind them. With each set of doors, the screams grew louder. I did not know if I was strong enough to face the cause of those screams. I was ushered into a dark room that held five beds, and each one occupied by screaming men. It took a moment for my eyes to adjust to the dim light, but once they did, I wished I had been stricken blind and deaf. I did not want to see or remember what I saw. Joseph was out of his mind in pain, as were the others. Their screams of pain were agonizing. He did not know me nor could I do anything for him. He lasted only one more hour, and to say I was relieved when he gasped his last breath is an understatement. I could not bear to see him in such agony.

I learned that these five men had been ordered to uncouple the last four fully loaded flatbed cars attached to the train before it was to go on northbound. Once the cars were uncoupled and the train had pulled away, then the horse-drawn wagons would be pulled alongside so the cars could be off-loaded. All five men were down between the cars, uncoupling them when the engineer misunderstood the flagman's signals. He mistakenly put the train in reverse, crushing all five men.

Because this was the second time this engineer had done this, the railroad had a lawyer sitting in the waiting area of this rundown clinic to ambush each wife as she came out of that terrible room. I had not even been able to arrange for Joseph's burial, and this offensive man was already in my face. He was a very large man who obviously believed the cologne he splashed on himself would hide the fact that he desperately needed to bathe, let alone change his suit more often than he did. It was not yet the height of the day, yet his neck was already covered with sweat at the labor of carrying around so much weight.

He stepped in front of me, blocking my exit and demanding a few moments of my time. He actually took hold of my arm and pushed me toward a table where all of his papers were spread out. I took a seat across from him and simply stared back at him. He did not say a word; he merely unbuckled his leather satchel and began laying out $100 bills. When he had finished, he sat back and said, "Mrs. Lagolaei, do you know how much money this is? It is $1,000—a huge amount of money. The railroad usually does business by check, but you Negroes have a hard time grasping the amount when written on a check. Besides, none of you have bank accounts, and you would have a hard time cashing such a large check."

I wanted to scream at this man's rudeness. I wanted to defend myself, showing him I indeed knew how to read a check and could comprehend the value of this amount of money. Instead, I remained silent. I did not want to show my anger, and I was certainly not going to gush over that money placed on that table. I was not going to give this man any response. I didn't touch the money. Actually, I did not even look at it. I continued to stare directly at him.

"Mrs. Lagolaei, this is a huge amount of money. Even for a white man, this would be a huge settlement. All the railroad wishes in return is that you talk to no one about what happened to your husband. Do you understand? No newspaper people—no one. The railroad is willing to pay this amount to ensure your silence. If you refuse, trust me, Mrs. Lagolaei, even if you could secure a representative, no court in the city would grant you this much money—not for a Negro with no future. You have funeral expenses, don't you? You are now a widow; how are you going to survive without a husband if you refuse this very generous offer? All the other wives have signed this document. If you refuse, they will not come to your aide in court without having to repay the railroad. Don't you see how foolish it would be for you to refuse this very generous offer?"

I knew I had no stomach for such a fight, but I also knew I would never touch a penny of this blood money. I took the pen and signed the paper. He was so arrogant, he had no idea he had insulted me. He smiled at me as he placed his final signature into his satchel. His work was completed. He had done the same for all five widows. As he picked up his satchel, he said, "For a moment there, I thought you might not sign. You are a very lucky woman, Mrs. Lagolaei. Even white people don't get this kind of money. I told my boss I could get all the signatures for half that amount, but the railroad is bidding on a new line contract next week and cannot afford any bad press right now. If this had happened week after next, the railroad would only have paid for the funeral—if that. So you see how lucky you are?"

I was given $1,000 for Joseph's life, which was a large sum for the day. However, no amount could come near his loss to me. Who could put a price on a loved one? I never spent a penny of that money. I felt I would somehow be dishonoring Joseph. Not being a person who cares to show her emotions, I did my grieving in private. I thought I had settled my heart over the loss of our little girl. I had gotten busy and went on with life because that is what I do. But now, with the loss of Joseph, I felt like I was drowning in a sea of emotions. I pulled Joseph's clothes out of our wardrobe cabinet, buried my face in them and wept bitterly over my loss. I cried for him, for Caramel Hannah, and for all those children we would never have. I think I cried for three whole days—until there were no more tears left to cry. I never realized how much I always held inside, not willing to show anyone how I truly felt about things. I knew it was wrong, but I have always had a hard time showing my emotions. I think it's because when I was little, I was the volatile one. Momma would scold me about my quick temper and tell me, "Pearl, you gunna get yerself sold if'n you keep that up. Ms. Victoria won't allow her slaves to disrespect her. You best keep what you think'n to yerself, girl."

I think I have bottled up my feelings for so long I don't know how to be open and free. I am thankful I was able to show Joseph how much he meant to me. I really don't believe I could have done that had we not come together to grieve over our little girl. I know he died knowing that I loved him deeply.

I knew I needed to pull myself together. I decided I had to go on with life, so I went on working and caring for Estée for three more years before Ruby returned home.

CHAPTER 22

Ruby Remembers Arthur and I Had A Dream

TOBIAS REPLACED HIS tin box on the shelf next to their suitcase. The water closet was beckoning him, and he again needed a few moments away from his vivid memories. As he returned to his seat, he knew the real reason he needed a short break was because his Auntie Ruby's story was always difficult to review. He remembered how angry he had gotten the first time he heard what Uncle Arthur had done to his beloved Auntie Ruby. No matter how often she warned him to be careful, it took years before he could forgive that man. Some lessons are just harder to learn.

Of Grandpa and the sisters, the one who lived the longest was fragile little Ruby. Tobias stared out the train window and thought, "Auntie Ruby, I cannot believe eight years have passed since I lost you. I was forty-eight years old when you died, and I cried like a baby. I loved my Grandpa Samuel, and I loved Auntie Pearl, but you, Ms. Ruby, are the one I miss the most. Even though your story is the most difficult one to review, review it I must. You lived it, Ms. Ruby. You not only lived it, you became even stronger because of it."

Tobias took a deep breath and allowed his mind to return to the day when Ms. Pearl asked Ruby to tell me her story. Aunt Ruby started this story the same way she would tell it a dozen more times to me. She'd get this twinkle in her eyes, and she would try not to smile as she opened her story with…

Everyone liked Arthur right away. He was a very likeable man, but a quiet man. During one of our Sunday dinners, Brother Samuel was surprised to learn through a slip of the tongue that Arthur had been married before. Everyone could all tell he was sorry the minute it came out of his mouth. Arthur enjoyed hearing everyone else's story, but he was not forthcoming about his. This fact bothered Samuel, who knew that Arthur was pressing me to set a date and that he intended to take me far away from Atlanta once we were married. Therefore, Samuel decided to be very direct with him.

Samuel waited until the dishes had been cleared, and I was out of the room, to ask, "I like you, Arthur, and I know Ruby does. I only have one serious problem with you. What are you hiding that you don't want us to know about you?"

Arthur responded rather defensively, "Why? Because I won't lay out my pain in front of all of you? Why do I have to talk about something I vowed I would never think about again?"

"Arthur, you don't have to tell me anything—ever, that is, unless you want to marry my sister. Then you had better start talking because I'm telling you if I tell Ruby she is not going to marry you, she won't marry you."

Brother was telling the truth. I never would have gone against my brother's wishes. I returned to the table, shook my head in agreement and said, "Arthur, we need to hear your story."

✤ Arthur's Story ✤

"Okay, okay," he said, feeling rather cornered. "I was twenty and six when the war ended, and I was set free. I about starved that first year because I refused to become a sharecropper. I never wanted a white man to order me around again. My daddy didn't feel strong enough to hold out. He had my momma and my three sisters to feed. He went back with his hat in his hand, hung his head and begged our old owner to take him on. I think that was the hardest thing he ever had to do. The second hardest thing was watching me walk down the road, leaving my family behind.

"I was sure I was going to get hanged that first year. I was forced to steal just to get a bite to eat. I slept where I could and went barefoot for three months after another boy stole my shoes while I was sleeping. I can't tell you how many times I thought about going back with my hat in my hand, hang my head, and beg for work. I was just about broken when I came across this girl with the sweetest smile. Her daddy was one of the few black farmers who owned his own land. It wasn't a big place, but it was his. Celia offered me one hot meal a day and a clean, dry place to sleep if I would come out and help her daddy clear a field.

"A few months later Celia was with child, and her daddy told me he would kill me if I didn't marry her. He didn't need to threaten me because I wanted to marry her. I agreed to work the farm as long as Celia, the baby, and I could live there and have enough food to get by. We were really happy. I liked the work, Celia was getting big, and we were anxious to see our baby.

"One night I woke up to Celia's screaming something awful. I knew something wrong with the baby, but all I could do was hold her hand and hope it would come out soon. Celia's daddy didn't know what to do either. Her momma had been dead for three years by then, so no one was around who would help us. I watched my woman and my baby die that night. After her daddy and I buried them, he asked me to stay on, but I couldn't. I never wanted to climb back into that bed. I said my goodbyes, and I walked away. I never wanted to think about that pain ever again. I kept busy working for other farmers.

"I got good at clearing land. I would finish one field, and two more would be waiting for me. I didn't stick around long enough to see those fields planted, let alone see a crop brought in. I kept moving—until I met Ruby, and I guess I got tired of moving on. I want to own my own land, Samuel. I want to clear my own fields and plant my own crop and have a family. I know lots of clearing jobs are available in the Carolinas. If Ruby and I work hard and save our money, I know we can get a place of our own in about ten years. Samuel, I was good to Celia, and I will be good to Ruby."

Tobias remembered the look in Aunt Ruby's eyes whenever she repeated her Arthur's story. I was a mix of pain and pride; pain at knowing her man had been hurt so deeply, and pride, being able to bring the shine of hope back into those eyes by her loving him.

Aunt Ruby would always announce, "Brother Samuel was satisfied with Arthur's answer, and two weeks later, Arthur and I were married and on our way to the Carolinas.

Arthur and I were happy and excited as we made our way to the Carolina's. He was certain there would be plenty of work for an experienced field clearer. We spent our first two years near Charleston, living in field houses on the land he worked. By the end of the second year, Arthur had made the acquaintance of two strong and able-bodied men who were willing to travel with us. Gilbert, a massive boy of twenty, had a quick temper. He had been on his own since the age of ten and had been cheated by both blacks and whites alike. Arthur suspected the boy possessed more brawn than brain, making it easy to confuse him and thereby cheat him. Once Arthur proved himself to Gilbert, a more loyal helper couldn't have been found. Besides Gilbert, our best treasure was Theo, a man well into his forties who was not afraid of hard work.

Arthur spent that second year teaching his men the proper way of clearing fields. He explained how most men wasted too much labor, not realizing that saved labor is money in their pockets. Once they were sure their system would work, Arthur set out to bid on clearing jobs. Arthur taught me how to drive the team, which freed all three men to work the fields. Arthur said this was money in the bank, and I felt happy because I was helping us get our own place sooner. Knowing they could do the job quicker than others, Arthur included one additional entry in his bids. His first four bids were not only lower than all of the others, Arthur's bid included a promised date of completion. A clause stated that if the land was not cleared on time; the bid would be cut in half. After coming in on time,

Arthur did not have to bid again. A new field job was always waiting for us. The four of us worked hard, lived thrifty, and loved our life. Arthur and I put most of our share of the clearing fees into a large glass jar we kept under our bed.

For six years we had more work than we could accept. We moved often and had worked our way all the way up to the Virginia border before clearing jobs began to slow down. Knowing we needed to keep busy, Arthur began studying the different crops in the area. He, Gilbert, and Theo realized that tobacco was their best bet. If I drove the team, the three of them could clear a field quickly. At first, Arthur approached several tobacco farms about hiring his crew, but no one was interested. They had never hired outsiders and saw no need to start doing so. Arthur knew if he could get one farmer to give them a try, he was sure it would be just like the clearing jobs—but no one would budge. He had approached the seven largest growers, and none were interested.

He came home exhausted and discouraged, when Theo suggested that Arthur might be going about this matter all wrong. The big growers were fat and sassy and didn't need our help. We decided to go to the small farmers—the ones who needed to get their crop to market before the big farmers' harvests drove down the prices. If we could cut, bale, and dry the tobacco faster, these small farmers could get their crops to market ahead of the larger growers. All we needed was one farmer to see how we could make our plan work for him.

That night all four of us packed up the flatbed wagon and headed six hours south to where the smaller farms were located. Arthur not only offered to help bring in the crop; he also offered our wagon to double the amount delivered to market. We were hired on the spot. For the next three years we cleared fields, brought in tobacco, and joyfully added to our money jar. We were sure we would have enough money to buy our own place in another year or two. Arthur was a man on a mission. In many ways he reminded me of Pearl. Going after big goals thrilled his heart. Setting a plan in motion and seeing it come to pass made him happy, and making him happy made me happy.

Arthur figured for us to thrive, we needed eighty acres of cleared land. The government would only consign off parcels of forty acres in South Carolina, so Gilbert and Theo offered to throw in with us and get a hundred acres. Arthur refused, knowing we could not clear and plant that much land in one year, for that was the government's requirement. If you bid on government land, you had to clear it and plant it within one year or it went to auction, and you lost everything. Many a farmer lost his life savings because his farm was auctioned off after a year of grueling labor. Arthur did not plan to risk our eight years of savings.

We moved further south and were working a small farm right outside of Spartanburg. The government had expanded its land grants, and a flood of new, young farmers started buying up the parcels. This, again, was great for us. As soon as these city boys realized they could not meet the deadline, we had plenty of work, but we also had to deal with untrained city folk who thought they were farmers.

We were working hard on a small farmer's land, located very near the Natahala National Forest. This part of the country was especially hard to clear because the trees were deeply rooted and so plentiful. Even Gilbert had trouble with the large intertwined roots. The common practice was to use blasting powder, and no one thought ill of those who did. Anyone who had spent a day working in the hot South Carolina sun, digging out one of these massive stumps, would be the first to submit to its benefit. Obviously, the rules for its use were strict. For instance, none could be set off before eight o'clock in the morning or after six o'clock at night. Any time a charge was to be set off; the farmer was required to blow a loud whistle as a two-minute warning. Most everyone followed these orders, but there were always a few who forgot. Usually those who forgot were young new farmers who would not, or could not, afford to hire help clearing their fields and were getting desperate. The whistles provided by the gunpowder sellers were very loud and distinctive; the sound could not be missed.

The farm on which we were working was adjacent to one owned by a new young farmer. Many a night we would hear a gunpowder blast well after dark, which was a dangerous practice. We could tell he was desperate and had been setting off several blasts close together. He was clearing his fields alone, save for his two young boys who were of little help. Gilbert believed the man was overusing the blasting powder in order to reduce the stumps and roots to a more manageable size. We never reported the farmer because we all understood his problem. As it turns out, we should have turned him in. Those rules were in place for a reason, and we would live with the knowledge that the reason had been overlooked for the rest of our lives.

One morning I was walking our horses through our half-cleared field while Arthur, Gilbert, and Theo loaded the blasted roots, rocks, and stumps onto the flatbed. We dared not let the wagon wheels stay in one place very long because the Carolina clay could quickly suck in the wheel and the horses would have a terrible time freeing the wagon. If I walked between them and kept them rocking back and forth five or six inches, the men could get the wagon loaded without getting stuck. This method, which we had perfected several years earlier, worked well for us.

In the course of another full day on the job, we had worked our way to the far edge of the field and were just about ready to pull the loaded flatbed out of the field and offload it. Right then a very loud blast was set off just beyond the clump of trees separating the two farm parcels. The neighboring farmer did not blow a warning whistle, and he set his blast much too close to his property line. Our horses had grown used to steadying themselves for the loud blasts when they heard the whistle blow, but this blast was far too close, and without any warning. Custer, our more skittish horse, kicked his back legs and began to bite at me. Max, our usually gentle giant, began pulling against his bridle, kicking his back legs. I tried to hold onto their leads but they jerked away from me, and when their back legs hit the wagon, they panicked and tried to run. Max's head came across and knocked me silly as I bounced off of Custer, lost my balance and fell under their feet. I was knocked out and have no memory of being trampled by our panic-stricken horses. Thankfully, the wheels of the fully loaded flatbed missed my body, but my body had been crushed by our horses.

I was told that Gilbert picked me up and carried me back to our field shack. All three of them thought I was going to die. With no available hospital or doctor for miles around, everyone knew you did your best, and if you lived, you lived. Arthur and Gilbert pulled the still-loaded wagon up next to the shack, unhooked the horses, and Gilbert tied up Custer while Arthur climbed up on Max and headed to the nearest town. Wealthy white folks could get their hands on opium for such injuries, but Negroes were relegated to whiskey. Neither Arthur nor I had ever gotten into drinking. Arthur always said that people with goals and dreams don't waste their money with such things, but now Arthur was desperate to find all the whiskey he could buy.

For months Gilbert and Theo worked the fields without Arthur's help. I could not be left alone, and Arthur took very good care of me. Many of my bones had been broken, and none of them knew how to straighten them without causing me even more pain, so they mended the way they were. For months I could not be moved without pain, so Arthur kept me filled with whiskey. I have little memory of those first four months. On one of Arthur's whiskey runs, he brought back a set of used crutches. I began the difficult task of making my broken body move around the shack. Once I was strong enough to move around without whiskey to dull the pain, I learned that Gilbert and Theo had finished clearing that farm and had moved on. Arthur, unable to go with them, struck a deal with the farmer. We were allowed to rent the shack for an outrageous sum until I was strong enough to move on. I set about pushing myself every day, trying to increase the range of my movements.

Arthur refused to touch me for fear of breaking me, and I began to notice a serious change in him. Even though I no longer took whiskey to relieve my pain, we were still going through our supply at an alarming rate. Arthur would sit on the porch for hours, staring at the crops being grown in our cleared fields. At six months, Arthur believed I was strong enough to be lifted onto the flatbed. If he drove slowly and avoided deep ruts, we could get to the nearest town and rent someplace more reasonable. Every time Arthur had to pull money out of our jar, he became quiet and sullen. This went on for almost three years. Nothing was going into our money jar, and rent, food, and whiskey money was fast eating into our funds. It had taken us eight long years of hard labor to put that money in our jar, but only four short years to deplete it.

I tried to talk to Arthur about his drinking, but he would just walk away. One morning I woke up to an unusually sober Arthur sitting at our kitchen table with all the contents of our jar stacked in front of him. I did not say a word. I took the seat across from him and waited for him to speak. "Ruby, it's almost gone. I am too old to start all over again. My dreams are gone, and I can't do anything about it."

I remained quiet. I knew Arthur was hurting, and I had nothing to offer him, except gratitude for four years of priceless care. Arthur set aside everything to care for me, and now the cold truth that we would never see our dreams come true was sitting on the table between us. Arthur began picking up the money and returning it to the jar.

With a look of resolve, he said, "Ruby, I sold the wagon and horses three years ago because we couldn't afford to feed them when they weren't bringing in money. I think we should do something before it's all gone. I think I should look around for a used buggy and horse. I want to take you back to Atlanta. You need your family now that you are hurt and injured. I love you, Ruby, but you are broken in body, and I am broken in spirit. I have nothing left to take care of you. I'm just too worn out to try again. Ruby, honestly, I simply want to die."

I tried my best to convince Arthur that I still loved him and wanted to stay with him. He knew I loved him, but he needed his freedom; I needed to love him enough to let him go. I tried not to cry in front of him. I knew Arthur had simply endured too much and had given up. I wanted to shake him and scream, "What about me? Don't you love me enough to try again?" But I didn't ask these questions because I already knew the answer. It was not about me; it was about Arthur. He had fought a valiant fight, recovering from the loss of his first wife and child. He worked hard to rebuild his dream of having a family of his own, a place of his own, and a life of which he could be proud. Then I went and got hurt and destroyed all of those dreams again. The money was gone, I was never going to be able to have children, and I was too crippled to help him start over. I knew

I was too much of a burden for Arthur to handle. I could do nothing about his broken dreams—except to love him enough to make this decision as easy for him as possible. I worried about what would happen to him now that he had found that whisky could dull the pain. However, he didn't care to discuss the issue, and he couldn't bear to think about how I was feeling; he was too broken.

A few days later he loaded what little we had, helped me into the buggy and off we went. Six days later we pulled the buggy up in front of Pearl's house. As Arthur helped me out of the buggy, Estée saw us and came out to greet us. She ran up to me and tossed her arms around me before she realized how broken I was. She froze and cried, "What happened to you, Ruby?"

Not wanting to go into the details of the accident in front of Arthur, I ignored her question and asked, "Estée, is Pearl or Joseph home from work? It's been a long journey, and I am quite tired."

We had moved so often that I did not know what Pearl and Joseph had gone through. Estée did not want to be the one to tell me, so she let us go into the house to wait for Pearl. Arthur had no intention of facing Pearl. He felt bad enough leaving me; he did not want to see Pearl's disappointment. He offloaded my belongings and helped me into the house. While I got us a much needed drink of water, I saw Arthur take out our money jar, pull out three twenty dollar bills and replace the lid on the jar. I thought to myself, "Sixty dollars for twelve years of hard labor?" but I was wrong—oh, so wrong. Arthur stood, smiled at me and said, "I know this is not fair to you, Ruby. You deserved a home of your own and a husband who could keep you safe. I have done neither." He walked over to me, slipped the sixty dollars in his pocket and handed me the money jar, which contained almost five hundred dollars.

"No, Arthur, I can't take it. At least let us share it equally.'

Arthur just smiled and said, "Let me do this, Ruby. I need to do this for my sake, as well as yours. I will take the horse and buggy though, if you don't mind. You can't handle a horse anymore, and I am certain that Pearl won't." He bent down, kissed me and walked out the door. I never heard from him again. The pain in my body didn't compare with the pain I felt watching him leave. To this day, I still love that man.

Rummaging through her goodie bag, Ruth brought Tobias back to the present. "I'm sorry, Ruth, I didn't even notice you had returned to your seat. My mind was a thousand miles away."

"That's all right; I suspected you would be thinking about your family today."

"I'm sorry I have been ignoring you. Did you have a nice talk with that woman?"

"Honey, I still am. I just came back to get a few more cookies for the children. How are you holding up? I think we have at least two more hours before we reach Lynchburg, Virginia. We will have a one-hour dinner stop there while they change the locomotives."

"I'm holding up quite well. I have been sitting here remembering all of the reasons I'm thankful for my life and proud of my family. Ruth, I was nine years old the first time I heard Arthur's story. I still remember how angry I was when I learned he quit on my beautiful, sweet Auntie Ruby. I could not wrap my mind around his decision. I had loved his story and him—up until the point where he brought my Ruby back to Atlanta and left her there. Who could do such a thing?"

"Tobias, all I can say is he must have been incredibly broken to do that to Auntie Ruby."

"I know, Ruth, but it is still hard to imagine. Aunt Ruby knew I would react with loyal indignation, but she decided to tell me the whole truth and then use it to teach me a valuable lesson. All these years later, I still remember what she said: 'Toby Boy, when people disappoint you, you have to try to understand their *whys* and love them anyway. No one is capable of acting like a hero all of the time. Some can most of the time. Some can some of the time. Sadly, some have been so broken, they never can. Everyone will let you down sometime. You have to decide what kind of person you want to be, Toby Boy. The biggest hero is the person who can still love those who have disappointed him.' "

With tears welling up in her eyes, Ruth leaned over and kissed Tobias, "What a godly woman she was! I still miss her every day."

"Ruth, you know I do. Whenever I struggle with anger or disappointment, and you know how often that is, I remember this lesson from my Auntie Ruby, and I try to understand their *whys*."

Digging into the tin box, he pulled out the four photos, which were taken the day all three couples got married. "Ruth, I know you have seen these photos lots of times, but right now, thinking about their lives, I am overwhelmed with gratitude that Grandpa Samuel hired a photographer the day they all got married. Aunt Pearl, always the practical one, admitted to me once that she thought spending that money was wasteful—until she lost her Joseph."

Taking the photos from him and studying each couple, Ruth mused, "You know, Tobias, they are all our family. CeCe, Joseph, Arthur, and Little Estée. We owe them all because they were loved by Samuel, Pearl, and Ruby."

Taking back the photos and placing them into the envelope to keep them safe, he choked, "I wish I could have known Joseph, Arthur, and especially Estée, that little broken bird named Estée. Because of her generosity, I was able to come live with the sisters."

Patting Tobias on the cheek, Ruth agreed, "We both owe Ms. Estée a huge debt. If not for her, you and I would never have met. That is a life I do not wish to imagine."

Tobias let out a deep sigh, "Arthur's story was hard enough for today, Ruth. I cannot handle the thought of not having you in my life."

Trying to lighten the moment, Ruth suggested, "Tobias, you have been reviewing some difficult stories this morning. Why don't you spend some time remembering the sisters' happy years with Estee? I am going to leave you to your thoughts. I told Clara I would be right back. I will probably sit with her all the way to Lynchburg. She needs lots of love right now."

CHAPTER 23

✢

Pearl Remembers
A Home for Us

As RUTH WALKED back to Clara, Tobias pulled out the fourth photo—the one taken of the broken little bird Estée the day of the weddings. He had heard her story so many times he felt as if he knew her. Even in the photo, he could see her shy, withdrawn demeanor. He also remembered how the sisters had told him how Estée came to life while Ms. Pearl had read all those exciting novels to her. Staring at her photo, Tobias let his mind drift back to the day the sisters first told him the final story about sweet little Estée.

He remembered how angry he was that day and how he had announced that he was going to quit school. He thought that Ms. Pearl was going to tan his hide, but instead, she sat him down at the kitchen table and said, "Toby, I understand how you feel. Life will bring some hard things, but you must never give up. Life is too valuable to just sit down and give up. Oh, I wanted to after Joseph died. I think I might have—had it not been for Estée.

✢ Pearl Shares Estée's Gift ✢

Even though she was a broken person trapped by her own fears, Estée loved me and was right by my side when we lost little Caramel Hannah. She also stood by me as I grieved over Joseph's death. She had been there for me when I most needed her, and because she needed me, I dared not give up on life.

Estée had lost her father three winters before Joseph died, and we took over caring for her. Estée had dinner with us every night, and she and I loved sharing our novels with Joseph. When faced with the task of selling her father's business, I agreed to work with the lawyers to get the business ready to sell. I taught Estée how to take over her father's bookkeeping to make sure she would not be cheated. Estée still refused to go beyond the yard, so I did her banking.

Once we found a buyer, the new owner decided to keep me on since I knew every aspect of the business. Because of all my help, Estée demanded to drop the rent in half as payment for my help. Her generosity made it possible for me to stay in this house after Joseph died. For three years, Estée and I helped each other endure our grief. We had our dinner meals together, continued reading novels, and kept each other company. Not until Ruby came home did I realize exactly how much I had missed her.

Life settled into a calm, predictable routine. Ruby had dinner ready when I arrived home; afterward, Estée and I did the dishes. Ruby gathered her evening's handwork so she could work while enjoying our current novel. During the next five years, we read the complete works of Jane Austen, Mark Twain, and Charles Dickens. The book cart man began to make regular stops at the house, knowing we three women were always good for a sale. He would occasionally remind us that he was also in the market to purchase used books. Estée would always reply, "We could never do that, Mr. Josiah. We could never sell our friends."

As our library grew, so did our understanding of life beyond our little world. Learning how hard life was for Oliver Twist, Tom Sawyer, or Huckleberry Finn was both entertaining and enlightening. One evening as I was reading about Tom Sawyer in the caverns, I stopped and told Estée all about Ruby's and my experience when we survived in the caverns and our life above the livery.

In great earnest, Estée declared, "You need to write down those stories, Pearl. They are every bit as exciting as Tom's experience."

Frowning at her, I replied, "Estée, no one is interested in what happened to three little black children."

More confident than I had ever seen her, Estée admonished me. "A good story is always a good story. We love reading about Edmond Dantès even though he was a Frenchman. We loved the March sisters, even though they are white. We love Huckleberry, even though he is an ornery white rascal."

"I don't know, Estée. Maybe someday people will be able to hear stories about black people and see them as people just like themselves; I sure hope so."

Trying to convince herself, as much as me, Estée pleaded, "Pearl, we can't be so very different. We can love these characters, and even see things in their stories that remind us of ourselves—even though they are white, and we are black. But even if white people can never see how alike we really are, I want to keep reading these stories because I love them." As if thinking hard, Estée paused and then declared, "I don't think there is a single real white person whom I like or trust. I can't leave my yard for fear of running into one of them. But all these characters in all of these books we have read are now my dear friends. I would be sad to think that any one of them might have lived right down the street from me, and my fear because of the color of their skin kept me from knowing them. Wouldn't that be sad, Pearl?"

"Yes, it would be, Estée. Reading is a safe way to get to know what others have gone through and realize we all hurt in the same ways. I think once we know that, it might be harder to hurt people. At least I hope that is true, and who knows, maybe someday, someone will write our story."

Just the hope that someday, someone might write our story seemed to make Estee happy, but there was still something bothering her. A few days later, Estée came to us with a plan; a well thought-out plan. "As you both know, I receive a fair payment each month from the new owner of my father's business. It is sufficient for my needs. Both houses are paid off, and I am able to live in my house quite well, but I am lonely. What would you two think if I were to sell my house and move in here with you? I could take some of the house money and have a third bedroom added to the back. That way I am far away from the street, and no one has to share a room with me. What do you think?"

Neither Sissy nor I answered right away, and Estée feared she had overstepped her boundaries when I asked, "Estée, how would we settle the rent?"

"Oh, Pearl, I would not charge you rent. I would be so happy here with you two that I could not think of charging you rent. Also, you do know that my father intended to leave this house to you when I pass, don't you? He loved you both so much for your kindness to me; he said he could never repay you. So I will have the lawyer prepare the deed in such a way that all three of us own it equally. The last one to outlive the others will own the house, and that must not be me. I do not want to outlive either of you."

Estee's generous offer went a long way in allowing Sister and me to keep our pledge of never touching Joseph or Arthur's money. I always considered Joseph's death money to be blood money, and Ruby always hoped that Arthur might one day return, and she would be able to give his money back to him. Ruby knew if she was going to keep her promise, it would require her earning her own way again.

After several months of recuperation, Ruby found the old handcart she had used so many years in the past. It was now rusty, and even when it was empty, she could not manage it. She could no longer conduct her personal door-to-door service anymore. She decided to try something new and had me place an ad in the local paper.

**Mending • Alterations • Personal Embroidery Services
All work must be dropped off and picked up.**

I was surprised at the response she received from that ad. Ruby worked quickly and neatly, but what set her apart as a seamstress was her ability to take a drawing from a client and embroider it exactly as drawn. Soon even Ruby was paying her own way.

The year was 1886 when the house was placed in all three names. Sister and I were now thirty-seven and doing well. Brother Samuel, on the other hand, was not. Work was hard to find, and he yearned to take his family somewhere with plenty of opportunities. He and CeCe had been married for twelve years and had lost three babies before Little Ruby Girl came along. She was now three years old, and her daddy felt the pressure to provide for her. At the same time, with feeling responsible for us, he would not entertain the idea of leaving Atlanta.

After Joseph died, I had depended heavily on Brother Samuel—not for income, but for emotional support. But once Ruby was back and we were secure in a house of our own, Brother Samuel began to rethink his options. After talking with us, Samuel packed up his little family and headed to New York City.

For the next fifteen years Estée, Ruby, and I lived a quiet, comfortable life. We saw the dawn of a new century arrive, but our life remained unchanged—just as we wanted it. Then in 1901, Estée was given her most ardent wish, to be the first to pass. She always feared being left alone, so when the end was near, she made her final preparations. She had turned seventy-six the week of her passing, and on the nightstand next to her bed was her most prized possession, *The Count of Monte Cristo*. Inside this book was a letter from her lawyer. Estée apparently realized she was ill and had her lawyer write up her will, leaving the balance of payments from the business and her note for the sale of the house next door to us.

"For three years we refused to spend Estée's funds and simply added them to Joseph's and Arthur's money. The house was paid off, and we made sufficient money to meet our own needs. It wasn't until we received the telegram from Brother Samuel, asking us to take in his grandson that we felt the full blessing of Estée's generosity, which made it possible for us to welcome you, Tobias, with open arms, knowing we would be able to support you."

Sitting here all these years later, holding this photo of Estée Washington, Tobias allowed the full weight of her generosity to sink in. We were never well-off, but we never went without our necessities. As a youth, whenever the Aunties told Estée's story, my heart struggled. I know that it was because of her passing I was able to live with the sisters. I longed to know this wonderful lady, whose love for my aunties made my life in Atlanta possible. I think about Estée in heaven, free and whole, living with people of all colors without any fear. "Ms. Estée, thank you, and say hello to my family for me, and tell them I am well."

Tobias' heart was filled with emotion as he returned the photo to his tin box. Knowing what these two aunts had gone through and how they both had overcome issues that should have crushed them, filled his heart with pride. He thought about the speech he had prepared for this event and knew there would never be enough time to properly tell these people all the things that Ms. Pearl had accomplished in her lifetime.

These hours on the train spent in reviewing all of the family stories drove home the huge responsibility he had felt after Aunt Ruby passed away. He knew he had to keep his promise to all three of these amazing women—to write down their stories. The book was not simply to address what they had endured; rather, this book would tell all of the wonderful things they did for others because all three of these women did not simply endure; they overcame. They used their experiences to teach me and many others, that lying down and giving up is never the answer. They taught me that quitting is for cowards. That doing right—even when everyone else is doing wrong—is always right.

TOBIAS:
Life Must Go On
1906-1922

Anger Took Hold of Me

THINKING ABOUT THESE three women reminded Tobias of one of the hardest times in his young life. It was a time when he had to stand tall and face the pain of loss instead of quitting. He reached in the box and pulled out the little white button and the marble. He had been nine years old the night Ms. Ruby handed him that little white button and told him, "You have a choice, Toby Boy. You seldom get to choose what hits your life, but you do get to choose how you will respond. Put these in your box as a reminder that life is seldom fair, but on this day, you have decided to stand tall and live right anyway."

Holding the button and the marble brought back all the pain he had felt that day he had to decide to stand tall—regardless of how he felt.

Two weeks had passed since the riots had ended. All the black women and children had been ordered to remain inside, while all of the able black men were busy helping clean up our part of town. Two weeks of hunkering down in fear takes its toll, especially on a nine-year-old boy. I tried to stay focused on the good, but the reality of what had happened rattled my world. I tried not to think about all the terrible things going on out there, but I knew *out there* was waiting for me, and the thought frightened me. I didn't want to believe that innocent people could be hurt. I remember thinking, "Maybe the black men got mouthy and talked back. Maybe they were the shiftless bums who wandered the downtown streets. Ms. Pearl said they were always up to no good, stealing from those who work hard for what they have." I needed a good reason for this to have happened. If I could figure out what they had done wrong, and if I just did not do whatever it was that they had done, I would be safe. But then my mind went back to Miss Buttons, my beloved teacher. What in the world could be the reason for her death? What could she have done to deserve being killed? Then my mind would fill with fear and rage because, if she was not safe, then I would never be safe.

The first day back to school was filled with tension. As I walked down the street, I studied everyone, wondering what they had seen and had done during the riots. I was anxious to see all of my friends, but I feared that some of them might be gone. I didn't know what to think; I only knew that Miss Buttons would not be standing at the door that day. I would never again see her beautiful smile and shining eyes greet me as I entered her classroom. Even my aunties could not shelter me from this cold, hard fact. I was nine, and life was hard.

To be fair to our new teacher, I don't think there was anything she could have done to win us over. In our eyes she was an interloper; she did not belong in our schoolroom. Sulley's eyes blazed with anger as she waltzed into our room as big as life, leaned against Miss Buttons' desk and called the class to order. He could hardly contain himself when she tapped the desk with Miss Buttons' pointer and demanded the class's attention.

Of course, all of the girls quickly sat up straight and tall, but this attention only fueled Sulley's rage. He stood up and let his chair crash to the floor. He did not pick it up; instead, he just glared at Miss Jackson while he fought back tears. Miss Jackson stepped down off the platform and began walking toward Sulley, but he did not want anything to do with her. He picked up his cap, shoved it into his back pocket and stormed out the back door without saying a word. We all knew he was hurting at the loss of Miss Buttons; we all were.

If only we had been given a few minutes alone to mourn the loss of Miss Buttons together. We knew it wasn't Miss Jackson's fault, but since she was the one standing there, she felt all of our anger. I knew my feelings were wrong, but my loyalty to Miss Buttons and then to Sulley clouded my judgment that day.

When the class stood for the pledge, I remained seated. I did not want to pledge allegiance to a country that would allow someone to hurt my teacher. I remember feeling overwhelmed at everything I was thinking. I felt that a firestorm was in my mind. Only two weeks had passed since the Atlanta riots. Miss Buttons was dead, and I had finally heard all about what slavery had done to everyone I loved...and I was an angry boy.

All of Ms. Pearl and Ms. Ruby's warnings to me now fell on deaf ears. I wanted to lash out and hurt someone like I was hurting. I wanted to scream until all of the pain poured out of me. I wanted to slap that smile off Miss Jackson's face. How dare she smile at me? I wanted to go find Master Stewart's grave, dig him up and kick him as hard as I could. I wanted my grandpa, how I wanted my grandpa. I placed my head down on my desk and began to cry. I didn't care who saw me cry. I WANTED MY GRANDPA! I knew if I held in those tears, I would choke on them.

Thankfully, Miss Jackson did not approach me that morning. She allowed me to grieve without interruption. After the pledge, Ruth Naomi Johnson led the class in a hymn as she always did. But this time, she stood right beside my desk and laid her hand on my back. I had been smitten by her the first day of school, but that day—that was the day I fell in love with sweet, kind, understanding Ruth. I felt no condemnation from her. She did not say a word, but the feel of her hand on my back that day was priceless to me.

That evening I told my aunties what had happened at school. I knew I was in for a lecture from Ms. Pearl, and I knew I deserved it. "Tobias..." (She always called me 'Tobias' when she was serious), you have to understand something. You have a right to be angry. Losing your teacher was terrible, Tobias. Miss Buttons was a wonderful young lady, and she did not deserve what happened to her."

I did not want to start crying again, so I said, "Ms. Pearl, can we please not talk about Miss Buttons tonight?"

Ms. Pearl's gaze softened, and she came over to sit beside me. She placed my head on her lap and confessed, "Toby Boy, this has been a long hard day for you, but I think that Ruby and I are partly responsible for all the rage and anger you are feeling. Remember, we warned you that hearing the whole truth about our family was going to upset you? Maybe we should have given it to you in smaller doses. It is never easy to hear about injustice. You are only nine-years-old, Toby Boy. Most adults cannot handle the truth about slavery and hatred. I wish we could have sheltered you from the truth, but you need to understand that life is not fair. There is hatred in this world, Toby Boy. There is injustice and racism. This is our reality. This is why we need you to learn self-control and self-determination. Most of this world believes they have a right to control you and to determine for you what your life should look like. Toby, even though I hate it, sometimes we have to go along to get along. Maybe someday, things will change and the rules for everyone will be the same, but that day is not today."

Triggering on these last words, I sat up, wiped my eyes and said, "That is what Grandpa Samuel said to you in the livery."

Pearl smiled and patted my head, "That's right, Toby. It is when things are not fair that we need to be wise. You can get angry and storm out like Sulley did today; or you can be a good friend and place your hand on a hurting person's back and bring him comfort, like Ruth did for you today. We can't always remove the injustice, but we can always be a good and true friend."

Ms. Ruby slid off the couch and sat on the floor in front of me. "Toby Boy, do you think Sulley needs a good and true friend right now?"

"Yes, he does," I said with confidence, "but I don't know if he is ever coming back. You didn't see the look on his face today."

Ms. Ruby smiled, "I've seen that look. I've even given that look. When a friend is hurting so deep he cannot imagine ever feeling any other way, he needs a good and true friend to remind him that he is not alone. Toby, here is a brand-new, shiny white button. I think you should put it in your tin box, along with the button you have from Brother

Samuel. This button will always remind you of Miss Buttons. She should be remembered."

"You are right, Ms. Ruby. I will also put one of my marbles in my tin box as a reminder of my friend, Sulley."

The next morning I left for school thirty minutes early. I didn't really know where Sulley lived, but I had an idea. I knew he did not have a momma anymore. He lived with his daddy and his two older brothers. Sulley said it was every man for himself at his house. I had seen him turn the corner by the leather shop several times, so I decided I would walk real slowly, hoping Sulley would see me and come out onto his porch. Sure enough, out came Sulley, but he was not dressed for school. It looked like he was wearing an old pair of his daddy's overalls. He had rolled up the legs four or five times to keep from tripping over them. He had taken an old belt that looked like it had seen its share of kid beatings in its day. Sulley tightened the belt around his waist and let the extra leather hang in the wind. I stepped onto his porch and asked as casually as I could, "You coming to school today, Sulley?"

"Nah, no more school for me, Toby. I'm gunna start painting houses with my daddy and brothers. My daddy said schooling is a waste of time anyway. I only went because I liked Miss Buttons. She always told me I could learn if I really wanted to; but now that she is gone, there is no reason to go."

"Sulley, can we still be friends?"

"Sure we can, Toby. Not so sure how, now that I'll be working all the time and you being in school all the time. You're an all-right boy, Toby. Maybe I can stop by your house on Saturday mornings sometimes. I like your Auntie Ruby's biscuits. My brother, Jethro, makes bricks instead of biscuits. If you aren't careful, you can break a tooth on 'em."

I knew Sully was only half joking as I offered, "That's a deal, Sulley. I'm sure Ms. Ruby will even have lots of strawberry jam for your biscuits. See you Saturday." I heard Sulley whistling as he headed back into his house. I knew his brothers were always mean to him, but on that day, Sulley knew he had a good and true friend.

It was not easy warming up to Miss Jackson, but I promised my aunties that I would try, and I did. It slowly began to feel normal, but it would never again be the wonderful experience I had had with Miss Buttons. I focused on my studies and making friends. Without Sulley around, I had to reach out to the other boys and make myself forget how hard they had been on Sulley. I had to learn early that no one is perfect and that I had to give these boys another chance. It was not their fault that my friend was no longer at school.

Sulley came around nearly every Saturday. His father and brothers worked him hard and paid him very little. Ms. Pearl offered to school Sulley on Saturdays, but he was not interested, so we just fed him and remained his friends. Ms. Ruby would often mend his torn trousers and replace missing buttons. Eventually, Ms. Ruby found some used clothes that fit Sulley. Since his daddy and brothers did not believe in washing their clothes, Sulley would bring his wash over, and Ruby taught him how to use the washtub. He even began to wash himself while his clothes were hanging out to dry. I could see how much Sulley liked spending those Saturdays with us. At first, he ate fast, as if he had never eaten before. After a few Saturday dinners, Ms. Ruby came up with a trick. About thirty minutes before our dinner was ready to serve, she called Sulley into the kitchen and placed a whole plate of buttered biscuits in front of him. By the time we were called to the table, he was smiling contentedly, ready to enjoy his dinner instead of inhaling it.

Sulley loved story time. At first it was short stories that could be finished that same evening. He had a hard time remembering stories from week to week, and he would get frustrated when it took too long to finish. Sulley couldn't keep track of the different characters, always interrupting and asking someone to remind him who was who—until the Saturday that Ms. Pearl started reading *Treasure Island*. From the first page, Sulley was hooked. "Is this why my teacher, Miss Buttons, said it was so important that I learn how to read? So I could read stories like this?"

Ms. Pearl smiled, "This one and hundreds of others that are just as exciting, Sulley."

I chimed in, "Sulley, wait until she reads *The Count of Monte Cristo*. It is all about a young Frenchman named Edmond Dantès, who was sent to a terrible prison where he met a priest who taught him how to read, do mathematics, and how to fight with swords."

"You're joshing me, right?"

"No, Sulley," Ms. Pearl promised. "The world is full of wonderful books that can take you away to interesting places. When you know how to read, no one can stop you from going anywhere you want to go." Ms. Pearl walked over to the bookcase and began pulling out books. "Sulley, you want to go to France and find treasure chests filled with gold? *The Count of Monte Cristo* is the book. Do you want to follow the artful dodger through the streets of London? *Oliver Twist* is the book. You want to go sailing the open seas and fight a great white whale? Then *Moby-Dick* is the book for you. Sulley, do you want to be shipwrecked on an uncharted island, build an amazing tree house, and fight pirates? Then *The Swiss Family Robinson* is the book for you!' Turning back to Sulley, whose eyes were wide with wonder, she asked, "Where would you like to go next, Sulley?"

"Ms. Pearl, right now I would like to get back on that ship with Jim Hawkins. Do you think there really is a treasure? Is the map real? Will Jim survive?"

We all started laughing at how many details Sulley had remembered; he was hooked indeed. In a very serious tone, Sulley asked, "Ms. Pearl, how long would it take to learn how to read?"

"Sulley, it will take some time, but once you learn, no one can stop you."

It took about five years to teach Sulley how to read, and Ms. Pearl loved every minute of it. However, those five years were not without problems. At first, Sulley's only splurge from the meager wages his daddy paid him was to go down to the thrift store and buy *new* used clothes. Ms. Ruby did her best to alter the trousers to fit Sulley's large frame. We made sure not to laugh at him as he strutted around the house in his new outfit and proudly announced, "Ms. Ruby, now I can go to church with you all. No more globs of paint and belts to hold up trousers that don't fit me."

Sulley now had three whole outfits to wear to church. He even bought himself two pairs of dress shoes, but even Ms. Ruby could not get him to wear socks. "Ms. Ruby, my feet can't take being boiled in them socks. My feet need to breathe."

It was fun watching Sulley strut around, proud as a peacock. I don't believe he had ever felt so proud. The night before his first Sunday church meeting, Sulley asked, "Ms. Ruby, do you think you could give me a haircut? I can't even get a comb through this nappy mop of mine. I bought myself a jar of hair wax, but I need someone to cut off all these dry, dead knots first."

Ms. Ruby gladly sat him down out on the back porch, wrapped a towel around his shoulders and went after that mop of hair in earnest. She had wanted to tackle it for months but did not want to hurt his feelings. Sulley ordered me to stay inside so it would be a surprise when it was all cut and slicked back, neat and clean. Ms. Ruby even talked him into shaving off all the peach fuzz he had been sporting for months.

We invited Sulley to sleep over so he could have Sunday breakfast before walking to church with us for the first time. Looking at him all dressed up, with his hair slicked back, clean-shaven, and smiling, it was easy to forget that Sulley was only thirteen. He was a young boy, trapped in a grown man's body, but that morning all was right with the world.

Sulley studied all the men at church and whispered, "Toby, with my next payday, I'm gunna get me a tie. All the men here wear ties. I'm gunna get me one."

I was only ten years old, and the last thing I wanted to wear was a tie, but I could see how much the idea meant to Sulley. All the ladies at church made such a fuss over him—all neat and clean as he was.

As exciting as this time was, watching Sulley change was not without its difficulties. The next Saturday morning Sulley showed up for his lessons a heartbroken, angry boy. "Ms. Pearl, you know what my brother Jethro did? Last night he was going out dancing and wore my clothes. He didn't even ask if he could. He just took 'em. I begged my daddy to stop him, but he wouldn't. He just told me to shut up. He came home about two hours ago, smelling awful."

"Oh, Sulley," Ms. Pearl consoled, "we can wash the smell out of your clothes."

"Won't do no good, Ms. Pearl. Jethro caught my trousers on a nail and tore a big hunk out of the seat. His feet were too big for my new shoes, and he stretched them way out of shape and scuffed them up something awful. He just threw my clothes on my bed and went to sleep. It didn't matter to him that I had worked all summer to earn those clothes."

As he recounted his story, I could not help but remember how proud he felt in those clothes only the week before. Now they were ruined, and I got angry. "Sulley, you should go burn Jethro's favorite stuff. Show him how it feels."

"He will do no such thing, Tobias!" When Ms. Ruby used my name in that tone, I knew I was in for a lecture. Instead, she sat a plate of biscuits down in front of Sulley and smiled. "Sulley, it's not fair that your daddy and brothers don't respect your things, and it is not likely that they will ever change. Your burning their things won't teach them a lesson. It will only make you just like them. So Sulley, how are you going to respond to this injustice? Do you fight back—take their prized possessions? Do you run away? If you start running, Sulley, you had better be ready to run for the rest of your life because there is lots of injustice in this world. Or, do you find a peaceful way to limit the injustice, all the while living a life you can be proud of?"

Auntie Ruby softened her voice and asked, "Sulley, do you remember how proud you felt last Sunday? Boy, it was not the clothes that made you proud. It was the fact that you had worked hard, earned those clothes, cleaned yourself up, and stood tall and proud of the young man you are becoming. Your daddy and brothers will never understand or feel what you felt last Sunday."

"But Ms. Ruby, now I can't go to church with you. I don't have anything to wear, and it will take too long to earn enough to buy new clothes."

Standing up and displaying his painting overalls, he sorrowfully said, "I can't wear these to church."

"And why not, Sully? Are you ashamed of being a hard-working painter? Do you think those ladies at church cannot see past the paint-stained overalls and see a good, clean, proud young man standing in those overalls? It's never the clothes, Sulley. It's the person in those clothes that matters."

Then Aunt Ruby suggested, "So how do we limit the injustice of your daddy and brothers? As soon as you earn enough to buy something new, you can keep your new clothes here. Your family is never going to change, so you work around them. You come here every Sunday and get dressed for church. After church, you come back here and carefully put away your clothes for the next Sunday and change back into your overalls. That is one way to limit the injustice. Don't retaliate, but also, don't give them another bite at the apple. Sometimes keeping the peace is just not tempting the other person to take advantage of you."

That first Sunday wearing his painted-coveralls was not easy for Sulley, but the women of the church acted great. One lady actually commented on one of the paint colors, saying she'd like that color on her shutters. Before we headed home, Sully had his first customer.

By the time we were walking back home, Sulley was walking as straight and tall as the week before. Two weeks later Sulley was able to buy a pair of trousers, and Ms. Ruby took leftover material and made up a nice dress shirt that fit him perfectly. One week later, Ms. Pearl struck a deal with Sulley. She would buy the paint and every Saturday, after his reading lesson, Sulley would scrape and paint all of the trim on the house in exchange for a new suit, an extra set of trousers, and a pair of dress shoes. I remember suggesting, "Sulley, you need to have the sisters throw in a tie with that deal;" which they agreed to gladly.

CHAPTER 25

Dissension in The Church

As THE TWO sisters cared for Sulley, they also had to make other hard decisions in life. For several years after the riots, no other topics of discussion were addressed. Many people would have thought the issues were simply black versus white, but they would have been wrong. The lines had been drawn; you were either with them or against them. You were either militant or passive. If you were not willing to risk everything you had to fight this injustice, you were considered, "one of them tokens"—a name hated by everyone, on either side.

Everyone had an opinion about how unfairness should be addressed. The one matter everyone did seem to be in agreement on was the unfairness. However, unfairness was about the only matter everyone could agree upon.

Most colored churches in Atlanta became embroiled in this discord. The militants were loud and demanded that every sermon be a lesson about injustice, which would fire up the congregation to a fever pitch, sending them out to do brazenly foolish acts to prove that they were not tokens.

Many a promising young man was lost to the hangman's noose during those terrible years. Every time one of these fired-up young men went out and refused to "shuffle and duck," he became the target for many a white man's rage. The year was 1913, and white folks were not yet ready to surrender their rights. "How dare a darkie not show me the respect I deserve!" With every hanging, the camp lines were drawn thicker. For some, the unjustified retribution signified a need to slow down and to protect the young men from danger; for the militant, the reprisals fueled their fire to fight back.

One thing everyone of color agreed upon was things needed to change. The arguments grew out of when and how to bring these changes into being. My mind returned to the uncertainness of life in Atlanta in those days.

We all attended Cleveland Street Baptist Church. The sisters had been going there since Ruby returned home so many years earlier. The Right Reverend Jonah Gates had been the sisters' pastor for the past fifteen years, and up until the riots, their church was perfect. They had been known for their community outreach, and Rev. Gates was a true soul winner. His fiery sermons had driven more than a few lost souls to the altar, but everything changed after the riots.

Rev. Gates and his only son had been out checking on members of the church on the second night of the riots. They had taken supplies from the community pantry and were trying to deliver food to the shut-ins. On the last block, he and his son split up so they could finish more quickly and get back home themselves. They had agreed to meet under the twin oaks at the entrance to the city park. Rev. Gates found Mrs. Carlyle barricaded in her living room, and she had been without food or water for two days. He filled her water jug and gave her a loaf of bread and a jar of jam. He did not feel right about leaving her alone immediately, so he spent more time with her than he had intended, leaving his son, J.G., Jr., alone and unprotected. By the time the pastor made his way to the twin oaks, he found the lifeless, badly beaten body of his only son.

Rev. Gates never really recovered from his loss. His once open and loving spirit became hard and bitter. All of his dreams had died with his son, and he wanted justice for J.G., Jr. The longer that justice was denied, the deeper his bitterness grew. His sermons were now filled with bitter recitations of how every black person must fight back against these injustices. With nothing else to lose, Rev. Gates used his pulpit to incite the young men to action.

I was only nine when all of this unrest started, but I remember several funerals of young black men who, once fired up by Rev. Gates, had gone out to prove they were no longer willing to "shuffle and duck" in the presence of white men. I remember Rev. Gates' saying how proud he was of these young men, but then I looked over at their mothers and wondered, "How proud are they? They have also lost a son, but to what end? There must be a better way to press for change."

I do remember the night this argument came into our house. I had quickly finished my homework that night because I was anxious to hear the next chapter in the book Ms. Pearl was reading to us. Normally, all of our books were purchased from the used book cart, but this novel was purchased new as a gift to me. Before sharing this new book with Sulley, Ms. Pearl wanted just the three of us to enjoy it. Jack London's novel, *The Call of the Wild*, was set in the Yukon during the 1890s Klondike Gold Rush—a time when strong sled dogs were in high demand. *The Call of the Wild* was a story to capture the heart of mind of every young boy of eleven. We were only a few chapters into the book, but I already knew I wanted to go to the Yukon, get a team of dogs, and have an adventure!

Ms. Pearl had only read the opening line of the next chapter when, frustrating both of us, Ms. Ruby interrupted. "Pearl, we need to talk."

We could tell she had been out of sorts throughout dinner. Something was definitely on her mind, and she needed to talk. Pearl set down the book and looked at me. "Tobias, I think we should forego our reading tonight. Ruby and I need to talk, and I do not believe you should be part of this conversation. Would you please pick up your schoolbooks and go to your room?"

Even though I was only eleven, I was seldom banished from any conversations in that house. Our family was open and loving, always careful to respect the other person's viewpoint. I started to protest, but with a smile and nod of her head, Ms. Ruby dismissed me without any further discussion. I made my way to my room, knowing something big was up between my aunties. I heard Ms. Pearl order Ruby to stop pacing around and to take a seat. "So what is bothering you, Sister? It must be something huge for you to interrupt our story time."

"I'm sorry, Pearl, I just can't concentrate on make-believe stories of great adventures when we have so much trouble to deal with right here at home."

Once I was certain they were deep in conversation, I slipped out of my bed and opened my bedroom door. I knew Ms. Ruby was upset about something, and I wanted to know what that something was.

"Pearl, doesn't it bother you what the preacher is saying every week? Don't you feel responsible to do something about it?"

Confused, Pearl asked, "Ruby, what was so different about yesterday's sermon? Pastor has beaten that same drum for two years now. Nothing ever seems to change. Rev. Gates lost his son in the riots, and you and I are trying to be patient and understanding with him."

"Pearl," Ruby almost cried in frustration, "I understand his anger, but church is supposed to be about God's love, not about hate."

"Ruby, I know I have always been pushier than you. It has gotten me into more than one difficult spot. You, on the other hand, can patiently sit and wait for things to be righted, where I cannot help but boil up in anger when I see a wrong and feel compelled to step in to fight for justice."

"Sister, we all fight against injustice in our own way. Just because I don't react like you do doesn't mean I'm not doing my part."

"I know that, Ruby. I'm not calling you a coward."

"But others do! Right, Pearl? I don't care what others call me as long as I know I'm doing what I am supposed to be doing."

"I think you misunderstand what is bothering me, Sister. You and I both agree that things need to change. Things have needed to change since our time above the livery."

Now confused, Pearl asked, "What are you talking about, Sister? I thought you were saying we needed to join Rev. Gates in protesting all the wrongs we see."

"On the contrary, Sissy, I believe you and I need to make a decision tonight. We are responsible for two young boys. God has put their care in our hands. It is up to us to rear these boys into godly young men who will love God, love their fellowman, and live honorable lives. Rev. Gates, for whatever his reasons, has turned his back on the Gospel. Instead, he is preaching a dangerous message of hate, rebellion, and civil disobedience. I'm not saying there is not a place for such talk. Somehow, this country needs to face what is happening, and change needs to come. I am saying what does it matter if all our young men have been hanged from the nearest tree and go into an eternity without God? All Tobias and Sulley are hearing each week is hate and war. Sissy, our loyalty must first be to these two boys. We need to find a church where redemption of the soul is the focus—not the redemption of our rights."

With the sound of great relief in her voice, Aunt Pearl responded, "Oh, Sister, I have been thinking this for months. Now that Sulley is coming along with us, we need to find a place where both of our boys can grow and learn."

One week later Ms. Ruby and Ms. Pearl invited Pastor Johnson over for pie and coffee. I was allowed to sit at the table and listen, but I had been instructed to remain quiet. As he entered our living room, I thought to myself, "So you are Ruth's father"—a detail I kept to myself. I watched as the sisters peppered the pastor with questions from salvation to social injustice.

Pastor Johnson had obviously been grilled on the topic of social injustice many times throughout his ministry, and he was ready. "Ms. Pearl, Ms. Ruby, we all know there is a lot wrong with how things are right now. It has always been so, and it will always be so. I pray every day that God would send a strong, godly man who can lead the way to force fairer laws and that God would change the hearts of those who look at us as less than human. That being said, ladies, I do not believe that I am that man. God had given me a heart to teach His Word and win the lost. For that, I do not apologize. While everyone is looking for justice and fairness, I can boldly say, I know exactly where you need to go to find the fairest spot on earth. Jesus did not die on a white cross, nor did He die on a black one. The Bible says He died for the sins of the whole world—black, white, Jew, or Greek—Jesus died for all of us. When we stand at the foot of His cross and accept His payment for our sins—that ground at the foot of the cross is level ground. There are no second-class believers. There are no special bloodlines, except for His blood, which was shed for all of us. If I preach the cross of Christ, I am preaching the truest form of social justice.

"Ladies, what does it matter if we fight for our rights but stand wrong and condemned before our God? It is my job to win souls."

Once satisfied that this man had not abandoned his first love, the sisters made their decision. Two weeks later, the four of us walked into the Second Methodist Church of Atlanta, where the father of Ruth Naomi Johnson pastored.

CHAPTER 26

The Whippoorwill Calls

WE SETTLED INTO a calm routine, and time passed by quickly. I turned thirteen the year I completed my six years of school. Ms. Pearl then arranged for me to take correspondence classes from Spellman College. I was much too young to attend, but the college had a wonderful program of mathematics, languages, and history.

Sulley was now sixteen and beginning to read well enough to read on his own—as long as the stories were uncomplicated and exciting. His daddy and brothers continued to take advantage of him, but Sulley was learning ways to protect himself without losing his dignity. One day he stopped by the house to ask a question. "I would like to bring by a girl to meet you. I know you will like her."

Ms. Pearl, always so direct and to the point, asked, "Where did you meet this girl, Sulley?"

"Oh, she lives down the street from me. I've known her since she was eight."

"Okay," paused Ms. Pearl, trying to figure out where this was going. "So how old is she?"

"She's fourteen, I think. She has had a hard life, Ms. Pearl. I want her to meet you and Ms. Ruby. I don't think she believes there are really people as kind as you two are."

Obviously embarrassed at questioning his motives, Ms. Pearl backpedaled, "We'd love to meet this girl, Sulley. Why don't you bring her around this evening about seven for a piece of pie and conversation? She might not feel comfortable sitting down to dinner on her first visit."

Sulley picked up his hat and headed for the kitchen door with a huge smile on his face. "I'll go ask her right now," and out the door he went.

He wasn't ten steps from the door before Ms. Pearl was all over this situation. "Sissy, you don't think Sulley is in love, do you?"

Always more cautious and careful not to jump to any conclusions, Aunt Ruby suggested, "Pearl, let's just wait and see. No sense in borrowing trouble. Besides, now I have a pie to bake—thank you very much."

We finished dinner a little early that night, and while I dried the dishes, I heard Ms. Ruby suggest, "Now Pearl, why don't you let me take the lead? We both know that you tend to drill down to the point way too quickly, and you might scare her off."

"Would that be such a bad thing, Sissy? Our Sulley is not ready to get serious with anyone just yet."

"Pearl, we are not going to fix, or break anything here tonight. We are just visiting with a young girl and getting to know her."

Pearl smiled at me as she walked back into the kitchen. "I do tend to push a little hard, don't I, Toby?"

I did not say a word.

Promptly at seven o'clock, the front doorbell jingled. Sulley pushed the girl forward and said, "Hi everyone, this is Whippoorwill Gumm. Whippoorwill, this is Ms. Pearl, Ms. Ruby, and this is my best friend, Tobias, but everyone calls him Toby."

Ms. Ruby guided the shy girl into the living room and said, "Good evening, Whippoorwill, it's nice to meet you."

Aunt Ruby's smile softened the moment, and before long Whippoorwill relaxed and began telling us all about herself. "You probably wonder about my name, right? That's okay, everybody does. I usually get something like, 'You gunna sing for us, Whippoorwill?' Everybody thinks they are the first one to think of that."

Aunt Ruby chuckled, "I'm glad I didn't say that—although I must admit I thought of it. So child, how did you come about that name?"

"You see, I was born in North Carolina, the third daughter, born one month after my daddy was hanged for stealing chickens. I was named such because the night I was born, the whippoorwills were singing their mournful song so loud outside that my momma said she could not think of anything else. She said their song was so sad, all she could think about was how I was never going to know my daddy and that made her sad too. So I got the name Whippoorwill Gumm. About a month after I came, my momma wanted to get us away from there because she didn't want us girls to be known as the daughters of a chicken thief, so she made her way back here to Atlanta to be close to family."

"So you have family here?" Ruby prodded gently.

"We did. Momma's momma was here, as was her older sister. But they are both gone now."

"I am so sorry, child," Ms. Ruby consoled; "it's hard when people we love die."

"Oh, they didn't die, Ms. Ruby. They just did not like the man my momma married, so they up and moved to Mobile, Alabama."

"Oh," Ms. Ruby chuckled. "So your momma got remarried, did she?"

"Yes, ma'am. My grandma said my momma didn't even wait until her man was cold in the grave. I don't rightly remember a time when Mr. Bartholomew wasn't married to my momma."

"So he became your new daddy?"

"No, ma'am; he married my momma, but he made sure us girls never forgot we wasn't his. I guess my momma was right to name me Whippoorwill. They say the whippoorwills' mournful song in the wee hours of the morning is the sound of them dreading the beginning of another painful day; that about sums up my life."

Softhearted teddy bear, Sulley, was all mush at the telling of this story. It was obvious to all of us that Sulley wanted to rescue Whippoorwill from her circumstances. Even though he had now lived in a man-sized body for three years, he was still a boy and not ready to take on the responsibilities of a family. Sulley was far from ready to strike out on his own, let alone take care of another person.

That evening, after Sulley and Whippoorwill left, we sat at the kitchen table and talked about this situation into the wee hours of the morning.

We knew Sulley felt responsible for this girl. We also knew that if we did not help Whippoorwill, Sulley would do something rash and ruin his life because of trying to save her. Ms. Ruby finally said, "That Whippoorwill is a child without an anchor, and she will tether herself onto anyone she feels is steady and true. We need to get her into church where her only true hope can be found. We need to keep Sulley busy so he does not mistake concern and pity for love."

True to his word, Sulley began bringing Whippoorwill to church with him. Ruth quickly introduced herself to the new visitor and soon they became fast friends. A week or two later, at Pearl's suggestion, Pastor Johnson invited Sulley to go fishing and talked to him about the difference between caring and loving. He was able to talk to Sulley about things two older women could not talk about—and certainly things his daddy and brothers never bothered talking about to him. Sulley paid attention to what his pastor said. He stayed her friend, but after that talk, he stayed her *distant* friend, always making sure Ruth was close by whenever he needed to be rescued himself.

For four years, the four of us were inseparable. At the beginning, Ruth and I believed we were sort of chaperons for Sulley and Whippoorwill. We worked at the community pantry, delivering necessities to families in need and sharing the gospel whenever we had the chance. But somewhere along that journey, the tables turned. Ruth and I both knew our affection for each other was getting dangerously strong. As with Sulley and Whippoorwill, we were much too young to act upon these feelings. Pastor Johnson kept a close eye on Ruth, and the sisters were ever mindful of my whereabouts. We had both been reared to believe we had important work to do—not necessarily great work, but important work. I, for one, loved working alongside Ruth and did not want my devotion to her to rob me of my ability to continue our association. I knew if I did not keep my passion under control, I would lose her forever.

Ruth found Whippoorwill a job at the hospital bakery. The two of them were caked in bread flour all day long, giggling and talking as they turned out bread, rolls, pies, and cookies. Ruth would talk about how much

God loved Whippoorwill, and that her name was just a name—one that did not destine her to a life of mournful sadness.

One Sunday, when Sulley had just turned twenty, he came to me and asked, "Toby, would you walk down the aisle with me this morning? You have been my best friend. I would like you with me when I walk down and ask Pastor Johnson to baptize me."

The two of us stood in the last pew, waiting for the altar call to begin. Sulley was excited and kept moving from one foot to the other, like a race-horse's waiting for the chute to open so he could take off.

Pastor Johnson's invitation was especially long that morning, explaining what it meant to accept the gift of salvation. Little did Sulley and I know that while waiting for our turn, someone else was also waiting for exactly the right time. Suddenly, Whippoorwill stepped out of her pew, took hold of Ruth's hand, and walked down to the altar. Pastor Johnson smiled as he greeted her and quietly talked with her before announcing, "Brothers and sisters, Miss Whippoorwill Gumm has come forward this morning to accept Jesus as her Savior. Ruth and I have talked with her, and we believe her confession is sincere. We extend the right hand of fellow-ship to this young woman."

Sulley stood there stunned. "Toby, I don't know what to do. Should I still go forward?"

I knew what he meant. He did not want to take away Whippoorwill's moment, so I whispered, "Sulley, there is always room at the altar for everyone. You made your decision before you knew about her decision. Nothing has changed. Come on, let's go."

That morning, Ruth and I stood next to our friends, Sullivan Dunbar and Whippoorwill Gumm, listening to their statements of faith and com-mitment. Little did either of us realize that this would be the first of many that we, together, would bring to our Lord's altar. I was just seventeen years old, but I had loved this girl since I was seven.

CHAPTER 27

My Faith Was Tested

EVEN THOUGH WE continued to hear terrible stories about violence happening around the country, thanks to the sisters, my life remained unaltered throughout my teens. I did not experience the daily unfair treatment that Sulley experienced at the hands of his own family. I was kept busy with correspondence lessons, church work, and chaperoned youth socials. In a word, I lived in a bubble. I was not naïve about the world around me, simply protected from it. It is funny how, at eighteen, you have an answer for everything; but by the age of twenty, you realize how much you do not yet know.

There are times, as I look back upon my youth, when I realize how much more like Ms. Pearl I was than I would care to admit. I had been schooled well. I knew things, and I was quick to share what I knew. To be fair, I guess that is the toxic nature of youth. Although I had benefited from the gentle nature of Ms. Ruby for most of my life, I found myself short-tempered and frustrated with those who could not, or would not, see matters as I saw them. I was quick to point out the error of their thinking, and if that lack of knowledge or understanding shamed them, so be it; truth was truth. Oh, how even remembering my bluntness all these years later embarrasses me.

On the other hand, Ruth was much more like Ms. Ruby, and she became a huge mirror for me. When I would get frustrated, she would gently step in and smooth over the feathers that I had ruffled. She always told the truth, but somehow, Ruth's ability to tell the same truth that I was attempting to tell with her gentle and humble spirit made it far easier for the listener to accept.

I knew my pride and arrogance were going to get me into trouble, so I began tapering them. I remember walking into meetings, determined to be humble and quiet, only to end the meeting with a frustrated declaration of exactly how wrong these people were. More than once, I would catch Ruth's eye, and she would smile at me and shake her head in disappointment at my behavior. Those were long, long nights.

In my youthful arrogance, I could not understand, if truth was standing right in front of him, why that person couldn't choose truth. It seemed so simple to me…until the night Truth was standing right in front of me.

Sulley had been saving every penny of his hard-earned wages for almost two years. Fearing his brothers would steal it, he kept his savings at my house. Sullivan "Sulley" Dunbar was twenty-three when he proposed to Whippoorwill. They had a quiet, intimate living room ceremony at my house because they wanted to use his savings to buy everything they would need to set-up housekeeping. Although he invited his daddy and brothers to the wedding, only his older brother, Jethro, showed up.

Ruth and I helped them get their place in shape, and we were their first dinner guests. Sulley was so proud to be sitting at his own table in his own home, which was clean and neat as a pin. After dinner he guided us into the living room, but since their place was so tiny, it was actually just a step or two away from the kitchen table. But that did not matter to Sulley. It was his place, and Whippoorwill sat right beside him, just as proud as he was.

After coffee, Sulley suggested he read a chapter from the book he and his bride were now reading. Ruth and I held hands and rejoiced with our friends. I, for one, could not resist thinking about having a place like this to share with Ruth one day soon. As we said goodnight and I walked Ruth home, I remember feeling that all was right with the world.

That night I was awakened at four in the morning to pounding on our front door. There stood Sulley, drenched in sweat and filled with rage. At first I could not even understand what he was saying to me. All I knew was something terrible had happened to Whippoorwill, and he needed my help. I threw on some clothes and followed Sulley back to his tiny place. Everything was in ruins. The kitchen table was busted up, the settee he had worked so hard to reupholster was ripped open, and all of the stuffing scattered around. Their dishes had been thrown around the room, shattering into little pieces as they struck the walls. "Sulley, who did this?"

"My brother, Neville. He got drunk and came over here to teach me a lesson. He kept screaming at me things like how I think I'm so much better than Jethro and him. I tried to stop him, Toby, but Neville was out of his mind drunk. The more I got in his face, the meaner he got. I was afraid he was going to hurt Whippoorwill. He said he was going to take her and show her how a real man makes love. I got her into the bedroom and stood in the doorway. He was not going to get by me. If I had to kill my own brother, he was not getting past me."

"Sulley, where is Whippoorwill?"

"She is in there." Sulley nodded his head toward the bedroom. "I have never seen her so scared, Toby. I couldn't get her to come with me. It was like she couldn't hear me talking to her."

"Sulley, where is Neville? Why did you leave Whippoorwill alone when you came to get me?"

"Because, Toby, Neville can never hurt Whippoorwill ever again."

"What did you do, Sulley? Where is Neville?"

"He is out in the bushes, Toby. He would not stop. He was going to get by me and hurt my wife. I could not let that happen. I am her protector. That's my job, right?"

Calmly taking his arm, I suggested, "Sulley, let's go see Neville. Are you sure he is dead?"

The reality of what he had just done began to settle in, and Sulley began to shake. "I broke his neck, Toby. I didn't mean to, honest. He just would not stop, and I grabbed hold of him and lifted his feet off the ground so I could carry him outside—away from Whippoorwill. I guess I must have turned his head too far to the side because when I got him outside and dropped him, he just crumpled to the ground and didn't move. That's when I came running to you. What am I going to do now, Toby?"

My brain would not work. All of a sudden I had no answers—no absolute right or wrong. My best friend just killed his brother. It was 1917 in Atlanta, Georgia. We both knew what the white police would do to Sulley. It wouldn't matter that Neville broke into their place, tore it up, and threatened Whippoorwill. Sulley was a black man, and he had just killed someone.

Still with no answers, I at least regained my voice and suggested, "First of all, Sulley, we need to get Whippoorwill out of here. We need to get her to Ruth so she can take care of her. Once we know she is safe, you and I have to figure out what to do."

I waited in the living room while Sulley struggled to get clothes on his bride. I could hear her confused mind asking, "What just happened, Sulley? Where are we going? Sulley, I don't want to go out into the living room. That man wants to hurt me."

Whippoorwill's mind was all muddled. The fear of seeing Sulley fighting off that attacker was more than she could handle. I decided I could help Sulley by keeping my voice calm and calling out to her from the living room, "Whippoorwill, it's me, Tobias. I am standing here in the living room. It's safe now you can come out here. Sulley and I want to take you to Ruth. Would you like that? Would you like to see Ruth?"

Sulley carried his exhausted wife all the way to Ruth's house. Pastor Johnson answered the door, and I saw both Ms. Pearl and Ms. Ruby standing behind him. They did not know any details, but they all knew the situation was bad, and they had been praying.

Ruth pulled back the sheets and told Sulley to place Whippoorwill in her bed. Ruth then promised, "I won't leave her side, Sulley. You go do what you need to do. Don't you worry about your wife."

As we reentered the living room, I was not sure how much we should say just yet, but Sulley told them everything. Everyone stood silent and stunned. Finally, Sulley asked, "Should I go to the police? It is almost light out, and someone is going to see Neville."

Pastor Johnson grimaced at the thought of his going to the police. "I sure wish there was a policeman we could trust. Do you ladies know any by name?"

Sulley spoke up, "Doesn't really matter right now. When Neville doesn't show up for work this morning, my daddy is going to come looking for him. Neville never held much importance to our daddy, but he sure held a sight more than I ever did."

Needing to say something, Ms. Pearl offered, "Sulley, you have God on your side; don't you forget that."

Instantly, I was at war. My head agreed with Aunt Pearl, but this time my heart would not go along with it. Any other time I would have said exactly that. Black and white, right and wrong, good and bad—simple, right? Suddenly, all my lines began to blur. I knew what Ms. Pearl was saying was factually true. Sulley was a child of God, and God takes care of His children—true. But facing the reality of taking my best friend to the white police of Atlanta and expecting fairness… Can God really overcome that?

I was standing face to face with what I knew was true, but I was having a hard time putting my trust in it. I was having a hard time placing my best friend's future in that truth. Could I actually trust God to bring Sulley through this ordeal? If I could not trust God here, then where? If not now, then when? Suddenly my pride and arrogance were gone. I realized it was never about *my* answers, but about the One in whom I had trusted. I humbly began to ask for just enough faith to trust my God enough to stand in His truth.

Also feeling at a loss, Pastor Johnson suggested, "I believe we need to gather up all the men of the church and escort Sulley to the police station. Maybe, if they see that he has a large support group behind him, they will not dare mistreat him."

As we all started thinking of men to contact, Sulley's voice brought everyone to attention. "Pardon me, Pastor, but remember the Bible story you taught last Sunday? In Numbers, Chapter thirteen, the spies were sent into the Promised Land and came back fearful because they saw giants. They said they felt like grasshoppers in their sight. Ten of them warned that the giants were too big, but two of the spies said the people should go in and face the giants. They said, 'If God is for us, who can stand against us?' Pastor, you said that when we feel like grasshoppers facing the giants, we need to stand with God because grasshoppers plus God are always greater than giants.

"Pastor, I am feeling like a grasshopper right now, and the police are my giants. I am not walking into that police station all alone. I am not green enough to think I can trust the police to be fair to me. I know, in my heart, that I am not guilty of murder. I also know that my personal belief alone will not save me. I want to stand and see the salvation of the Lord; I want the Lord to fight for me. I don't want to try to outsmart the police or to show up with so many men that they back down. I want my God to rescue me—His poor little grasshopper. Will you stand with me and pray that God will give me the courage to do this?"

"Of course I will, Sulley," Pastor Johnson cried out. "I am so proud of you, young man. I might have preached that sermon, but you are wise enough to want to live it. I would be honored."

I stood there amazed at Sulley's faith. I could have repeated Pastor Johnson's sermon verbatim because I knew it; but Sulley was willing to live it. I had been trying to taper my pride and arrogance with pride and arrogance. Pride is believing we are giants, when in fact, we are but grasshoppers. Arrogance is believing an insignificant grasshopper can fight a giant. But true faith is realizing that a grasshopper who trusts in God to fight for him can stand up to the giants of this world.

Thirty minutes later, on Saturday morning, May 19, 1917, the three of us walked into the police headquarters on Decatur Street in Atlanta. Sulley asked to speak with a detective and told him his story. Pastor and I remained in the lobby, praying quietly. We knew, from other men's experiences, that the first twenty-four hours were going to be the most dangerous for Sulley. If some rough officers were going to pull him out the back door and exercise their own form of justice, it would be then.

We did not talk. We did not question. We prayed. All day Saturday, we prayed. As other men found out about what was going on, one or two at a time joined us in silent prayer for Sulley's protection. By late Saturday, Neville's body had been taken away, his father notified, and the police had been in and out of Sulley's place all day long. It was obvious to all that

Sulley's story rang true. However, in 1917, the police were less interested in defending a black man's rights than bringing about swift and total justice—as they perceived it. We kept praying.

First thing Monday morning, Sulley was shackled and delivered before the circuit judge. The police intended to charge Sulley with manslaughter. Five of us were sitting in the balcony of the courthouse when Sulley was escorted in. As best as we could determine, he had not yet been beaten.

We waited while the judge heard every case involving a white defendant or victim. At noon, without hearing Sulley's charges, the judge closed the courtroom for the lunch hour. Sulley was returned to police headquarters to wait for the afternoon session to be reopened. We prayed.

Anyone who knows the history of Atlanta, Georgia, knows what happened shortly after noon on Monday, May 21, 1917, a clear, warm and sunny day with a brisk breeze from the south. A small fire at the Candler Warehouse across the tracks from West End broke out around 11:30 a.m.. At 11:43, embers flew seven blocks north and destroyed three houses, and at 12:15, south of the Georgia Railroad from the big fire, ten homes were destroyed before being extinguished. At 12:46 a call came from a small warehouse just north of Decatur Street between Fort and Hilliard, and the crew sent to inspect it found a stack of burning mattresses but had no firefighting equipment with them. If the fire department had not already been spread across so many different parts of the city, the fire would have been put out there; but by the time reinforcements arrived, it was quickly leaping north.

Because eighty-five percent of the buildings in downtown Atlanta were roofed with wooden shingles, the fire spread quickly. By the end of the day, over 300 acres and much of the Fourth Ward had been destroyed, including nearly 2,000 homes, businesses and churches. At least 10,000 people were displaced. The city's losses were estimated at about $5.5 million dollars.

The courthouse remained closed that whole week. Once it reopened, the judge heard the charges against Sulley and shouted at the district attorney, "What do you think you are doing here, Carlton? Even your own officers say it was self-defense. This city has just had a terrible disaster that is going to cost millions of dollars to rebuild what was burned down. If you want to go coon huntin', you do it on your own time. I am not going to waste this city's resources on a trial like this." Turning to Sulley, the judge said, "Boy, you are free to go."

Around the dinner table that evening, we all discussed the fire. It had not been deliberately set by anyone. Everything pointed to a merging of weather, materials, and an electrical short. Did God cause that fire, or did He simply use the event that was already going to happen to protect and free His child?

Sulley brought the discussion to a close with, "If God can part the waters of the Red Sea, drop the walls of Jericho, and close the mouth of a lion, He can take care of His children."

Tobias smiled as he rolled the marble around in his hand and calculated to himself, "It has been thirty-seven years since Sulley taught me that having all the right answers is never as important as living out the right answers that you do know."

Looking out the window, Tobias thought about all the times since 1917 that Sulley had responded in simply faith. Being right is never as important as responding right—that it is not *what* you know, but *who* you trust. As a kid, although he had always cared about Sulley, he knew he had always felt quite superior to him—until that experience with the law. Sulley had always been a humble boy, whereas he had struggled with pride. Seeing Sulley's strong faith back then was an important lesson he never wanted to forget. Knowledge without faith is arrogance. After that experience, he never again felt superior to Sulley.

CHAPTER 28

The War in Europe

THE PORTER CAME through the car, announcing, "Lynchburg, Virginia, in twenty minutes. Lynchburg, Virginia, in twenty minutes. Ladies and gentlemen, this will be a one-hour layover. All passengers must leave the train while the locomotives are being changed."

Tobias secured their belongings on the upper shelf and put on his suit coat again. Since nothing in the suitcase was of any real value, he did not worry about leaving it behind; however, his tin box was quite another matter. Though it contained nothing of monetary value, to him, its contents were all priceless. The tin box contained his whole world, and he did not want to lose it. He tucked it under his arm and walked back to Ruth and Clara. "Clara, would you and your grandchildren like to join Ruth and me for dinner?" A look of concern washed over her face and Tobias quickly added, "It will be our treat."

"We would like that, Mr. Bascom, but is there somewhere close that will serve us?"

Every colored traveler knows exactly what Clara was asking. Tobias offered a reassuring smile, "The porter said there is a nice place called Warren's Café on Buchanan and 12th that will serve us. It is located only one block from the station. He said Mr. Warren is a nice man, and they have a side door for coloreds. We have plenty of time to walk there, eat, and return before our time is up."

Clara, a woman of some mass, did not like the idea of climbing off the train or walking up the hill, but a free meal convinced her it was worth the effort. Besides, she had no choice about climbing off the train. Everyone had to disembark before the conductor could change engines.

242

Ruth walked with Clara while Tobias walked with the children. Ten-year-old Rodney and seven-year-old Sheila were silent all the way to the café. Even simple chatter seemed beyond their comfort level, so Tobias decided not to push them to talk and focused on walking. He could feel Rodney's eyes studying him, but every time he looked over, Rodney turned away.

Both children were silent throughout dinner, and Clara ignored them. Suspecting that this was their regular routine, Tobias decided not to ask about dessert. Instead, he called the waitress over and asked, "What kind of ice cream do you have today?"

He watched the children's eyes as the waitress rattled off several flavors, then said, "Well, I would like two scoops of chocolate." Turning to Rodney, he asked, "What flavor would you like, Rodney?"

Rodney turned right to his grandmother with a pleading look—not a word, just a well-practiced look. Clara shrugged her shoulder, and Rodney smiled, "Chocolate too, and Sheila likes strawberry."

Turning to Clara, Tobias smiled and asked, "Would you like some ice cream or would a piece of pie better suit you?"

Clara actually smiled as she turned to the waitress and said, "I like chocolate."

After dinner Tobias walked up to the counter and paid the bill. Looking back at the table, seeing Rodney and Sheila polishing off their ice cream after a hearty dinner of meat loaf, mashed potatoes, butter beans, and all the milk they could get down them, he couldn't think of a better way to spend their vacation money.

As they walked back to the train, Rodney seemed more open than before. Tobias could tell he was studying the tin box, and he finally asked, "Mr. Bascom, is you rich?"

"No, Rodney," Tobias chuckled, "I am not rich. Why do you ask?"

Rodney twisted his mouth, as if trying to pull his facts together. "Well, Mr. Bascom, you be dressed right proper in that suit. Your wife gives away cookies and milk because you have more than enough, and now you paid for our dinner, and even ice cream. You must be rich."

"Well, Rodney, I am not. My wife and I love to share what we have with others. God has blessed us with a little bit more than what we need, so we try to bless others. Rodney, did having a good dinner tonight bless you?"

He did not answer in words, just a quick nod of his head. His eyes filled with gratitude.

Tobias felt good, knowing these two children were going to sleep tonight with full tummies. Providing their meals was such a small thing on his part, but such a huge matter for these children.

As they re-boarded the train, Tobias couldn't help but feel proud of Ruth. Her ability to love and care for hurting people always amazed him. Oh, sure, he had paid for the dinner, but Ruth had made it possible. Married to her for thirty-four years, he had known her for fifty years, and apart from Auntie Ruby, he had never known a more loving and gracious woman. Tobias sighed as he retook his seat, "I am overwhelmed that God allowed me to marry this woman."

Ruth continued to sit with Clara, wanting to share her journey of faith with this lost and lonely woman. They knew they only had about an hour before the train reached Culpeper, Virginia, and Clara and the children would be gone. Two hour later they would reach Washington, D.C.

Ruth wanted to use this time well, caring for Clara. Tobias let his mind return to the past, but this time it was all about Ruth. His life has not been without its struggles, but Ruth has always been there for him. She had always been a bright light of hope and understanding—especially during times of darkness and fear. As a young man dealing with World War I, Ruth was a constant, steady rock for him...soon he was back in his youth.

Most of 1917 and 1918 were consumed with thoughts of World War I. Every newspaper was filled with lists of the dead and stories of Army hospitals filled with wounded. Everyone dreaded seeing the Western Union bicycle coming through the neighborhood. Someone was being told that a son, a husband, or a father was not coming home.

About twenty-five percent of America's young boys were off fighting the war or returning home wounded. Tensions were at an all-time high; but on a personal level, life was moving along rather well. Sulley and Whippoorwill were settling back into life. Several of the women of the church had gathered up dishes, furniture, and knickknacks to replace what Neville had destroyed. Although expected, Sulley's father and brother never came looking for trouble. Finally, word came around that Jethro had joined the Army, and their father had left town. Only then did Whippoorwill feel she could stay home alone while Sully was working.

Just when we thought things were settling down, disaster hit again. In September of 1917, the headlines switched from the war in Europe to a gruesome murder of one of Atlanta's own. No one talked of anything else. A year earlier a local white boy from a prominent family had been found tortured and murdered, and everyone wanted answers. For months the police had been out in force, looking for eyewitnesses. The mayor had been quoted as saying: "We will leave no stone unturned until we find who did this. Rest assured, this killer will be found."

The mayor intended for this issued statement to bring a sense of comfort to the citizens of Atlanta—at least to the white citizens. To the rest of us, his pronouncement brought terror. We all understood that, if the perpetrator could not be found, any black man would do. For most of 1916, the police combed the black neighborhood where the boy's body had been found. The newspaper assumed his killer had been a black man and even hinted that the police had items left at the scene, but they refused to talk about them. For months the tensions grew, until finally, a young black girl came forward with information. She said that, several weeks after the murder, she had been at a party where a boy bragged to some other boys that he had killed that white boy. She did not know his name, but she gave the police a good description and provided the names of the boys who had attended the party. At first, the police did not believe her, thinking she was

simply trying to get the reward the victim's parents had offered for information leading to the arrest and conviction of their son's killer.

The police began rounding up the boys, and soon they had a name,
but they could not find him anywhere in the city. His grandmother was
shown some items of clothing, and she confirmed they belonged to her
grandson. The police then had a photograph and a name, but for months,
they could find no sign of him.

We all worried this situation might ignite another riot. As long as this
black boy was out wandering around, none of us were safe. To all of our
relief, word got round that right after that party, he had hopped a bus and
had headed north. The police had been told he had relatives in Chicago
and hoped the police there might find him. Almost a year had passed before he was found and returned to Atlanta to stand trial. The year 1916 was
not a good one to be black in the city of Atlanta. None of us dared to be
alone when walking the streets. People wanted something to happen, and
they really did not seem to care who it happened to. For many months, the
newspapers remained filled with the gruesome details of the murder, and
once the man was found in Chicago, we all hoped the police had the right
man. Black or white, no one wanted a person who could do such awful
things to another person to be walking our streets.

Just as things finally began to settle down, I received a letter from
Harlem. Excited to read news from home, I opened Momma's letter—to-
tally unprepared for what I was to read.

May 1918
My Dear Toby,

In just a few months, you will be turning 21 years old. I do not know
how to tell you this, so I will just say it. Last night your Grandpa
Samuel passed away in his sleep. Toby, he was almost 73 and had

been in that wheelchair for 16 years. He came down with a cold about a month ago and could not shake it. I am thankful he did not suffer.

Toby Boy, no grandpa ever loved his boy as much as Daddy loved you. He was so proud of you and was always talking about you to anyone who would listen. I am so sorry we were never able to afford to come down to Atlanta to visit you, but with Daddy in the wheelchair, the doctor always said it was not safe.

Your grandpa was such a special man, and I know you have lots of good memories to hold onto.

Be well my boy.

Love,

Momma Ruby

For the next three months, I walked around lost. The idea that my grandpa was gone shook me to the core. The last year had been so hard, watching every step for fear of drawing attention to myself, and now this. As much as I loved the sisters, I desperately felt the need to get away for a while. I had finished up all my correspondence courses, and no jobs were available.

On Saturday, July 28, 1918, I turned twenty-one, and Ms. Pearl finally agreed to let me enlist. Ruth was already doing her part. She had volunteered as an aide at the downtown hospital. She worked with the black soldiers who were not yet ready to go home, encouraging them, handing out Gideon Bibles, and singing to the men. I was desperate to do my part.

That Monday I walked into the downtown recruiting office and enlisted. After completing basic training two months later, I was on a ship in Savannah Harbor, waiting to set sail on September 30, for Halifax, Nova

Scotia. There, to ensure our safety against U-boat attacks, we joined a large convoy of ships heading to France.

When we left Halifax Harbor on October 20 for France, I had difficulty adjusting. Experienced sailors encouraged me, "The first few days are the hardest. You will get your sea-legs, but until you do, make sure you are never too far from deck."

Being a private in the United States Army, I was not too concerned that I was having trouble adapting to the ship's motion. We were now five days out at sea, and I still felt squeamish below deck. The mess hall was the worst. All of the various smells overwhelmed my senses, causing my stomach to start churning. The heaving of the ship made my keeping anything down nearly impossible—unless I got involved in a conversation that would take my mind off how I was feeling.

One night I was scheduled for watch duty at 2200 hours. I actually looked forward to watch duty because the brisk salt air helped calm my stomach. As I was heading aft, Corporal Sanderson came out of nowhere, shoved me against the wall, and warned, "Private Bascom, you are causing more than a little talk on this ship. Mind you, I really don't care who you eat with, but Sergeant Williams has ordered me to warn you to mind your manners and stick with your own kind."

"Excuse me, Corporal," I answered back rather cheeky, "but I am sticking with my own kind. Karl Carter is a private in the U.S. Army, and so am I."

"Boy, don't you get funny with me. You know good and well what I mean. The sergeant is going to control your every move out on the battlefield. You really don't want to get on his bad side. You just consider yourself warned, and watch your back."

I made my way up on deck and began my watch. Everyone took his turn on deck, searching for any signs of U-boats. During my watch, I realized that no one on deck cared what color I was. We had a common enemy, and as long as I did my job, I thought I was just another soldier. That was not to say that everyone believed this, but most did.

The private about whom I was being warned was a fellow soldier from Atlanta. We hit it off right away, enjoying talking about home, boot camp and our mutual fear of what was ahead for us. I'm not really sure why, but you meet some people and automatically say to yourself, "I could really like this guy." That was the way I felt about Karl Carter. What I really liked about him was the very thing that was causing the problem; Karl treated me like an equal. In his mind, we were both simply privates, who were facing the same enemy. Our camaraderie did not go over well with others, but Karl didn't seem to care what his fellow white soldiers thought about his breaking bread with the likes of me.

This did not surprise me. I fully expected we would get rousted by the white soldiers. What I did not expect was being harassed by my fellow black soldiers. One or two of them warned me, "You think those white guys are going to watch your back out on the battlefield? They'd as soon shoot you themselves, boy. You best keep with your own. You keep hanging out with that white boy, and you will find yourself all alone. You think any of us will lift a finger to come to the aid of a white-lover?"

Karl and I decided it was best to keep our conversations limited to our time on deck. Neither of us wanted to paint a target on our backs; but that did not mean we were willing to end our friendship. How dare anyone think they had the right to tell us who we could call a friend? Karl and I had both been willing to go to war to protect the rights of people we did not know. We enlisted in order to stand up to those who wanted to use their power to deny these people the right to govern their own lives. Yet here we were, receiving death threats if we did not submit to the authority of those who considered themselves our superior. I thought the uniform would make us equals. I was wrong.

That night I stood at the rail, staring out into the pitch black, wondering why I was on that ship heading for France to fight the Germans. Yes, they were the big world bullies, but they were not the only bullies in this world. In frustration, I looked up into the dark sky, and in a rage that had been boiling for weeks, I said, "God, I'm tired of having to watch my back.

When will it be their turn to watch their backs? Why do I have to mind my manners and quietly surrender my pride because *they* say so? I am tired of being treated like an insignificant little grasshopper."

As soon as those words came out of my mouth, my thoughts went to Ms. Ruby. I knew exactly what she would have said—had she been standing on that deck beside me. "Tobias, my boy, you are giving those people too much power. No one can make you feel like an insignificant little grasshopper. Yes, they can disrespect you and mistreat you. But Toby, they cannot control how you think about yourself. Remember, self-control and self-determination are within your hands. Who you are is determined by how you act—not what others think."

I did not want to submit to this truth. I wanted to be angry, and I wanted to lash out at someone. I remembered Pastor Johnson's sermon and thought about all of the giants in this world. I thought about Master Stewart's lording his power over my family. I thought about the three boys back in Harlem who had lorded their power over my momma, and their fathers who had bullied my grandpa. I thought about Sulley's daddy and brothers who had disrespected his rights and hated him for bettering himself. I thought about the people back home who rode around under white sheets taking the lives of black men simply because they could get away with it. I thought about all the courtrooms that had turned a blind-eye to those hateful little giants, effectively giving them permission to take away the rights of others. There are all sorts of giants in this world.

Part of me wanted to take a gun and fight these giants instead of the Germans. I wanted to go find that sergeant, who was now sound asleep in his berth and pound some sense into him, but I had no more than thought this than Ms. Ruby's words began to ring in my ears, "Oh, no, you won't, my beloved boy. You might be a grasshopper, Toby, but you will never be insignificant as long as you conduct yourself with honor. I would rather you be an honorable grasshopper that walks with God than the greatest giant this world has ever known. Toby, there will always be giants. When you slay one, another will take its place, but always remember, a grasshopper plus God is always greater than giants. You focus on your character, Toby, and let God deal with the giants."

I would like to say that I settled that issue that very night, but I would be lying. I had that same argument every night for several nights before I was able to surrender my pride to God. On the fourth night, I was yelling at the sky, "God, I am their equal; this isn't fair. Why must I surrender my pride to them?"

In my heart I heard, "No, you are not insignificant, Tobias. You are never going to be their equal. You are My child—a child of the King of kings and the Lord of lords. I have not called you to surrender your pride to men; I have called you to surrender your pride to Me. If you will do that, I will handle the giants in your life. Yes, you are a grasshopper, but you are My beloved grasshopper—not theirs. Tobias, will you let Me fight your giants?"

That night, while standing on that deck and leaning against the rail, I surrendered my pride and gladly accepted the honorable title of "God's Little Grasshopper."

We arrived in France on November 1, 1918. Every young man on that ship fully expected to engage the enemy and prove his mettle. As we were standing at attention on deck, Sergeant Williams, right in front of the entire troop, walked up to me and handed me a clipboard, "Private Bascom, I've assigned you to motor pool duty." As a young man of twenty-one, my embarrassment and disappointment was huge; I knew the sergeant had done this just to show me he could. In my youthful thinking, I wanted to prove my mettle and earn my comrades' respect, but I quickly got over it.

As a motor pool driver, I was to arrive at the harbor, fill my truck with medical supplies, deliver them to the hospital, then move my truck around to the patient loading dock, where I would help load the wounded who were lucky enough to be sailing back home. I would make two or three trips a day. The hospital had the soldiers in wheelchairs already lined up along the hallway. Each man had an envelope of his medical records sitting on his lap, waiting for me.

I found it interesting that these same soldiers, who would not consider sitting at a dinner table with me, were now exceedingly glad to see me show up with the truck that was delivering them to the safety of a home-bound ship.

One by one, I wheeled these soldiers down the ramp of the hospital and up the ramp of my truck, buckled them securely in place, and then headed back to get the next patient until my truck was filled. I would drive these boys down to the harbor and wheel them up the gangway to the waiting hands of the ship's medical team. Almost every boy grabbed hold of my hand and thanked me. I could see in their eyes that they had seen things I could never imagine. Most of these boys were missing one, if not both, of their legs. I truly did not care what color they were. They were hurting and scared, and I was there to help them. I doubt that my being black even registered with them. I thought about Ruth back home, trying to comfort soldiers and share God's love with them and how I had wanted to do the same. It dawned on me that God had done just that for me. He had placed me there to share His love with these hurting men of every color. I smiled as I climbed up into the truck because I realized that my sergeant had not made me a grasshopper; God had done so because He had a job for me to do. I realized that as long as I humbly shared the love of God with people, I would never be insignificant. I might never be great in the world's eyes, but I would always be important.

That afternoon I had a two-hour break. I made my way to the Salvation Army tent that stood at the opening of the harbor entrance. Sharing that tent was a team of Gideons, men who were dedicated to the task of giving Bibles to the soldiers. I was given three boxes of New Testaments, and for the remainder of the war, every soldier I loaded onto my truck got a Bible and heard the message that God loved him.

Only after several of these trips did the thought occur to me that God had indeed rescued me from the threats of one of my giants. Although I had been disappointed in being assigned to the motor pool, I never had to worry about one of my giants not watching my back on the field of battle.

Seventeen days later, on November 18, 1918, the Armistice was signed; the war was officially over. I am profoundly thankful that I was never called upon to shoot a gun or take a life nor did I ever have a gun pointed at me or have my life threatened. I know that I was one of the lucky ones, and I would never again complain about being one of God's little grasshoppers.

CHAPTER 29

Surprised by A Visitor

AT THE END of the war, privates who had not been wounded were immediately mustered out of the military and issued an honorable discharge upon landing on American soil. My ship reached Savannah Harbor on the morning of January 10, 1919, and I caught the first bus heading for Atlanta. I could not wait to see Ruth and tell her how much I had missed her. I knew it would be a long time before I could act on my feelings for her. In the best of times, being black would make it hard to find work, but now that the city would be flooded with returning soldiers looking for work, I knew it would be a long time before I could take a bride and support her.

Just as I had suspected, every job for which I applied had five white boys who had also submitted applications. I thought about how hard it had been for Grandpa Samuel after the Civil War. Every time I was tempted to feel sorry for myself, I remembered that he had been willing to do anything to keep a roof over the sisters' heads and food in their bellies. Unlike most blacks who were applying for jobs, I was well-educated and well-read, but my abilities did not impress anyone but me. I still had most of my muster pay, but I knew it would not last long. I needed to find work—any work.

Adding to the general unrest of so many men looking for work, Atlanta was also embroiled in a messy murder trial. In September of 1917, the city had been dragged through the ringer when the police had been searching for the killer of one of Atlanta's prominent sons. It had taken eight months to find him and almost twenty months to bring him to trial. The newspapers were again filled with every detail of the grisly murder and, even though the killer's picture was plastered on the front page, no black man felt safe walking the streets of Atlanta. I knew it would be nearly impossible for me to find a good job with all of this unrest.

Although I was well-educated, I decided to swallow my pride and stand in line for day labor crews. Twenty months had passed since the Great Atlanta Fire, and now that the war in Europe was over, the rebuilding was in full swing. Physical labor was not something I was used to, but I knew my Grandpa Samuel would have been proud of me for doing whatever it took to earn a day's wage. I learned how to lay foundation forms, pour concrete, frame walls, and shingle roofs. Of course, because of the Great Fire, the city banned wooden shingles, believing they were the cause of the quickly-spreading fire. Like my grandfather, I had to get over my fear of heights. Climbing up the tall ladders with a stack of asphalt shingles over my shoulder wasn't so bad, but swinging my body out over the edge of the roof and taking that first step back onto the ladder just about killed me. I did not dare freeze in fear. The foreman was looking for any reason to get rid of me, and I was not going to give one to him.

I came home every day utterly exhausted. Ms. Ruby would always have a basin of warm soapy water and a clean towel waiting for me. She also had a hot plate of biscuits and honey ready for her boy. No young man, striving to prove his manhood, ever felt more loved than I did.

In early spring, I had just polished off my plate of biscuits when a knock sounded at the front door. Knocks on our front door were never welcomed. Friends always came to the kitchen door at our house, so this meant it was not going to be a friend. I made my way into the living room, steeling myself for whoever it was at our door. When I opened the door, to my surprise, a smiling Private Karl Carter stood there and held out his hand to greet me. Taking a quick assessment, I noted that he had both arms and legs, and I was glad. We had been separated the day I was assigned to the motor pool, and I didn't think I would ever see him again. "Karl, what are you doing here?"

Still standing there in the doorway with a smile on his face and his hand out to shake mine, he joked, "Well, Private Bascom, you going to just stand there, or are you going to shake a fellow soldier's hand and invite him in for a visit?"

I did not shake Karl's hand that day. Instead, I grabbed hold of him and gave him a huge bear hug and said, "I am so happy you made it home in one piece, Karl. Come inside. I want to introduce you to my Aunties, Ms. Pearl and Ms. Ruby. They know all about you."

As Karl took a seat on our sofa, it dawned on me that this was the first white man ever to be seated in our living room, and I could not think of a better person to break that line. "Karl, how did you find me?"

With a twinkle in his eye, Karl confessed, "Well, I remembered your telling me what church you went to, so I stopped by there yesterday. I asked a lovely young lady who gave me your address, "You wouldn't happen to be Tobias' girl, Ruth, would you?"

Beaming with pride, I said, "So you have met my Ruth; quite a lovely young lady, right?"

Karl grinned, "I thought you were going to marry her as soon as you got back home, Tobias."

"I wanted to, Karl, but I have to be able to support her first. Day labor is about the only work I can find, and it pays the lowest wages in town; but work is work, and I am getting along. How about you? Have you found any work?"

"Actually Tobias, that's why I am here. My father was friends with the man who owns a big warehouse down in the Fourth Ward. It was one of only three that didn't go up in the fire. When all the others were burned to the ground, his warehouse became overrun with orders. When I returned from the war, a job offer was waiting for me. I was given a crew of men, and we manage all the loading of the 10:00 and 2:00 freight trains. We started out with just the ten of us, but there is so much work, the foreman told me to find two more able-bodied men to add to my crew. Naturally, I thought of you. Would you like a job, Tobias?"

Uneasiness settled over my excitement, "Karl, how many blacks work at that warehouse?"

Karl frowned, "Nothing much ever changes, does it, Tobias? I find it is sad that you have to even ask that question, but I understand. Nothing will ever change until we change it. You went to war and did your part. Why shouldn't you have a chance to earn a fair day's pay for a fair day's work? But to answer your question, no, there are no other blacks on my crew—yet. Several are on the midnight freight crew, so you won't be the first. So, Tobias, how about it?"

I stood up and took hold of Karl's hand, "I accept. If it doesn't work out, Karl, I won't blame you. I can always go back to the day labor lines. When do I start?"

Karl put his other hand on my shoulder, "Welcome aboard, Tobias. Who knows, maybe someday, this won't be an issue. At least I hope so. Do you know where the Sutterhill Warehouse is located?"

"Yes, down on Cloverhill Road and Court Street, right?"

"Right, are you free to start tomorrow? If you take Cloverhill, come through the second gate away from Court Street. Then come to the third loading dock; I will be waiting for you at 7:00 a.m. That will give us thirty minutes to fill out your paperwork before our shift starts at 7:30. Be sure to bring along a thick pair of gloves and some hard-toed boots."

After this matter was settled, Karl walked over to the sisters and said, "You have reared a good man. While we stood watch, I heard all about your family. It is truly a pleasure to finally meet you both."

I could tell that Ms. Pearl was skeptical—as she usually was. Her distrust of white men ran very deep, and it would take more than an oil-slicked tongue to take down her guard. On the other hand, Ms. Ruby was all smiles. Any friend of mine was a friend of hers. "Karl, our Toby told us all about you when he got back. I wish I had known you were coming because I would have loved to share a dinner meal with you. Maybe we can do it next time?"

As soon as Karl was gone, Ms. Pearl climbed all over Ruby, "What were you thinking, Sissy? It is one thing for that white man to offer our Toby a job; it is quite another to ask him to dinner. Do you realize that is the first white man ever to step foot in this house, and you went and invited him to sit at our dinner table? What if that had offended him? You need to be more careful, Sissy."

I knew there was nothing I could say to relieve my Aunt Pearl's long-standing fear of white men. I understood where it came from, but I trusted Karl. I knew he had a good heart and would not betray me. I smiled at Ms. Ruby and said, "Just give her time. Karl will win her over—just as he did me. Not all white men are bad, and at least we can now say that we have entertained one good one in our home."

That evening I walked over to Ruth's house to share my good news. I was not concerned about Karl, but I was concerned about all of the others with whom I would be working alongside. Nothing much had changed since the days when my grandfather, Samuel, worked the rail-road loading docks. I would be lying if I said I was not worried. Everyone in the city was scrambling for work. If one of these men on Karl's crew had a brother or a friend who had been turned away, I would be a target for their frustration.

Ruth joined me on the front stoop while her father remained in their living room. Her eyes twinkled with excitement as she said, "I've been praying that you would find steady work, Tobias."

I couldn't resist teasing her, "Why? Because now I might be able to pop a certain question?"

Ruth grew very serious, "Tobias, you could have asked that question a long time ago, and I would have said yes. Don't you know that I have loved you ever since the day in first grade when I watched your kind heart reach out in friendship to Sulley?"

"Ruth, there has never ever been anyone else for me but you. I cannot imagine living my life without you by my side. When I am with you, I am a better man than I could ever be without you." Turning directly toward her, I pledged, "I am not in a proper position to ask for your hand tonight, Ruth. You know that I love you, but I want to be able to care for you and provide a home for you. I am not there yet; but I promise you, Ruth, it will not be long."

Kissing me with a passion I had not yet experienced, Ruth pledged, "I know you are the man I am supposed to marry, Tobias. I will wait, but please," she giggled, "don't make me wait too long."

I walked back home that night, thinking about my earlier fears that evening. None of those white men were going to scare me away from that job. Every time that concern arose, I thought of Ruth's passionate kiss and her plea to not make her wait too long. By the time I reached our kitchen door, I was whistling with pure joy.

CHAPTER 30

Pushing the Color Barrier

I WAS STANDING at the loading dock at 6:45 a.m., gloves in hand and ready for a hard day of labor. Just in case they might help, I had tucked my honorable discharge papers in the top of my lunch bucket. I could see Karl inside the large bailing door, talking in earnest with someone who was obviously his superior. The man kept thumping the middle of Karl's chest with his finger, and I did not have to hear his words to know it was most likely about me. As soon as he stormed off, Karl gave me the signal to come on in.

"Karl, are you sure this is a good idea? I don't want you getting into trouble on my account."

"Don't you worry about him, Tobias. He is just mad that I didn't give his son-in-law the job. That guy can't read, he has been fired from two other jobs in the past year, and he was dishonorably discharged from the Navy. I don't care if he knows the governor; he is not working on my crew. I told Guilford it had nothing to do with you. My crew must be able to read. We have manifests, bills of lading, shipping confirmation forms—none of which his son-in-law can read or fill out. When I told him that, he pointed at you and said, 'You gunna tell me that black boy can read?'"

"You should have seen his face when I rattled off all the novels you have read. I don't think he believed me, but it sure shut him up." Karl then confessed, "You have read more books than I have. Let's go into the office and get your paperwork done before the rest of the crew shows up."

The first few days were uncomfortable but quiet. Even though none of the men liked my being there, it helped that Karl was respected by his men. He and I agreed that, just like any other new crewman, I would be assigned the tasks that everyone hated—not because I was the only black crewman, but because I was the newest crewman. I had no problem with that.

Whenever possible, I tried to offer a helping hand to anyone who needed it. The large pallets of Georgia bricks were the most unyielding and getting them down the warehouse ramp was a two-man job. Most of the crew accepted my help without comment, but Sammy staunchly refused any help from me. I gave him a wide birth, letting him struggle with his loads, and made no comment when he finally had to ask one of the other crewmen for help.

About two weeks in, we were loading three boxcars with pallets of bricks. We were under a deadline to get all of the pallets loaded so the freighter could pull out of the yard before dark. At first, every man took his own pallet and manhandled his way down the ramp, across the yard and up into the freight car all by himself. By noon, everyone's body was so fatigued, we started doubling up and helping each other. I stood at the top of the ramp, waiting for the next pallet so I could help that crewman control it down the steep ramp and push it across the yard. Then I would head back to the ramp and help the next man. Sammy would refuse my help, so I would step back and let him head down the ramp all alone. Karl yelled at him once or twice, but Sammy was obstinate about not needing any help. We were on the last boxcar and had about six pallets left. Everyone was exhausted from the hard day's work, but Sammy still refused any help. I came back up the ramp and offered one last time, "You must be tired, Sammy. You are the only one who has worked all day without any help from anyone. You sure you don't want help with this last pallet?"

"Don't need no help from the likes of you," was all he said.

I shrugged my shoulders and moved on to the pallet behind him. If he didn't want my help, that was fine with me. Just as Luther and I maneuvered our last pallet of bricks to the top of the ramp, Sammy lost control of his pallet. He could no longer force it into the middle of the ramp and when it began to shift, he had nothing left to fight the load. The front right wheel of the dolly dropped off the side of the ramp, and that was all she wrote. No one was able to stop that dolly from plummeting over the side. The load shifted as soon as the wheel dropped, and bricks began sliding everywhere. Sammy just stood watching the disaster his pride had caused.

Every crewman ran to help. First, we needed to get the dolly back up on the ramp and clear away any bricks that were still on the ramp. We had four more pallets that needed to be loaded onto the boxcar. Once those were loaded, we would all try to salvage as many unbroken bricks as we could. We managed to save about half a load of bricks and got them loaded onto the freight car before the whistle blew. When the train pulled out of the yard, Karl told Sammy to count the broken bricks and to write out a short-load manifest for the office. All the crewmen knew that Sammy would be docked for all those bricks.

The whole crew was quiet as we walked into the office to sign out for the day. Sammy sat down and began writing out his paperwork when Karl walked up and said, "Sammy, are you ready to join this crew?"

Sammy put his pencil down and glared at Karl, "What do you mean?"

Karl stood right in Sammy's face and said, "I know Tobias here thinks it's because he is black that you refused his help all day long." Then turning to me, he said, "Isn't that right, Tobias?"

I simply shrugged my shoulders.

Karl then said, "Sammy, we are a crew. What one man does; so do the others. If you don't stop trying to prove you don't need anybody's help out in the yard, you are not going to last very long. We expect you to accept help when it is needed, and we expect you to offer help when you can. Do you understand? I try to be a fair foreman. You might have to pay for the loss of those bricks, but I am the one who will have to answer for that short-load. It didn't need to happen if you would have been a team player."

Sammy hung his head and said, "You are right, Karl. I just hate to admit it when I need help. I've never been much of a team player, but I promise I will try."

"Okay then," Karl thundered, "this is what we are going to do. Twelve of us were on the crew today. To show you how a good crew pulls together, we are going to divide the short-load between all twelve of us. That is what a team does. The work is lighter when we work together. The loss is less when we all share it. Do you understand now, Sammy?"

From that night on, we were a team. We quickly earned the reputation of having the fewest number of errors and losses of any of the freight teams, and this record kept the big bosses off Karl's back. You cannot argue with success—at least we were counting on that.

Most of the men settled into having me on the team rather quickly. A monthly bonus in their pay envelopes for being on the top-producing team certainly helped. My being on the team did not necessarily assure this ranking, but because they all knew that Karl would not stand for any race baiting and they did not want to be moved to another team, they tolerated me. We were all treading on new territory here. They did not trust me and I did not trust them, but as the weeks went by, our banter became more lighthearted as we were forced to work together. They learned that I was not stupid, shiftless and lazy, and I learned that not all whites were standing at the ready to beat me down and string me up.

Karl worked hard at making us a cohesive team. Most teams would do this by going out for a beer at the end of their shift, but there were no places around the loading dock that would allow me to join them. Karl decided to start a team family collection. Every Friday he passed a hat and asked for a donation equal to how much each man would have spent on beer. At first the donations were skimpy, but Karl kept at it. This practice went on for several months before the men realized the benefit of their contributions.

One Monday morning, Luther McGillus, one of the team's most respected members, showed up for work completely undone. That Sunday, his little boy, Jackson, had run out into the street to retrieve a toy and had been struck by a passing car. Thankfully, his only injury was a broken arm, but even that expense was more than Luther could manage, and he said, "Living hand to mouth, payday to payday, I don't know how I can make up for this. Either the doctor gets paid and my children go without food, or the doctor sends the collectors after me, and we all know what they will do to me."

Karl walked over to his locked desk, pulled out the envelope where he kept the donations and handed it to Luther. "We are a family, Luther. Just like at work, what happens to one happens to all, so it is with our families. You take this money and pay Jackson's doctor bill. None of us are willing to let your children go without food."

After that, the hat was never returned empty. When someone was in need, the team stepped up to help.

For the first few months, I made sure I did not intrude during lunch. Everyone had been stretched enough, and pushing them to sit with me during their lunch break was asking too much. I found if I went to the washroom and took my time, everyone was already seated and halfway through his lunch by the time I came over. I would sit quietly at the far end of the table and focus on eating. I did not try to join in their conversation. As long as I respected their boundaries, we got along fine. Karl was bothered by this ostracism something awful. I asked him not to push the point, but just as in the Army, his sense of justice would not be quieted. I knew he was just trying to change the long-standing rules, but I was the one who would eventually pay the price when someone felt pushed too far.

This was no exercise in social justice for me. I needed this job. I was on a mission and did not want to make trouble because trouble would mean I could not ask Ruth to marry me. Finally, Karl agreed to stop pushing me into everyone's face. He understood my concerns and wanted to respect my wishes. I appreciated Karl's heart, but the issues that threatened me were not going to go away simply by sitting at a lunch table with these men. The color barriers ran very deep and were going to take more than I was honestly willing to sacrifice at that time.

In my world, I believe that Karl was the first white man to be color-blind. I am certain there were others, just not in my world. This was a real blessing in our personal relationship, but it was dangerous in public. Karl had not grown up experiencing the backlash of being an uppity black man. At first, he did not understand why I was so resistant to pushing the color barriers. I had attended many a funeral of young black men who thought the time had come to take a stand. We all knew the time was coming, but we also knew the terrible price to be paid by those who pushed against those barriers.

Having this steady job meant I could finally ask Ruth to marry me. Except for my contribution to the household account and my offering at church, I saved every penny of my pay in the hopes of marrying Ruth and setting up our household very soon.

One evening I invited Karl to the house for dinner. Since he had already met Ruth, I also invited her. I knew Karl was lonely. His father had died in a hunting accident when he was ten years old, and it was just he and his mother at home. None of the other men on the crew would dare invite their boss to dinner, so Karl felt cut off and alone.

During dinner Karl told us how he got his job. "You see, my father and Mr. Sutterhill were boyhood friends. They both grew up just outside of Atlanta and had gone hunting and fishing together for years. Mr. Sutterhill's father was a successful businessman in town, whereas our family came from meager means. When I was ten, my daddy took off for their annual hunting trip. While flushing out birds, Mr. Sutterhill's foot was caught in a hole, causing him to fall. As he fell, his gun discharged, and the bullet hit my father in the head, killing him instantly. Everyone knew what happened was an unfortunate accident.

"Mr. Sutterhill swore he would never again go hunting or even hold a gun in his hand. Although my father's death was an accident and he was not obligated to do anything for us, he was an honorable man. He set up a monthly allowance for my widowed mother. He never came to our house or spoke directly to me, but I know he kept his eye on me. When I returned from the war, a letter from Sutterhill Warehouse, offering me a job was waiting for me.

"I have never tried to take advantage of Mr. Sutterhill's kindness. I know my job is the direct result of his sense of guilt at causing my father's death—not because he cares about me on a personal level. I work extra-hard at his warehouse in order to show my gratitude."

Ms. Ruby was the first to comment. "Mr. Sutterhill must be a good man. He did not have to do anything for you or your mother, but he did when many would not. I am glad our Toby is working for such a man."

Ruth then added, "The Bible says that taking care of the widows and orphans is the purest form of Christianity."

Karl smiled, "I wouldn't know about that, Ruth. My mother and I are not church goers. Being widowed at the age of thirty, her bitterness runs deep when people talk about God."

Ruth, always the one able to step right into the heart of someone's pain without offense, suggested, "And yet, Karl, might it not have been God who put the idea of caring for your widowed mother into Mr. Sutterhill's heart? Sometimes we give man the credit, when it is really God who is causing the blessing."

Karl studied Ruth's face, "I never thought it could be God's doing. It simply has been easier to think that Mr. Sutterhill felt guilty about the accident. Maybe that was what God used to take care of my mother all these years."

"Well, Karl," I offered, "If you ever want to get to know this God who cares for the widows and orphans, I would love to share His story with you."

"I would like that, Tobias. If there is a God, and if He cares about me, I should try to get to know Him."

TOBIAS:
With Ruth by My Side
1922-1941

CHAPTER 31

Ruth and I Got Married

FOR SEVERAL MONTHS we had a gathering at my house. I led the Bible study and Sulley, Whippoorwill, Ruth, and Karl were in attendance. We sat around the kitchen table while Ms. Pearl and Ms. Ruby sat in the living room listening intently. Ms. Pearl was still having trouble trusting Karl, but she was glad that he seemed so interested in the Bible. It is never easy to lay down our deeply held fears. Pearl had seen so much hatred, she had a hard time believing that any white person could ever be trusted. She was thankful to Karl for giving me a much-needed job, but having him sitting at her kitchen table in her house stretched her beyond her comfort zone. She allowed it because I insisted; but I knew it was always hard for her.

After about three months, Karl finally expressed his desire to become a follower of Jesus. His prayer was so sincere that even Ms. Pearl had to admit it was real. At the end of the evening, she walked up to Karl and welcomed him into the family of God. I remember smiling as she gave Karl a hug. What she could not do in her flesh—trust a white man, she found she could do in her faith—trust a fellow believer. From that night on, we were all family.

I had been working for almost a year, and Ruth and I started seriously planning our future together. I had saved enough to secure a rental for us, and we began collecting pieces of furniture. Sulley was a great help. While doing painting jobs in people's homes, in lieu of payment he would often be offered pieces of furniture. If it was a piece he knew Ruth would like, he would accept it, knowing I would pay him a fair price for it. One of the older ladies of the women's society had lived in Pennsylvania for several years and suggested the women do what the Amish do for newlyweds—work together to make a wedding quilt. Since none of the women had ever made a quilt, they settled on an old slave tradition of making a braided rag rug for us. The ladies began collecting colorful scraps of material and spent a month making us a much loved rug for our future living room. Ruth and I both knew this rug would always be in our home as a reminder of how much these women loved us. Whippoorwill also organized several of the younger ladies of the church, and they began knitting and crocheting doilies for Ruth.

In 1921, if a black couple were churched and wished to be married, they would simply invite their pastor to the parents' house. He would perform the marriage in their living room. Blacks who were not churched walked to city hall and paid a judge to perform the marriage. Ruth's father, Rev. Johnson, insisted that our wedding would be at the altar of our church. Everyone had watched Ruth grow up and loved her as much as I did. Ours would not be fancy, like the wedding photos of the rich and famous which were published in the Sunday social section of the Atlanta newspapers, but it would be special. Having so many people stand together as witnesses to our vows meant a lot to both of us.

Aunt Ruby asked if she could make me a new suit for the wedding. I knew this request was important to her, and even though my old wool suit would have cleaned up sufficiently enough not to embarrass my bride, I accepted Ms. Ruby's offer of love. I knew Sulley was out looking for the perfect tie to go with Ruby's suit. Sulley always had a soft spot for bright-colored ties, so I asked Aunt Ruby to help him pick out one that I would actually be able to wear on my wedding day.

Besides the tie, as a wedding gift to us, Sulley offered to paint the living room of our new little rental, while Karl and I cleaned up the woefully neglected yard. While pulling weeds, Karl again mentioned his friend. For several months now, Karl had been asking for prayer for this particular friend of his. He had dated her a few times, but he had decided to stop dating her and only be her friend. At first, this was all he said about her, so we prayed. Eventually, Karl shared that her name was Gladys Thomas and that she did not believe in God. We began to pray more earnestly for Gladys.

Over the months, Karl's faith had grown, and he did not want to get involved with a woman who would not share his faith. Once or twice Karl started to share his other concerns but stopped short of telling us his real apprehension. While pulling weeds in my new yard, I decided to ask Karl some more questions. "Karl, what is your real fear? Has this Gladys lived a terrible life? Do you fear we will not accept her? Remember my momma's story, Karl? True faith forgives everything."

Karl stopped pulling weeds and sat back, "You don't understand, Toby. Gladys hates black people."

"Most white people do," I responded glibly. "So what is so different about Gladys?"

Karl reached over to grab my arm, "Toby, I mean she really hates black people. Remember the murder trial a year or two ago that about started another riot in this city? It was the torture and murder of a prominent white boy by a black boy. Well, that white boy was Gladys' older brother. Her hatred is so profound, she actually gets sick when she sees a black person."

"Wow, Karl, this young woman has really been hurt."

"Toby, it's more than that. Your Auntie Pearl had a very hard time trusting me because of all the hurts white people had caused her, and I understood. I realized that my presence upset her, but Pearl was always polite to me—cold, but polite. She gave me a chance to show her I could be trusted. It took months, but look at us now. She was polite, and I was patient. We both had to accept the other person's wounds until real healing could take place."

"Karl, do you fear we might react badly to Gladys' hatred?"

"No, Toby, I don't. What I fear is that Gladys will not give you a chance to get close to her. She is outspokenly hateful of blacks. I could not ask you to take the kind of rude behavior I know Gladys would dish out. I could not sit there and listen to my dearest friend be so disrespected by a girl about whom I care. Toby, I hate this ugly and cruel part of her. A few weeks ago I told her I was done with her. I could not allow myself to fall in love with someone who could behave like this. I know it all comes from her wounded soul. She loved her brother so very much, and I believe her hatred is how she pours out all her pain. If only God could heal her wounded soul, I believe her hatred would go away."

"But Karl, you told Gladys you were done with her, right? But here you are pouring out your heart to me about her. So Karl, let me ask you a question. If you don't try to reach out to Gladys and share God's love with her, who will? If no one does, what will happen to Gladys?"

Karl sighed a huge, heart-aching sigh. "That is exactly the problem, Toby. I don't know enough to help her. I know what she needs. I just don't know how to tell her." Then, the question that had been sitting on Karl's chest all morning came out. "Tobias, would you be willing to talk to Gladys? Would you try to love her—in spite of her rudeness—for my sake? I know I am asking a lot of you—more than you can really imagine right now. Will you help me to help her?"

I told Karl I would pray about the matter. I had lived my whole life with the cold rudeness of white people. I knew how to brace myself and not react to their malice; after all, my survival depended upon it. But here I was, being asked to deliberately put myself face to face with pure hatred, and not only not to react, but to love her for Jesus' sake. Should I? Could I? Would I?

I wish I could say I responded immediately with a hearty, "Yes, of course I will." I have to be honest; this request wasn't that simple. It took a lot of prayer and a lot of talking with Ruth before my heart was willing to surrender to this task. Once I did, Ruth said, "Tobias, it's not how long it takes us to surrender; it's only that we do surrender."

I knew I was a fortunate man. Even when I struggled to do right, neither my God nor my Ruth condemned me for struggling.

In between wedding plans, Karl and I devised a plan. He knew Gladys would never agree to come to the Bascom house. That would be asking too much of her. We also knew that nowhere in Atlanta, Georgia, could blacks and whites sit together and share a meal in public. Karl knew his mother would allow him to entertain guests, but the neighbors on either side of them were outspoken members of the Ku Klux Klan. He knew I would not be safe walking in his neighborhood.

After several days of planning, Karl decided the Sutterhill Warehouse would have to be the place. Before approaching Gladys, Karl and I moved one of the wooden lunch tables over to the far side of the loading yard. We placed it under a tree in order to provide us with some shade from the hot summer heat. Out of habit, most of the men sat at the table right outside the bailing door. At first, they didn't even notice that we had moved one of the tables, but once Karl and I started sitting out there, one or two other workers came to join us.

After our lunch, Karl and I started a short Bible study around the table and very quickly, these two men stopped coming to our table. Karl and I sat together at that table for two full weeks before we felt confident the other men would not bother us. Karl laughed, "Toby, remember how hard it was for the team to accept a black man sitting at our lunch table? It didn't take long for them to change their long-held aversion to eating with a black person—so much so, that when you and I pulled this table away from the others, those two had no problem walking over here and joining us. But pull out a Bible and start talking religion, and watch them scatter."

Our wedding day was fast approaching, but Ruth and I were determined not to let it consume our every waking moment. Sulley and Whippoorwill were expecting their first child, and we were just hoping the baby would wait until after the wedding to join the family.

Both Ruth and I wanted Karl at our wedding, but knew we needed to be cautious. Most of our church family carried deep wounds and feared white men. We did not want our wedding day to be marred by our insensitivity. We wanted Karl there, but we did not want to shove him into the faces of people about whom we cared and loved. We decided that Sulley and Whippoorwill would stand with us, and Karl would just be a guest sitting in a pew. He would be there, but not up front and in the face of our beloved church family.

I had invited my mother and Brother Jubilee to come, but I knew it would be impossible. Being a street preacher in Harlem meant he lived on donations and the meager pay my mother made cleaning office buildings, but they were happy; that was all that mattered to me. Momma Ruby's letters were filled with joy and peace. She knew Brother Jubilee loved her, so I was content to send them a wedding photo.

On Thursday afternoon, Ruth and Whippoorwill baked our wedding cake. Although not fancy, no one had ever tasted a better cake. On Friday afternoon, they were busy frosting it when they heard someone knocking on the front door. Ruth called me in from the back yard where I was polishing my shoes for my wedding day and said, "Tobias, someone is at Pearl's front door. Could you please answer it?"

I wiped off the black shoe polish from my fingers as I made my way to the door. Even though very few of our friends were able to buy us wedding presents, one or two gifts had been delivered, and I assumed another gift had arrived. Ill-prepared for what I would see, I swung open the door, let out a loud yelp, and then hollered, "Ruth, come quickly, it's my Momma Ruby and Brother Jubilee!" My momma just stood there on my front porch, smiling back at me. Brother Jubilee was right behind her with a suitcase in each hand. "Surprise, Toby Boy, we've come for your wedding."

"Oh, Momma, both Pearl and Ruby are at the church right now. They wanted to make sure everything is just right for tomorrow. Boy, are they going to be glad to see you again and to finally meet Jubilee."

Taking the suitcases from Jubilee, I carried them into my bedroom while Ruth guided my mother and Jubilee into the living room. "Did you walk from the train station?" Ruth asked. "You must be hungry. I can fix you some lunch. We are about to finish frosting the wedding cake, so you just relax a moment; I will be right back."

Ruth rang back into the kitchen, and I heard her excitedly exclaim, 'Whippoorwill, can you finish up the frosting while I make some lunch for my future mother-in-law?"

Whippoorwill ran to the kitchen door and stared at the couple resting on the sofa. Before returning to her task, she giggled as she called out to them, "I love your boy, Toby, Ma'am. He is my husband's best friend. I'm Whippoorwill, Sulley's wife."

Momma Ruby called back, "I know who you are, Whippoorwill. My Toby has written me lots of letters about you and Sulley. I am so happy to finally meet you, and I can't wait to meet Sulley."

Whippoorwill returned to her frosting as I returned to the living room and sat next to my Momma and wrapped my arms around her and gave her a kiss on the cheek. "This is the best wedding present I could ever get. How long are you able to stay here in Atlanta?"

Jubilee leaned forward and said, "We have our return tickets for Wednesday morning. We're sorry we were not able to give you any notice. We didn't know ourselves until three hours before the train was leaving the station. Several of our friends knew how much Ruby wanted to be here for your wedding, and they all did extra jobs in order to buy our tickets. They surprised us, and we were able to surprise you."

When Pearl and Ruby returned home an hour later, no one stopped talking all evening. It was as if we were all racing to get every story told and every memory shared before we ran out of time. We all had a lifetime of stories we wanted my momma to hear. I felt so good to be able to go up to her and put my arms around her. When I had left New York City at the age of seven, she and I were barely polite strangers. Throughout the years, our letters had drawn us closer, and I really got to know my momma. Now as a young man, to be able to hug and kiss her with absolute freedom was precious to me, and I could not get enough of her. The photos she had sent did not show what I was seeing in her eyes that night—no fear, no shame, no anger—only love.

In the wee hours of the morning, Jubilee and I headed for bed. Since I was now sleeping on the sofa, Auntie Pearl and Auntie Ruby took Momma out into the kitchen so I could get some sleep. They lowered their voices, but I could hear my aunts telling my momma all about her daddy. As I drifted off of sleep, I heard my momma's voice asking the sisters the same questions I had asked as a child. That night, my momma was seeing her daddy in a new way, and my heart was full.

The next morning was very busy. With two additional people getting ready for the wedding, I decided to take all of my clothes over to

Sulley's place, drop them off, and then head to the church to make sure all of Ruth's plans were being followed. People began bringing in fresh-cut flowers from their gardens. Each bouquet was that person's gift to us, and notes of congratulations were tucked into each bouquet. Ruth and I were going to love reading all of those notes together. By noon, the sanctuary looked like the big flower shop downtown. Once I felt everything was in order, I headed back to Sulley's place, put on my new suit and tie, and walked back to my house so I could walk my family back to the church.

Ruth had decided to wear her mother's wedding dress. She had lost her mother when she was only five years old and wanted something of her mother's at the wedding. When most of the people were seated, I walked in with Sulley at my side, knowing I was making the best decision of my life. I smiled at all of the guests as I waited for my bride to enter. My two aunties, beaming with love and pride, sat in the front row. I blew each of them a kiss and mouthed, "Thank you for everything." I then turned to my momma and mouthed, "I love you, Momma." My heart was filled to overflowing as I waited for my bride to appear. I was reminded of the declaration my Grandpa Samuel gave the day I was born: "May this boy never live a day without knowing he is loved."

I bowed my head and prayed, "Lord, would You please tell my Grandpa Samuel You answered his prayer?" As I lifted my head and wiped the tears from my eyes, I saw Ruth standing at the end of the aisle with her father, and she was smiling at me. As they both approached me, I stepped forward, took her arm and said loud enough for everyone in the church to hear me, "I am indeed a blessed man."

"Not yet you aren't, young man," Ruth's father smiled as he announced, "I have waited twenty-two years to give this girl away, and you are not going to rush it!"

The whole church exploded in laughter as I blushed. That day my beautiful, wise, loving, gracious, and patient Ruth was going to be mine forever. As Sulley handed me Ruth's wedding ring, I leaned over to him and said, "Sulley, now I know how you felt the day you married Whippoorwill."

Sulley's eyes welled up with tears as he smiled back at me. I took the ring from Sulley, turned back to Ruth, and slid the ring on her finger. I have no memory of anything else until her father said, "Tobias, you may now kiss your bride."

The ladies of the church brought out the cake and punch as everyone came around to congratulate us. I felt like a giggly school girl that afternoon. I could not stop smiling, and I kept whispering in my bride's ear, "Hello, Ruth Bascom, I love you."

Since honeymoons were for the rich and famous, Ruth and I decided we would spend our wedding weekend locked away in our new rental. I had arranged to take that Monday off of work but did not dare ask for more. As a wedding gift to us, several of the church women told us they were going to stock our kitchen with food. The night before our wedding, Ruth baked several special treats for us and took them over to the rental, along with all of her clothes. I had taken all of my clothes over a few days earlier. After we had greeted all of our guests, Ruth and I walked to our new home. Still in our wedding clothes, we were laughing and talking non-stop all of the way there. I knew my momma would be well cared for by my aunts, but we did arrange to get back together on their final night in town. Ms. Ruby said she would prepare a big family dinner on Tuesday night. With all of that settled, I could focus on my bride.

As we reached the back door, a wonderful smell greeted us. One of the ladies had come to the house that morning and had placed a cast iron pot in the oven filled with a pot roast, potatoes, carrots, and onions. A tray of yeast rolls was rising on the counter, ready to pop into the oven. The kitchen table was already set and ready for us. Oh, how we felt loved and cared for.

Our three days flew by. We knew we would have a lifetime together, but neither of us wanted this glorious weekend to end. But end it must, and life goes on. We both had responsibilities to attend to, but we always knew that the other one would be waiting for us at the end of every day.

I returned to the freight yard bright and early Tuesday morning, while Ruth returned to the bakery. That evening we celebrated our family history over dinner. Ms. Ruby told Momma the story about their time of living in the cavern. Afterward, Momma cried, "I'm so glad to know all these stories. Daddy never liked to talk about the past. He really was an amazing man."

The next morning they boarded the train back to New York. We didn't have a lot of time together, but the time we had was precious.

CHAPTER 32

The Battle For Gladys

OUR LONG WEEKEND had been wonderful, and now that the wedding was over and my momma was gone, I needed to start thinking about people other than myself. After all, Whippoorwill's baby would be coming soon, and the situation with Karl and Gladys still remained. Would our friend have his heart broken? Would Gladys respond? Would she become our friend or remain our life-long enemy simply because of the color of our skin?

One week after our wedding, Karl had invited Gladys to come to the warehouse to join him for lunch. Karl did not ambush Gladys. He straightforwardly told her that his purpose for having her come for lunch was in order to introduce her to his best friend. Gladys knew this was a deal-breaker for Karl. The fact that she had even agreed to come was a victory of some sorts.

The night before that first lunch, I was beside myself. Ruth's gentle words did not reduce my anxiety. I confessed, "Ruth, Karl has painted such an ugly picture of Gladys' anger, and I do not want to let Karl down, but a man can only take so much disrespect, especially when it's right in his face."

True to form, Ruth just smiled at me and said, "Tobias Bascom." I knew I was in trouble when Ruth used my full name. "You cannot do this on your own. Loving the unlovely—black or white—can only be done with God's grace. God has poured out His grace on you, and He expects you to share His grace with Gladys. This young woman has been put in your path, and you need to ask God to give you the strength to control your pride and love her like God loves her."

That night, Ruth and I prayed for my pride and for Gladys' wounded soul. If we were never to see her again, we wanted an opportunity to share God's love with her while we could. That night as we were getting ready for bed, Ruth said, "Toby, you have built Gladys' anger into a huge giant, and you are feeling like a grasshopper, right? Remember, Gladys is not the giant. It is her anger, not her, you are fighting. You walk up to her tomorrow and imagine yourself a grasshopper sitting on God's shoulders. When you see that flash of anger, just imagine God taking control of it. This is not your battle to win or lose. It is God's alone."

Again, I realized how blessed I was to have Ruth in my life. By the time I was leaving for work the next morning, I found myself almost excited to finally meet this Gladys.

The lunch whistle blew right at noon, and Karl headed over to the main gate to escort Gladys to our table. I found myself fidgeting with my lunch box—not so much out of anxiety; rather, today was a day of excited anticipation. After struggling to do what is right, and the struggle is finally over, something good will come from that struggle. By the time Karl and Gladys walked up to the table, my heart was sincere, and my soul was calm.

I did not extend my hand to Gladys because I did not want to offend her. I simply smiled and said, "Hello, Gladys, it's nice to meet you."

Gladys did not look directly at me. She nodded her head and took a seat as far away from me as she could. Karl decided to ignore this choice and said, "Gladys, this is my best friend, Tobias. Tobias, this is Gladys, the girl I wanted you to meet."

Gladys and I both caught the fact that Karl did not introduce her as his girlfriend. As Gladys opened up the picnic basket she brought with her, I opened my lunch bucket and placed my meal in front of me. I wanted Gladys to know that I did not intend to eat her food—not because I feared she might have tainted it, but because she wanted nothing to do with me.

Karl suggested he pray for our lunch, and, for several minutes, things remained quiet as Gladys began removing her lovely spread from the basket and placing each item in front of Karl. She had obviously gone to a lot of trouble to impress him. By the time she had everything laid out, the

280

ten-minute warning whistle blew. Karl started eating quickly, and Gladys joked, "I guess I need to be faster next time if you're going to be able to eat everything before the whistle blows again."

"I'm glad you want there to be a next time, Gladys," Karl responded. "I really do want you and Tobias to get to know each other."

Gladys just smiled but said nothing. I don't think she ever actually looked at me during that first lunch or for several others that followed, but she did keep coming, so there was hope.

I could feel her seething rage boiling under the surface, but I remained calm. After a week of just enjoying our lunches, Karl suggested that I lead us in a short devotional. I had been preparing them since we had first started planning these lunches. I would open with a Bible verse that talked about how much God loves us and would make only one or two comments, then close in prayer. I kept it simple, nothing profound, just sharing the simple truth that God loves us all.

For several weeks Gladys sat quietly, not engaging with me at all. She would not look at me or talk to me. She would not respond when I addressed her directly. Several times, she even leaned over to Karl and asked if they could eat their lunch alone. Karl remained steadfast. "Gladys, if you're not going to even try, why are you still coming around? Do you think I will change my mind? Do you think you can bat your pretty eyes at me, and I will ignore your serious problem? For weeks you have sat here hearing all about how much God loves you, yet you would rather hold onto your rage than to open your heart and accept God's love."

For the first time, Gladys got very real and very serious. Casting a quick smile my way, she confessed, "Karl, I really don't mind listening to Tobias talk about God's love. I've actually gone home a few times and looked up the verses he used and liked what they said." Then turning directly to me for the first time, Gladys asked, "I want to believe what you say about God, Tobias, but how can you say that God loves us when He allows such terrible things to happen to us?"

This was a truly honest question from Gladys, but before I could even gather my thoughts, the lunch whistle blew. With all the compassion God had poured into my heart for this woman, I said, "Gladys, if you will come back tomorrow, we can talk about your reasonable question. You have asked a fair question that everyone asks at one point in their life, and a quick, glib answer would not be fair to you."

That evening, Ruth, Karl, and I prayed for wisdom. Gladys' pain was real and deep, and only God's grace could reach that deep into her to heal her wounds. We knew we needed to talk about her pain, but we needed more wisdom than any of us possessed. I knew I could find lots of Bible verses that said how much God loves Gladys. I also knew I could find lots of Bible verses that would tell her she needed a Savior. I did not think I could, as a black man, be the one to talk to Gladys about the torture and murder of her beloved brother by a black man.

No, let me rephrase that. I did not want to be the one who would look Gladys in the eyes and dare to talk to her about her brother. One wrong word and the gates of hell would open up and try to swallow me. Again, I struggled to surrender my rights to protect myself. Somewhere, deep inside of me, I knew it had to be me—the black man. Not Karl, but me.

I knew if God could direct my words and bring healing to Gladys' soul, the healing would be so much more complete if it came from a person who represented her biggest giant—a black man. That night Ruth and I again prayed for God's grace over my life and that of Gladys' life. We prayed for eyes to see Gladys the way God sees her and to close my ears to the words that would inflame my feelings of pride.

Karl and I were both quiet as we clocked into work that morning. We were both concerned that Gladys might not even show up, but then if she did, how was she going to respond? We hardly spoke all morning, trying to stay focused on the work at hand so the morning would go by more quickly. I found myself checking the big clock on the freight yard tower several times. I still had no idea how I would begin my conversation today. Ruth had already warned me about the dangers of setting my agenda in my head. "Toby, you need to let Gladys lead the conversation. People respond better when you answer questions that they have asked, rather than giving them a lecture about what you think they need to know."

At times like this, I feel like a puny grasshopper. Nothing is in my control. Gladys might have gone home and regretted even asking that question. I wondered what to do if she goes back to her stone-faced countenance. Then I remembered Ruth's admonition, and I smiled at my continual need for control, and admonished myself, "Tobias, this is not your battle. You are simply the tool that God is using to show His love to this girl. This is not about you, Toby; it is about Gladys. If she requires patience, then you extend God's patience to her. If she needs wisdom, it is God's wisdom—not yours—that she needs. You surrender your heart to God and let Him direct the conversation." I repeated this admonition several times that morning.

Shortly before the lunch whistle blew, we looked over and saw Gladys standing at the freight yard gate. Karl gave me a wink as he loaded the last box on the dolly and made sure the dolly's brake was set and safe. By the time the lunch whistle finished blowing; Karl was half way to the gate to escort Gladys in.

I went inside the bailing door, grabbed my lunch and headed out to our table. We had been doing this for five weeks with nary a peep from any of our crewmen. They knew we were talking religion at our table, and they wanted nothing to do with it. As I walked out onto the deck and began walking down the wooden stairs that lead to the lunch area, I noticed two of our crewmen sitting at our table. They never did that. I immediately got irritated and grumbled to myself, "Didn't they know how important today was for Gladys? Why, today of all days, did these men decide to join us at our table?" My mind began to race, and I asked myself, "How can I get rid of these men?" I no sooner asked myself this question when Ruth's words repeated in my mind, "This is not your battle to win, Tobias. You let God direct things. He will always do a better job than we can."

This plan made no sense to me, but then I remembered that I am but a grasshopper, and I must trust that God is in control. I reached the table just as Karl and Gladys arrived, and I heard myself calmly saying, "Good day, Gladys, hope you had a restful night."

As I took my seat, I thought about what I had just said and thought, "Where did that come from? Why did I ask that?" I had no more than questioned it before I heard Gladys say, "Actually, I didn't get any sleep last night and almost did not come today because of it. After our conversation yesterday, I got home last night and found it was all I could think about." Gladys glanced over at the new men at the table before continuing, "You see, I can't really talk to my parents about it. Talking about Charlie in our house is a lightning-rod topic. I don't think my parents even talk to each other about Charlie anymore."

Luther suddenly sat up straight, "That's where I know you from. You are Charlie Thomas' sister, right? Charlie used to bring you around during our senior year of high school. You were just a kid back then."

Gladys' eyes filled with tears at the mention of her brother's name. "Yes I was, but I had to grow up fast. Charlie died when I was a senior in high school and my younger brother, Bill, was only eight. So you knew my brother, Charlie?"

Luther smiled, "I sure did!" Then as if weighing his words more carefully, Luther added, "What happened to Charlie was horrible, and I am glad they caught the guy. I couldn't imagine going through life wondering if every person you talk to might be the one who did it. At least now you know who he is and that he will never walk the streets ever again. At least that's something to be thankful for."

Gladys gave Luther a polite smile. "I guess you have a point there, although I hardly think there's anything about my brother's murder I can be thankful for."

Luther quickly corrected himself, "Oh, I didn't mean that, Gladys. I just meant that knowing who did it and that he is locked up means you can begin to move forward."

"You'd think so," Gladys responded with a rather acid tone, "but not really. I live with this all the time. Every single day I relive the night we found out my brother had been tortured and killed." Gladys then turned toward Karl and defiantly declared, "I not only hate the black man who tortured my brother, but now I hate all black men. You can't trust any of them."

Karl glanced over at me for help, but somehow I knew I was to remain silent. I thought it strange that I wasn't struggling to control myself. I was so focused on praying for Gladys' wounded heart that I could not take what she was saying personally.

Karl said nothing, just reached over and took Gladys' hand as she pleaded, "I'm so sorry, Karl. I tried; I really did. It is funny actually because I kind of like Tobias. I have enjoyed listening to him talk about God. I just cannot get past the fact that he is black. Everyone tells me blacks are all the same. They blame us for everything bad that has ever happened to them."

Before Karl could respond, we heard Luther ask, "Isn't that what you are doing, Gladys? Tobias did not murder your brother, yet you seem to be holding him responsible simply because he is black, and the man who murdered your brother is black. Personally, I have never had much use for blacks, but I've come to realize after working with Toby for almost a year now that they aren't all thieves nor are they all shiftless and lazy. My own brother has been in and out of jail for years. He hasn't done an honest day of work in his whole life, but that is the way he is. He's white, and he's my brother. We grew up in the same house, but who he is does not make me guilty of any of his crimes. Why is that true for whites and not for blacks?"

Gladys studied Luther's face as she considered his words. "Luther, it's not the same. You knew my brother, Charlie. You must have read how he was tortured by that black man?"

Undeterred, Luther answered right back, "Yes, my whole family followed the trial. I loved your brother, Gladys. He was everyone's favorite friend. But Gladys, what if it had been a white man who did it? Would you turn on Karl here? What if it had been one of those German immigrants who have been moving down here from Chicago? Would you hate all Germans? What if it had been the son of one of those Jewish New York jewelers who moved into Atlanta that same year to open up a shop down on Fulton Street? Would you hate all Jews?"

"Actually, Luther, I think I would." Gladys' voice broke as she said this. "Luther, my pain is so great and my anger is so all-consuming, I need to have somewhere to dump it or I will explode. It is too much to pour onto one single man. Since the first day I saw him in shackles at his arraignment, I promised myself I would never say his name ever again. The truth is..." Gladys confessed, "even if the courts would have allowed me to torture him the way he tortured my brother, I know it would never be enough to empty out the rage in my heart."

I was amazed at how this conversation was going. I kept praying for Gladys, and I knew Karl was praying. Then we heard Luther, the crewman who did not believe in religion, say to Gladys, "Then it appears to me, Gladys, that that black man killed more than your brother that day. Your brother, Charlie, lived an amazing life for twenty-two wonderful years. I have hundreds of great memories of Charlie; yet you only remember one—the day he died. Why are you giving that man so much power over your life? Didn't he take enough from you that day?"

Knowing his lunch break was quickly coming to an end, Luther stood up, gathered his lunch bucket, and asked one final question: "Gladys, what would Charlie think about how you are living your life now? Would he be happy for you?"

Luther was only three steps away from the table when the five-minute whistle blew. Karl, Gladys and I sat there quietly for a minute. None of us had even unwrapped our lunches, but none of us were hungry. We had too much to chew on to be thinking about food right then.

Karl finally stood up and took Gladys' hand, "I have to get you back to the freight yard gate, Gladys. I only have three minutes to get you there and be back to work before the final whistle blows."

Turning to me, Gladys said, "Can I come back tomorrow? My question from yesterday is still unanswered. Tobias, I'm not saying I have changed my mind about blacks, but I do recognize how unfair it is to you. I don't know if I could change even if I wanted to, but I'm willing to listen if you are willing to keep talking to me."

No one was more amazed at my calm and loving reply than I was. "Gladys, you are always welcome here. Maybe we both can learn truths about God's love."

After work Karl and I talked about how the lunchtime had gone. I confessed, "Karl, I was so frustrated when I saw Luther and Sammy sitting at our table. I just knew they were going to mess up our chance to talk with Gladys. But upon reflection, it could not have been more perfect."

Karl smiled, "'I doubt that Luther understands just how *on the money* he was. It is funny; Luther hates it when people talk religion, but God used him today, didn't He, Toby?"

"He sure did, Karl," I chuckled. "If you had been the one to say that, Gladys might have resisted because you want something from her. If I had said that, I would have been a black man defending all black men in her eyes. But Luther's love for her brother gave him permission to talk on Charlie's behalf. Gladys thinks she is showing her love for her brother by hating everyone she blames for his death. Luther reminded Gladys of Charlie's character and what he would have wanted for his kid sister."

After we clocked out that day, I turned to Karl and said, "Karl, you and I both know that Gladys' real problem is not with blacks. That is really a secondary issue. Her first and most important issue is her relationship with God. We cannot get so focused on how she feels toward blacks that we never get to the most important question in her life. Even if we could turn her into a radical lover of black people, but never introduced her to God's Son, we will have failed her."

CHAPTER 33

⚜

Suffer or Surrender

TRUE TO HER word, Gladys was standing at the gate the next day. Luther and Sammy returned to their old seats without a comment. Over breakfast that morning, Ruth and I had talked about what happened the previous day. Having a neutral third party at the table, getting Gladys to open up about her anger and hate, in front of me but not directed at me, had laid it all out in the open. Both Ruth and I were amazed that God had used Luther that way. He really didn't much care about Gladys. He said his piece and moved on, but God used him to prepare Gladys's heart, and he wasn't even aware of his role.

I decided I was not going to bring up Gladys' hate today, unless she brought it up. I wanted to get to her original question, but the day before reminded me that I could serve God better by not trying to control things. After all, I would have booted Luther and Sammy off the table if I had been in control of things the day before. I took a deep breath and lightheartedly prayed, "God, Grasshopper Private Bascom here, reporting for duty."

As soon as Gladys finished laying out Karl's lunch, she said, "I spent last night thinking about what Luther said yesterday, so I made myself remember lots of good memories of Charlie. Every time I slipped back and started rehearsing the trial, I made myself go back to when we were kids and thought of a fun day memory; it really did help."

Karl suggested, "Gladys, when you feel up to it, I sure would like to get to know Charlie. Maybe we could sit on your steps, and you could tell me some of those memories."

"I'd like that, Karl. Luther was right. I have allowed that man to rob me of all my good memories." Then taking on a more serious face, Gladys turned to me and stated, "Now, back to my unanswered question. Tobias, for years, your people suffered horribly under slavery. How can you believe there is a loving God who cares about you when He did that to your people?"

"Wow, Gladys, that's exactly what my Grandpa Samuel used to say until someone shared God's love with him. Many black people hold that belief. Actually, I don't think it is exclusively a black issue. Gladys, everyone has something terrible to overcome. It might not be the terrible death of a beloved brother or hundreds of years of forced slavery, but everyone has experienced something painful and feels the need to blame someone. The bigger the pain, the bigger the target must be for us to blame, and what is bigger than God? Gladys, you asked me how I could trust a God who allows bad things to happen. Gladys, it's because bad things happen to us that I know I must trust God's love. Every bad thing that anyone does, and that includes you and me, only proves that we are all sinners in need of a Savior. Oh, most of us would never kill someone. Most of us would never own another human being or sell a baby away from its momma or sell the baby's daddy. We justify our ugly sins because we can point to others who have done much worse, so we think we are good.

"Sin is like poison, Gladys. Imagine ten people being lined up at a table and told to drink the glass of water standing in front of them. However, murderers and those who hurt little children are given a glass full of poison to drink. That would be okay, right, Gladys? The next person in line is someone who captured and sold slaves for a living. How much poison should be in his glass? Same as the murderers, right? Of course right. Next to him stands the man who represents all of the men who use their power to control and oppress the common man. They build their wealth by cheating others and destroying lives through oppression and depression. Oh, they would never physically kill a man, but many a man has taken his own life because he could not endure what happened to him. Might we say that man's glass should be half full of poison? The next is a mother who is so full of her own pain and selfish desires that she pours out her pain on her own children. Her cruelty, both physically and emotionally, destroys that child's will to live. How much poison should be in her glass? Gladys, all of these examples represent terrible people, right?"

"Of course they are," responded Gladys.

"Gladys, you, Karl, and I are nothing like any of those people, right? As long as we compare ourselves to the likes of these terrible people, we are good people, right?"

"Well, we are good people, Tobias," Gladys cried out in defense. "We don't do bad things."

"No, we don't do terrible sins, do we, Gladys? We are never selfish. We have never been cruel to anyone. We have never walked past a needy person and ignored his need because we were too busy. We have never used our words to make anyone feel small and insignificant, right?

"Gladys, can we both agree that, sometime in our life, we have all done something, said something, or even simply thought something mean and hurtful?"

Obviously uncomfortable with where this was going, Gladys admitted, "Well sure, we would be kidding ourselves if we thought we had lived a perfect life, but I'm not a terrible person like those people."

"Gladys, you've seen the meat scales at every butcher shop in town, right?"

"Sure."

"Most of us believe that at the end of our life, all of our bad stuff—Gladys, can we agree to call the bad stuff *sin*?" Gladys nodded her head in agreement. "Good, so we believe that if our sin is placed on one of those meat scales, and if any one of those other people's sins are placed on the other side, we would win, right? As long as we are better than *them*, we are good.

"The problem is, that is not how we will be judged at the end of our lives. It will not be anyone else's sins on the other side of that scale; rather, it will be God's perfection sitting on the other side of that scale. God loves us with a perfect love. He loved us so much that He sent His Son to die for our sins. That's the kind of love that will judge us or redeem us. Have we loved others with that kind of love? Of course we haven't, but if we accept

His love and His sacrifice, He promises to remove our sins from the scale and make us perfect in His sight.

"Gladys, if you have not done this, then you are still standing at that table with a glass of poison sitting in front of you. It might not be filled to the brim with poison, but it still has poison in it. Any amount of that poison will kill you. Would you really care if the person beside you is drinking pure poison while you only have a little in your glass, especially if you are required to drink your glass and die? God's love promises to remove all the poison. He offers us a perfectly clean glass because His love is perfectly clean.

"You asked why God causes bad things to happen to us. God does not cause it; He allows it. There is a big difference between the two. Man has been allowed to choose for himself the path he will take. Will he choose hate and selfishness, or will he choose God's love and forgiveness? So, Gladys, I'm asking you that same question. Which will you choose?"

"Tobias, when you gave the example of the mother, were you thinking of me? Are you saying that because I am so filled with hate about my brother, that I would hurt my own children?"

"Gladys, God did not cause what happened to your brother, yet you hate Him for it. A sinful black man did the crime, yet you now hate all black men for what he did. He was so filled with hate that he poured that hate out on your brother. Hate is a poison that destroys the hater. Do you honestly believe you can keep from poisoning your children when you harbor so much hate yourself?"

"Tobias, I want to believe that God loves me. I know my hate is destroying me; I just don't think I can let it go."

"Gladys, you can't—not without God's help. Aren't you tired of carrying this hate around with you? If you knew exactly how much God loves you, would you be willing to allow Him to cleanse out all that hate and bring peace and calm to your soul?"

Gladys looked from Tobias, to Karl, and back to Tobias before saying, "Tobias, if you can be patient with me and keep teaching me about God's love, I'm willing to listen. I know I need help, but I'm scared that I'm too far gone. I think I killed off the old Gladys, and there is nothing inside of me now but hate."

"Gladys, all God asks of us is to give Him a chance to prove His love to us. If you will keep coming, I will keep sharing God's Word with you. Do we have a deal?"

Just as the lunch whistle blew, Gladys reached out her hand and said, "Let's shake on it, Tobias. I want to believe."

For the next few weeks Gladys faithfully came every lunch hour. She peppered me with questions, but now they were not challenges. She was wholeheartedly seeking truth. Several times I felt she was at the brink of surrender, but something always seemed to hold her back.

Ruth and I continued to pray for Gladys' heart. She was no longer aggressive toward me, but that did not mean she was truly changing. At dinner, I suggested that Ruth might come and join us for our lunchtime study. Ruth had been praying for Gladys for almost a year, and I felt it was time for the two women to meet, so Ruth agreed to come the next day.

At noon, Gladys was at the gate, anxious to begin our study. Karl looked around for Ruth but did not see her, so he brought Gladys to the table. I came out of the bailing door just as Karl and Gladys reached the table. I looked back at the gate, and there stood Ruth, calm and smiling, and excited to finally meet Gladys. I raced over to the gate to let her in, and I brought her to the table. "Gladys, I would like to introduce my bride to you. Gladys, this is Ruth Bascom. Ruth, this is Gladys Thomas."

Ruth, Karl, and I were shocked at Gladys' response. She immediately recoiled from Ruth's extended hand, and the look on her face turned hard and angry. Gladys pushed past us and ran for the gate with Karl running quickly at her heels. Ruth turned to me and said, "Let's pray, Toby. I believe Gladys is in the battle of her life right now."

At least fifteen minutes passed before Karl and Gladys returned to the table. Gladys had obviously been crying, and Karl's eyes were ablaze with fear as Gladys tried to explain to us why she had reacted the way she had. "I'm sorry I was so rude just now. I was just shocked to meet your wife, Tobias. Instantly, you turned from the teacher I have come to admire into just another black man who has a wife. I know that does not make sense, but it seemed so logical to me at the moment. I was instantly filled with rage that you get to have a life, and my brother will not. I don't know why I reacted that way. I truly am glad that you have found love in your life, but at that moment, all I could feel was rage."

Ruth and I remained quiet. We both knew that Gladys needed to talk through her feelings. "For weeks now, Tobias, I have struggled with my pride. Several times I have been tempted to ask you to pray with me. I wanted to surrender to God's love, but I just couldn't give in. I talked myself out of it because I didn't want Karl to think I was doing it just to win him. I also couldn't give in because I am afraid that after I do, nothing will really change for me. Then what will I do? I know I cannot stay as I am. I want to believe that God's love can change me."

Ruth leaned forward and with all the love God had poured into her heart for this woman, she suggested, "Then Gladys, test Him. Surrender yourself to God and let Him show you that He can be trusted. What do you have to lose?"

"I want to, I really do. I want God to clean out my soul and take away all of this poison I have inside of me. I know I'm a sinner and that my only hope is in God's love." Turning to Tobias while taking Karl's hand, Gladys asked, "Tobias, will you pray with me? I am ready to surrender my heart and soul to God."

The four of us held hands and prayed. None of us cared who was watching or what they were thinking. God's work was being done at that table, and Gladys' heart was surrendering to the loving God of the universe. Ruth and I prayed for her healing and redemption from the slavery of hate and rage. We asked God to flood Gladys' being with His love and to show her how much she could trust Him. When we were done, we stood quietly with our heads bowed, hoping Gladys would also pray. Quietly at first, but quickly becoming more confident, we heard her speak.

God, I love all the Bible verses that talk about Your love for me. I know I deserve to drink that glass of poison because I have so much poison inside

of me. But God, You sent Your Son to drink that glass for me, and I sur-
render myself to You because You loved me that much. I want to become
Your child, God.

Gladys expected an immediate transformation with bells, whistles, angelic singing—the works. She stood there a moment with a look of disappoint-ment, but Ruth sat her down and explained all that had happened during her prayer. "Gladys, God just purified that glass of poison for you, and you will never again have a glass of poison placed in front of you. God adopted you into His family and wrote your name in the Lamb's Book of Life. He just sealed your salvation for all of eternity. All of that was completed be-fore you even said amen."

Gladys' eyes welled up in tears. "But I don't feel any different. I need to see a change in me. I cannot stay the way I am."

Ruth smiled and corrected Gladys, "You mean the way you were. You have been forgiven. Those feelings will come, Gladys. You can trust God to keep His word. You are now His child."

Several months passed before Gladys fully realized exactly how profound-ly she had changed. She had wanted immediate change, but God was mak-ing it permanent. She wanted an emotional display, but God was quietly changing her heart. We could see the changes much more quickly than Gladys could, but soon even Gladys began to realize that her heart was be-ginning to mellow and soften—not toward black people alone, but toward life, love, acceptance, peace, and mercy. We were seeing a new woman de-velop right before our eyes, and her transformation was exciting to watch.

CHAPTER 34

Surrendering Our Dream

DURING THAT FIRST year as we worked with Gladys, life continued as usual. Sulley and Whippoorwill's new baby son arrived, and we all celebrated with them. I thought Sulley's heart was going to explode with pride as he carried his son into his living room to show him off. "Toby, I would like to introduce you to my son, Sullivan Tobias Samuel Dunbar. We are going to call him Van, for short."

"He is a beautiful boy, Sulley," I replied with tears in my eyes. "I feel so honored that you gave him my name and my grandpa's name."

"I would have left off the 'Sullivan' part, but Whippoorwill insisted. Besides, when you have your son, he will be Tobias."

"Sulley, I am sure your son will live up to all three names. He will certainly be loved and cared for."

"Toby, I have always remembered the story of what your Grandpa Samuel did the day you were born. Ever since I first heard that story, I wanted to do the same when I had my children. But Whippoorwill warned me that she wants to be present when I do it, and she can't get up for a few more days. Would you and Ruth, Ms. Pearl and Ms. Ruby, and Rev. Johnson please come over after church next Sunday? My wife and I would like all of you here when we present our son to God and pronounce a blessing upon his life."

That Sunday we felt honored to stand as witnesses as Sulley and Whippoorwill stood under the open sky, lifted up their firstborn son, presented him to God, and asked Him to bless their son's life. Once word got around about this sweet ceremony, it became a tradition in our church that still goes on today. After the third child, the parents started keeping the child's name a secret until the ceremony, making the time of dedication even sweeter.

Ruth and I spent as much time as possible with little Van. We had been named his godparents, but in truth, we wanted as much practice as possible holding a little one since neither of us had any experience in that area. Months went by without any signs of hope. At first, we were able to set our hopes aside and focus on Gladys. We assumed our baby would come in due time.

On our second anniversary, Karl and Gladys were married. Even though we were busy with their wedding plans and happy for them, the fact that we were still not expecting was a hard pill to swallow. As with most matters, Ruth handled it better than I did—at least she did at first. Several of the older women shared how their first child did not come until well after their first year of marriage. This news brightened her spirit, and Ruth was able to pour herself into other people's lives and wait patiently—that is, until after only six months of marriage, Karl and Gladys announced they were expecting. I could see that this news rattled Ruth's usually calm spirit. She remained gracious and happy for Gladys, but I did not take my eyes off of her that whole evening.

We barely got into our kitchen door before Ruth collapsed in my arms, "Toby, I am glad for Gladys, I really am. But I don't think I am strong enough to endure this. What if we are never meant to hold our very own child in our arms? What if we are never to have a naming ceremony and ask God to bless our child's life? Toby, I don't think I can bear this."

As I stood there in our kitchen, knowing my wife's heart was breaking in sorrow, my mind raced to think of something that would calm her heart and dry her tears. I wanted to quote the perfect verse that would fix everything, but I knew that Ruth already knew all those verses and she did not need me to lecture her right then. Suddenly, the memory of my Auntie Pearl's story about how she comforted Uncle Joseph at the loss of their only child came to my mind. Ms. Pearl and I are so much alike—both in our strengths and in our weaknesses. I remembered her saying that God shut her mouth that day because Joseph needed comfort—not instruction. She knew the hope of other children someday would not remove the pain of losing their child that day. She said that it was in their grieving together that God bound their hearts as one.

Standing there holding the strongest woman I ever knew, I realized that that was a moment for us to bond together in our greatest fear. I allowed myself to feel Ruth's fear and pain at possibly never having a child of our own. Eighteen months of disappointments now loomed into a lifetime of possible disappointment. Ruth and I both cried and held onto each other. Neither of us gave the other one false hope or hollow platitudes. We knew we were standing at an altar and being asked to trust God with our dreams. Neither of us was questioning God's love for us, but we were both struggling to accept what might be God's plan for us.

Without saying a word, I finally pulled our two kitchen chairs away from the table and guided my beautiful wife down onto our knees. "Ruth, we don't know what God's plan is for us. There still may be children in our future, but I believe you and I need to lay our dream of children at God's feet. If we hold onto this dream like some right we are owed, it will cripple us. We need to release the dream and trust God through our pain, so God can fill our hearts with His peace and joy."

I would like to think that we only had to do this one time, but that would not be the truth. Ruth and I struggled many times—usually when a close friend had a baby. Loving them enough to be happy for them, while we mourned for the babies that never came to us, was the hardest trial Ruth and I endured, but endure it we did. Over the next five years, Sulley and Whippoorwill had two more children; Karl and Gladys had a second son. We loved these children and would never wish our sorrow on our dear friends. God used these trials to stretch our love for others, for it was in those times of struggle that Ruth and I asked God to pour His love into our hearts so we could be glad and celebrate with our friend's during their times of greatest joy.

By 1928 we had been married for six years, and life was good. Ruth's father began to turn some of the preaching over to me, and I loved it. I still worked full-time at the railroad yard because our church family could not afford to support two pastors, but I didn't mind.

Our weekly Bible study was going stronger than ever. If it were not for our annual remembrance day—the day we took stock of all the answers to prayers, I could have easily forgotten how far Gladys had come. The hardheartedness was gone, and, in its place, stood a gracious, kind, loving woman. People who had not known her previously would have a hard time imagining exactly how hateful and hard she could have been. Gladys' family was the most impressed. Although never religious people, her parents could not help but see the difference in her, which caused them to begin seeking out this God who changed their daughter so very much. Her younger brother, Bill Thomas, had been only eight years old when Charlie was killed, and, for several years, she had filled his head with her hate. He was twelve years old when Gladys surrendered her anger to God, and she worked hard trying to undo all the hatred she had poured into her little brother. Gladys' complete change intrigued her family, and soon they were joining her at church. Her father said, "If God can make that kind of change in my Gladys, maybe there's hope that her mother and I might find our way out of the dark pit we have been in since we lost our boy."

Karl and I continued with our lunchtime Bible study, and three of our crewmen were now regulars. First, it was Luther and Sammy who joined us, but then Luther brought Hank along. For two full years, the yard foreman, Ed Gardner, stayed on Karl's case about the Bible study, but Karl knew his real beef was with me. Ed wanted me gone, and he made it clear to Karl that, with or without his help, I was on my way out. He had already replaced the three blacks on the late night shift, but because our team continued to be ranked on top, he needed Karl's help to get rid of me.

In October of 1928, Sammy's mother who lived in Baltimore took ill, and he came to Karl and me after work and said, "I have to leave right away. My mother is sick, and there is no one up in Baltimore to take care of her. The doctors say she won't survive this, but it might take a year before it takes her. I'm sorry about the short notice, but I have to go."

As the crew captain, Karl had every right to hire Sammy's replacement, and he knew exactly who he wanted. Sulley's painting business was really struggling, and with three little mouths to feed, he needed a good paying job. Besides, with Sulley's size, he would be a great asset to the crew. That evening Karl offered the job to Sulley, who accepted without any hesitation. "Karl, I can finish up my current paint job in two days. Would that work for you?"

"Sure, Sulley. You can start this Thursday." Karl knew his replacement was going to get him into hot water with Ed. Not only was he not getting rid of me, he was bringing on another one. Karl kept all this to himself, and I didn't know how much pressure he was under until it all came to a head a week later. Sulley had been on the job for four days and was doing a great job. His size and power ensured the heavy pallets were off-loaded quickly, which further infuriated Ed. It was more important to Ed to get his way than to have the top-producing crew on the yard.

I noticed that Karl was beginning to look a little haggard when he came out of Ed's office after our shift. I asked him about it several times, but I always got, "Oh, it is just business. Ed is never happy. He thinks he isn't doing his job unless he is pouring on the pressure."

Karl did not want to bother either me or Sulley. He had no intention of firing us and hoped that our crew reports would eventually make Ed back down; it didn't happen. Instead, Ed began writing up Karl for negligence. He would walk through the yard and find dolly wagons fully loaded without the safety brake set. At first, Karl called the crew together and yelled at all of us about the safety rules. One mistake was one mistake too many, but when the third dolly in two weeks' time was found without the safety brake set, Karl knew something funny was going on, but it wasn't funny. A fully loaded runaway dolly could kill a man. One afternoon, Karl noticed Ed's moving around behind the weight landing. Once the men loaded a dolly, they would roll it onto the weight landing and record its weight before moving it out onto the deck. Once the weight has been recorded onto the bill of lading and pasted on the outside of the top crate, it was ready to be taken down the ramp and pushed over to the loading dock beside the freight car.

Karl made his way around behind the crates that were ready to be loaded and kept an eye on where Ed was and what he was doing. He watched as Ed moved around and released the safety brake of the first dolly in line. Sulley had just taken the dolly in front of it and was halfway down the ramp when Ed gave the dolly a hard shove and then took off running. Karl screamed at Sulley to get out of the way as he made a mad dash for the ramp still screaming at Sulley. At the last minute, Sulley let go of his dolly and dove off the ramp. The runaway dolly slammed into Sulley's dolly, and they both picked up speed as they crossed the freight yard. Luther heard the screaming and saw what was happening. He grabbed an anchor pole, a wooden pole six feet long and about three inches in diameter, which is used to strap down the dolly inside the freight cars. Luther jammed the first pole under the front wheels of the first dolly, but the speed was too great to stop the forward motion. He grabbed a second and third pole, shoving the first in front of the wheel, and then he shoved the second pole under the first pole like a pole-vaulter, jamming the first pole right into the dolly's axle. Luther used all of his body weight to bring both dollies to a stop. Everyone stood there stunned by what had happened—everyone except Ed. He was back in his office as if nothing had happened when Karl walked in and accused him of sabotage. "Ed, I watched you release that brake and push that dolly. You could have killed Sulley just now. Was it also you who released the other brakes?"

Ed's face was beet red as he yelled, "I don't know what you're talking about, Karl. I have been in my office this whole time. Your crew is just sloppy, and you are trying to blame me for their mistakes. This will be your fourth infraction in as many weeks, Karl. I think there is going to be some changes made around here. Toby and Sulley will be gone by tomorrow."

Karl leaned against Ed's desk, slammed his fist down and shouted, "You have been trying to get rid of them since day one, but I never thought you would put men's lives in danger. I saw you release that brake and shove the dolly, Ed."

With a smug face, Ed replied, "Prove it. As a matter of fact, I think you will be gone tomorrow as well. Blaming your supervisor for your crew's shoddy work is grounds for firing."

Sulley and I were standing at the doorway and heard the whole thing. Even if we both volunteered to quit, it would not have saved Karl's job. I felt so helpless standing there. I knew there was nothing I could do, when suddenly I felt a hand placed on my right shoulder, and I was being moved aside. I looked up and saw Mr. Sutterhill, whose eyes were blazing with anger as he slipped between Sulley and me and walked up to Ed Gardner and said, "I saw you release that brake, Ed. I was standing up on the catwalk and wondered why you were walking around behind the crates. I want you out of here within the hour. Turn in your keys and empty your desk, and, by the way, you will not be getting a letter of recommendation from this company. You are just lucky no one was killed."

Mr. Sutterhill took hold of Karl's shoulder and marched him out of Ed's office before saying, "Karl, I want you to write up Luther. He earned a triple bonus today. Those runaway dollies would have crashed into the freight car if he hadn't risked his own life to stop them. He saved this company a lot of money today."

"I will be more than happy to tell Luther you said that, Mr. Sutterhill," Karl beamed with pride. "I am so thankful you were up on that catwalk today. No one would have believed me."

"Yes, I would have, Karl. It was no accident that I was up on that catwalk. Your crew has had a clean record for five years, then suddenly all these safety infractions. I knew something was up."

"Thank you, Mr. Sutterhill. We have all tried to do our very best for you."

"I know that, Karl,'" Mr. Sutterhill said with a strange look on his face. "I've kept my eye on you over the years, and I will be sad to lose you as a crew captain."

Stunned, Karl just stood there. *"Am I still going to lose my job?"*

Mr. Sutterhill slapped his hand on Karl's shoulder and laughed, "Well, Karl, you cannot be a crew captain and the yard foreman at the same time, can you? Tell Luther that he has your old job, and tomorrow morning you move into your new office."

Life was good again, and we were all thankful. Ed was gone, Sulley and I were secure in our jobs, and Karl received a much-deserved promotion. For the next twelve months, we all enjoyed the fruits of our labor. We worked harder than ever to make sure Mr. Sutterhill would not regret his decision.

One year later, in October of 1929, the Great Depression hit hard. Men were jumping out of windows in New York, bread lines began forming everywhere, and lots of men were out of work. About a month later, the full weight of this disaster sank in. At Bible study one night, Sulley shared an idea with the group. "You all know that I struggled to put food on the table and keep a roof over my family's head when I ran my own painting business. I thought I just needed to work harder with three little ones to feed, but I had no idea this terrible disaster was coming. I am so thankful to Karl, but mostly to God, for providing this job at the freight yard. During this Depression, as they are calling it, no one has any money to paint anything. There are no painting jobs going on anywhere in the city, but freight cars are still moving and someone is needed to load them. I feel so blessed that God gave me this job so my three little ones will not go hungry."

CHAPTER 35

The Great Depression

SULLEY'S THANKFUL HEART would not stop churning. Every Friday, Karl stood at the bailing door as the shift whistle blew the ending of our work-week. As he handed out the pay envelopes, Sulley would almost tear up as he said, "Thank you, Karl." The weight of this blessing was very real to Sulley. Being able to take that pay envelope home and put food on the table for his wife and three little ones, while other men were seeing their children go without weighed heavily on him.

After a week or two of contemplating his options, Sulley decided he would share his idea with Karl and me. "Because the three of us are employed, we need to do something for those who are hurting."

"What do you have in mind, Sulley?" I asked.

"Toby, there is a large vacant lot beside the church. I think we should gather up all the able-bodied men and start a community garden. People are struggling to get by, and if we can help out by stretching their food supply, I think we should do it. I also think we should get all the old men of the church who love fishing and start a 'Fishing-for-Jesus' ministry. I know none of us have a lot left over, but if we have anything left over and do not share it during this time, we are not being thankful. How about it?"

"Sulley, I can think of two or three other vacant lots in the city that we could also garden. My aunts have a very deep backyard, and so does Miss Fanny and Rev. Johnson. Our little leftovers, if pooled together, could be used to feed a multitude."

Ruth was quiet while we men banged out our gardening plan. When we were finished, Ruth said, "Toby, remember the story about how your Great-Grandma Hannah canned all the fruits and vegetables so they would not starve during the Civil War? Your aunts told about canning food to make them last. We don't know how long this depression is going to last. We could put together a team of women who know how to do canning, and they can teach the others. It is late October, but we still have lots of blueberries around, apples are still going strong and figs are available for at least another month. If we start this community pantry, we can also provide something sweet once in a while. We can ask everyone to gather up all their unused jars and build a canning closet in the back of the fellowship hall." Ruth stopped to catch her breath and then smiled and chuckled. "We could paint a big sign above the closet, 'I CAN do all things through Christ who strengthens me.' "

We burst out in laughter at Ruth's enthusiasm, but we all agreed with her idea. We knew this was a wonderful idea and a great opportunity to show the love of Christ to others.

We started with the vacant lot next to the church. In order to avoid the winter frost, we began by building raised planting beds. We started with carrots, beets, parsnips, rutabaga, onions, cabbage, leaf lettuce, and spinach. In one weekend, we had all twenty raised beds planted.

At my aunt's house, Sulley and several others built raised planting beds and started broccoli, cauliflower, mustard greens, and parsnips. These would grow all winter and could be harvested well into spring.

Ruth and Rev. Johnson decided their garden would be filled with herbs. They planted thyme, basil, chives, dill, lemon grass, marjoram, mint, garlic, and parsley. Ruth knew that their garden would make the other gardens produce perk up in soups and casseroles.

Although both of my aunts were now eighty years old, they wanted to help. Gardening and canning was simply out of the question. As word got around to other churches about our "Mercy Gardens," these churches began sending a small committee over to check out what we were doing. Ruth came up with a wonderful idea of how best to use my aunties. "Once a month we can invite people to our church who are interested in starting their own Mercy Garden. The men can share what we have learned about growing vegetables year-round. We can do the same for the women who want to start a canning pantry. Aunt Pearl and Aunt Ruby can tell them the story of how their Momma saved everyone on the plantation from starving during the Civil War. If we can get four or five other churches to join us, we can make sure food will always be available to share here in Atlanta."

Hearing Ruth's idea brought a new realization to me. "You know, Ruth, using that terrible situation my great-grandma went through to help bless people today is wonderful. First, it means that many other people will hear what she went through, but most importantly, her experience can help others overcome the struggle they are going through."

During the worst years of the Deep Depression, our church family experienced our greatest years of blessings. We had no idea how long this depression was going to last, but we all proved that when we stand united, care for the needy, and share the Gospel, life can be rich and full—even in times of great stress.

By the summer of 1930, our church was operating four Mercy Gardens. In addition to ours, we helped other churches start eleven more around the greater Atlanta area. Ms. Pearl and Ms. Ruby loved telling their momma's story. If a church was having a hard time getting their people to see the vision, the ladies of that church would call a meeting, and Ms. Pearl and Ms. Ruby would tell their story. By the time they were finished, the majority of the people were willing to sign up to help. Many were able to survive those first, and most fearful, years of the Depression. Many of those who benefited from Mercy Gardens began attending church, though church attendance was not required to receive our help. Once the people realized the love that was being shown to them, they wanted to find out more. Outside, in the garden, they received one kind of mercy, but inside the church building, they learned of God's great mercy. At first we fed their bodies, but then we fed their souls.

Ruth, Whippoorwill, and Gladys made sure the canning pantry remained stocked all year round. Because jars and lids were expensive to replace, Whippoorwill asked Sulley to build a lean-to beside the church. As people came up to the side door to receive their Mercy supply, they would drop off their empty jars and lids at the lean-to. One of the young men, usually Sulley's boy, Van, would gather up these used jars and carry them into Rev. Johnson's kitchen. There, Ms. Ruby would be ready with boiling pots of soapy water to clean the jars and set them out to dry so they could be refilled by the canning committee.

Ms. Ruby loved teaching the younger women how to can. Seeing the young men out in the garden brought back sweet memories of Brother Samuel, and passing along Momma Hannah's talent meant she would live on in these young women's memories.

Ruth and I kept a close eye on the two sisters. Their excitement tended to overtake their energy. Many an afternoon, Ruth would walk into the canning kitchen and make Ms. Ruby sit down. "You can instruct these young girls from here, Ms. Ruby. You have been on your feet for hours."

We knew the sisters felt they were running out of time, and they wanted to get in all the opportunities they could before their age closed the door. Pearl loved talking to the church ladies about getting their children educated. She had already been doing this for years. Once Sulley and I were grown, Pearl missed the thrill of teaching boys how to read. From an early age, girls were put to work and had no spare time for learning. Girls were busy caring for their siblings and cleaning their momma's house; or they were hired out in order to bring in much-needed money.

Pearl had started visiting the neighborhood schools back in 1921, reading to the children every Friday afternoon. She knew if she could just get them "bitten" by the love of reading, their desire would carry them forward. Pearl cherished sharing her love of books and spent nearly every day talking to one church group after another about the importance of sending their children to school. She was always distressed when a mothers said, "My boy can't never read. He's good for not'n but labor."

Pearl would tell them the story of Sulley and how black children are every bit as capable of learning to read. She would come home after one of these meetings and storm around the house, saying, "If their own parents have swallowed the lie, how are we ever going to convince the children? It's bad enough the white people think we are incapable of learning, but when our own people believe it—that mountain is almost insurmountable. We have to prove to them that they can learn. We also have to show them why they must learn. I love it when I sit in a classroom and start reading a book about some exciting adventure, watching all the boys leaning on the very edge of their seats. They are fairly beside themselves in anticipation of the next page. Once they realize that learning to read will open all these books for them, I have them!"

From 1921 through 1931, Pearl had been responsible for starting six different church- reading clubs. She had made it her mission to find good, exciting readers who were willing to help out. She collected copies of the best adventure books available and set up a club schedule, which accomplished two goals: 1) the boys became excited about reading, and 2) they stayed out of trouble.

By 1931, at the age of eighty-two, Ms. Pearl was a most beloved woman by all of the black boys of Atlanta. She would walk around town, stopping in to the reading clubs to pay a visit. She loved to see the boys piled on the floor at the feet of the reader. You could almost hear a pin drop until the excitement overtook the boys, and they would leap up and scream in pure joy.

During her final year, Ms. Pearl started four more clubs in the city. We tried to get her to slow down, but there was no stopping her. After all, she was on a mission. That winter was an especially wet one, but Ms. Pearl was determined to get these four clubs up and running. No one could read a story like Ms. Pearl could. While reading *Treasure Island*, young Jim Hawkins was right in the room, climbing the ship's mast and hanging on for dear life. Every boy could see him clear as day—just like I had so many years before.

Ruth was the first to notice the deep, persistent cough, but Ms. Pearl refused to stop. She would argue, "My boys need me today. We are right at the most exciting point, and I want to see their faces when they learn the truth."

In late fall of 1931, my eighty-two-year-old Auntie Pearl took to her bed with a bad headache—something she never did. After two days, we were all concerned and called a doctor. Pearl's vision was so blurry she could not read, and the headaches were getting worse. The doctor said he could give her something for the headaches, but he feared her blurry vision was a sign of a brain tumor. "At her age," he warned us, "There is really nothing we can do for her. Just keep her safe and warm."

Once the headaches were under control, Pearl enjoyed resting in bed while we all took turns reading to her. Aunt Ruby and I took our turns first, but then Ruth, Sulley, Pastor Johnson, Karl, and even Gladys took their turns. Over the past eight years, Gladys had become one of Pearl's closest friends. Seeing the change in Gladys' heart gave Pearl hope for a better tomorrow. She always said, "If God can change Gladys so completely, we dare not question what He can do for all of the others."

Ms. Pearl's last six weeks went by much too quickly, but the number of people who came to celebrate her life was a real blessing. At her service, I told her story.

Apart from my wife Ruth, my Aunt Pearl was the strongest woman I have ever known. She was born and reared a slave on the Stewart Plantation. At the age of six, my Great-Grandma Hannah would put my Auntie Pearl to work in the dry goods pantry, measuring flour, cornmeal, lard, salt, and sugar. As Pearl worked, she listened to the Master's children having their lessons, and Pearl was bitten by the desire to read. For two years, she quietly sat by the entry to the children's classroom and listened. She had a hunger to know words, and that hunger lasted until the day she died. Auntie Pearl was a determined, stubborn person, which were very dangerous attitudes for a slave.

My Auntie Pearl was given a rare opportunity for a slave. The Mistress of the house, Ms. Victoria, decided that Pearl would be taught how to read and write—not for Pearl's benefit, but for her own. She intended to raise Pearl to take over the household after Great-Grandma Hannah passed away. Ms. Victoria was tired of all the hours it took filling out supply lists for the kitchen, so Pearl was tutored for five years; she never wasted a single day of her education.

After being emancipated, Auntie Pearl insisted upon teaching my Grandpa Samuel and my Auntie Ruby how to read. She also taught her dear friend, Estée Washington, how to read. Many of you have heard the story of Estée and what she went through as a captured runaway slave. You've heard how broken she was and how her fear of white people kept her a prisoner in her own home. But through books, Estée got to see the world and sail the seven seas. Through reading, Estée had lots of wonderful friends—both black and white.

Throughout her lifetime, Ms. Pearl taught many in this room how to read.

As I made this statement, Auntie Ruby, Sulley and Whippoorwill each stood up and raised their hands in praise to Ms. Pearl. Suddenly, dozens of boys, who had been standing at the doorway, began to walk into the church and raise their hands. One boy announced, "There are many, many more of us. We cannot all fit into the church, but ten reading clubs of boys are standing outside. Ms. Pearl was our friend and our hero." With grateful tears in my eyes, I repeated one of Ms. Pearl's favorite mantras.

Reading will open doors that no one can shut. It will take you places you are not allowed to go. It will introduce you to people, both living and dead, who struggle with the same things we struggle with. Reading shows us that we are not so very different from everyone else.

Because Aunt Pearl had been so ill, Ruth and I had temporarily moved into my old bedroom to help care for her. After the funeral, Ruth suggested that we give up our rental house and permanently move in with Ms. Ruby. We did not want Auntie Ruby left alone, and since her house was paid for, the money we would save on rent could go into the supplies for the Mercy

Garden. Many families were joining forces during the Depression just to get by, but we were doing it out of love—not out of necessity.

We had barely recovered from Pearl's loss, when we lost Ruth's father. He had been in failing health for almost a year, but the Mercy Garden project had kept him going. For many months I had taken over most of his duties, but the first Sunday after his passing, I was embraced as the full-time pastor.

That afternoon, Ruth and I met with the leaders of the church. Because we were settled and happy with Ms. Ruby, we requested they offer the church parsonage to Sulley and Whippoorwill. Sulley was already spending every evening and weekend at the church organizing Mercy Gardens, and Whippoorwill had taken over the canning ministry when Pearl became ill, so it made sense to give the house to them.

The gardens' flourished under Sulley's care. The church family increased in numbers as people experienced the love our church showed in their time of need. Even though we were growing and flourishing, funds were still tight for everyone. Ruth and I decided that I would continue to work at the freight yard, using the pastor's salary to keep the church doors open.

Out of love for Aunt Pearl and love for her young boys, Ruth and Gladys decided to take over Aunt Pearl's reading clubs. Right after her funeral, one of the clubs decided to rename themselves, "The Pearl Bascom Reading Club," and soon all the others followed suit. Twelve chapters were located in various parts of the city, and the boys who formed the clubs were fiercely loyal to her memory.

One evening we invited Karl and Gladys over for dinner, and Ruth recounted her first meeting with one of the chapters.

At first the boys were uncomfortable with my presence. I'm sure they considered me an interloper until I started talking about Ms. Pearl. Once I showed them how much I loved her, I became one of them. One young boy, about nine years old, came up to me with the club's copy of *Treasure Island*. He did not say a word, just handed it to me. At first, I assumed he was telling me that this was the book they were currently reading, but I knew they had already read that book. The boy tapped his finger on the cover and with tears filling his eyes, he said, "Look inside."

On the inside cover the boys had written, "Miss Pearl Bascom read this book to us," and it was signed by all thirteen boys. The young boy smiled and said, "You might be a really good reader, Ms. Ruth, but no one can read a story like Ms. Pearl."

Ruth laughed, "I felt like I was being challenged. Ms. Pearl had set the bar very high, and these boys expected nothing less from me." Turning to Gladys, Ruth asked, "Did you get the same treatment, Gladys?"

Gladys smiled, "Not exactly, Ruth. It helped that I had been going to the club meetings with Pearl for the past several years. All of the boys were used to seeing me with her, so I was already one of them. Every few days, Ms. Pearl would hand me the book and say, "Your turn to read to them, Gladys," which would be greeted by a groan from the boys and from me!

Ms. Pearl would stop the boys and remind them, "Good readers are not born; they are developed. One day, all of you will become great readers. Give Gladys a chance."

Ruth smiled as Gladys confessed, "At first, I was embarrassed. I was afraid to let go, fearing I would look foolish, but Ms. Pearl taught me how to read with expression and emotion, lifting my voice to match the tension in the scene. Ms. Pearl told me, 'You have to give yourself to the story, Gladys. When you do, you will disappear, and the characters will be all the boys can see. A well-written story, read with great emotion, will transport those boys anywhere in the world.'

Karl sat at the dinner table beaming with pride at his wife. Only eight years had passed since she had given her heart to God and had surrendered her anger. "Tobias, can you believe how far our Gladys has come in eight years? None of these boys are BLACK boys to her. They are just boys who loved Ms. Pearl and now love her. Ms. Pearl knew she could trust Gladys with her boys because when God changes a heart, He changes it completely."

For the next ten years, Ruth and Gladys kept the reading clubs going. Many of the older boys took over some of the clubs. They loved telling the newcomers stories about the good ol' days. They would open a book and show the boys their name on the inside cover. "See, I was here when Ms. Pearl, herself, was the reader."

To this day, all over Atlanta, grown men still remember my Aunt Pearl with love and affection—not because she gave birth to them, but because she believed in them and took the time to invest in them. When Ruth and I struggle with the fact that we will never have children of our own, we remember Ms. Pearl. She was loved by countless children because she dared to believe in them.

CHAPTER 36

Shattered, But Not Destroyed

ALTHOUGH WE WERE experiencing great blessings throughout the Depression, the threat of racial tension was always present. Pastor Johnson had not believed in getting involved in the political arena. He felt strongly about sharing the Gospel and dealing with people's souls, rather than their rights. When I was a child, this was the main reason my aunties decided to join his church. For years, I felt this calling was also my mandate. I tried to stay out of social causes, believing I had a higher calling; however, times change, and sometimes, we must learn to change with it.

As I struggled with my thoughts and responsibilities, other issues forced their way in. In 1937, I received word that my Momma Ruby had taken ill. She only lasted a few weeks and then was gone. I spent days locked in my office, reading all her wonderful letters over the years. Each letter was a precious gift to me, and they brought me great comfort.

By 1938, talk of war in Europe began to cause tensions to increase at home. Years of going without and then talk of sending our boys to war again, brought out the ugly side of men. They seemed to need a scapegoat for their frustrations, and black boys had always been an easy target. Sulley's boy, Van, was now sixteen. Sulley kept Van close by his side. He was not allowed to wander around alone. Van was a gentle giant—much like his father. He loved helping with the gardens and would often carry the heavy boxes back home for the older folks. Sulley wanted to forbid him to do this, but Van's heart was determined to be helpful; Sulley knew he could not interfere.

Ruth and I watched as Sulley and Whippoorwill struggled to trust God to keep their boy safe. We also watched as Karl and Gladys feared for their two boys. Karl, Jr., and William had been reared to look at black people as being no different than themselves—a viewpoint that was not tolerated in the 1930s. Karl had always wanted to push back the color barrier, daring to risk his own safety to do so, but now his boys were standing in harm's way. Frustrated whites believed that "If you're not one of us, you're no better than the blacks." To break their long-standing code meant facing their wrath. Karl had always been more militant on the subject then I had been. He had always been willing to put his job on the line to stand for what he believed in, but now Karl wouldn't be paying the price; his boys would be the ones paying the price.

Ruth and I loved all three of these boys as if they were our own. We watched them grow up, and now we were seeing them face the same issues my Grandpa Samuel had to face back in 1865, what I had to face in 1918, and now they were facing in 1940. I realized that nothing was ever going to change if a change were not forced. Karl had been saying this for years, and even though all of our children would be in danger, I realized that the world could not remain as it was. I had no idea how that change would come about, but I decided I would begin praying for change.

Becoming political and demanding our rights as human beings went against everything I had ever been taught, and taking that stance did not settle well with me. I had always been taught to keep quiet, work hard, mind my own business, duck and shuffle aside, and be respectful. Back in the day, these rules were lifesavers. My grandfather came out of slavery at the age of twenty. None of our people were prepared for freedom. They did not know how to make a decision, nor did they know how to earn a living. They did not even know how to express how they felt without having the dreaded fear of calamity overtake them.

Ruth's father believed we should be good citizens and spread the gospel. He believed that if we did this, God would clear the path for us and bless us. I too believed the path he chose to be true. God had always watched out for me and those I loved, yet I was now wondering if that was all that God required of me.

Seventy-five years had passed since our people had been emancipated. I was tired of watching our sons and daughters being treated as if they were still ignorant slaves. Ms. Pearl knew the answer was education. She always said, "Once a black child is given the gift of reading, there is not a door that will remain closed to him." But doors were still closed, and I was not even knocking on those doors. I was standing at those closed doors, expecting God to open them for us; I knew that was wrong. Oh, I knew it would take all of God's power to open those doors, but I had to begin knocking before He would open them. But on which door should I knock first?

Karl, Sulley, and I were all in our early forties and began to pray for wisdom, realizing we were looking ahead to the next generation. We did not want our children to live under the same rules we had lived under. We wanted them to experience a freedom we could only dream of having.

In the summer of 1941, we learned of a city-wide group of pastors who were gathering together, praying together, and seeking God's wisdom. They were asking God to raise up godly leaders. The very idea of joining forces with such men thrilled my soul and drove away all of my doubts. I had been meeting with these men for six months when the news came of the attack on Pearl Harbor. That Sunday everyone was in shock. Every church prayed for all of the boys who lost their lives that morning so far away from home. No one was talking color that day. Those were *our* boys. Those were *our* ships. *We* had been attacked, and *we* all wanted to go after *our* enemy that day.

As we listened to the President on the radio, I worried about our boys. We all knew we would not be able to keep Karl, Jr., or Van from signing up first thing Monday morning. Karl and I both knew what it was like to be eighteen-years old during a time of war. Gladys was thankful that her Billy was too young to sign up. "One boy at a time is all I can take."

Sulley quietly hoped that his boy would be rejected because of his size—as he had been. He assured Whippoorwill that this would be the case, but when Van returned home and said he had three days to report for duty, Sulley was beside himself. He tried to hide his disappointment, but Van was so excited, and he knew he had to let his boy grow up. Ruth slipped a Gideon Bible into both boys' duffle bags. Van joined the Marines, while Karl had decided to join the Navy.

The men's prayer group I had joined so many months earlier now became a prayer vigil for all of the boys heading into harm's way. We all joined the war effort. Now, more than ever, Sulley's Mercy Gardens were needed. He changed their names to "Victory Gardens" and prayed for every family who had a son serving overseas.

After boot camp Van was shipped off to the Philippines. Sulley worried that his son would be a large target and that Van's gentle spirit would be broken by the horrors of war. As Van's letters began pouring in, we were encouraged by his accounts. I, for one, was glad to read how Van's military experience seemed to be quite different than mine. He talked about his buddies, and it was obvious that he did not feel like a second-class Marine. I read and re-read his letters, trying to understand how these same boys, who, in a foreign land under constant threat of death, could treat Van as a brother, but back home would probably not blink at hanging the likes of him.

Karl, Jr.'s, letters were far fewer. Where Van's letters were short and often, Karl's were fewer, but pages long. Out at sea for months on end, his letters took on a daily diary style. He was somewhere in the vast Pacific Ocean, and he was seeing lots of combat. Gladys could not wait to receive one of her son's letters, yet she dreaded the daily accounts of his war experiences. During these years, while watching our best friends suffering the terrible waiting game every parent must go through, Ruth and I actually felt grateful we did not have a son. We witnessed the daily dread of an unknown car pulling up to the house, the all-consuming anticipation of the daily mail delivery, and then the heartache of finally getting those precious letters—only to have the cold reality of what their boys were going through become very real.

Sulley began to notice a hardening of his boy. Van's letters took on a cynical tone. The war was changing him, and Sulley feared it was not for the best. After one such letter, I remember Sulley's saying, "Tobias, some men are just not made to take a life. I fear my boy might come home so broken in spirit, he won't ever be the same again." Then Sulley stopped for a moment and added, "That is, if we get him home at all."

By 1942 the newspapers were filled with accounts of what they were finding all over Europe. Even though the news sickened us, we felt compelled to read every article. Our young men were seeing, both in Europe and in the Far East, the worst of what man is capable of doing to his fellow man. We knew that Van was part of the forces fighting to defend Battery Point on the island's north coast, facing Bataan. The newspapers, which were filled with stories of Bataan, Corregidor, and the Philippines, sent Whippoorwill to her bed. Sulley refused to have a newspaper in the house anymore. Even though they were sure their son was not on Corregidor, hearing the reports that were coming over the radio of the valiant battles, but the great loss of life and our eventual surrender, became too much for Whippoorwill.

For two long months, none of us heard anything. No one could tell us where Van was or even if he was still alive. Eventually Sulley got word that Van had been taken prisoner in the Philippines, but reports were that he was alive. They learned that Van had never been on Corregidor, and for that news, we were all grateful.

Sulley tried to keep the news of how the enemy treated their POWs away from Whippoorwill. "Honey," he kept repeating, "at least he is alive. We have to hold onto that hope right now."

In February of 1944, the news we had all been dreading finally came. Ruth happened to be at Gladys' house when the black car pulled up in front, and two uniformed officers walked up to the front door. Several neighbors came running from their houses; everyone knew what that car meant. One of the women took off running for the train yard, knowing Karl needed to get home quickly. Karl's face turned ashen as he started running for home. I didn't even stop to clock out that day. I tried to catch up with him before he reached his house, but just as we turned the corner, we could see the two officers walking back toward their car. Karl simply stopped running and stared at the men who had broken the worst news a mother can receive, and he collapsed to his knees, crying, "Not my boy. Please God, not my Karl."

There are moments in your life when the wind shifts, and everything that ever was—is forever changed. Looking at my friend, I knew that his faith would hold true, and he would not turn against God for allowing this terrible loss. I knew it as assuredly for Karl as it would have been for me. I also knew that Gladys' faith, after twenty-one years, was just as rock solid. I knew they would endure this heartache; however, I knew they would never be the same again. Pain like this puts a mark on you that can never be removed. As I stood there praying for my friend, I could not help but think of the tens-of-thousands of other parents, on both sides of that terrible war, who had been, and were yet to be, visited by such news. How do any of them survive this experience without God's love and mercy? I had seen so many turn hardened and cold, their joy and hope of any future drained away, leaving only an empty shell in its wake.

I walked over to Karl, helped him to his feet, put my arm around him and guided him into his house. That day, more than any other day of my life, I was thankful it was not my responsibility to make everything right again. Ruth and I were simply to weep with those who weep. We knew that God was there in the midst of all that pain, and that He could be trusted. Although they would be scarred for life, He would bring our friends through this trial; it would not destroy them.

We learned that Karl Junior's body would never be coming home. His ship went down out in the vast Pacific Ocean, and all but twenty bodies went down with the ship. Gladys was the one who insisted upon having a memorial service. "I learned an important lesson by losing my brother, Charlie. Do not throw away his whole life in the grief of his loss. I want to remember my boy's life, all twenty years of it. I refuse to focus only on that one day when he died." Karl Carter, Jr., had a wonderful memorial service.

CHAPTER 37

The Gift of Wise Counsel

AFTER JUNIOR'S MEMORIAL service, Aunt Ruby invited Karl and Gladys, and Sulley and Whippoorwill to our house for dinner. No one wanted to sit at home alone that evening. During dinner, Gladys asked, "Ms. Ruby, I know you and Pearl both endured heartbreak that would have destroyed most people. Is there anything you can share with me that will help me endure this pain?"

Aunt Ruby leaned forward, put her elbows on the table, cradled her face between her aged, wrinkled hands and smiled. "Gladys, you know how much my sister, Pearl, loved and admired you, right?"

"Yes ma'am, Ms. Ruby, I do, and the feeling was mutual. Your sister was an amazingly strong woman."

Aunt Ruby leaned back and smiled. "Will you allow me to tell one of my favorite stories about my sister?"

The whole dinner party chimed in together, "Of course, Ms. Ruby, please do."

Ruby took a drink of water before starting. This needed to be a night where she would use all of her storytelling gifts. These friends were hurting and needed to hear this lesson.

"We have all heard the story of how Pearl lost both little Caramel Hannah and her husband, Joseph Lagolaei. I was not here for Pearl during the worst of her suffering at this great loss in her life. I came back home almost three years after it happened.

"During those three years, Pearl went to work caring for Estée Washington, while she nursed her grief. Because Pearl was a strong woman by nature, she endured her grief by sheer willpower, but a large part of

321

Pearl had been buried with Joseph. By the time I came back home, Pearl was an empty shell; I hardly knew her. No spark was left in her. Oh, she had accepted God's will in the matter, and she did not blame Him for taking Joseph, but there was no life left in her."

Gladys interjected, "I know how she felt, Ms. Ruby. I dare not turn to hate against those who took my boy's life. I have gone down that path before, and I know where it will take me. But this new path scares me just as much. I can't stand the pain I'm feeling, but to get rid of it, I fear I must die inside to quiet it. What did Pearl do, Ms. Ruby?"

Ms. Ruby reached over and picked up her well-worn Bible and opened it to one of Pearl's favorite verses. "Gladys, I will share the path that God took Pearl down to bring healing to her. This was quite a private path she walked, but because I know how much she loved you and if she were still with us, she would be the first one to share it with you. I pray what I know of her journey will help you."

✤ Ruby Shares Pearl's Healing Story ✤

Estée and I watched helplessly as Pearl kept retreating into her grief. We did not know what to say to her. Pearl had always been our fearless leader, so we prayed for God to guide us. One day the book peddler came by the house while Pearl was at work, and I was out on an errand. Estée had never been able to walk out front by herself, let alone talk to the white book peddler, but her love for Pearl gave her the strength that day to open the front door and step out onto the front yard. She asked the peddler to pull the cart into the yard so she could look through what he had for sale. As she leafed through his books, she prayed. She came across a collection of poems and songs written by Frances "Fanny" Crosby. The foreword talked about how this woman, who was born in 1820, had been blind since birth but had become an inspiring public speaker and champion for the education of the blind. Knowing how much Pearl loved education, Estée bought the booklet for her.

At dinner that evening, Estée gave Pearl the booklet and asked her to pick out one of the poems and to read it out loud. The first poem in the booklet was titled, "Blessed Assurance," written back in the year 1873. In the margin, someone had written a Bible verse—Psalm 22:3—so before Pearl read the poem, she opened her Bible and read, *"But Thou art holy, O Thou that inhabits the praises of Israel."* Below the poem, that same hand had written, "God inhabits the praises of His people." Then Pearl read the poem that God used to start her healing:

> "Blessed assurance, Jesus is mine! Oh, what a foretaste of glory divine!
> Heir of salvation, purchase of God, Born of His Spirit, washed in His blood.
> This is my story; this is my song, praising my Savior all the day long;
> This is my story, this is my song, Praising my Savior all the day long.
> Perfect submission, perfect delight, Visions of rapture now burst on my sight;
> Angels descending, bring from above, Echoes of mercy, whispers of love.
> Perfect submission, all is at rest, I in my Savior am happy and blest,
> Watching and waiting, looking above, Filled with His goodness, lost in His love."

That night Pearl re-read that poem three times before saying, "I need to be filled with His goodness, and I want to be lost in His love. Perfect submission, all is at rest, I in my Savior am happy and blest." She turned to Estée and me and said, "The Bible says that God inhabits the praises of His people. I know I cannot sing a note, but I am going to sing anyway, 'all the day long,' until He has filled this empty shell with His love and mercy. I want my God to inhabit my being."

Turning to me, Ms. Ruby chuckled, "By the time you came to us, Tobias, Pearl had become a rather good singer, but at first it was quite painful to the ears. Pearl did not care what note she hit, she was focused only on the words. Words were always special to her, and God was using them to heal her empty soul. Eventually, she began to improve, and all three of us would work around the house singing our favorite hymns."

Gladys smiled at Whippoorwill, "So singing hymns that praise the goodness of God will change these pain-filled hearts of ours. We have all witnessed what it did for Pearl, so I can trust that God will also do it for me."

My Ruth leaned over and placed her hand on Gladys' arm and said, "Our God is so wonderful. He used the change in your heart to convince Pearl that He could change the hearts of others. He is now using the story of how He changed Pearl's heart to convince you that He can be trusted to fill your heart with His perfect delight again."

Although not overnight, Karl and Gladys surrendered their pain to God. I watched as God used their understanding of pain and surrender to become great comforters to Sulley and Whippoorwill. They understood their friend's agony better than anyone. Not once in the twenty-two months that Van was a POW did they ever chide them with, "At least your boy is still alive."

Those two couples were bound together in mutual grief, praying, not only for Van's safe return, but for the safe return of all young men still in harm's way; just as Ruth and I had to learn how to be sincerely happy when others were blessed with babies we would never have, Karl and Gladys were able to celebrate with pure hearts the day the news came that Van had been liberated and was on his way home.

It was late August of 1945 before Van reached home. Two years of suffocating heat, rice and boiled cabbage had taken its toll on Van. He had lost so much weight he could not walk very far without resting. He was just shy of twenty-three and had already lost several teeth.

Whippoorwill, Gladys and Ruth set about putting some weight on him, while Sulley and I focused on his spirit. I had seen that same look in the eyes of so many young boys in France—eyes that had seen too much death and agony. I was happy to see that Van still had that Gideon Bible Ruth had tucked into his duffle bag. It was well-worn and never far from Van's side.

At first, Van was reluctant to talk about his experience. One day Sulley invited me over to the house, hoping I might get his boy to open up. I asked, "Van, how were you able to keep your Bible in the camp?"

Van picked it up and turned it over and over in his hand before answering, "When we were taken captive, the first thing they did was strip us of our backpacks and guns. They even took off our helmets and pulled out all of the pictures our boys had tucked inside of them. It wasn't enough that they took them from us, they set them on fire and made us watch them burn. I can't tell you why, but that morning I had taken my Bible out of my backpack—something I had not done in a year. I read a verse or two and put it into my thigh pocket instead of my backpack. That pocket was used to hold our flip-pads and pencils. We would write down our coordinates or some instructions we needed to remember. That morning our radio operator had used the last page of his flip pad, so I had handed him mine. It was more important for him to have one than for me to have one. My pocket was open, and I happened to slip my Bible into my pocket. Two hours later we were surrounded, stripped of everything, but no one checked my pocket. Over that year I had lost a lot of weight, and my pants were really baggy. They did not notice I had anything in that pocket."

Van smiled as he lovingly slapped his hand on the Bible. Turning to his dad, Van said, "Dad, I know you are worried about the horrors of war that I saw, but I would rather tell you a different story. You know, Dad, when we arrived at the permanent camp, none of us had a stick of anything from home. At first, I kept my Bible a secret, fearing the guards would find out I had it. After about a month, I could see the tension building in everyone. They were so homesick, we spent hours talking about baseball, or different cities the prisoners had visited—anything that would remind us of home.

"Finally, one day I showed my Bible to the guys in my tent. You should have seen their eyes. I passed it around and let each one look up a verse they were familiar with. It was great to hear those guys reading the Bible."

Sulley took the Bible from Van and studied it. "Is that why it is so worn out?"

"Kind of, Dad," Van confessed. "You see, when I first arrived in the Philippines, I never took it out of the backpack. I thought I was too busy to read it. From the very beginning, I saw a lot of killing. The more killings I saw, the less I wanted to read that book. I remember thinking that the whole world was going to hell—and it deserved to. I didn't care about anything but staying alive. It hurt too much to care about anyone. I had never felt so cold and dead in my whole life, and even though I was in a place where I was forced to kill or be killed, taking another person's life changes you."

Looking straight into his father's eyes, Van confessed, "Daddy, I don't think I lost my faith out there. The truth is, Daddy, I don't think I really left here with faith."

Both Van and I saw Sulley's body stiffen at this admission. "Daddy, please hear me out. I was not on the battlefield two days before I realized I was all alone out there. I had loved my life here in Atlanta. No child ever felt more loved than I did. I was cared for, protected, encouraged to follow my faith, and I had no reason to question it, so I didn't. But out on that battlefield, seeing the very worst of mankind, I began questioning everything, and I found I had no answers. For one whole year, I left this Bible in my backpack because I thought it was worthless to me.

"Daddy, I got so hard. When you realize that God's love is not in you, nothing is left to soften the harsh reality of war. I felt like I had been lied to. Life was worse than you told me it was. Simple answers would no longer work for me. I didn't even want my buddies to call me Van anymore. Van no longer existed, so I told them to start calling me Sullivan. Van was that gentle giant of a boy who behaved like his daddy, and I wasn't that person any longer. The Marine who walked into that

POW camp had turned into Sullivan Dunbar. It took me over a month to remove that Bible from my thigh pocket. I was convinced that it just represented home to me. It took a terrible hunger for a taste of home for me to open it up and read it, but when I did, Daddy, all my memories of home came flooding back to me. As I read it, I could actually remember the sound of your voice reading those verses to me as a little kid, and the memory brought great comfort to me. But Daddy, as I read it, I realized that I had never made it mine. It was always your Bible, so I began to pray and ask God to make it mine. I did not want to be in that terrible place all alone anymore; oh, not the camp, but in that hardened place where God does not exist."

Sulley's shoulders quivered as he remembered all those cold letters he had received from his boy. "I knew you were in trouble, Van. I could see the hard-heartedness in your letters, and I prayed for you."

"Daddy," Van cried, "While reading this Bible, I realized that I had not been lied to, I just had not accepted it for myself. I had accepted your faith, but I had not yet made it my faith. Daddy, I made it my faith while in that POW camp."

Van smiled at me and said, "Uncle Toby, I am not the only Marine who found his faith in that camp. I started passing it around so others could remember that there was something bigger than themselves out there, and that God's love was real. In all those twenty-two months, not one of our boys gave it away. Not all of them appreciated it, but they were all thankful we had it. I think, for some, it was just that we were getting something over on the guards. But for many of us, it was our *blessed assurance* that the whole world was not going to hell, that God was there with us, and His Word was a reminder that we had not been forgotten. Many a man read this Bible and cried out to God for help and strength during those terrible days in the camp."

Sulley smiled when he heard how his son talked about that *blessed assurance*. He couldn't wait to have Whippoorwill tell her son all about Ms. Pearl's story and how his momma had sung that very song every day while her boy was in that terrible camp.

327

TOBIAS:
A Legacy of Integrity
1945-1954

CHAPTER 38

⚜

Honoring a Great Lady

TOBIAS TRIED TO shake off the emotions that always came from remembering how Auntie Pearl's life had, yet again, helped those he loved get through difficult times. The conductor had already come through the car several minutes earlier, warning everyone to begin gathering up their belongings, but Tobias had ignored him because he wanted to finish his memory.

Noticing that Tobias was no longer deep in thought, Ruth leaned over and quietly suggested, "Tobias, we will be pulling into the station in about ten minutes. Maybe you should visit the water closet and then put on your suit coat. When we get off the train, we will be busy looking for our driver, and we don't know how long the car ride might be. I've already taken care of myself, so I will stay with our things."

Tobias noticed the excitement in Ruth's voice. She had never been outside of the state of Georgia, and here we were getting ready to drive through Washington, D.C. He quickly made his way to the line that had formed, and waited his turn, thinking, "This train ride has been a real blessing to me. Being able to spend all day going over all my family history and remembering all of the great lessons I have learned makes my heart swell with thankfulness."

As Tobias returned to his seat, three long whistle blows indicated that they were pulling into Union Station. A few minutes later, the conductor swung open the door, pulled the big lever that allowed the stairs to fold out of the floor and slam down, locking them into place. Tobias quickly pulled down their suitcase and his tin box and followed Ruth to the open door.

It was one in the morning when they climbed the wide set of stairs that delivered them up to the Union Station rotunda. It was pitch-black outside, and the yellowish glow of the lights in the rotunda gave the place an eerie feeling. "Tobias, just imagine how many important people have walked through this rotunda."

Tobias just smiled. Ruth had never been very impressed with titles or positions, but tonight, the idea of walking the same floors as people about whom she had read her whole life, was overwhelming her. "Ruth, I think we are supposed to walk out the northeast exit and just beyond Columbus Circle, we should find our driver waiting for us on Massachusetts Avenue."

Even though it was late, knowing this was their first trip to the Capitol, the driver decided to take them up Constitution Avenue so they could get a glimpse of the White House and the Washington Monument. Both Tobias and Ruth were quiet as they made their way through the city, crossed a bridge and traveled up to Fairmount Heights. The driver pulled up in front of a row house, sandwiched in the very middle of a set of five. All of the lights were on, and as they climbed out of the car, a woman came out the front door and made her way down the steep steps to greet them. "I am so glad you made it safe and sound, Brother Bascom. My name is Sister Eugenia Wilcox Allen. My husband wanted to stay up to greet you, but since he is going to be one of the first speakers at the event tomorrow, I told him you would forgive him. He isn't as young as he once was and cannot burn the candle at both ends—like you young ones can."

"He has nothing to apologize for, Sister Eugenia. Ruth and I are so grateful to you both for opening up your home to us."

Taking Tobias's arm, Sister Eugenia began leading them back up the stairs while her son followed with the suitcase. "Let's get you both out of the damp night air. Besides, at night our voices carry, and I don't want a visit from a disgruntled neighbor tomorrow morning." Then with a broad smile, she added, "Especially tomorrow morning."

No sooner were they inside the front door when a voice bellowed from the back hallway, "Is that you, Tobias? I've been resting, but I could not go to sleep until I knew you were here safe and sound." Then with an endearing chuckle, he added, "I'd come out and greet you, but I am in my nightclothes, so I will see you at breakfast. Goodnight."

Sister Eugenia smiled, "That was my husband, the Right Reverend Josiah Allen. Mind you, he is very old school. Most of the younger pastors like to be called 'Bishop' these days. Josiah worked so hard earning his degree and having the title, 'Right Reverend,' bestowed upon him means the world to him. He will never give it up."

"We look forward to meeting him tomorrow morning, Sister Eugenia," Ruth responded. Then removing a large container from her grip and handing it over to her hostess, Ruth added, "I hope you don't mind, but I was taught never to come empty-handed. Maybe you could add these treats to the breakfast table tomorrow."

With their hostess gifts delivered, Tobias and Ruth quickly unpacked and dropped into bed. Tobias had intended to go over his speech one more time, but as soon as his head hit the pillow, he was out.

The excitement in the house woke Ruth very early the next morning. She slipped out of bed and quickly got dressed and made her way to the kitchen where she caught the Right Reverend Josiah Allen sneaking a bite of her coffee cake. "Oh, my goodness, Mrs. Bascom, did you bake these treats?"

"Why, yes sir, I did. Glad you like them," Ruth responded with a bright smile.

After swallowing the last stolen bite, he said, "My wife says that Tobias is tall and lean. Just how does one accomplish that with a wife that can bake like this? My wife is forever telling me I cannot eat this or that because it all sits right here," as he rubbed his satisfied tummy.

"I am sure it will catch up with him, Rev. Allen," Ruth teased, "but I love baking for him, and he loves to eat, so we are a good fit."

Just then Tobias walked into the kitchen and introduced himself. "Good morning, Rev. Allen. I understand that you will be one of the speakers today. I cannot tell you how nervous I am to speak in front of all of you. I just wish that my Great-Aunt Pearl could have lived to see this day."

Quickly dusting the crumbs off of his dress shirt, Reverend Allen added, "Many of us have worked hard to get this law changed. It has been a long battle and we are excited to celebrate, but the war has not yet been won. There is much, much more to do before we see the end of separate but equal, but I do not dare get on that horse this morning, or we will all be late. We need to get you some breakfast and get on the road by 10:30. We need to be in the city and at our table by 11:30 so the celebration can be call to order by noon. After lunch has been served and the singers have performed, we will start the program promptly at one o'clock."

The next three hours became a blur. Tobias tried to go over his speech, but someone was always walking up to introduce himself. Names and faces began to merge, so Tobias leaned over to Ruth and whispered, "Can you help me keep track of names? These people have not even finished introducing themselves, and I can't remember their names."

"Just smile, Tobias," Ruth advised, "you are more nervous than I have ever seen you. Just remember why you are here. Ms. Pearl has earned this honor, and you are simply her representative."

Suddenly they heard a commotion behind them, and they both turned around to see Thurgood Marshall entering the dining hall. "That is a name you will remember," chuckled Ruth.

A chime was sounded, instructing everyone to take his seat, and the luncheon was served. Tobias had no intention of eating anything. His nerves would not allow anything to go down or stay down. He moved the lunch around his plate, feigning interest in the food, but nothing was brought up to his mouth. He had visions of choking on something and bringing the whole room's attention to himself. He was relieved when the servers cleared away the dishes, and he tried to enjoy the musical entertainment, but his mind kept trying to go over his talk. He was certain he would get up to the podium and go blank. His hands began to perspire, and the server had taken away his napkin. He slipped his hands below the table and under the tablecloth. He rubbed his hands on his trousers and then laid them flat on his thighs in order to stop their shaking. They remained there during the first five speakers. He knew he was number six in a panel of eight speakers. The event would conclude with Thurgood Marshall. Tobias was certain he would enjoy the others once his task was completed.

As speaker number five was drawing his talk to a close, Tobias pulled his speech out of his coat pocket and unfolded it just as he heard his name being announced. The master of ceremonies did a fine introduction, focusing on Ms. Pearl instead of him. As he listened and looked around, he realized how much these people already admired his Great-Aunt Pearl, and his stomach settled down; a quiet calm overtook him. He did not have to impress these people because Pearl's life had already done so.

As he walked up to the podium, he thought about how hard he had struggled to write his speech, not knowing what to include and what to leave out. Tobias laid his speech on the podium and smiled at the audience. After issuing his obligatory acknowledgments, he was ready.

Today we are joyfully celebrating the fine work of Mr. Thurgood Marshall, Esquire. His huge victory over the "Separate but Equal" laws of this country are monumental and have been covered by five wonderful speakers today. That law has ruled the educational system of this country for many years.

As part of this celebration, the lifelong work of my great-aunt, Ms. Pearl Bascom Lagolaei, is also being honored. Since I am the last surviving member of Ms. Pearl's family, I have been asked to speak on her behalf.

While pondering what I should say today, I realized that, since I am speaking on her behalf, I should tell you what Ms. Pearl would say if she were here. Ms. Pearl was nothing, if not direct and to the point, on all topics of education.

To understand her point of view, one must understand what she overcame in order to hold that point of view. When I was asked to represent Aunt Pearl, I knew what she would have said, "No, Tobias, you represent our whole family—not just me." Since this would have been her direction, this is what I have decided to do.

I am only the second generation of my family born into freedom, and the last surviving member of this proud family. I stand here representing the whole Bascom family. My great-grandmother, Hannah, was born into slavery in the year 1824. She lived her entire life, all forty-one years of it, as a slave on the Stewart Plantation, just outside of Atlanta, Georgia. Sadly, she did not live to see freedom, but her three children did. In 1865, my grandfather Samuel and his two sisters, Pearl and Ruby, were emancipated at the end of the Civil War. Grandpa was twenty, and the sisters were sixteen.

The Emancipation Proclamation had been signed into law in 1863. Laws on the books do not always translate into daily reality. It took two additional years of war and tremendous fear before my grandfather and his sisters were actually emancipated; today, many of us believe we are still waiting for the full effect of that law to be carried out.

This past May 17, 1954, segregation in schools was made illegal in this country, but just as with the Emancipation Proclamation law, it will take some time and hard work before that law becomes a reality to our people.

Ms. Pearl was convinced that the laws had to be changed before black children could be fully educated. Thanks to people of vision like Thurgood Marshall, that work has been accomplished. Now, however, the more difficult work stands in front of us—forcing the changes those laws demand. Laws which are on the books, but are not in everyone's daily reality, become impotent. The Emancipation Proclamation opened the door to freedom, but desegregated schools, giving every child a right to equal education, is the engine that will walk our people through that open door to freedom.

As I stand here, I cannot help but wonder how many years it will take to make the law for truly equal education a daily reality for everyone. These two powerful laws are now on the books, but the irony is, that yesterday, my wife Ruth and I had to stand in a line marked, "For Coloreds Only," in order to come here this weekend. We all understand much work yet needs to be done; Ms. Pearl would have quickly pointed out—"You best start out by cleaning up your own house."

Please allow me to explain what she meant by this statement. I was blessed to have a family that impressed the need for education throughout my life. Ms. Pearl was taught to read while still a slave—a practice that was against the law back then. She loved to read, and she taught my grandfather and her sister Ruby to read upon their emancipation. Pearl believed that reading could open doors that no man could close, that reading could take you places you were not physically allowed to go, and to meet great people of all colors, who are long since dead.

Holding up an old copy of *Treasure Island*, Tobias smiled at the audience. "Not much to look at, right?" In the year 1907, I was ten years old, and my best friend, Sully, was thirteen the first time she read this story to us. Ms. Pearl reread this story three times before we would allow her to move on to another story. She followed it with *The Swiss Family Robinson* and then Jack London's *The Call of the Wild*; these three stories made me want to board a ship and sail the seas, get a team of dogs and explore the frozen north, and build a tree-house in my backyard. She knew these stories would ignite both our imagination and our hunger to learn how to read.

Tobias then set down *Treasure Island* and picked up his well-worn copy of *The Count of Monte Cristo* for all to see. "This novel has quite a daunting look about it, right?" Leafing through the pages for effect, Tobias announced, "This copy was printed in 1859 and has 753 pages of old English—not something uneducated young black boys could follow, right?"

In the year 1910, when I was thirteen years old, and my best friend, Sulley, was then sixteen, Ms. Pearl read this very book to us. Oh, she knew better than to start out with this novel. First, she shared the simple adventures of the likes of Tom Sawyer, Jim Hawkins, and Oliver Twist. Once she had us hooked, we were glad to see this book had so many pages because we were saddened when the other stories ended much too soon.

When the book was finished, Auntie Pearl peppered both of us with questions, and Sulley and I were amazed at how much we had retained. Afterward, Ms. Pearl said, "Boys, look at what you have accomplished. You know this story inside and out. It contains 753 pages of complicated storyline, yet you both remember every little detail because it was exciting. Don't ever let anyone tell you that you are incapable of learning. This book proves that you are capable."

Replacing the book on the podium, Tobias let his eyes sweep over the crowd, "This copy has been in my family since 1883 and is my most prized possession." Ms. Pearl bought four other copies and did the same thing with every one of her Brigade Clubs.

As she began her Boys' Brigades, her greatest struggle was convincing the parents of those boys that it was not a waste of time. This reason angered Ms. Pearl, and she would rant, "We can change all the laws we want, but if our own people believe our children are incapable of learning, our children will not learn."

To prove the parents wrong, she knew she needed to get the boys so excited about the stories that they would beg to hear the story of Edmond Dantès. She captured the imagination of every single boy the same way she had for Sulley and me. She showed them that they too could understand this novel and remember hundreds of details. From then on, the older boys would proudly tell the younger boys, "Just you wait. One of these days Ms. Pearl will decide you are ready to hear the story of *The Count of Monte Cristo*; just you wait!"

Proud of his great-aunt's wisdom, Tobias again quoted Ms. Pearl, "White men were able to justify slavery because they believed that blacks were less than human. They believed blacks were incapable of learning anything but the simplest of tasks, treating them like children who needed white people to control them. Education will change how the world views you."

Tobias smiled. My Aunt Pearl was always preaching this truth to the parents of her boys. Ladies and gentlemen, when black people believe their children are incapable of learning, they are reinforcing the same lie that many whites still use to justify laws like Separate but Equal. It may have been separate, but it has never been equal.

Looking around this room, I realize I am preaching to the choir today. We are the select few who have benefitted from a good, strong education; but what about all the others?

We need more black lawyers like Thurgood Marshall, who will work within the courts to change the laws, but we also need to change the attitudes of our people. Blacks are every bit as capable of learning as whites are. We have had hundreds of years of limited education, and that practice must stop. We need to help every child reach his greatest potential—with or without the help of white people. We cannot wait until they decide our children are capable. If we educate our children, laws or no laws, educated people will make themselves be heard and will force a fair place for themselves in this country.

I will leave you with one of Ms. Pearl's favorite sayings, "Slaves had no control over their own lives; they had no choices. Emancipation set us free—but without the tools to flourish. Education is the tool that will keep the door to freedom open for us. If we neglect to educate our children, that door will close again. Self-control and self-determination are the hallmarks of freedom. Education is the key that will open the doors of our children's future."

Tobias took his seat to thunderous applause. He knew the task of accomplishing this would be left to other men; it was his responsibility to light the flame, and he knew he had accomplished that.

CHAPTER 39

Nothing is as it was Before

THE REST OF the weekend was wonderful. Josiah's son took them everywhere, and by the time they had boarded the southbound train, all they wanted to do was sleep. Even Ruth did not dare look around for a needy person with whom to chat. They quickly tucked their belongings on the luggage shelf and got comfortable. Ruth leaned against Tobias' shoulder and was out like a light within minutes, but as tired as he was, sleep eluded him.

As the train made its way along the Potomac River, swiftly carrying them southward, Tobias reviewed his speech and its impact on the audience. He was pleased. Watching the moonlight dance upon the water, he tried to ignore what was bothering him, but he knew what it was. He had deliberately taken his time on the train ride north, making sure he had finished reviewing his family history exactly where he stopped right as they had reached Washington, D.C. He knew he needed to get off the train two days earlier in a solid state of mind and not be an emotional wreck. He was bothered that the entire Bascom family history had not yet been fully told. Pulling his suit coat over Ruth's body, he decided that if he intended to get any sleep, he needed to cover the last nine years.

The first two years after World War II had undoubtedly been the most turbulent years of his life. As a young man, the winds of persecution had always been part of his life, but as long as he minded his own business, worked hard, and steered clear of trouble, he had felt safe; but World War

II changed everything. As the boys of war began returning home, many of them wanted to change the social order of things. Having served arm-in-arm together, lots of them refused to return to the old order of things; but the "good ol' boys" were not going to give up their positions quietly.

Soon sorrow and loss were running rampant, and even as our country was celebrating our great victory, few black people felt victorious. Yet again, just as it had been for Grandpa Samuel after the Civil War, and for me after World War I, jobs were scarce, war wounds were fresh, and men were desperate. None of these factors would bode well for the people whom he loved. This time, however, the young men were determined to see change; they began to challenge the old ways. Young white soldiers asked why, and the old guard fought back, desperate to hold onto what they knew, but it was our boys who would pay the price of freedom here at home.

As we began reading of an increase in lynchings, we worried about our boys. Men of my age were usually safe as long as we showed respect, but our younger generation was tired of showing respect when none was given in return. Discouragement tried to consume me, and there were long periods of time where the only thing I could hold onto was the witness of those who had endured before me. Their lives reminded me that God is always faithful, that trials and tribulations come to stretch us—not to destroy us.

The gift of seeing Van's settled faith becoming real to him was one of the anchors God placed in my life. It is easy to ignore the blessings when the enemy is screaming in your ears. Loss after loss, attack after attack, and I began to focus on the Enemy rather than on the One who held my future. I am not sure when it started, but I remember the day I realized how much I had allowed it to consume me.

It all started on January 27, 1947, the day we learned that old Mr. Sutterfield, the owner of our warehouse, had passed away. He had been ill for some time, and since he had no living children and had been a widower for many years, no one knew what would happen to the business. Quietly, I thought that maybe old Mr. Sutterfield might have left the business to

Karl. Of course, I never voiced this idea, but knowing how much the old man had looked out for Karl, I thought it might be possible; I was wrong.

Mr. Sutterfield was not even buried before the swarm of lawyers descended on the freight yard. Files were ransacked, freight contracts studied, appraisers were everywhere, trying to determine the value of the company. Karl was always being dragged into one meeting or another. They were going over employee records, asking him how best to streamline the payroll in order to make the bottom line look most appealing. They were putting the business up for sale.

At first, Sulley, Karl and I didn't worry about it. We had years with the company and were highly respected, but two months later, everything changed. The new owner took over with an iron hand. He was one of those men who would be heard, who would not listen, and who does not believe he answers to anyone. His first step was to call Karl into his office and announce, 'I don't care how you do it, but I want all seven of those darkies off my payroll by Friday. Lots of able-bodied vets are looking for work; you make room for them.'"

At first, Karl simply ignored this direct order. He did not say a word to Sulley or me. Friday came and went, and nothing changed. That next Monday morning, Sulley and I showed up, along with the other five, and clocked into work as usual. I barely had my lunch pail in my locker when the new owner flew down the stairs screaming at Karl, "I told you to get rid of these boys. What are they doing here?"

Sulley and I turned to look at Karl. "What is he talking about, Karl?"

"He ordered me to fire all of you, and I refuse to." Karl stood there with the most defiant look I had ever seen on his face. "Mr. Wilson, it isn't right to fire these men. They all have perfect work records."

Mr. Wilson was now toe-to-toe with Karl. His face was beet-red, and his nostrils flared like a stampeding bull, "I don't recall asking your opinion, Karl. The last time I looked, it was my name on the business loan of this company."

Karl did not back down. "I am not going to fire these men, Mr. Wilson, and don't you dare use unemployed veterans as your excuse. I lost a boy to that war. Sulley's boy spent two years in a POW camp for that war, and Cleveland's boy came home without a leg. Every one of these men defended this country every bit as much as those white men you want me to hire."

"I'll hire and fire whomever I wish," screamed Wilson. "This is still a free country, and if I don't want darkies working for me, I have that right. So since you are such a lover of darkies, why don't you head up to that office of yours and start packing it up? You are fired too!"

Karl stood there defiantly, "You can't fire me, Mr. Wilson, because first thing this morning I turned in my resignation and packed up my office. I would rather be a garbage collector than work for the likes of you."

We were all quiet until we passed beyond the security gate. Sulley grabbed hold of Karl's arm and asked, "Does Gladys know what you did this morning, Karl?"

"Yes, and she agreed with me. She knew I could not give that man one more day of labor if I was forced to fire you guys."

I remained quiet all the way home. I knew that the church would reinstate my pastor's salary, and Ruth earned a good living as the head baker at the hospital. I wasn't worried about us, but Karl and Gladys and Sulley and Whippoorwill were in real trouble. Somehow I knew things were going to change—but right then, I didn't know how much.

By May of 1947, no more available jobs remained in Atlanta. Returning soldiers had filled every opening. Gladys' brother Bill found Karl work within a month, but Sulley was struggling. Finally, Sulley and Van decided to look outside of Atlanta. None of us wanted to lose them, but we knew they had to find work. Sulley had been my close friend since I was seven years old. He had become a strong anchor for me. Sulley was never the student that I was, but Sulley's faith was grounded and as strong as he was. He was a man I had come to admire and depend upon, and I had not prepared myself for this loss.

In early June, Sulley returned to Atlanta to tell us that he found work in a small town about ninety miles outside of Atlanta. Both he and Van had been hired on by the school district as custodians and handymen. They were to maintain all of the buildings and the school grounds. "Tobias, it's a nice little town. Jefferson, Georgia, is not a bad place to live."

One week later, we said goodbye to Sulley, Whippoorwill, Van, Carletta, and Clare. They were only moving ninety miles away, but my world felt empty without them. I just didn't know how empty my world would soon become.

By the middle of June, we realized that my Great-Auntie Ruby was failing fast. She was ninety-eight years old, and we had known for many years that her time was coming to an end. How do you prepare to say goodbye to one of the two most important women in your life? Ms. Ruby had been there for me since I was seven. She was the keeper of all my stories. She was my encourager, my challenger—the one who would always help me set my compass to the correct course. How was I to go on in a world that no longer included Ms. Ruby or her wisdom?

Ruth and I sat by her bedside and stared into those eyes that had never judged, only loved. We remembered all of the old stories that had filled my childhood with pride and direction. I knew I was the man I had become because of those who had gone before and had set the course for my life.

A woman who was loved by many, Ms. Ruby had friends coming in to say their goodbyes. On the second-to-last day, she reminded me of my promise, "Toby Boy, please don't let Momma Hannah, Samuel, Pearl, Joseph, my Arthur, or little Estée down. You need to write their stories so, years from now, people can know what they endured and what they overcame. When people read their stories, they will come to life again in the hearts of the readers. Promise me, Toby Boy."

"I promise, Auntie Ruby."

She then pointed at her bookcase beside her bed. "Toby, get down our special book."

In a house filled with books, you might think that would be a vague request, but I knew exactly what book Ms. Ruby was referring to. I reached up and took down *The Count of Monte Cristo* and handed it to her. The only book in our house more prized than this one was the Bible.

Auntie Ruby caressed the book, remembering all the exciting hours this book took her so far away from here. Her precious wrinkled hands that had patted my back so many years earlier patted the book as she said, "Toby, my boy, there is a letter inside this book for you. I don't want you to read it until after you have kept your promise. Only then may you open it and read it. Do you understand?"

"I understand, Auntie Ruby."

Two days later, the last connection to my past was gone. I struggled as I prepared the message for her memorial service. How do you sum up a life like hers? I grew up in a home that honored self-control and self-determination, honorable behavior, a strong work ethic, and submission to God's will; but that day, I wanted to scream, "I am not ready to let go of her, God! I do not feel in control of myself. I know You gave me forty-three beautiful years with this lady, but it wasn't enough—not nearly enough. Please God, I cannot go through this again with my Ruth. Please, God, please take me first. I don't want to feel this deep loss ever again."

As these words came out of my mouth, the room became very quiet. I thought of all the losses I had experienced over the past few years, and a calm and peaceful thought, which I believe came from God, occurred to me. "That pain you feel when you lose these precious people you love is a gift. Love fills you up and expands your heart, Tobias. When that loved one is taken away, it tears at your heart because that person dwelled there. That pain is the price you pay for having a great love in your life. Embrace it, Tobias. It is proof of their value to you."

I sat for a few moments and pondered the message. I had had so many wonderful people in my life. I was blessed to have Grandpa Samuel. He was MY grandfather. Who else in this whole wide world can say that? Ms. Pearl was MY great-auntie. She loved me as her own son. Hundreds of grown men, all graduates of her reading brigade, would have given anything to be able to make that claim. Karl, Jr., had been like a son to me. I had led his daddy to Christ, and I had been privileged to baptize him. He had been a young man who had known where he was going when he died, and I will see him again.

My Auntie Ruby is not really gone; I know I'll see her again. Then it occurred to me that, for months, I had been staring into the face of the Enemy, focusing on all of my losses and feeling so sorry for myself. I was licking my wounds at the loss of my dear friends, Sulley and Whippoorwill, instead of rejoicing that I had been given so many years of their friendship.

I sat at my desk and chuckled.

God, You are correcting my compass yet again. My course was set on self-pity and loss, but today, You corrected it and now it is set on gratitude. Thank You for all of these precious people You have put in my life to teach me how to live and how to love. Please, God, make me worthy of these gifts. Thank You for loving us and for giving us others to love as well.

I tore up the message I had written that morning. Instead, I wrote a tribute of thanksgiving. On the top of my notes, I wrote a reminder to myself, "Its okay to let them see you cry," and I did.

As I spoke at Aunt Ruby's funeral, I made it a celebration—not a wake. I decided to set my tin box on the podium and tell everyone some of my favorite family stories. While doing this, I would open the tin box and pull out the keepsake that went with the memory. After several of these, I closed the tin box and held it up. "What does this tin box represent? It represents our heart. Every one of us have had both painful and happy experiences. Life is hard, and no one gets through it without some pain, but one of the most important lessons my Great-Aunt Ruby ever taught me was "Toby-Boy, only treasure the good memories. We remember the bad ones, but never hold onto them. That which you treasure you will become. Fill your tin box with memories that will make you a better man—not a bitter man."

I ended Ms. Ruby's funeral by asking everyone a question: "What is in your heart—*your* tin box? What are you holding onto so fervently that it consumes your box, making you just like it? I, for one, choose to hold onto the memory of my family and how they overcame slavery, ignorance, and injustice. They taught this thankful boy how to love God and trust His plan for my life. To live a life of self-determination and self-control. Yes, they were born slaves, but they did not remain slaves. They found their freedom, and they shared that freedom with many others, including this very thankful man standing in front of you today."

Looking over at Ruth, sound asleep on his shoulder, Tobias allowed the momentary sorrow of Ms. Ruby's loss to touch his heart. "That is the price I must pay for having had you in my life, Aunt Ruby. It has been eight years, and I still miss you—but I did keep my promise."

Being careful not to disturb Ruth, Tobias reached for the tin box and placed it on his lap. He undid the latch and took out the final item he had placed in the tin box before leaving home. For six long years he toiled over this item in order to keep his promise to Ms. Ruby. When the feelings of loss threatened to overtake him, he would write. Once his book was finished, he had opened the envelope Ms. Ruby had tucked inside the family's favorite book. Inside he found a bankbook with Joseph's and Arthur's money deposited into an account with his name on it. It had been deposited into this account the year he had turned twelve. Inside the bankbook was a note.

Dear Toby-Boy,

If you are reading this, you have kept your promise to Sister and me. Use this money to print our story so Momma Hannah, Daddy Charlie, Brother Samuel, Sister Pearl, Joseph, my Arthur, and sweet little Estée can live on in the telling.

Always stay my beloved boy.
I have loved you with my whole heart,

Great-Auntie Ruby

Tobias smiled as he held his book, *Lessons My Family Taught Me.* Grateful that he had kept his promise, he carefully tucked his book back into his tin box, placed it on the floor at his feet, then laid his head against Ruth's head and contentedly fell fast asleep.

About the Author

DOREY WHITTAKER WAS accidently poisoned by arsenic at age three, left virtually deaf until age twelve, and illiterate until age sixteen. She knows how it feels to face tremendous obstacles. She was told, "Just get over it and move on." Dorey knew how broken she was. She also knew that God was her only hope.

None of us get to choose our beginnings, but we all must decide our life path. Either we accept the label of "victim," with all its excuses readily at hand, or we can choose to follow God's path to true self-worth.

In all three of her novels, Dorey shines a light on God's path to living a victorious life.

Available on Amazon:
Book #1 Wall of Silence
Book #2 Hope Returns

Visit Dorey's website at: Doreywhittaker.com

CPSIA information can be obtained at www.ICGtesting.com
Printed in the USA
BVOW02s2255180416

444704BV00001B/14/P